Unicorn on a Roll

Another Phoebe and Her Unicorn Adventure

Unicorn on a Roll

Another Phoebe and Her Unicorn Adventure

Dana Simpson

Andrews McMeel
Publishing®

a division of Andrews McMeel Universal

INTRODUCTION

it was not long ago that if I suggested you should check out a clever, funny, sweet daily comic about a girl and her unicorn, I would have had to endure some eye rolls and serious questions about my maturity level.

But the times, they are a-changin'. Dana Simpson's *Phoebe and Her Unicorn* has arrived at just the right time to perpetuate an unprecedented shift in opinion and openness to the genuine thoughts, feelings, experiences—and humor—in the lives of authentic girls.

In modern media, women and girls are finally starting to be seen as regular plain old human beings. Fifty years ago—heck, fif*teen* years ago—almost any depiction of a young girl would be some sort of hyperidealized version of childhood femininity. Girls in comics and cartoons were either precocious little sprites; bossy, irritating nags; or ethereal, fragile beauties, even at their tender ages. They were characters created by observers and idealizers, and because of this vantage, the audience watched them from a distance. But the characterization of Phoebe is indicative of a very recent, very new, very refreshing change of perspective of who girls really are. Though she is a girl who has many interests that are the usual girlish things, she is relatable to all regardless of gender or age. We don't watch her from the cheap seats; we are right up there with her on the stage, flaws and all. She's not a little Kewpie doll to be protected or admired; rather, we see ourselves reflected back in her. She is not just every girl; she is every child. She is US.

Now let's talk Marigold Heavenly Nostrils. Vanity, the supposedly "feminine" personality flaw usually assigned to antagonists and villains, is turned on its head. Yes, Marigold is vain, but she is caring and attentive, she keeps her promises, and though she reminds us all that every creature is basically beneath her magical majesty, she certainly doesn't treat anyone that way. She is riddled with self-love and is utterly unapologetic. And couldn't we all stand to feel a little more free to love ourselves? Her vanity is not portrayed as a trait worthy of revile, but as something that makes her funny, fun to be around, and utterly endearing. Some would say these are some pretty essential qualities in a BFF.

And when paired together, these two very modern depictions of female archetypes not only demonstrate for us a heartwarming, true friendship—they show us a little of ourselves; a little of what we aspire to be; and, perhaps most important of all, they make us laugh.

So hopefully soon the days of rolling our eyes at little girls and their dreams of magic and unicorns will be gone. It's about time that all of us, like Dana, realized that little girls are onto something. That bringing a little magic into our world is all it takes to help us through the trials and tribulations of life. So sit back and enjoy—girl, boy, child, adult—*Phoebe and Her Unicorn* is for YOU.

— Lauren Faust
January 2015

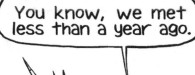

You know, we met less than a year ago.

It seems like such a long time!

I was so young and innocent, then.

And you are so **grizzled** now.

I have **TWO FEWER BABY TEETH.**

dana

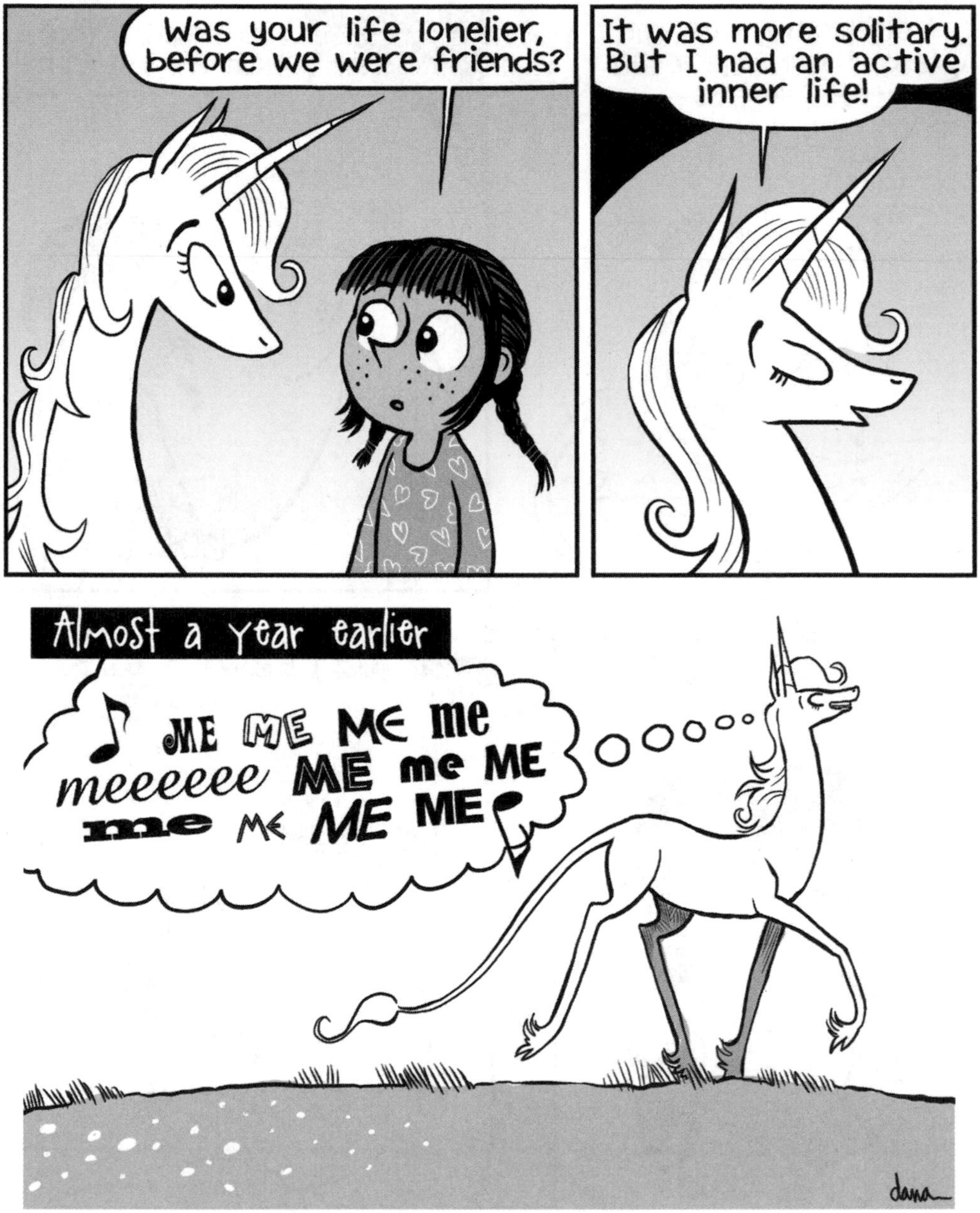
Was your life lonelier, before we were friends?
It was more solitary. But I had an active inner life!
Almost a year earlier
ME ME ME me meeeeee ME me ME me ME ME ME
dana

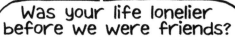

Was your life lonelier before we were friends?

NERRRRRRD!

Insufficiently so.

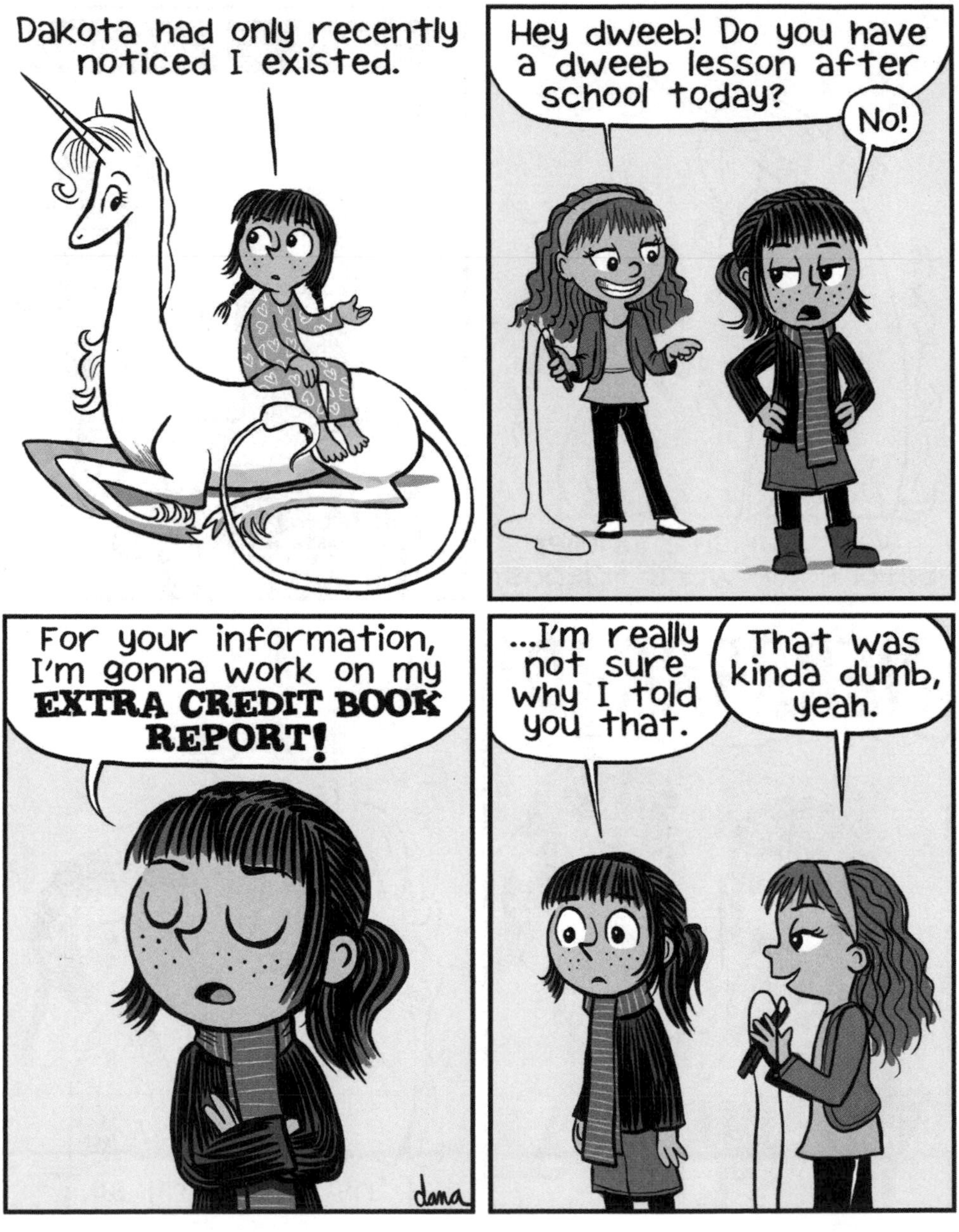
Dakota had only recently noticed I existed.
Hey dweeb! Do you have a dweeb lesson after school today?
No!
For your information, I'm gonna work on my **EXTRA CREDIT BOOK REPORT!**
...I'm really not sure why I told you that.
That was kinda dumb, yeah.
dana

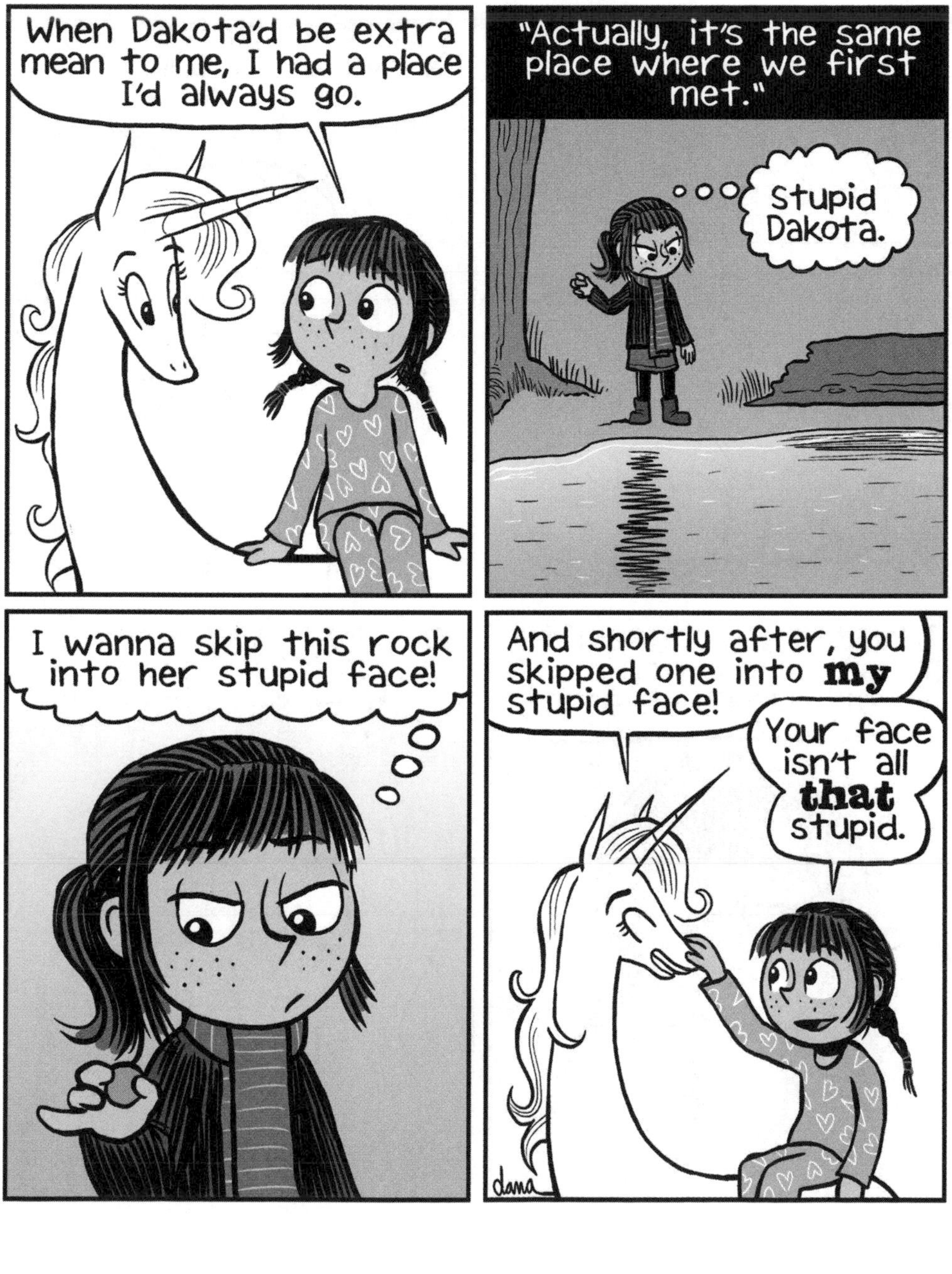
When Dakota'd be extra mean to me, I had a place I'd always go.
"Actually, it's the same place where we first met."
Stupid Dakota.
I wanna skip this rock into her stupid face!
And shortly after, you skipped one into **my** stupid face!
Your face isn't all **that** stupid.
dana

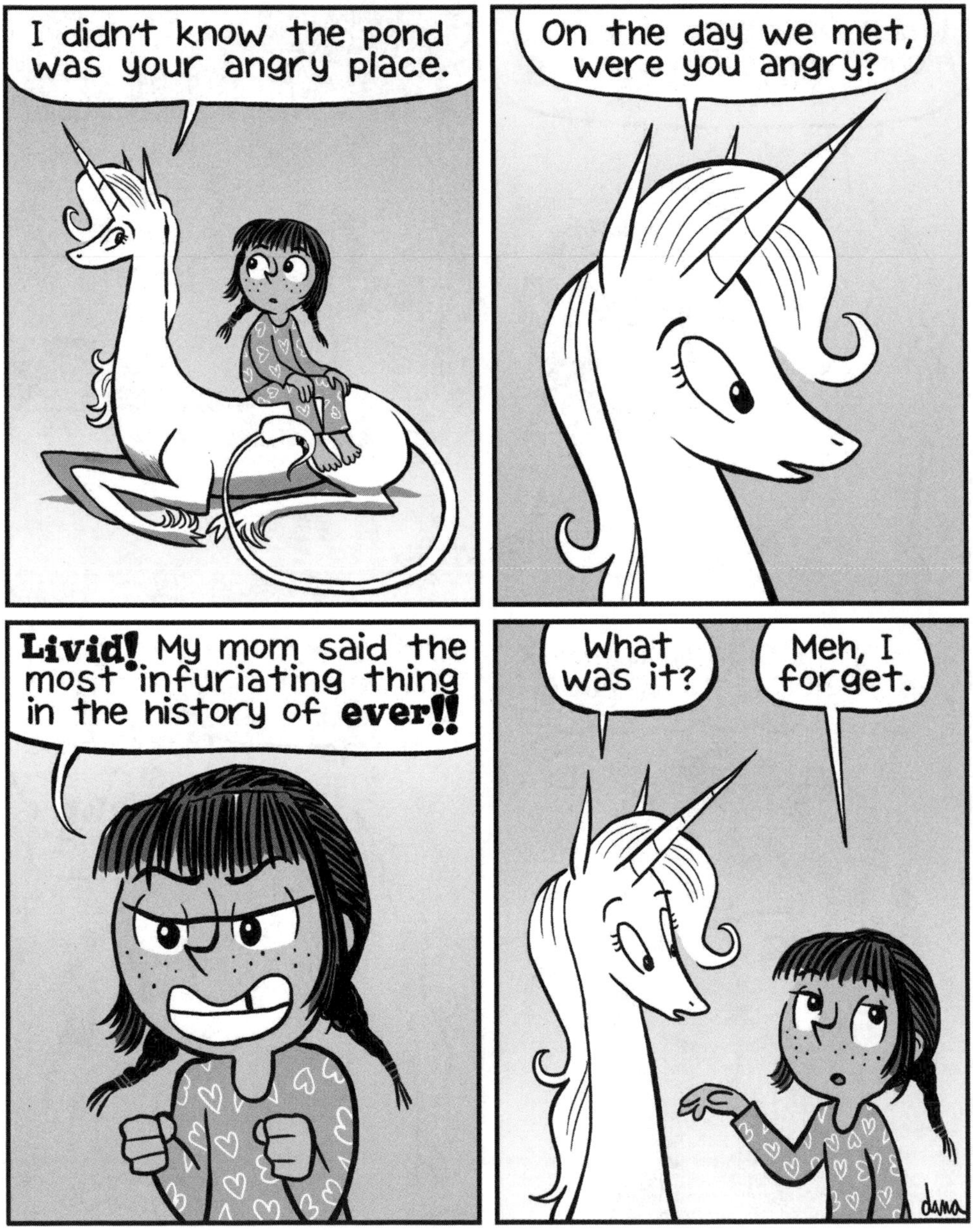
I didn't know the pond was your angry place.
On the day we met, were you angry?
Livid! My mom said the most infuriating thing in the history of **ever!!**
What was it?
Meh, I forget.
dana

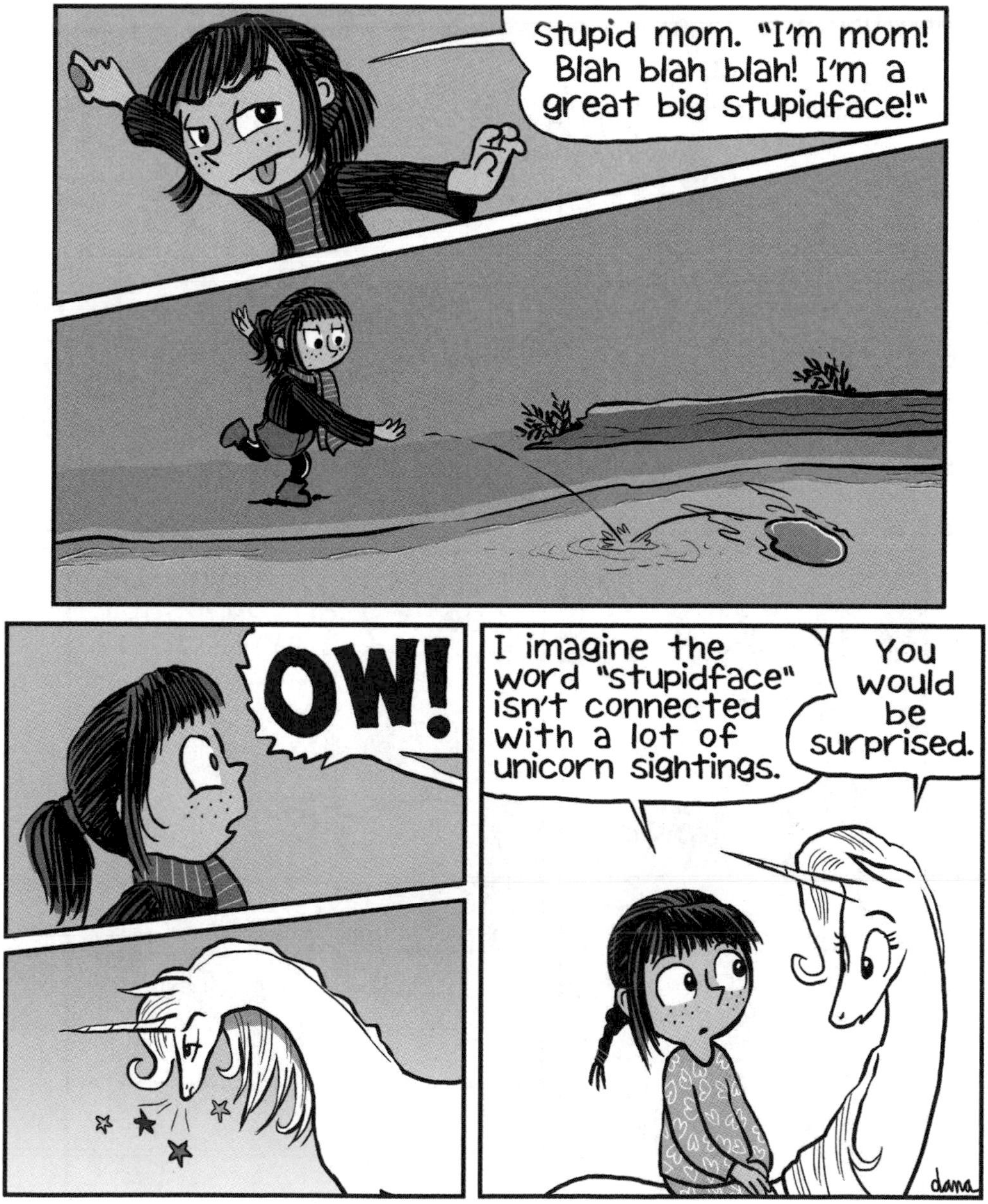
Stupid mom. "I'm mom! Blah blah blah! I'm a great big stupidface!"
OW!
I imagine the word "stupidface" isn't connected with a lot of unicorn sightings.
You would be surprised.
dana

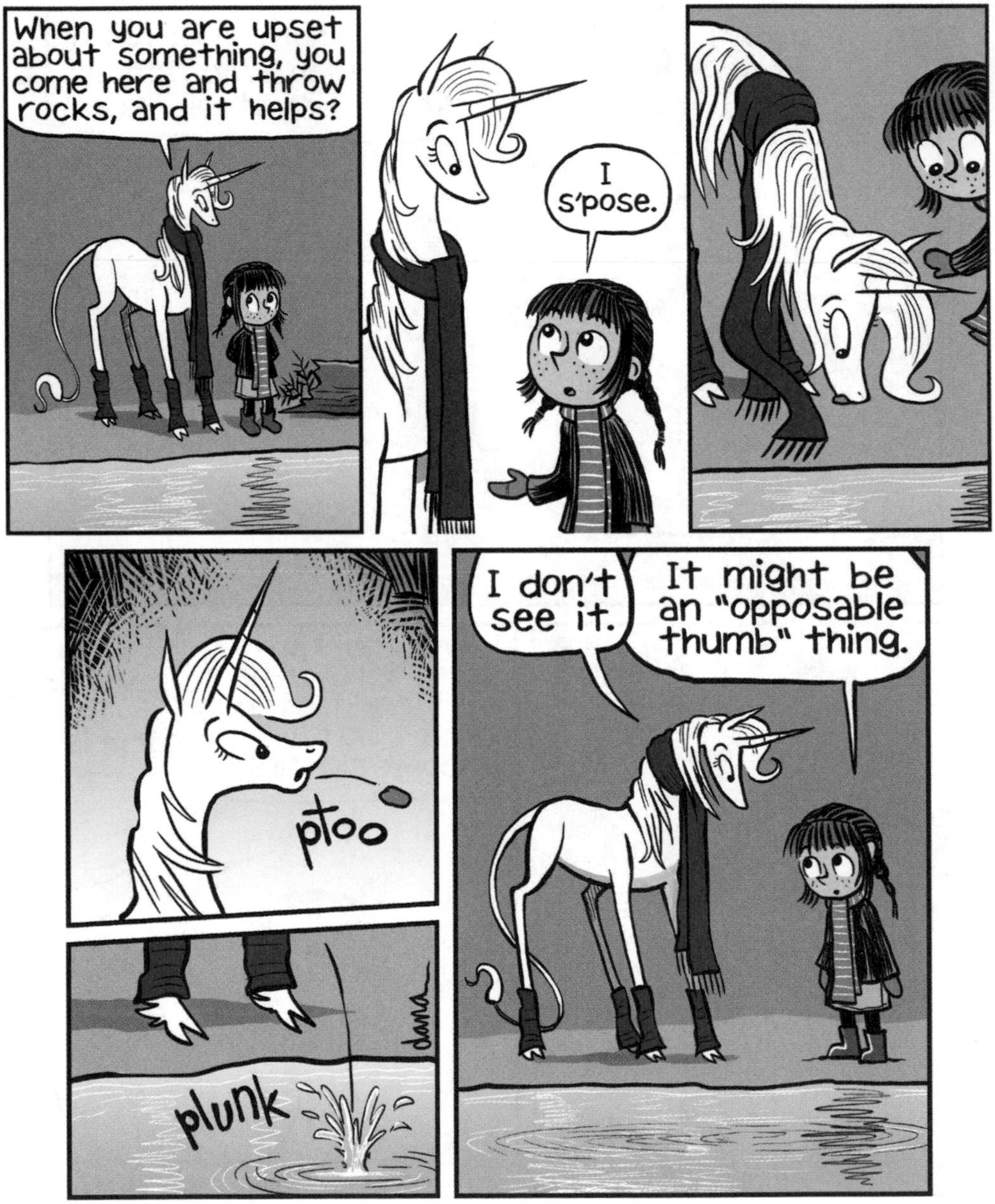
When you are upset about something, you come here and throw rocks, and it helps?
I s'pose.
ptoo
plunk
dana
I don't see it.
It might be an "opposable thumb" thing.

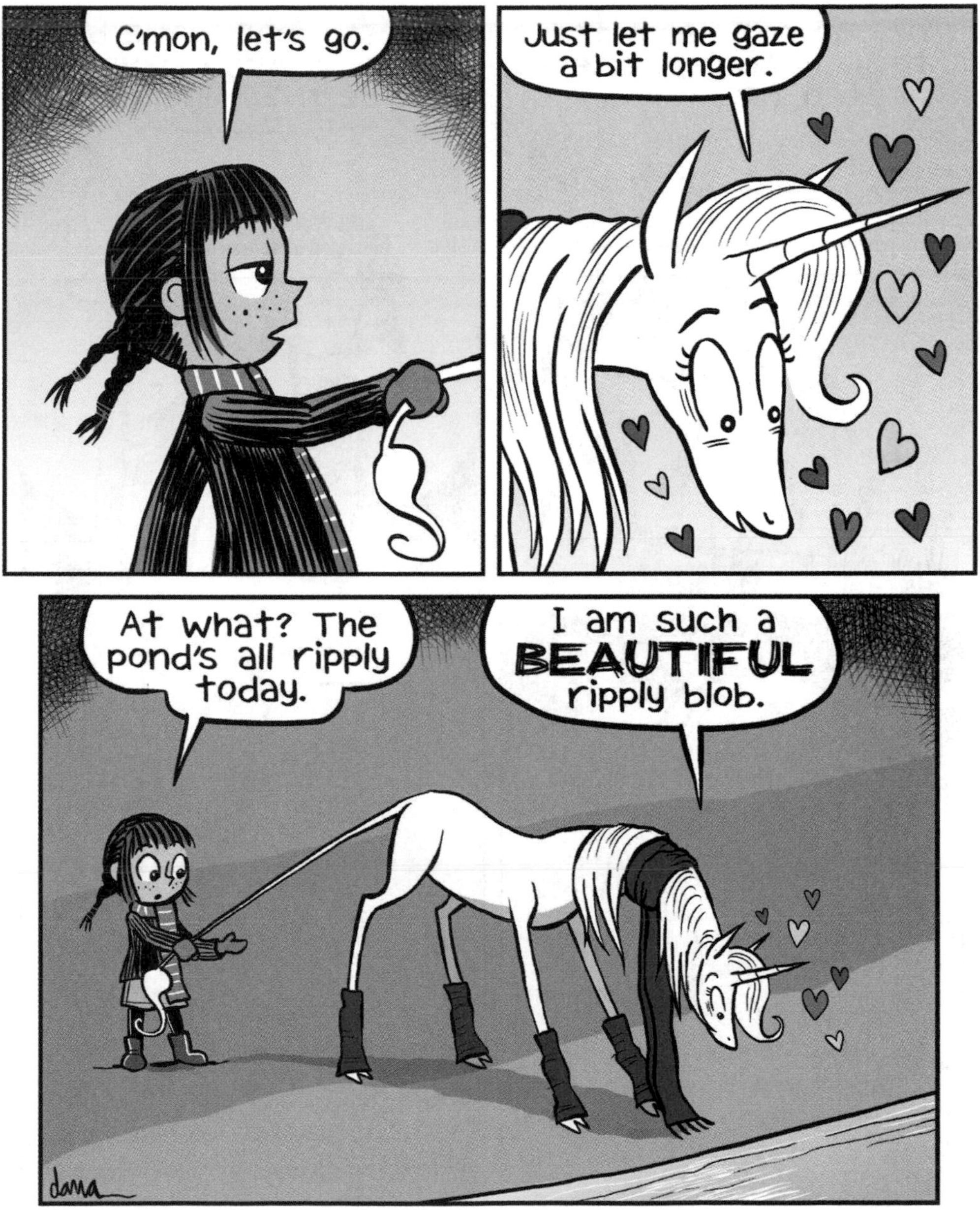
C'mon, let's go.
Just let me gaze a bit longer.
At what? The pond's all ripply today.
I am such a **BEAUTIFUL** ripply blob.
dana

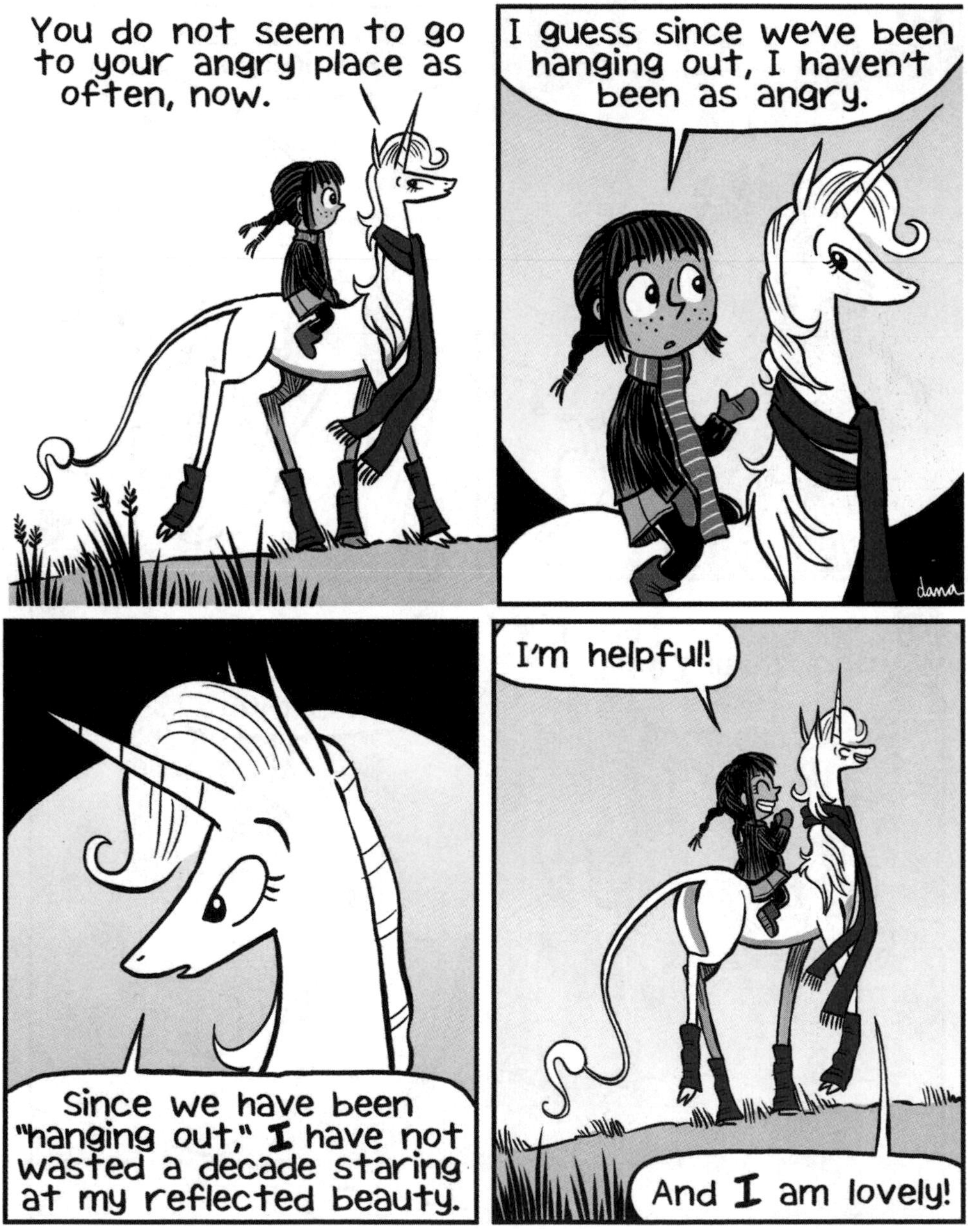
You do not seem to go to your angry place as often, now.
I guess since we've been hanging out, I haven't been as angry.
dana
Since we have been "hanging out," I have not wasted a decade staring at my reflected beauty.
I'm helpful!
And I am lovely!

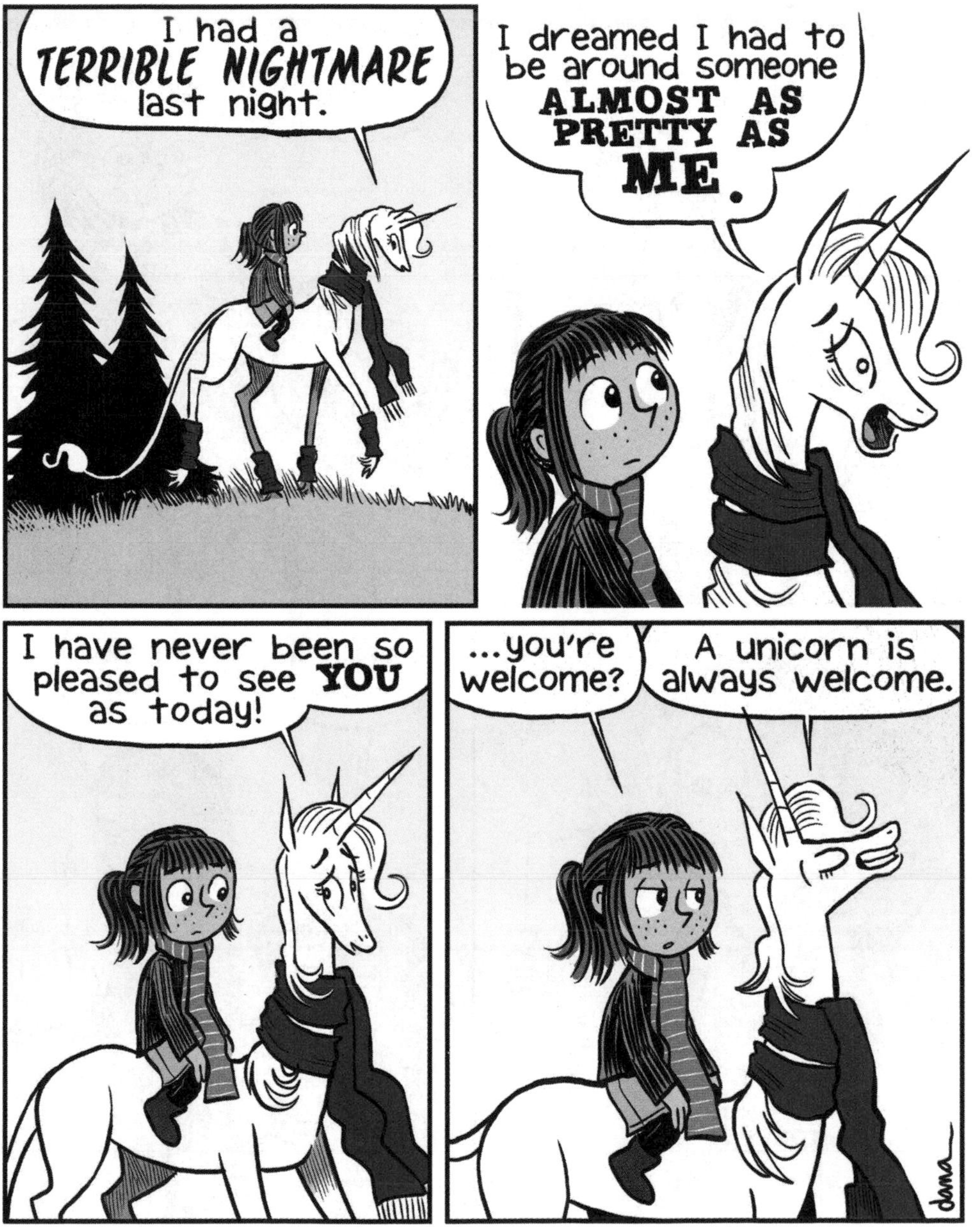
I had a TERRIBLE NIGHTMARE last night.
I dreamed I had to be around someone ALMOST AS PRETTY AS ME.
I have never been so pleased to see YOU as today!
...you're welcome?
A unicorn is always welcome.
dana

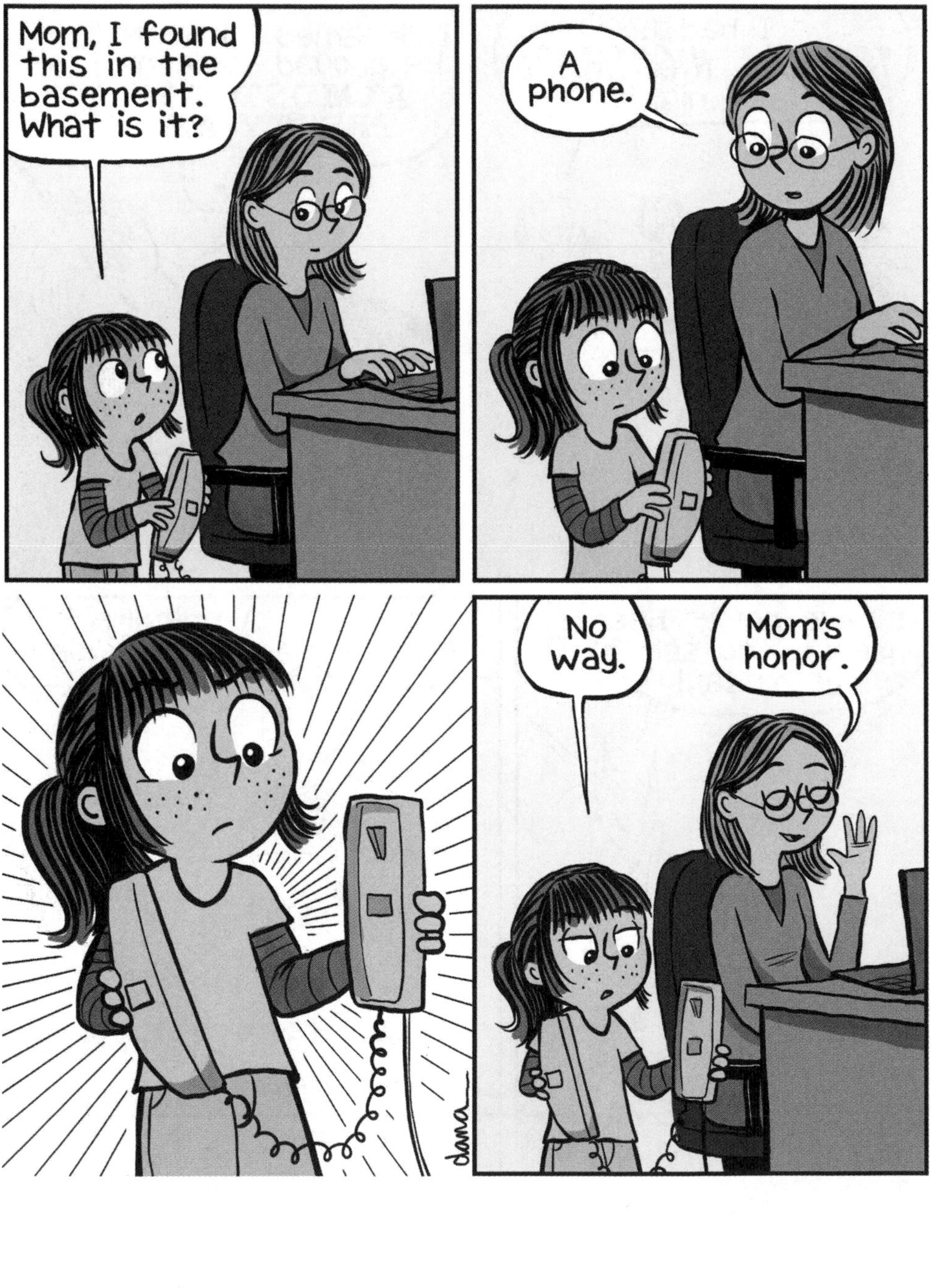
Mom, I found this in the basement. What is it?
A phone.
No way.
Mom's honor.
dana

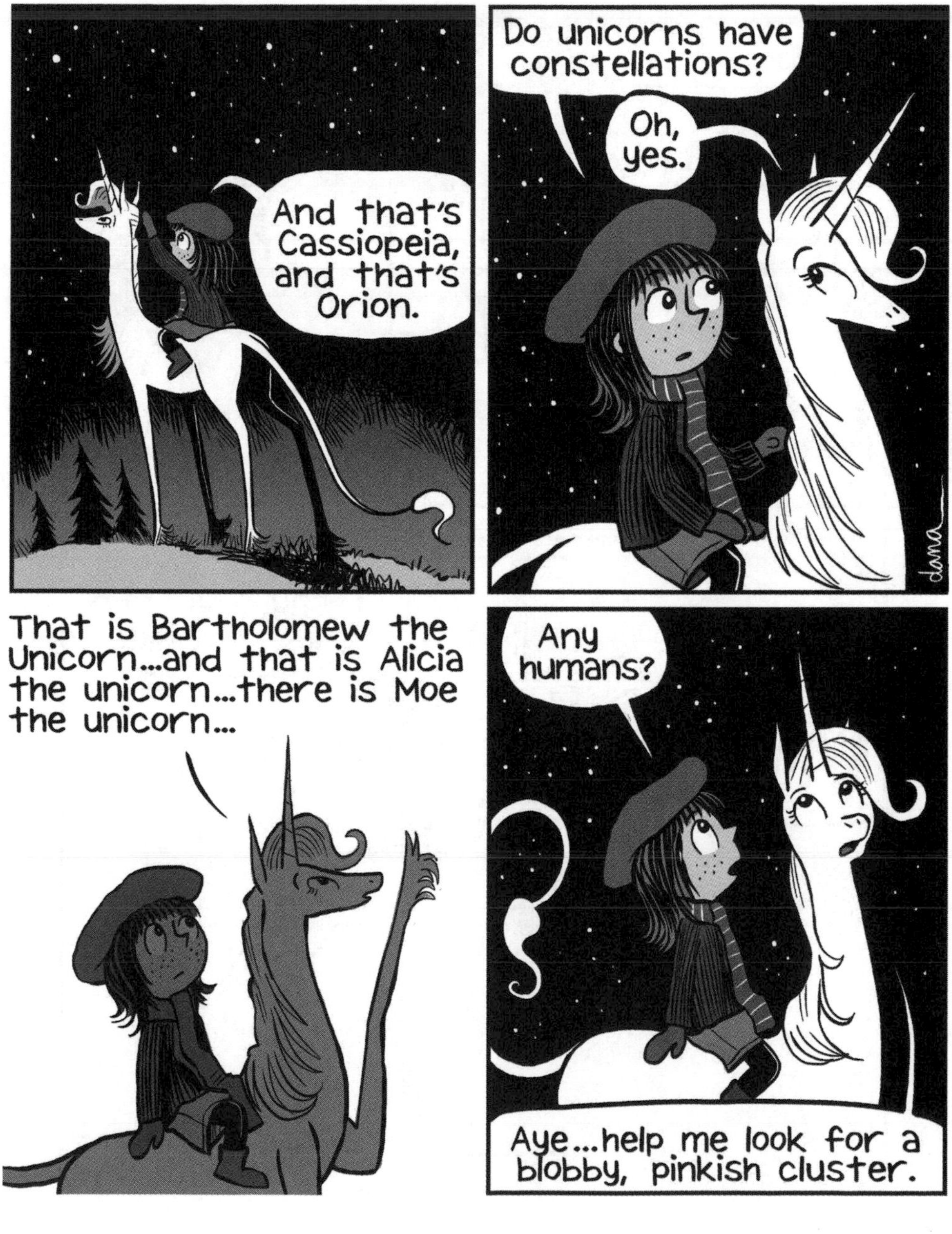
And that's Cassiopeia, and that's Orion.
Do unicorns have constellations?
Oh, yes.
dana
That is Bartholomew the Unicorn...and that is Alicia the unicorn...there is Moe the unicorn...
Any humans?
Aye...help me look for a blobby, pinkish cluster.

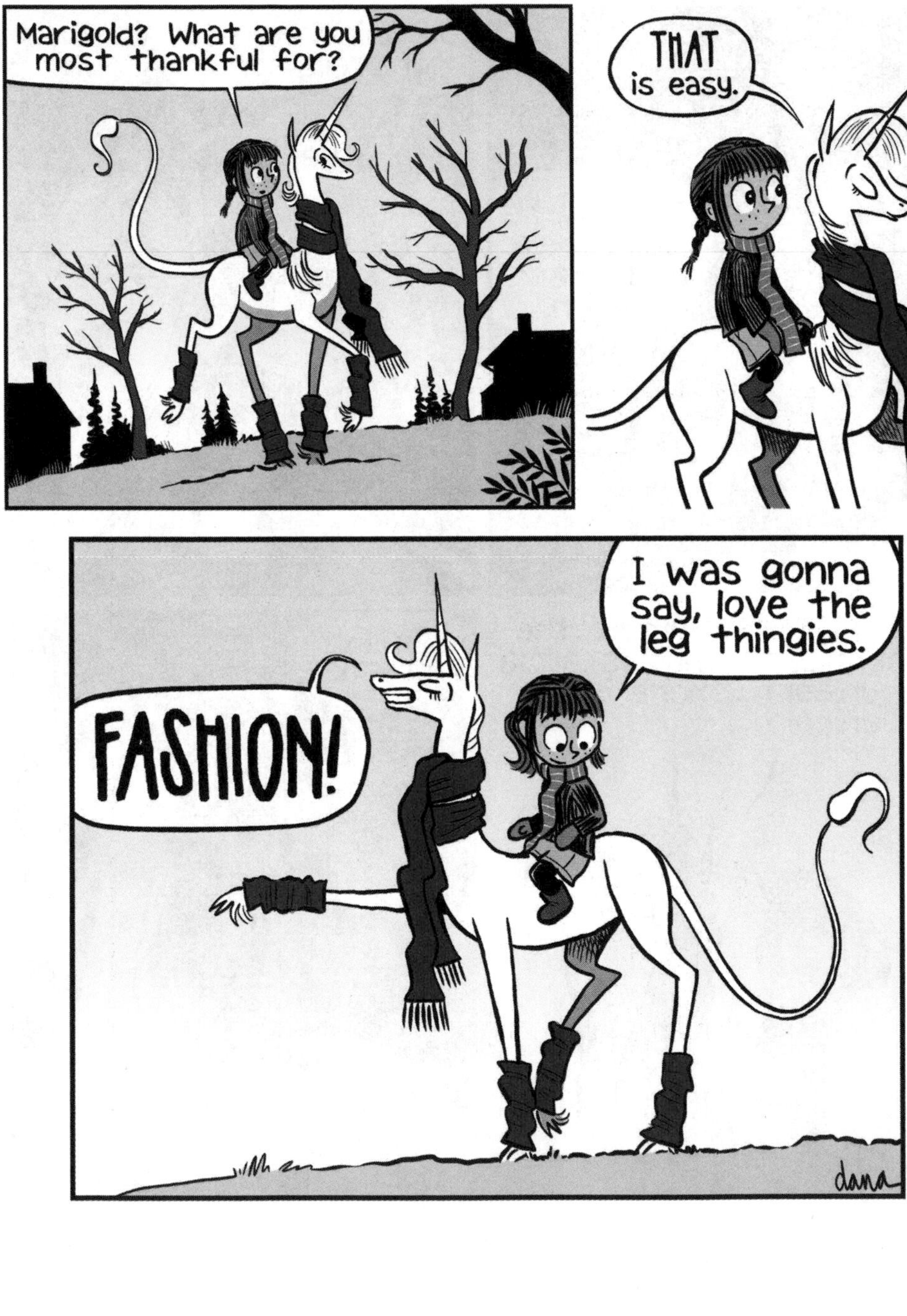
Marigold? What are you most thankful for?
THAT is easy.
FASHION!
I was gonna say, love the leg thingies.
dana

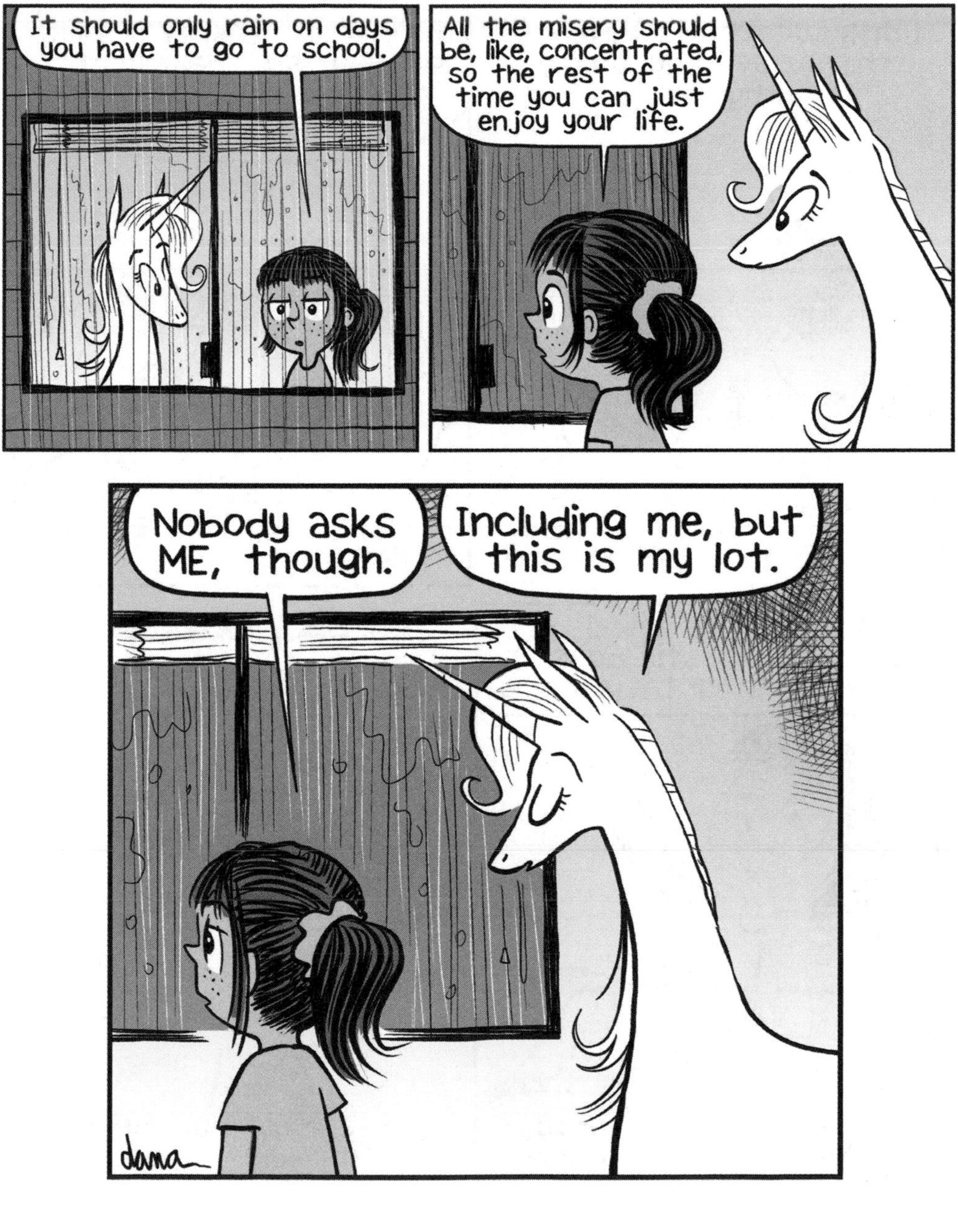
It should only rain on days you have to go to school.
All the misery should be, like, concentrated, so the rest of the time you can just enjoy your life.
Nobody asks ME, though.
Including me, but this is my lot.
dana

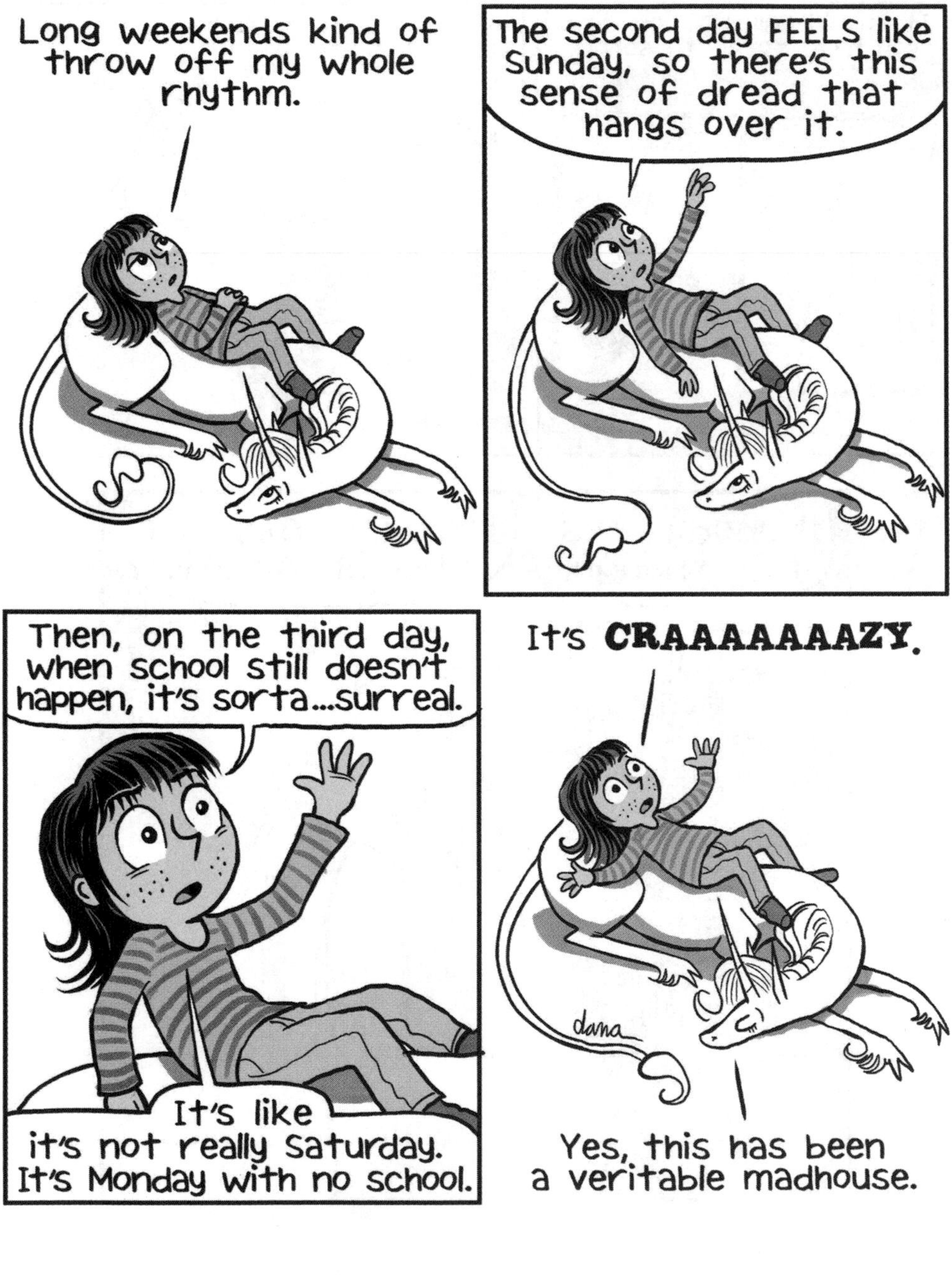
Long weekends kind of throw off my whole rhythm.
The second day FEELS like Sunday, so there's this sense of dread that hangs over it.
Then, on the third day, when school still doesn't happen, it's sorta...surreal.
It's like it's not really Saturday. It's Monday with no school.
It's **CRAAAAAAAZY**.
dana
Yes, this has been a veritable madhouse.

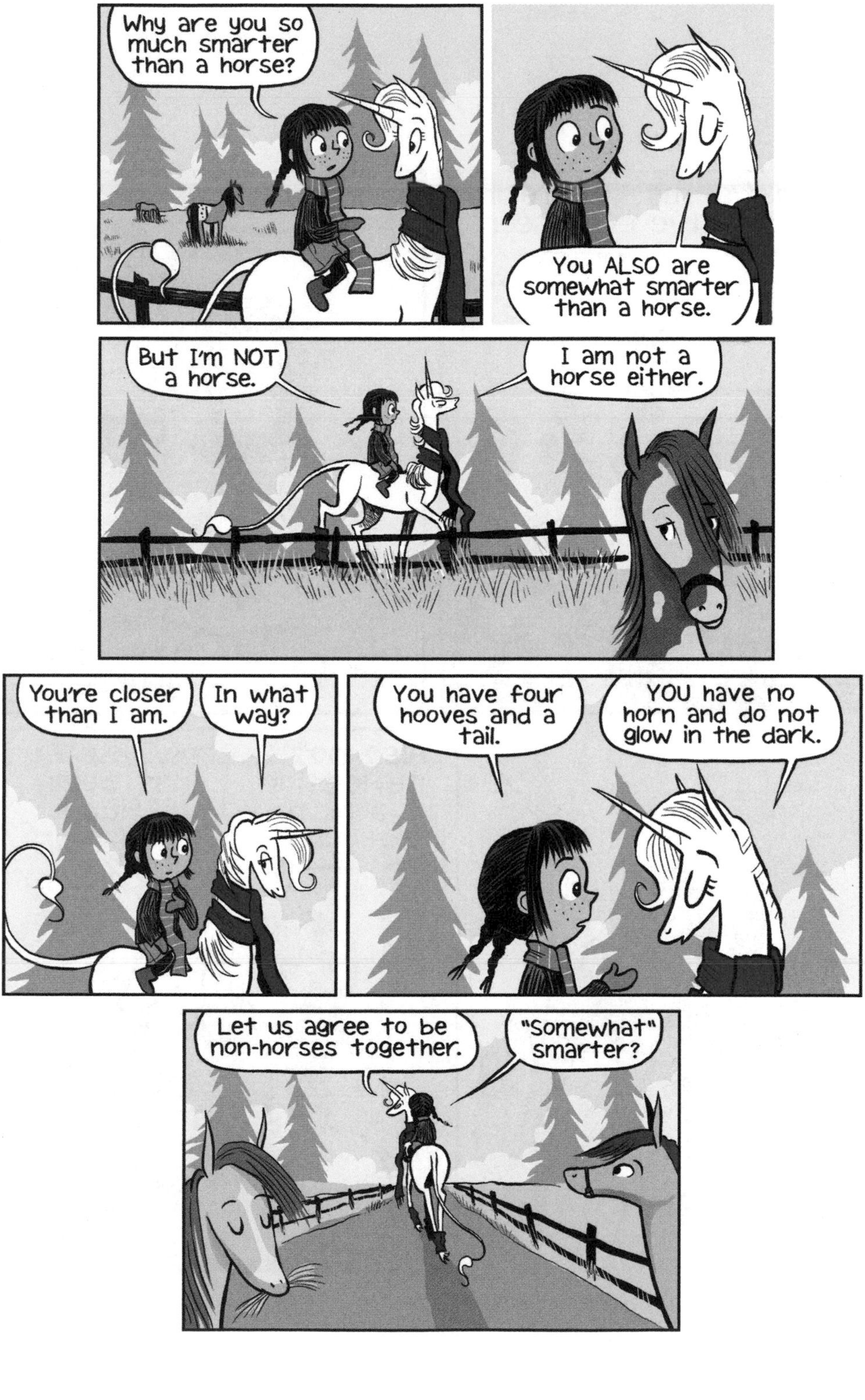
Why are you so much smarter than a horse?
You ALSO are somewhat smarter than a horse.
But I'm NOT a horse.
I am not a horse either.
You're closer than I am.
In what way?
You have four hooves and a tail.
YOU have no horn and do not glow in the dark.
Let us agree to be non-horses together.
"Somewhat" smarter?

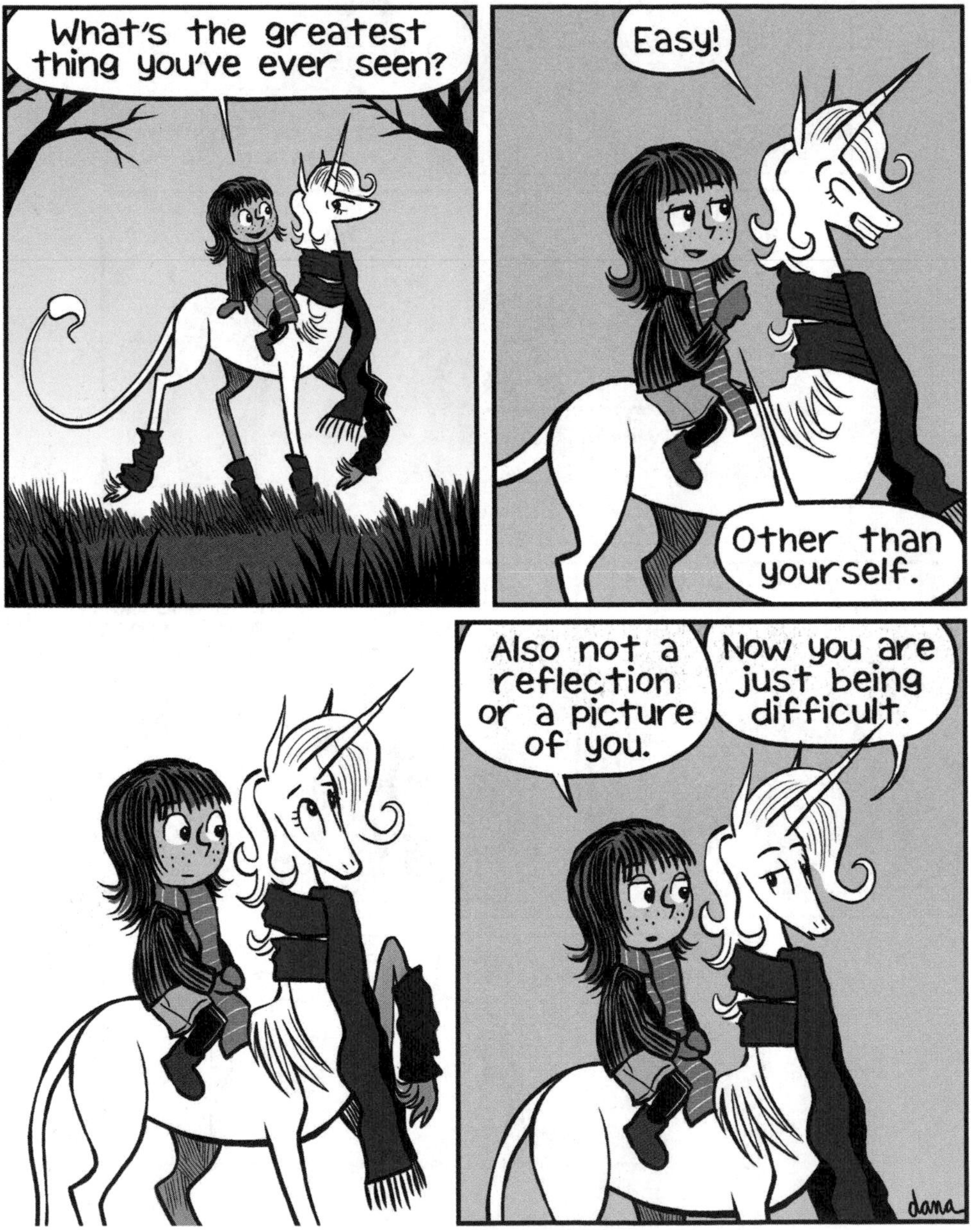
What's the greatest thing you've ever seen?
Easy!
Other than yourself.
Also not a reflection or a picture of you.
Now you are just being difficult.
dana

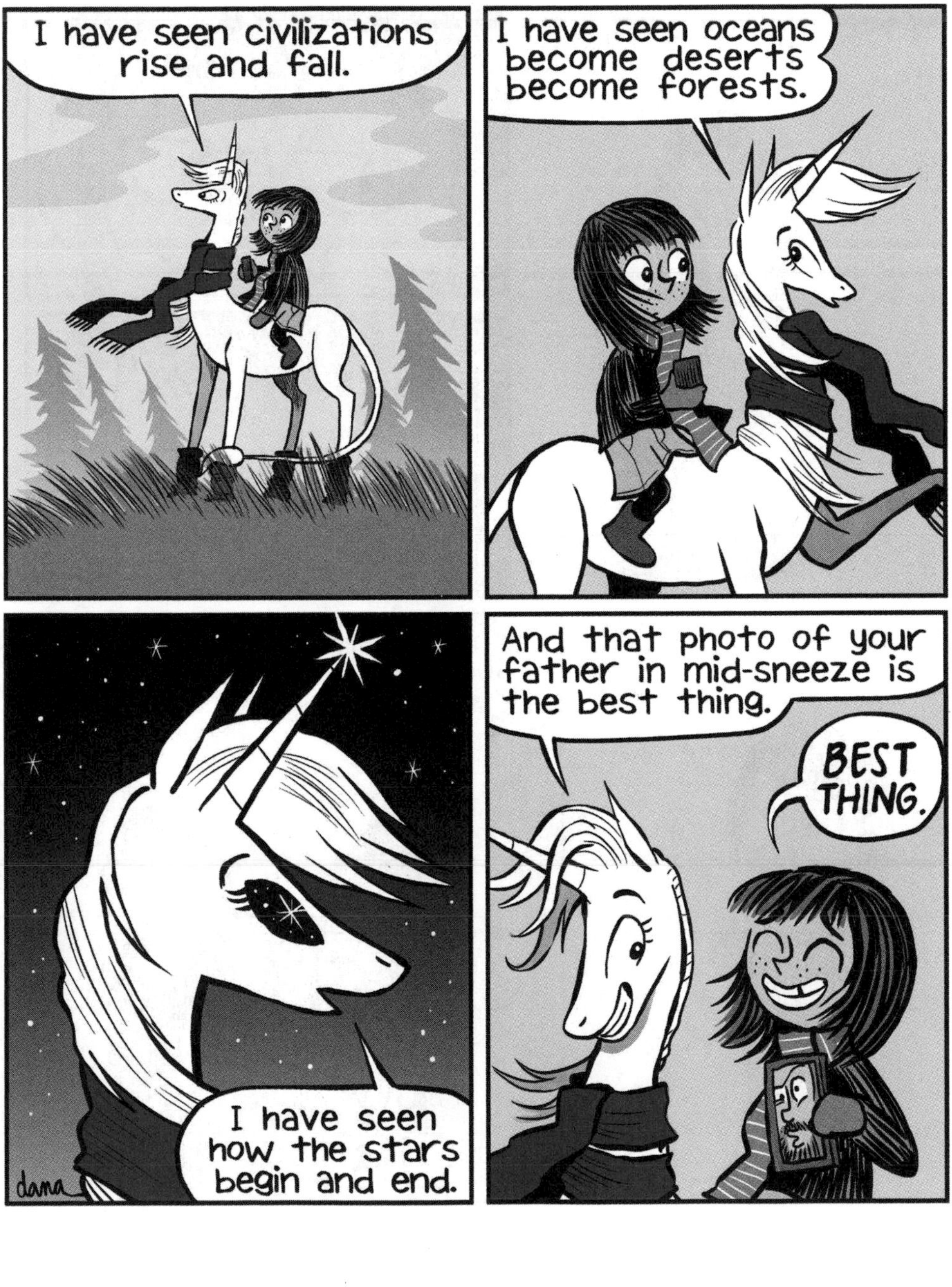
I have seen civilizations rise and fall.
I have seen oceans become deserts become forests.
I have seen how the stars begin and end.
dana
And that photo of your father in mid-sneeze is the best thing.
BEST THING.

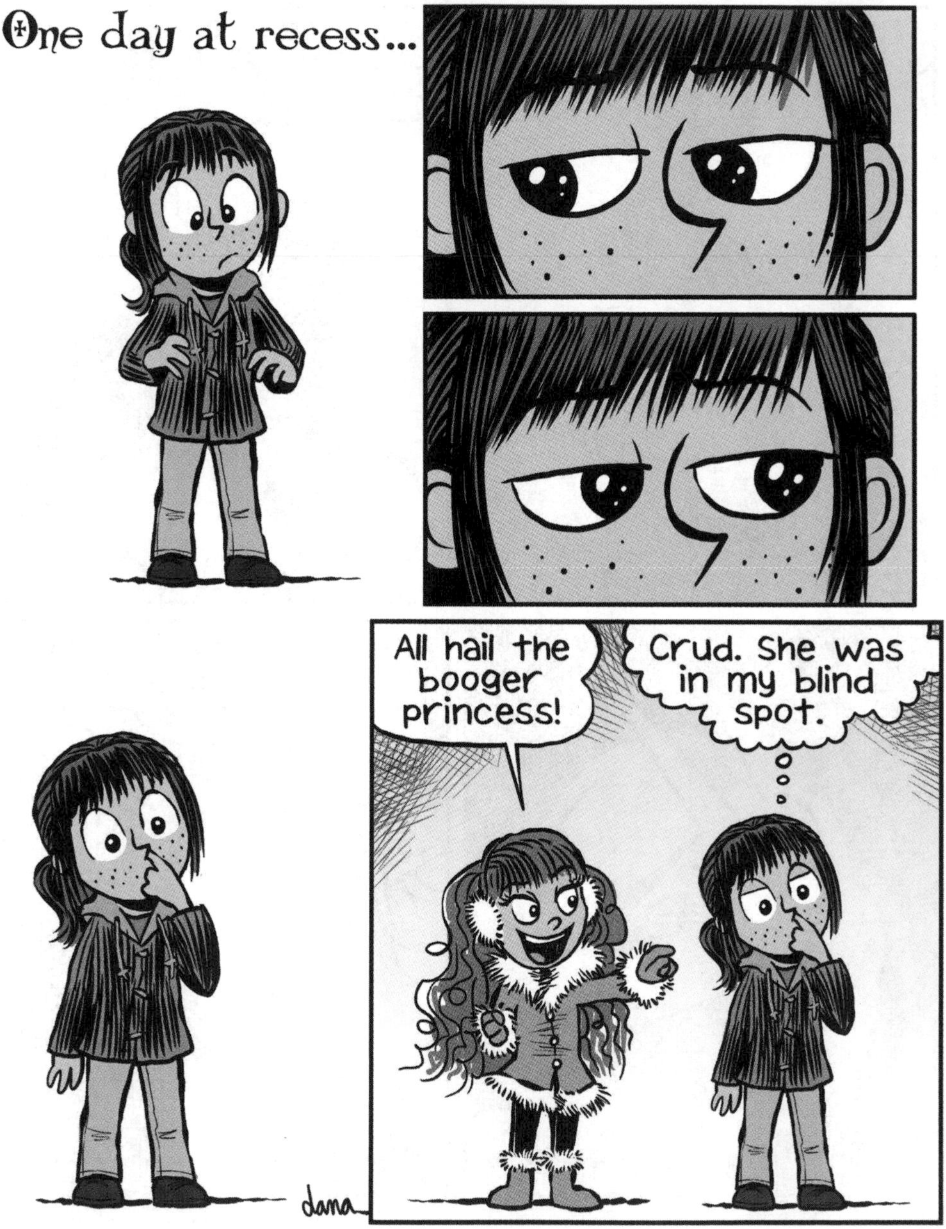
One day at recess...
All hail the booger princess!
Crud. She was in my blind spot.
dana

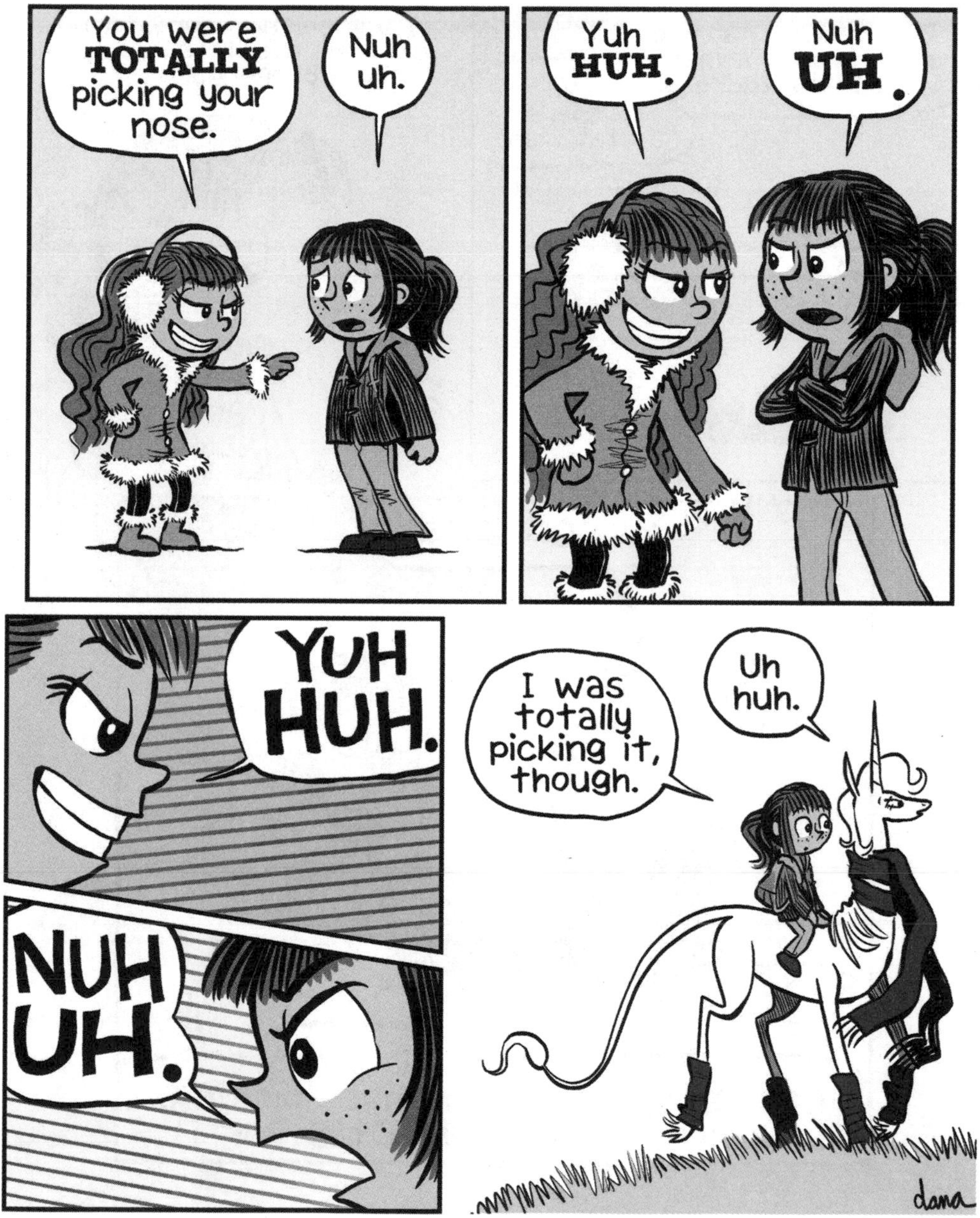
You were **TOTALLY** picking your nose.
Nuh uh.
Yuh **HUH**.
Nuh **UH**.
YUH HUH.
NUH UH.
I was totally picking it, though.
Uh huh.
dana

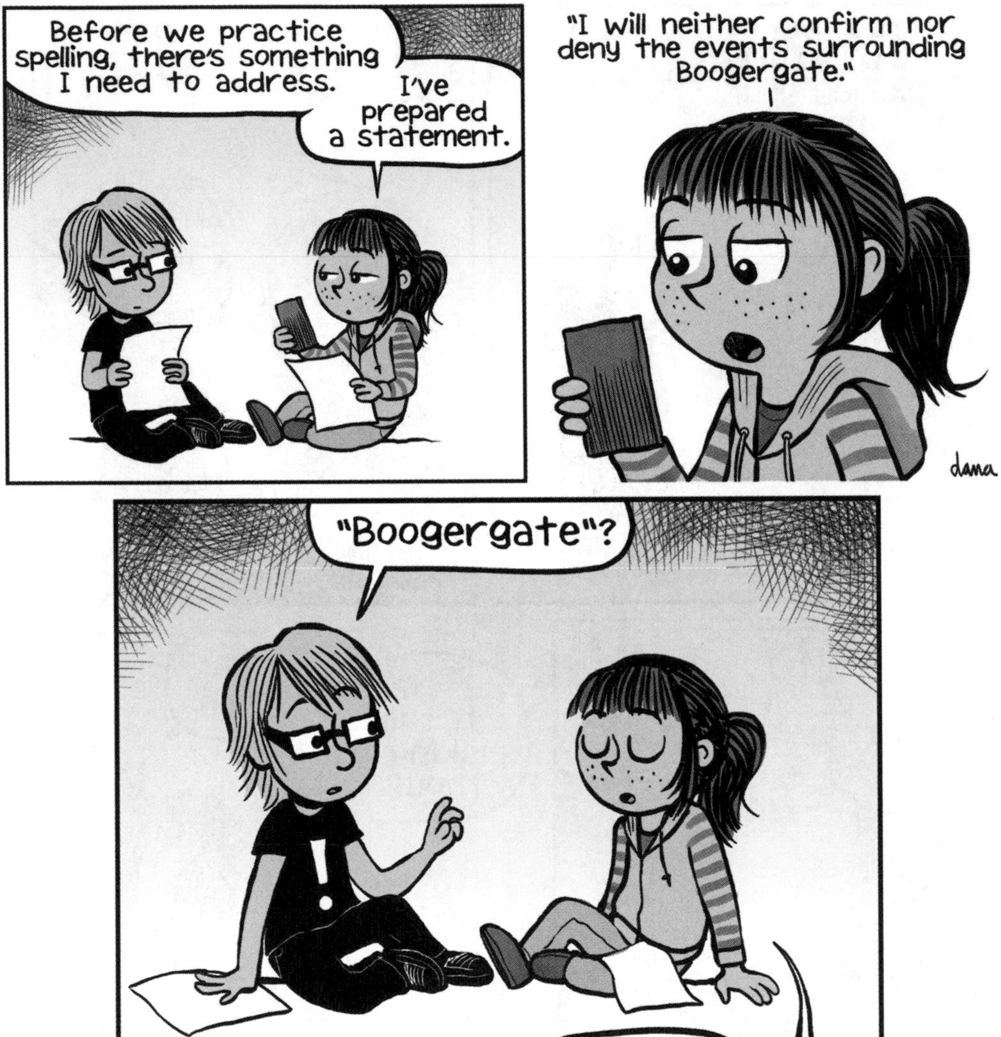
Before we practice spelling, there's something I need to address.
I've prepared a statement.
"I will neither confirm nor deny the events surrounding Boogergate."
dana
"Boogergate"?
If I'm gonna be known for nose-picking, I wanna be **NOTORIOUS** for it.

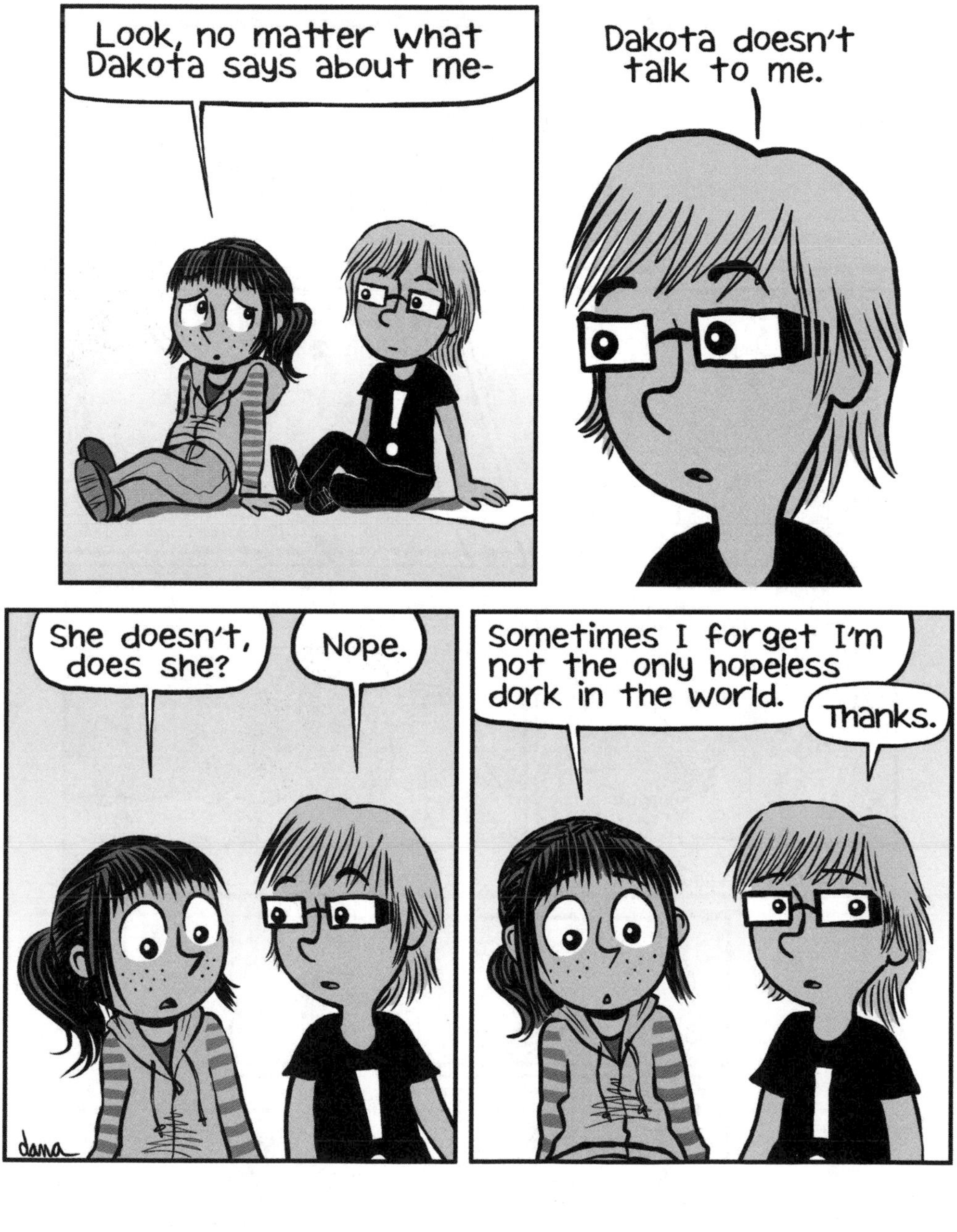
Look, no matter what Dakota says about me-
Dakota doesn't talk to me.
She doesn't, does she?
Nope.
Sometimes I forget I'm not the only hopeless dork in the world.
Thanks.
dana

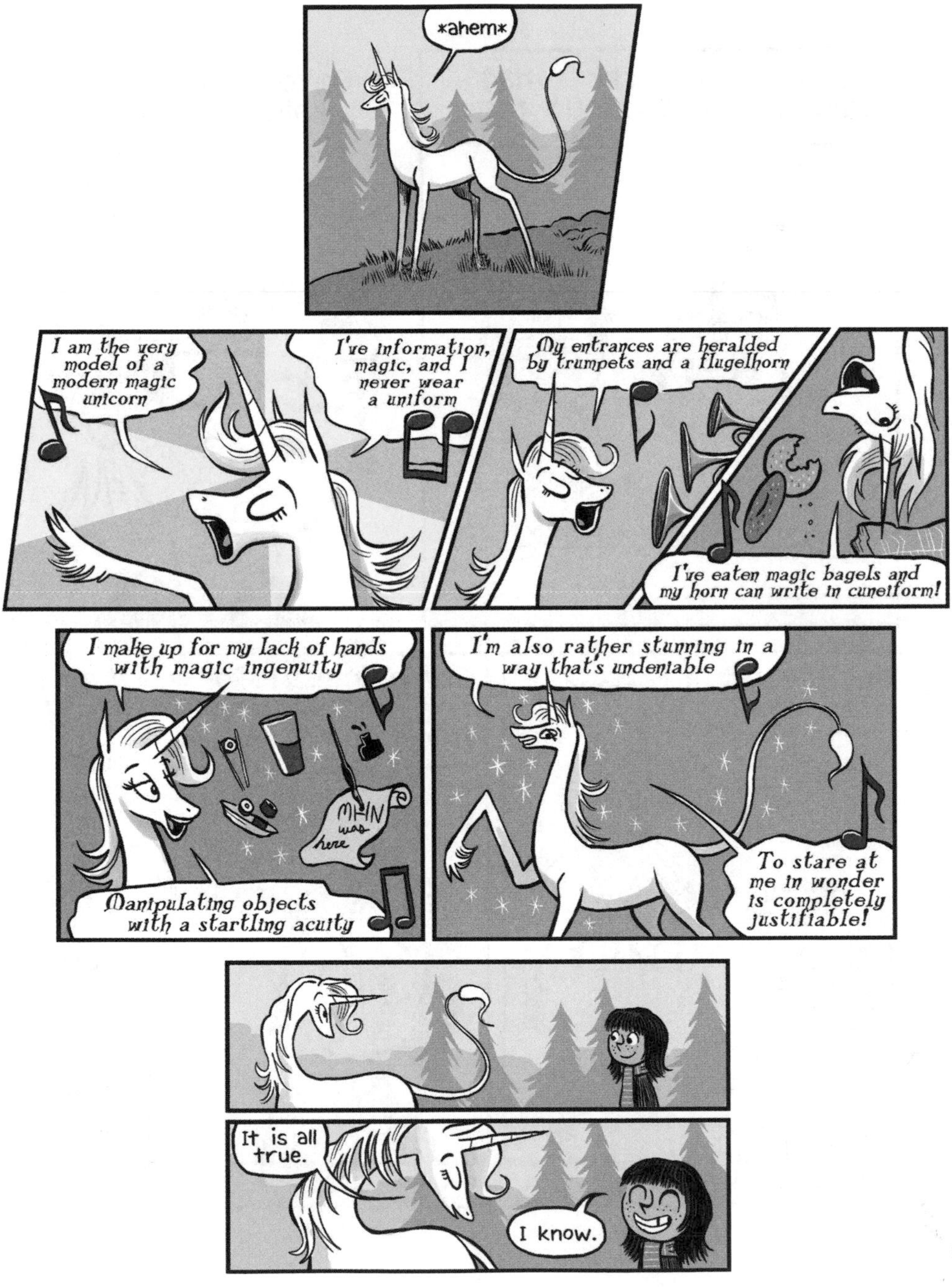
ahem
I am the very model of a modern magic unicorn
I've information, magic, and I never wear a uniform
My entrances are heralded by trumpets and a flugelhorn
I've eaten magic bagels and my horn can write in cuneiform!
I make up for my lack of hands with magic ingenuity
Manipulating objects with a startling acuity
I'm also rather stunning in a way that's undeniable
To stare at me in wonder is completely justifiable!
It is all true.
I know.

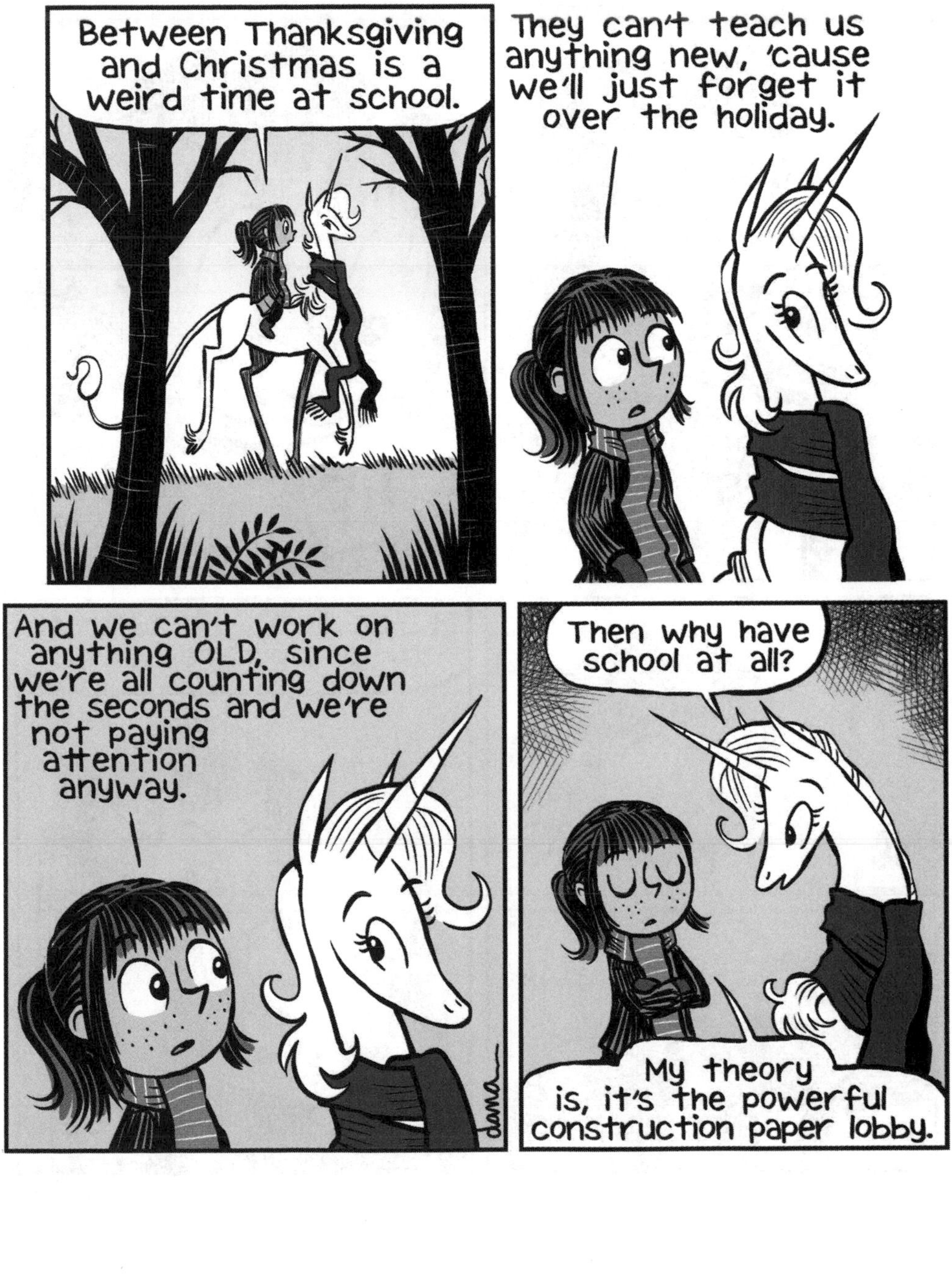
Between Thanksgiving and Christmas is a weird time at school.
They can't teach us anything new, 'cause we'll just forget it over the holiday.
And we can't work on anything OLD, since we're all counting down the seconds and we're not paying attention anyway.
dana
Then why have school at all?
My theory is, it's the powerful construction paper lobby.

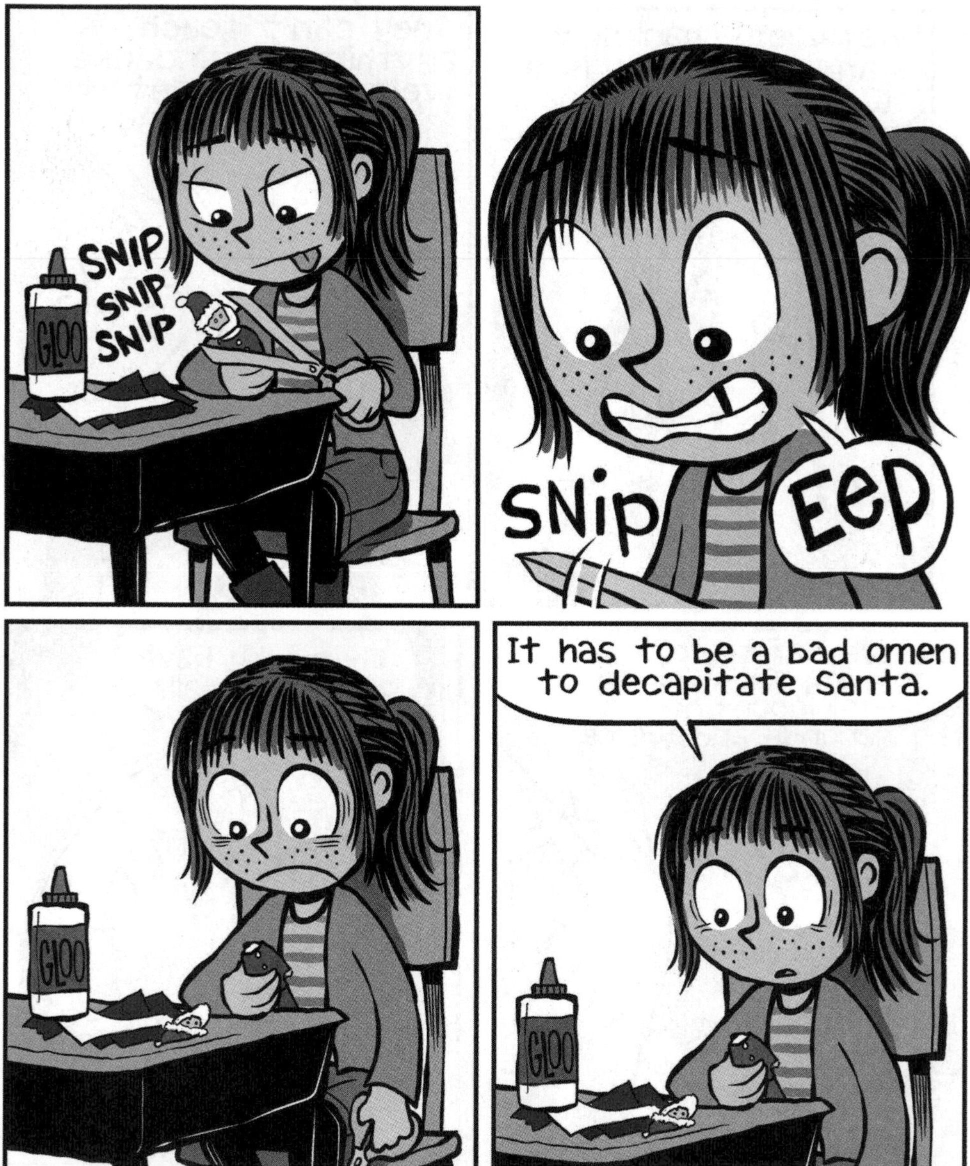
SNIP
SNIP
SNIP
GLOO
SNIP
EEP
GLOO
It has to be a bad omen to decapitate Santa.
GLOO
dana

Ew, you're gluing your Santa's head back on? How come? Why'd you cut it off?
Because he ASKED TOO MANY QUESTIONS.
dana
TEACHERRR!
When you give me these notes from your teacher, you could at least suppress that grin.

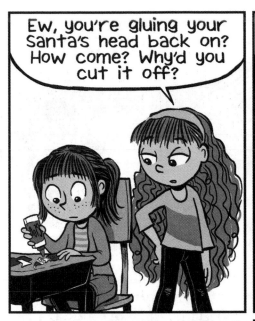

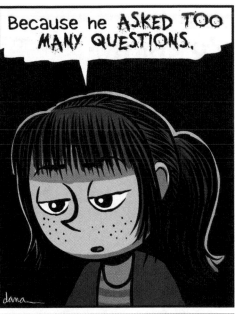

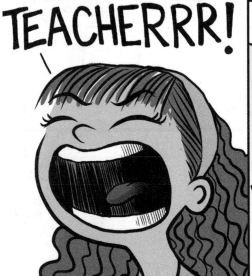

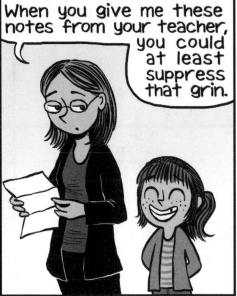

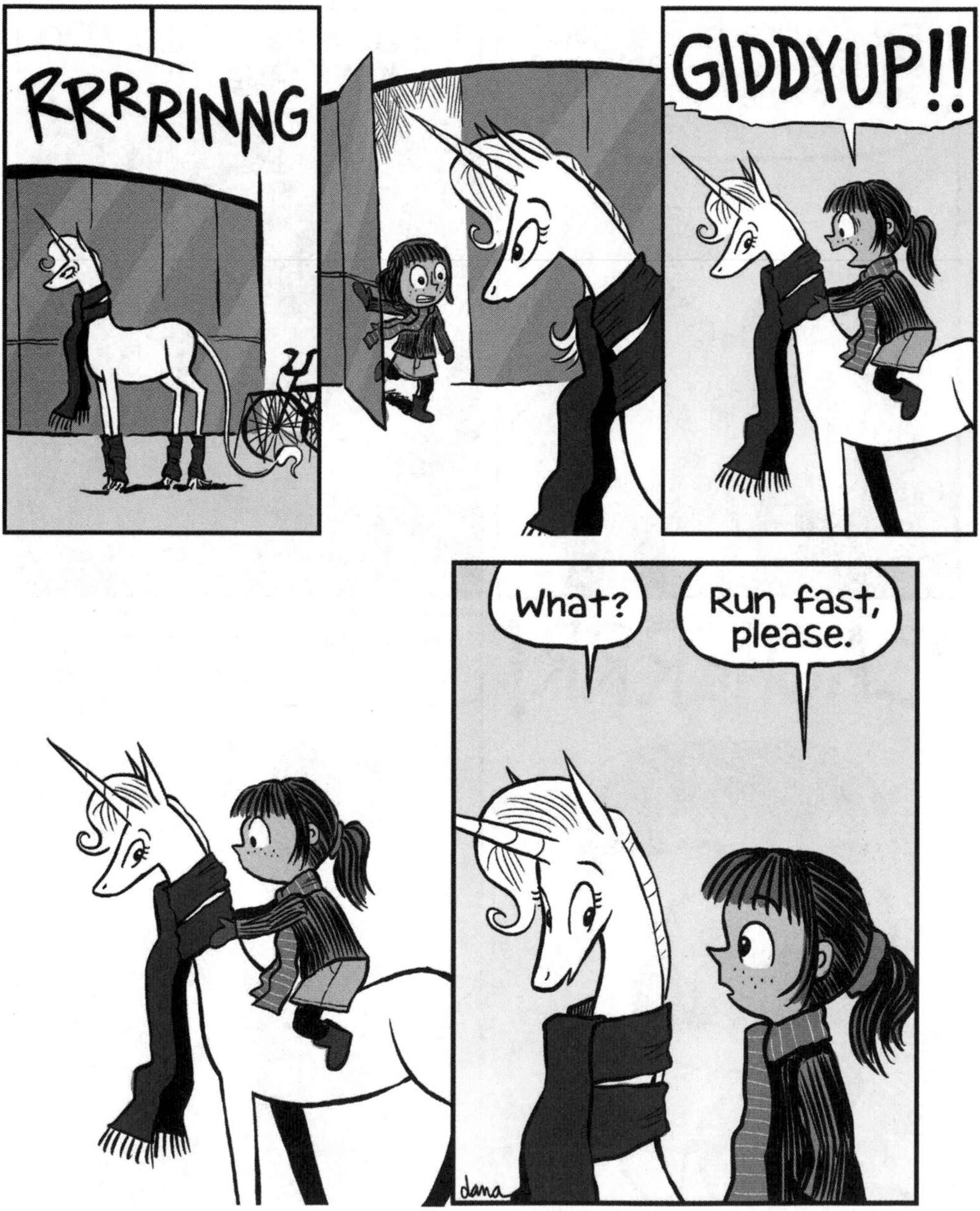
RRRRINNG
GIDDYUP!!
What?
Run fast, please.
dana

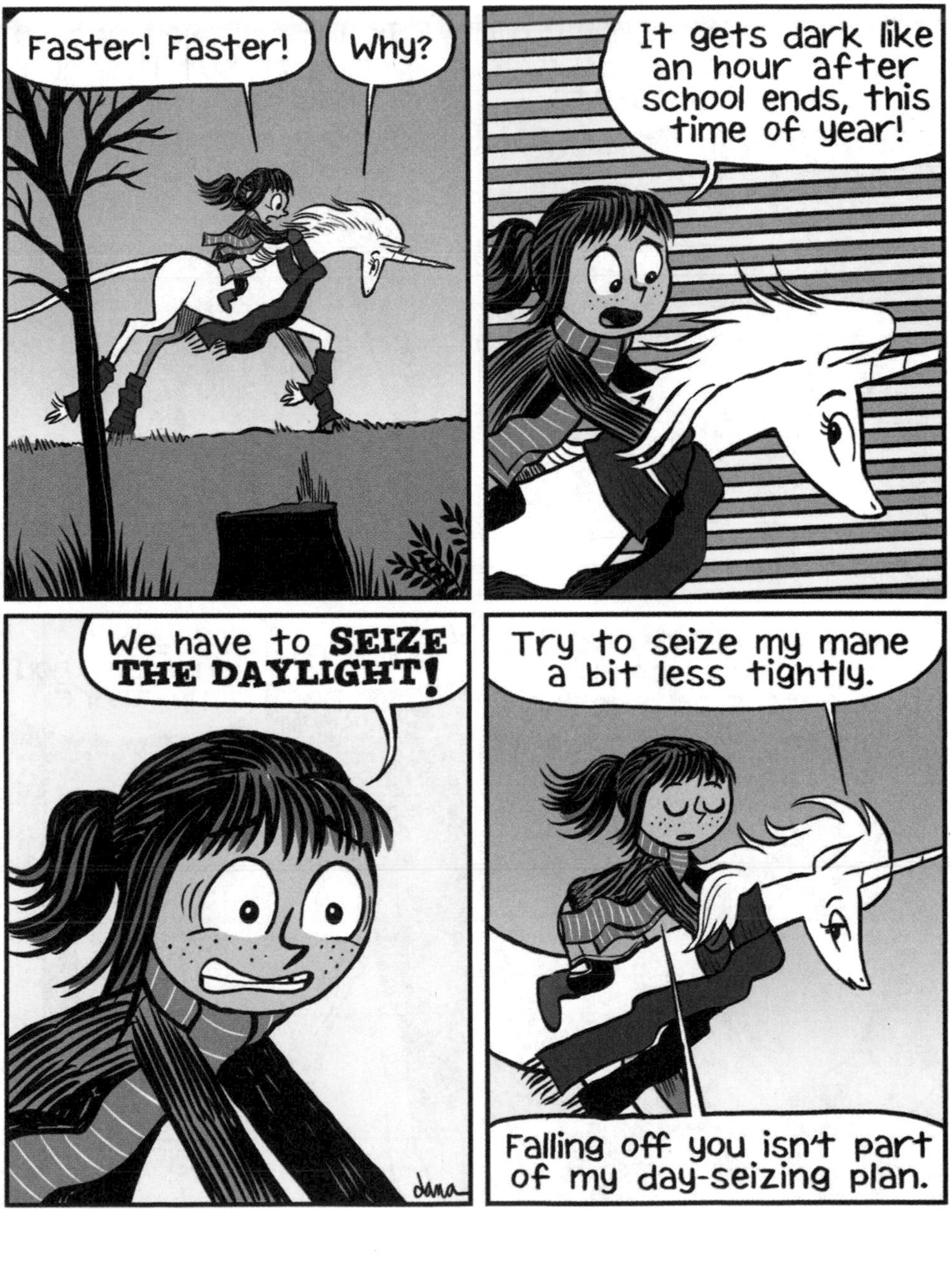
Faster! Faster!
Why?
It gets dark like an hour after school ends, this time of year!
We have to **SEIZE THE DAYLIGHT!**
Try to seize my mane a bit less tightly.
Falling off you isn't part of my day-seizing plan.
dana

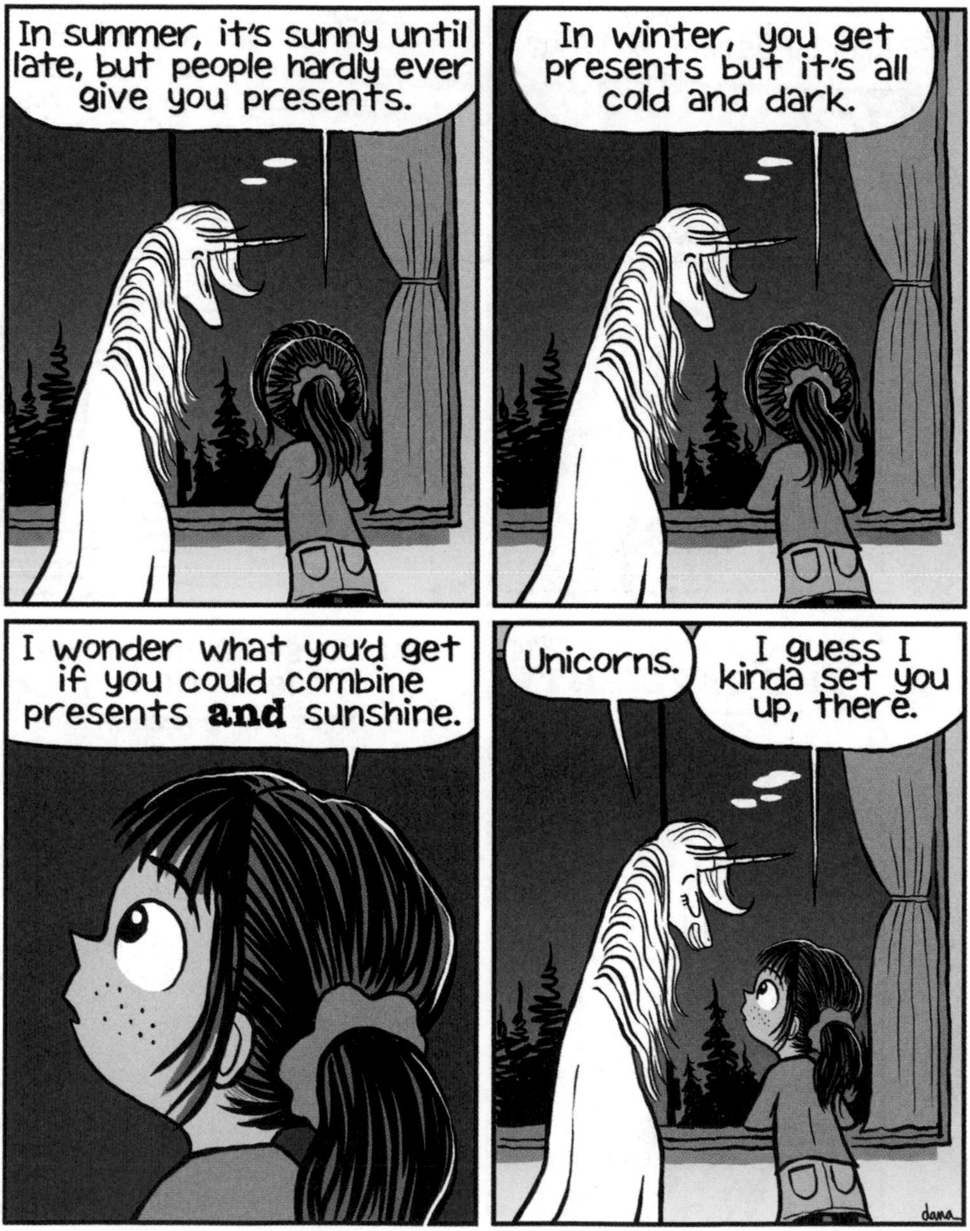
In summer, it's sunny until late, but people hardly ever give you presents.
In winter, you get presents but it's all cold and dark.
I wonder what you'd get if you could combine presents **and** sunshine.
Unicorns.
I guess I kinda set you up, there.
dana

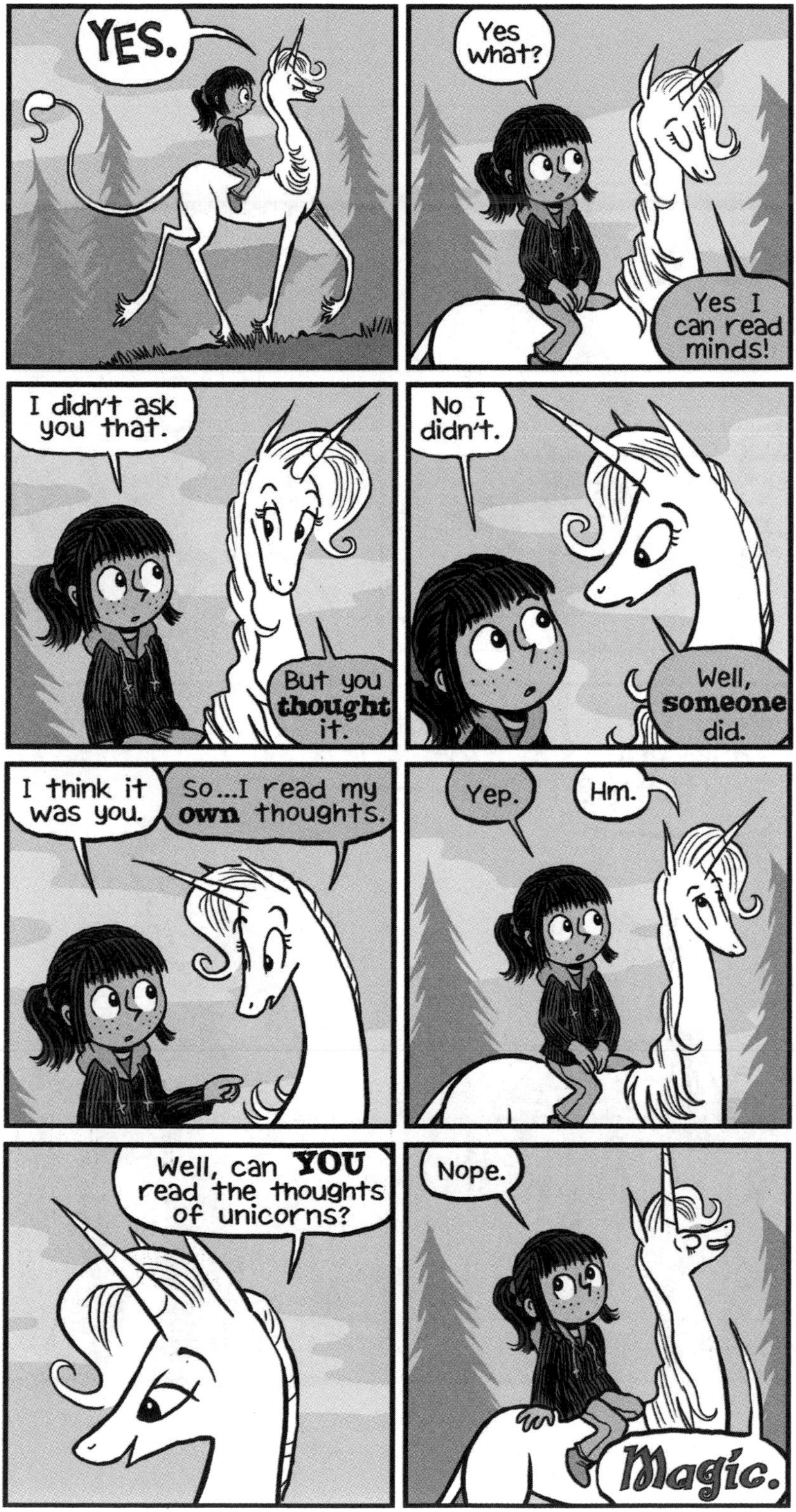
YES.
Yes what?
Yes I can read minds!
I didn't ask you that.
But you **thought** it.
No I didn't.
Well, **someone** did.
I think it was you.
So...I read my **own** thoughts.
Yep.
Hm.
Well, can **YOU** read the thoughts of unicorns?
Nope.
Magic.

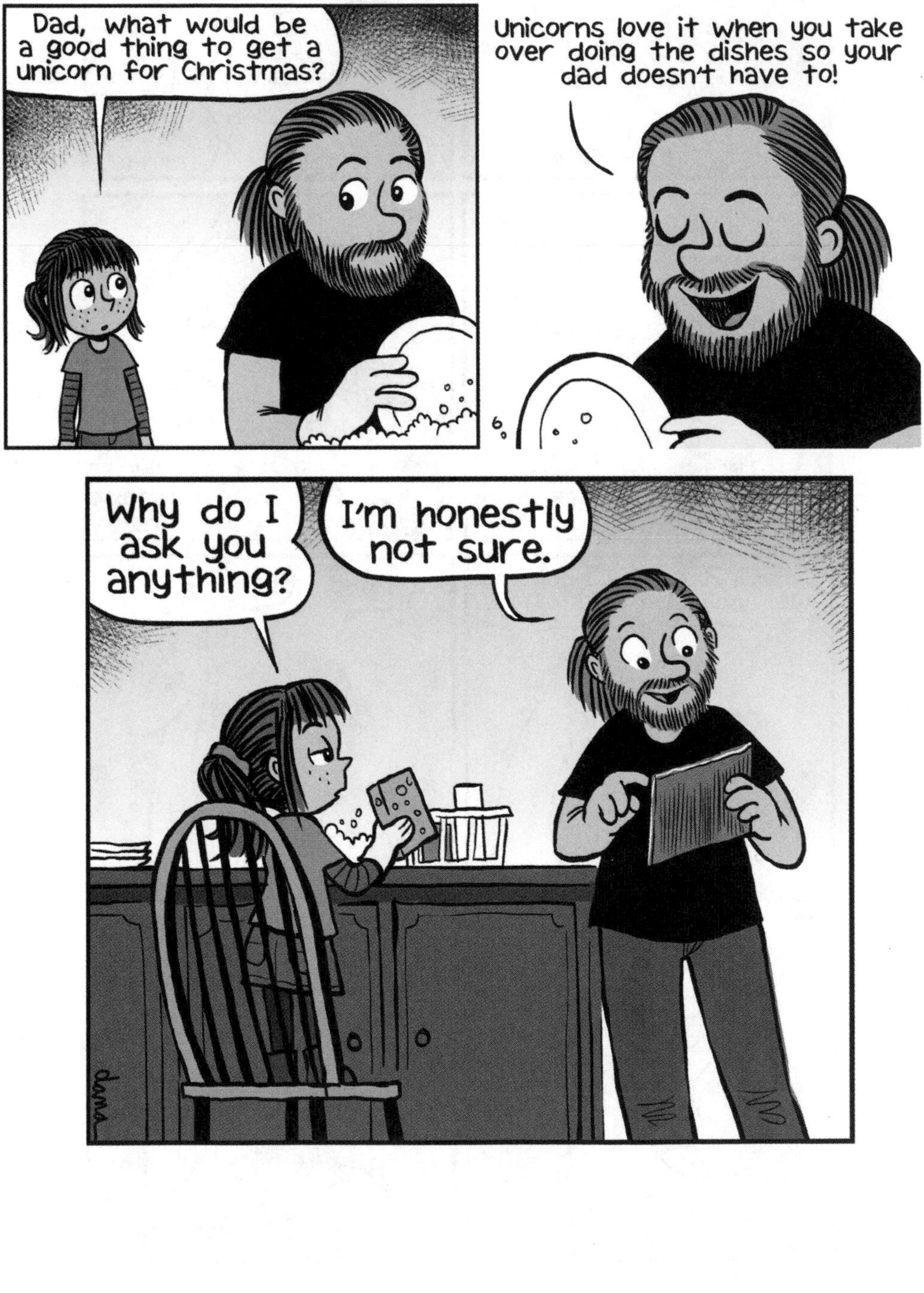
Dad, what would be a good thing to get a unicorn for Christmas?
Unicorns love it when you take over doing the dishes so your dad doesn't have to!
Why do I ask you anything?
I'm honestly not sure.
dana

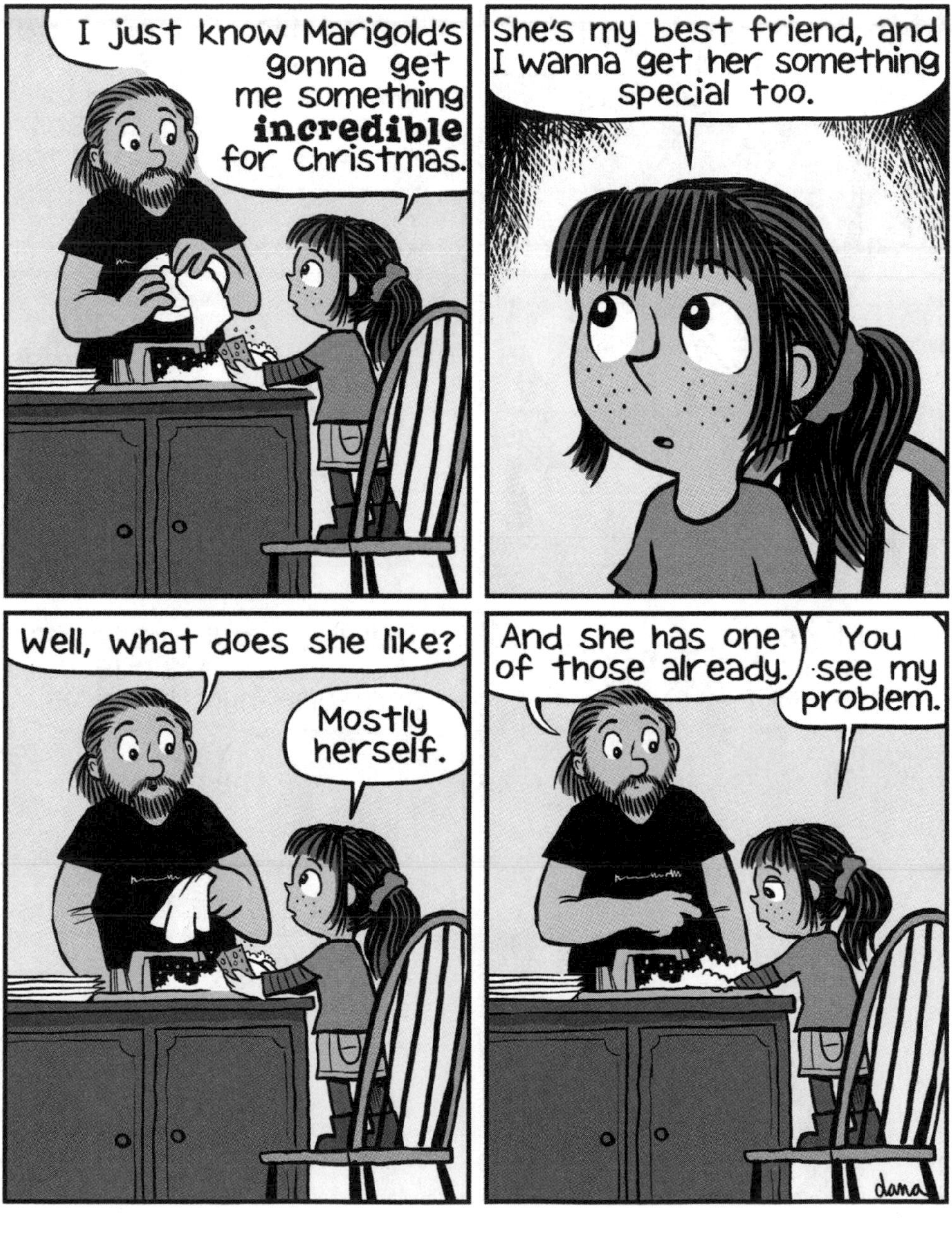
I just know Marigold's gonna get me something **incredible** for Christmas.
She's my best friend, and I wanna get her something special too.
Well, what does she like?
Mostly herself.
And she has one of those already.
You see my problem.
dana

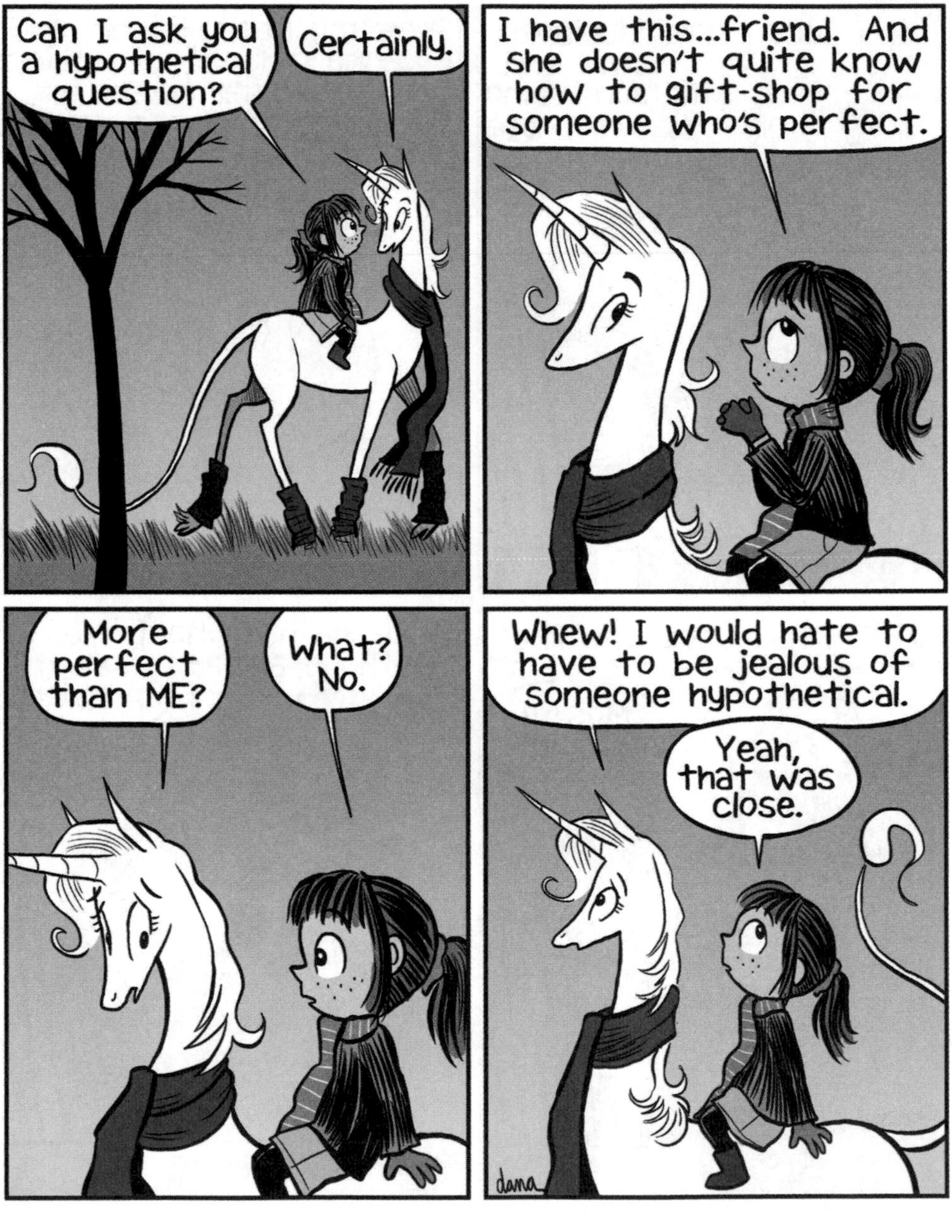
Can I ask you a hypothetical question?
Certainly.
I have this...friend. And she doesn't quite know how to gift-shop for someone who's perfect.
More perfect than ME?
What? No.
Whew! I would hate to have to be jealous of someone hypothetical.
Yeah, that was close.
dana

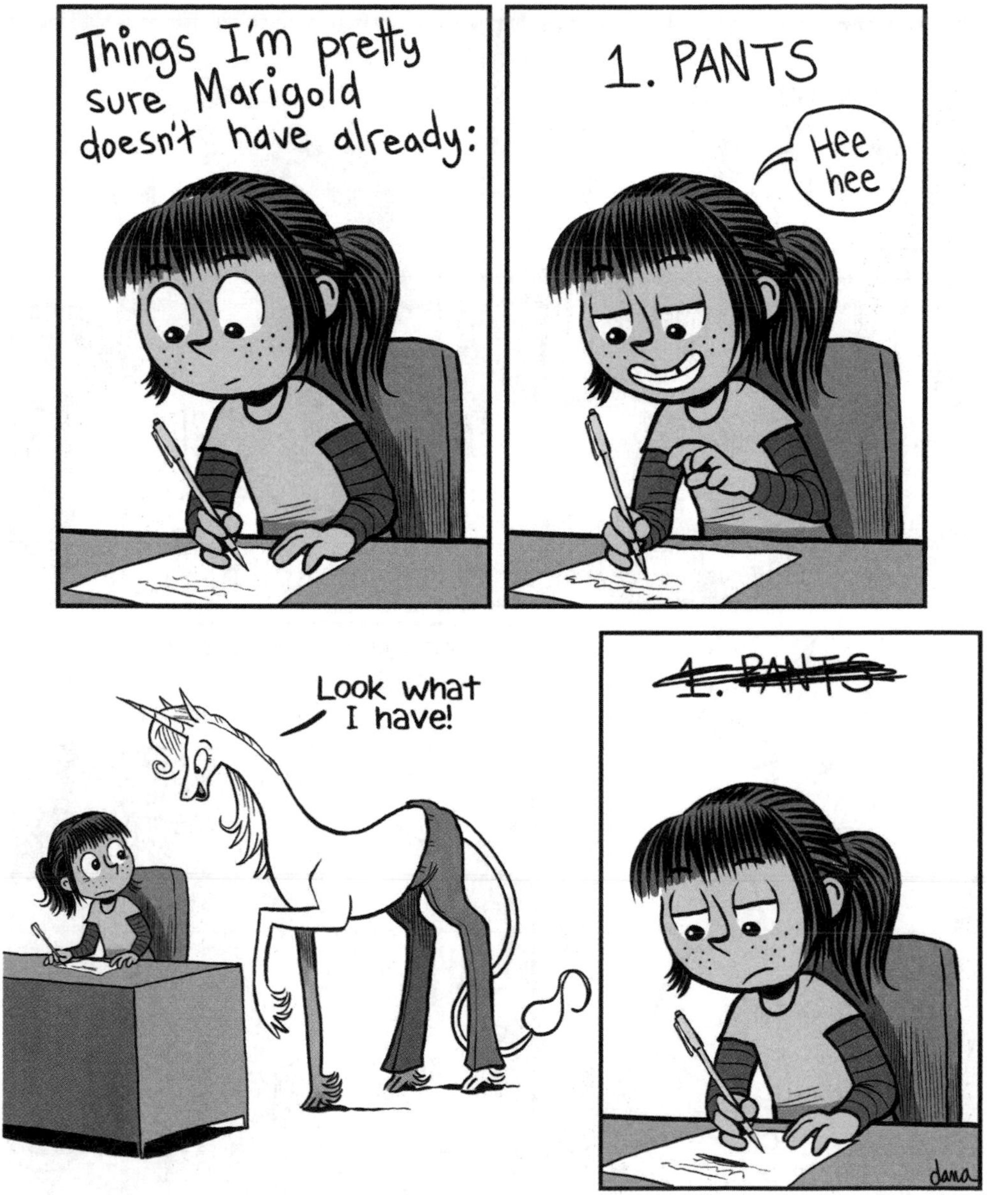
Things I'm pretty sure Marigold doesn't have already:
1. PANTS
Hee hee
Look what I have!
1. PANTS
dana

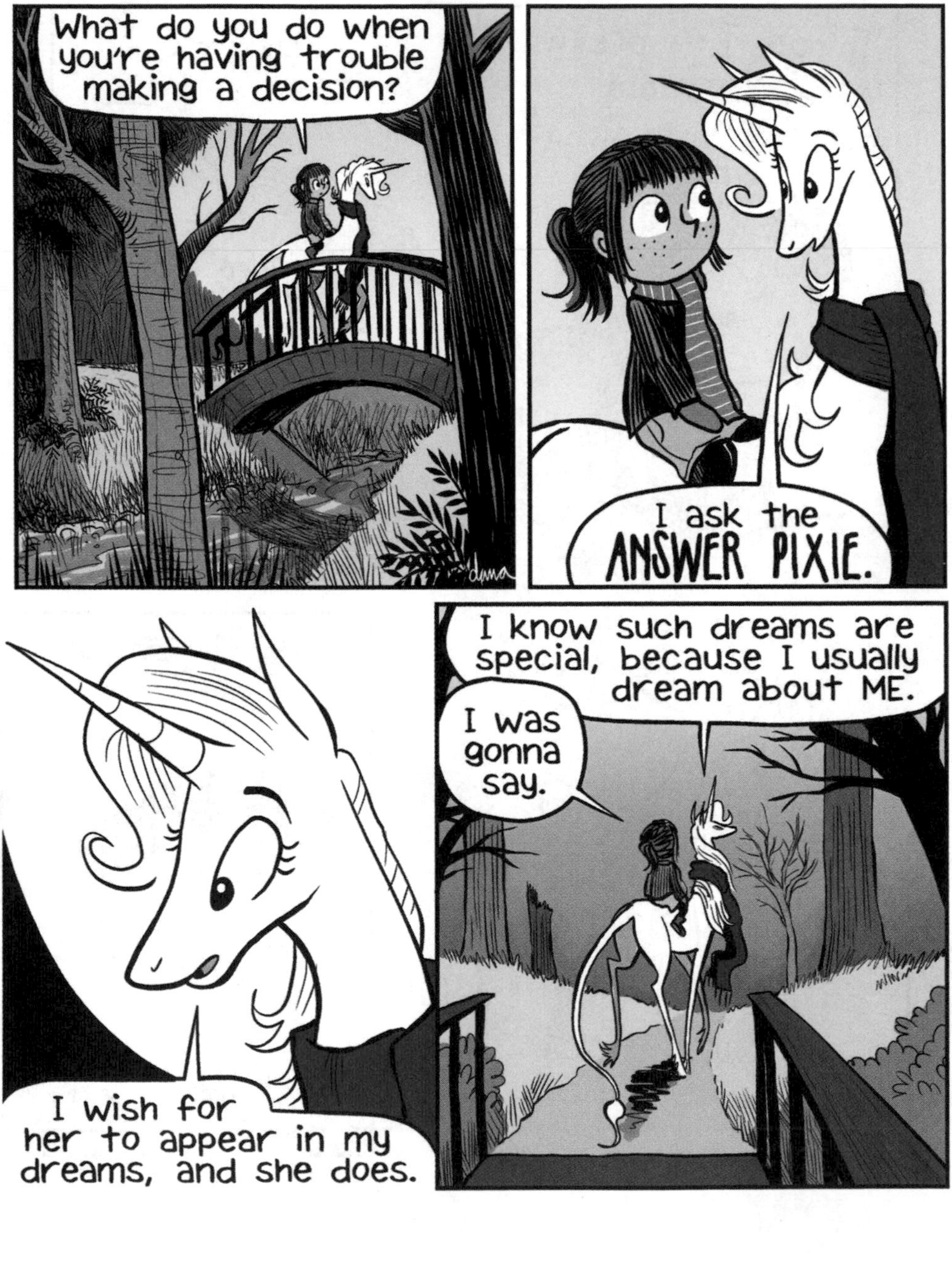
What do you do when you're having trouble making a decision?
I ask the ANSWER PIXIE.
I wish for her to appear in my dreams, and she does.
I know such dreams are special, because I usually dream about ME.
I was gonna say.

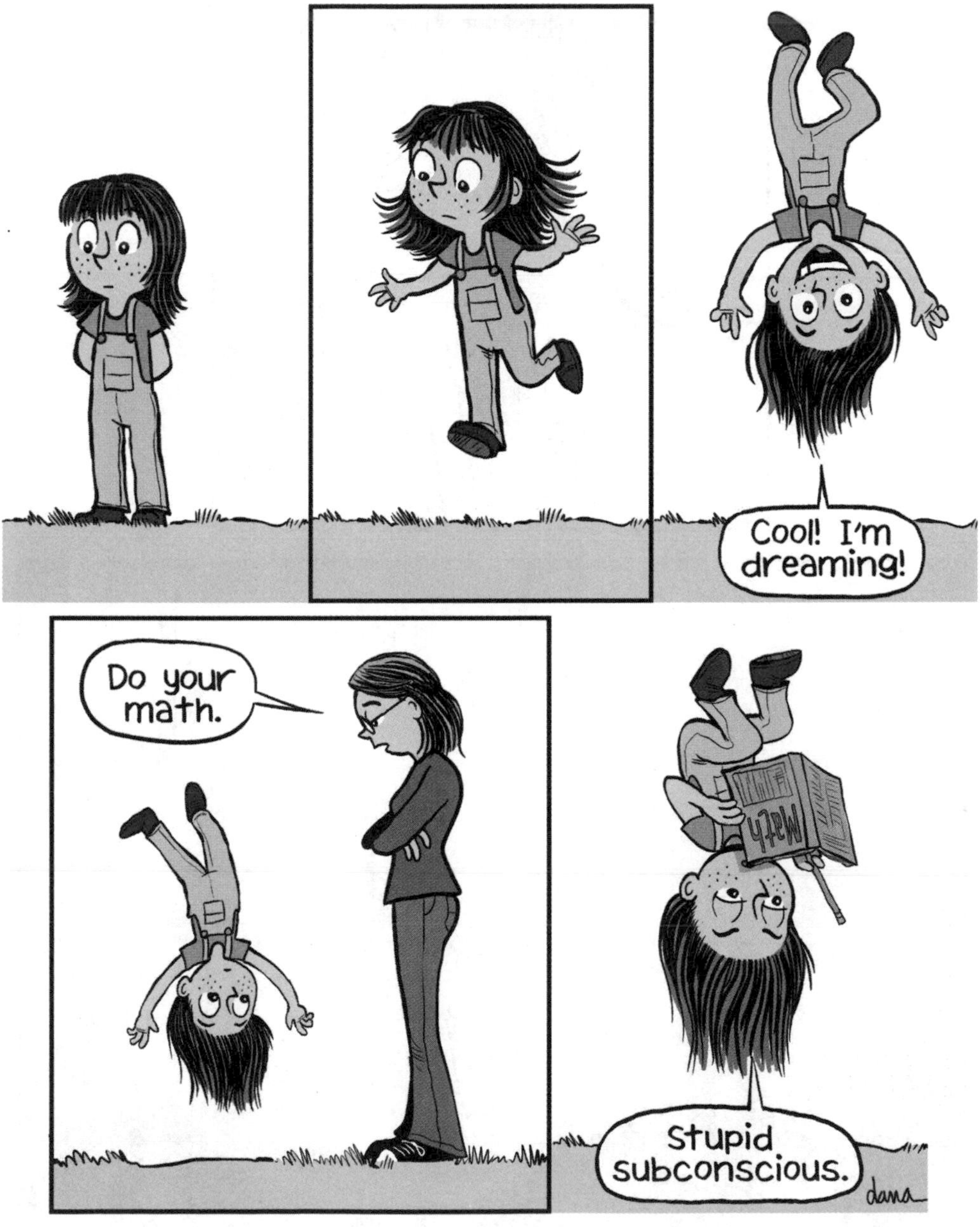
Cool! I'm dreaming!
Do your math.
Math
Stupid subconscious.
dana

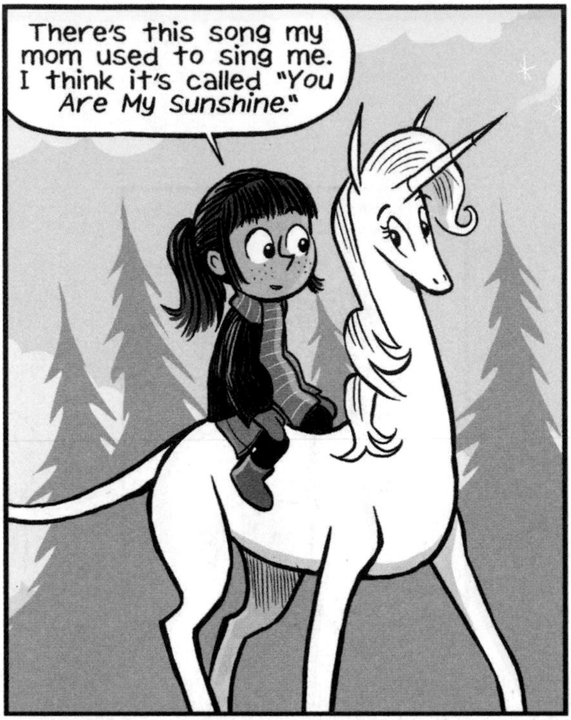
There's this song my mom used to sing me. I think it's called "You Are My Sunshine."

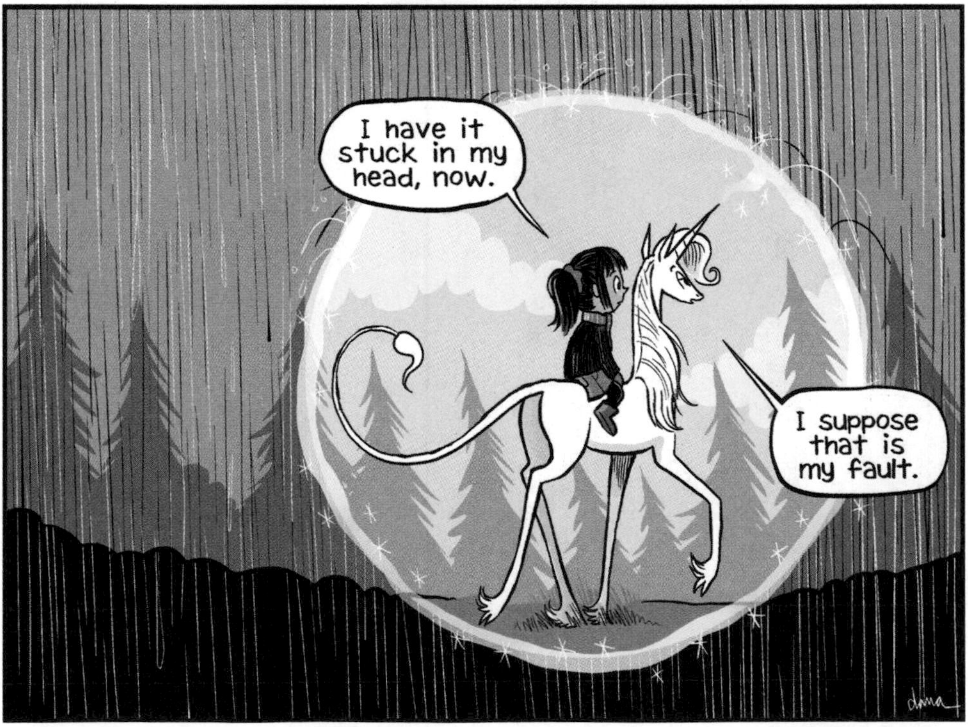
I have it stuck in my head, now.
I suppose that is my fault.

Math
dana
Hey.
What?
I am your answer pixie.
Why do you look like Marigold?
Because you only know one magical creature.

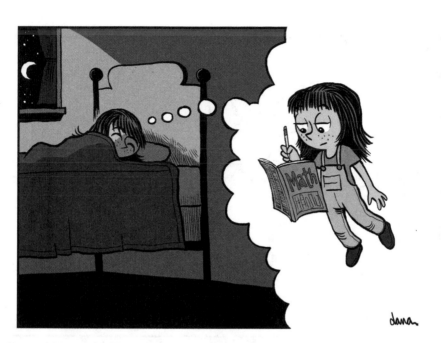

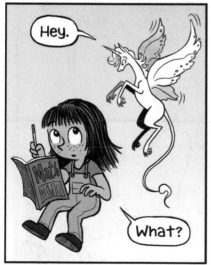

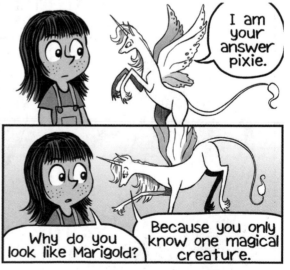

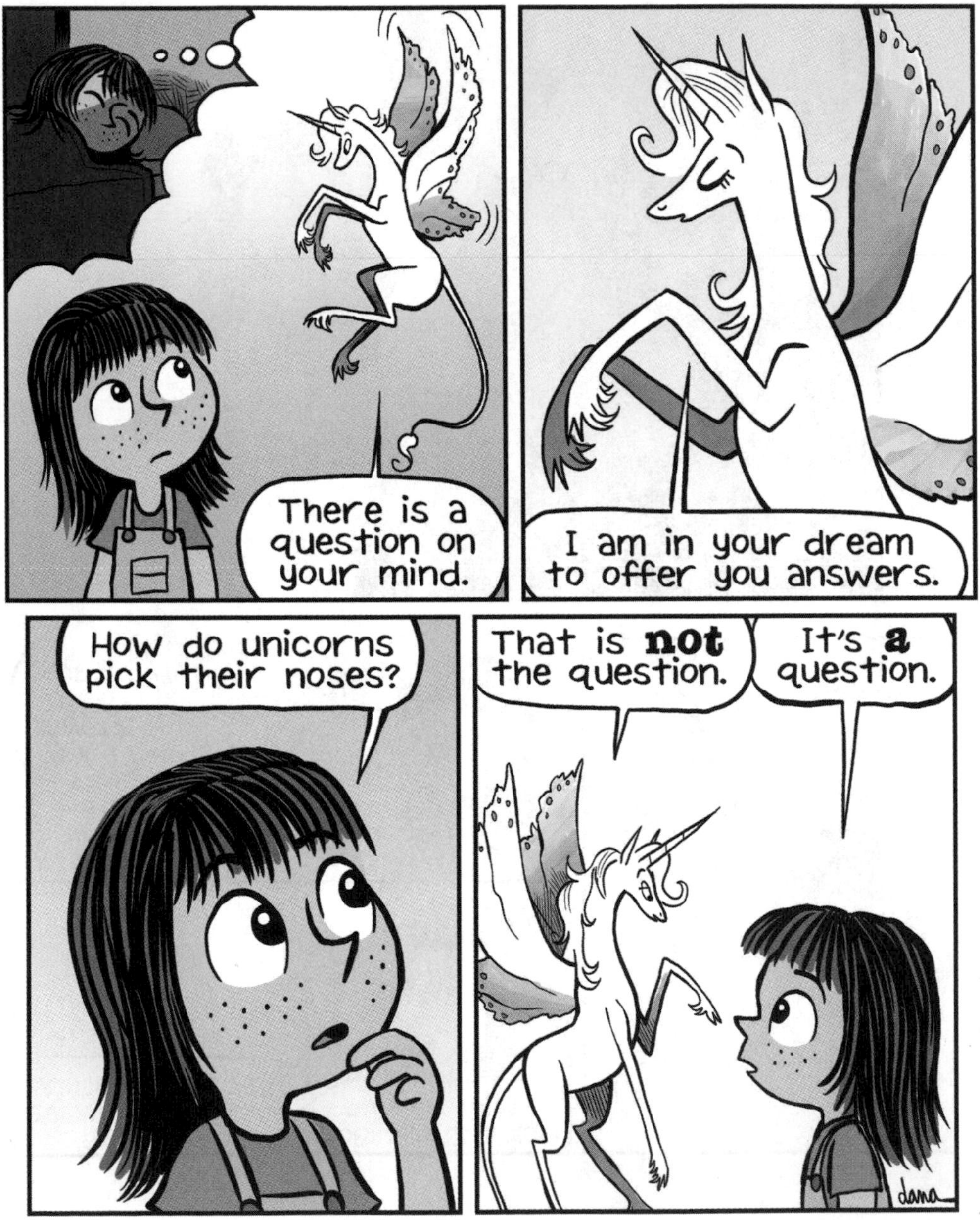
There is a question on your mind.
I am in your dream to offer you answers.
How do unicorns pick their noses?
That is **not** the question.
It's **a** question.
dana

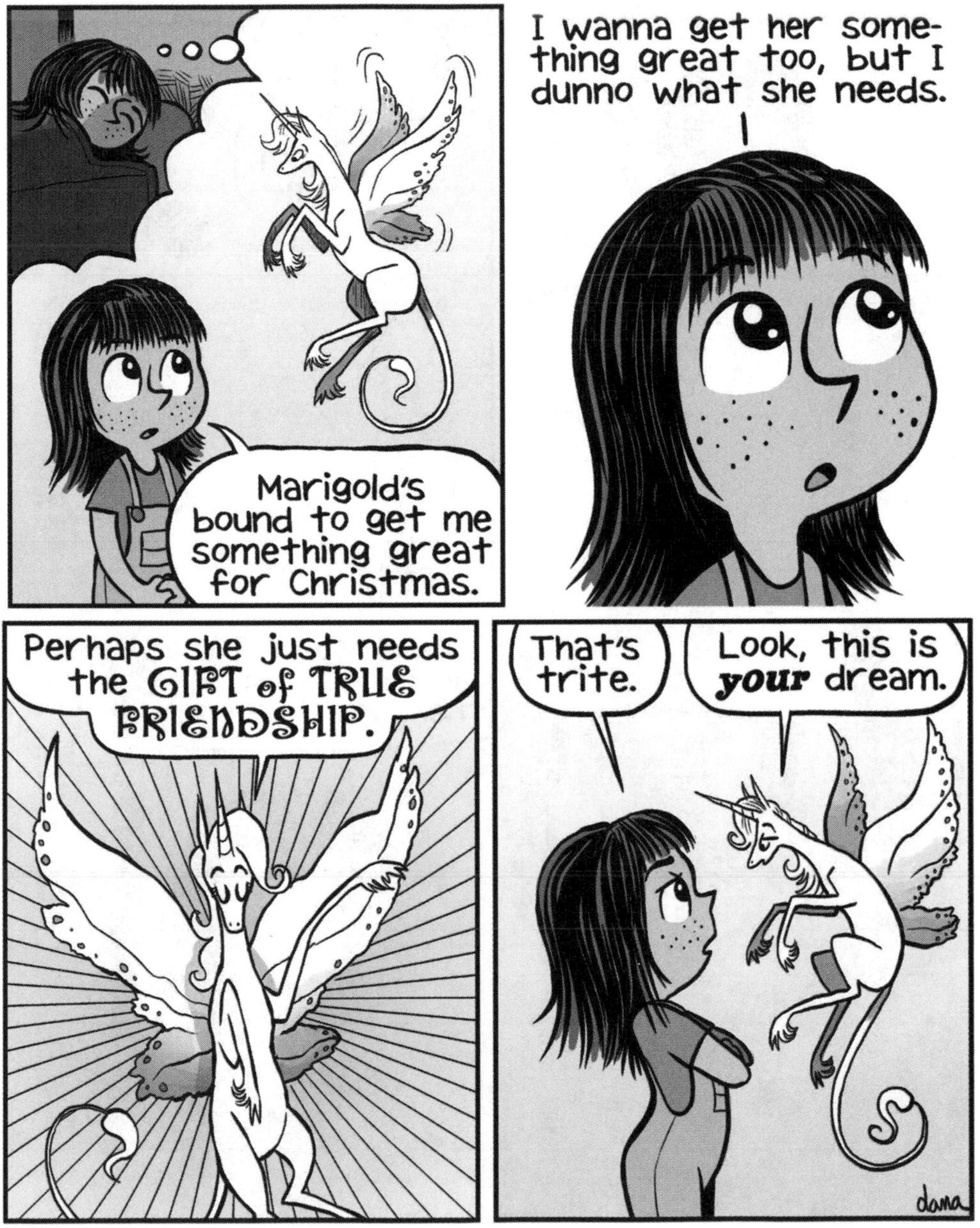
Marigold's bound to get me something great for Christmas.
I wanna get her something great too, but I dunno what she needs.
Perhaps she just needs the GIFT of TRUE FRIENDSHIP.
That's trite.
Look, this is *your* dream.
dana

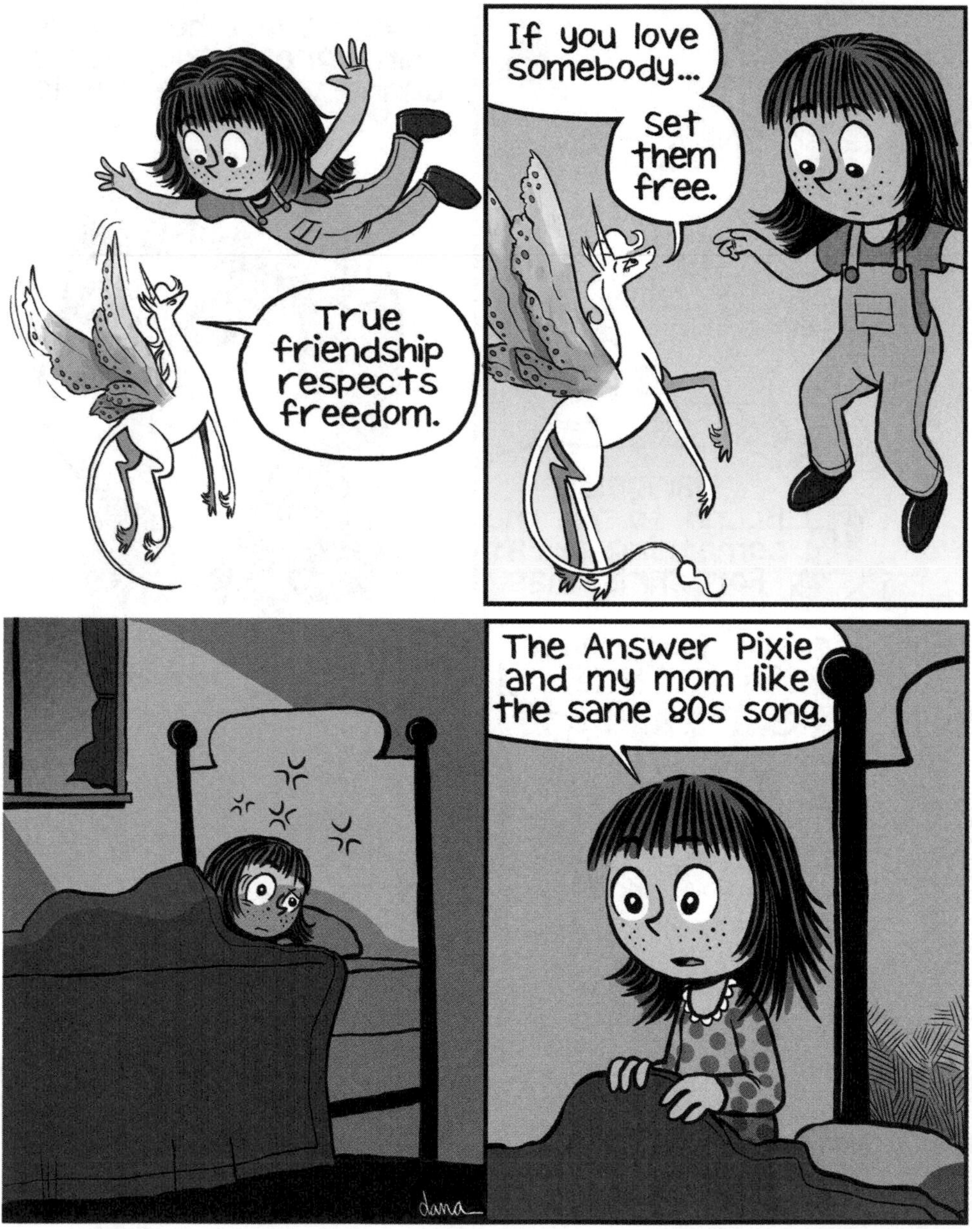
True friendship respects freedom.
If you love somebody...
Set them free.
The Answer Pixie and my mom like the same 80s song.
dana

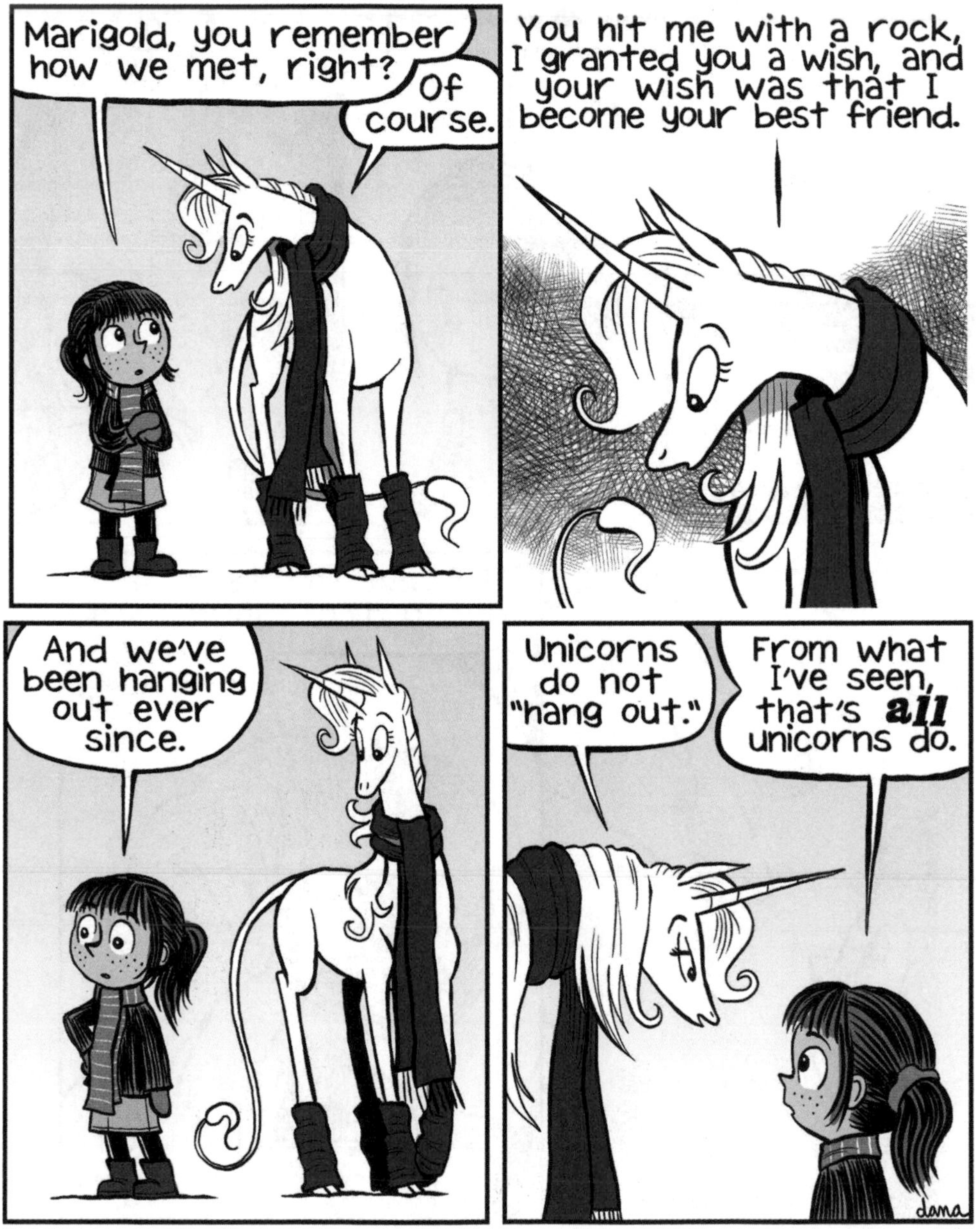
Marigold, you remember how we met, right?
Of course.
You hit me with a rock, I granted you a wish, and your wish was that I become your best friend.
And we've been hanging out ever since.
Unicorns do not "hang out."
From what I've seen, that's ***all*** unicorns do.
dana

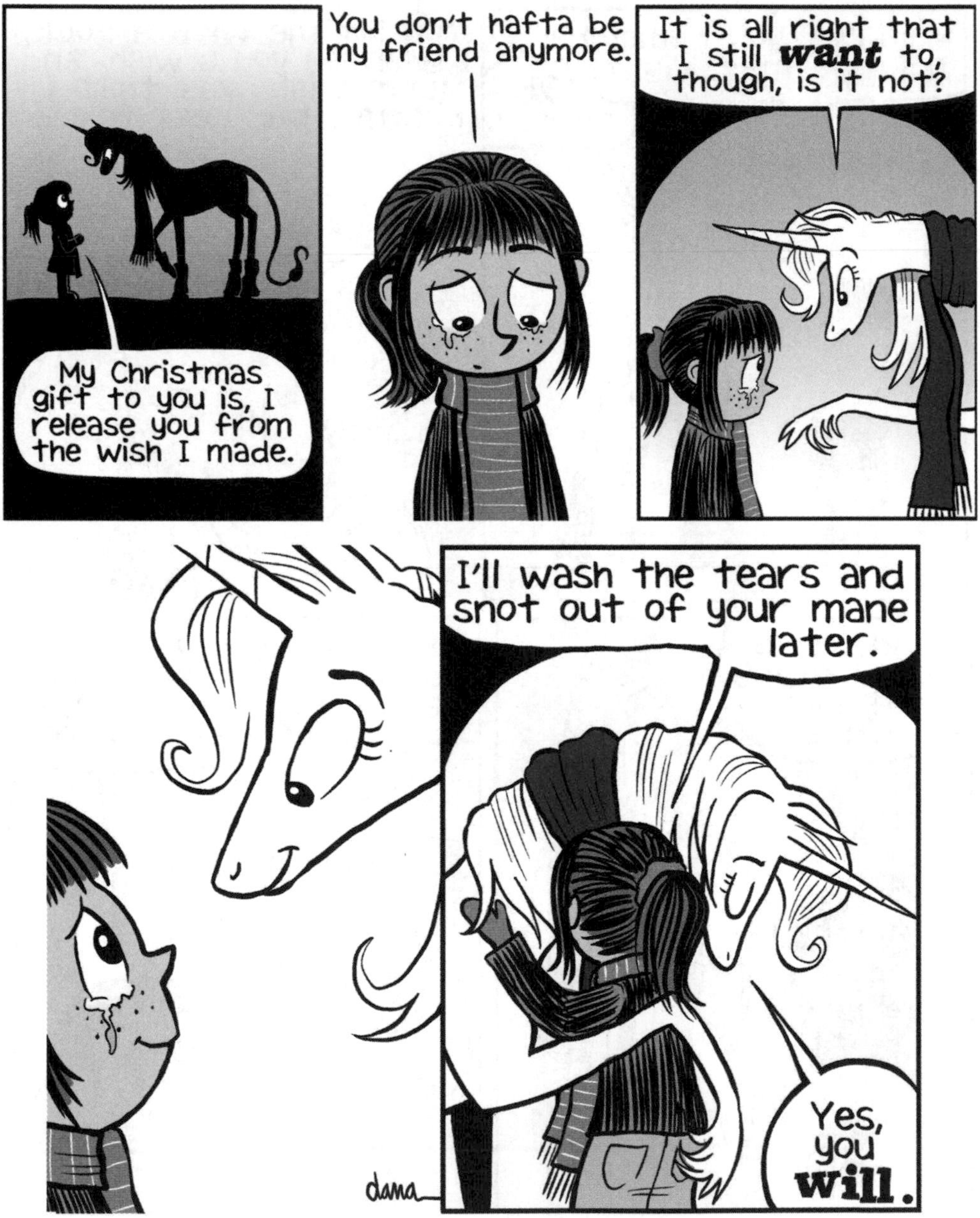
My Christmas gift to you is, I release you from the wish I made.
You don't hafta be my friend anymore.
It is all right that I still **want** to, though, is it not?
I'll wash the tears and snot out of your mane later.
Yes, you **will**.
dana

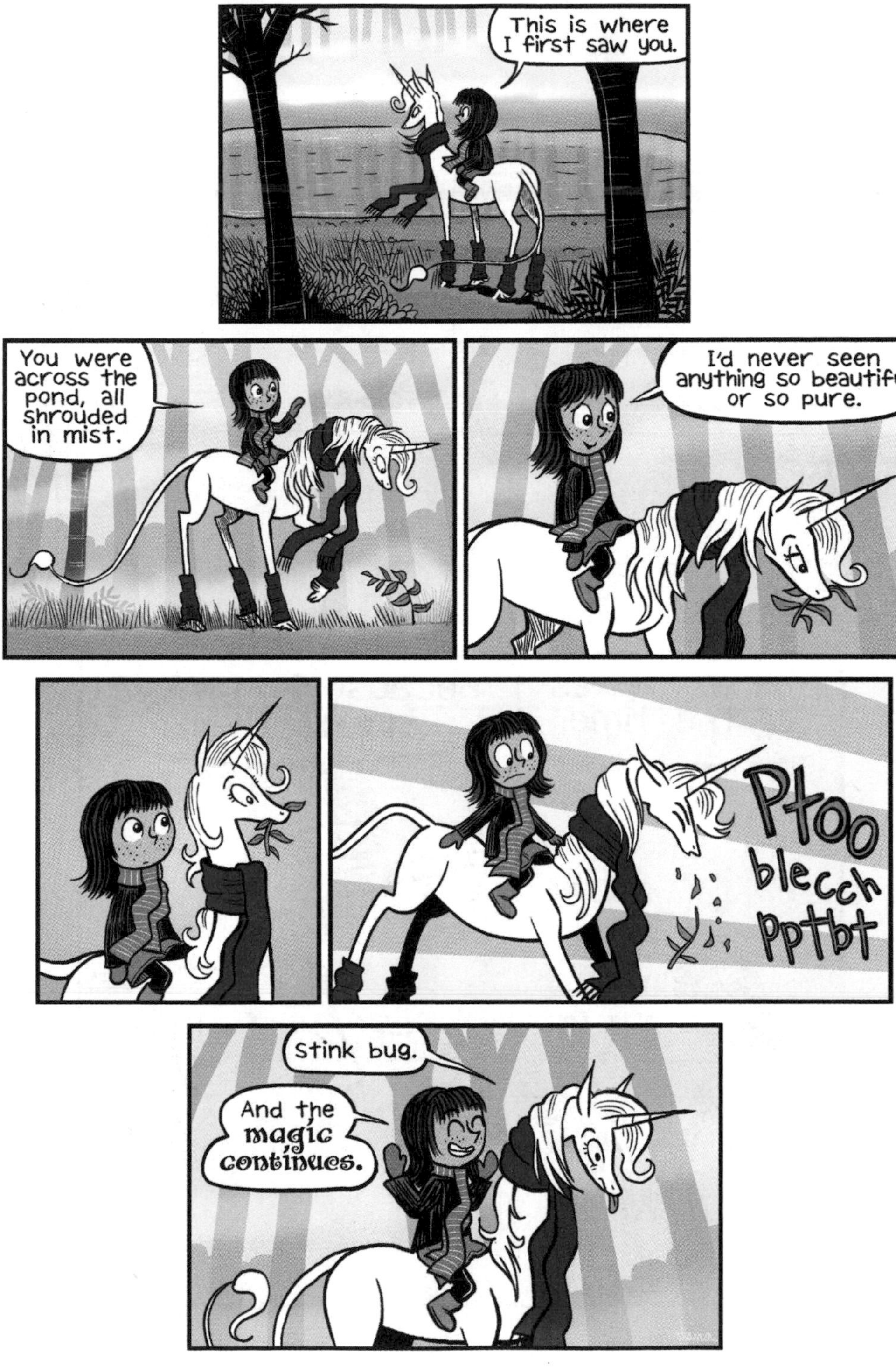
This is where I first saw you.
You were across the pond, all shrouded in mist.
I'd never seen anything so beautiful or so pure.
Ptoo
blecch
pptbt
Stink bug.
And the magic continues.

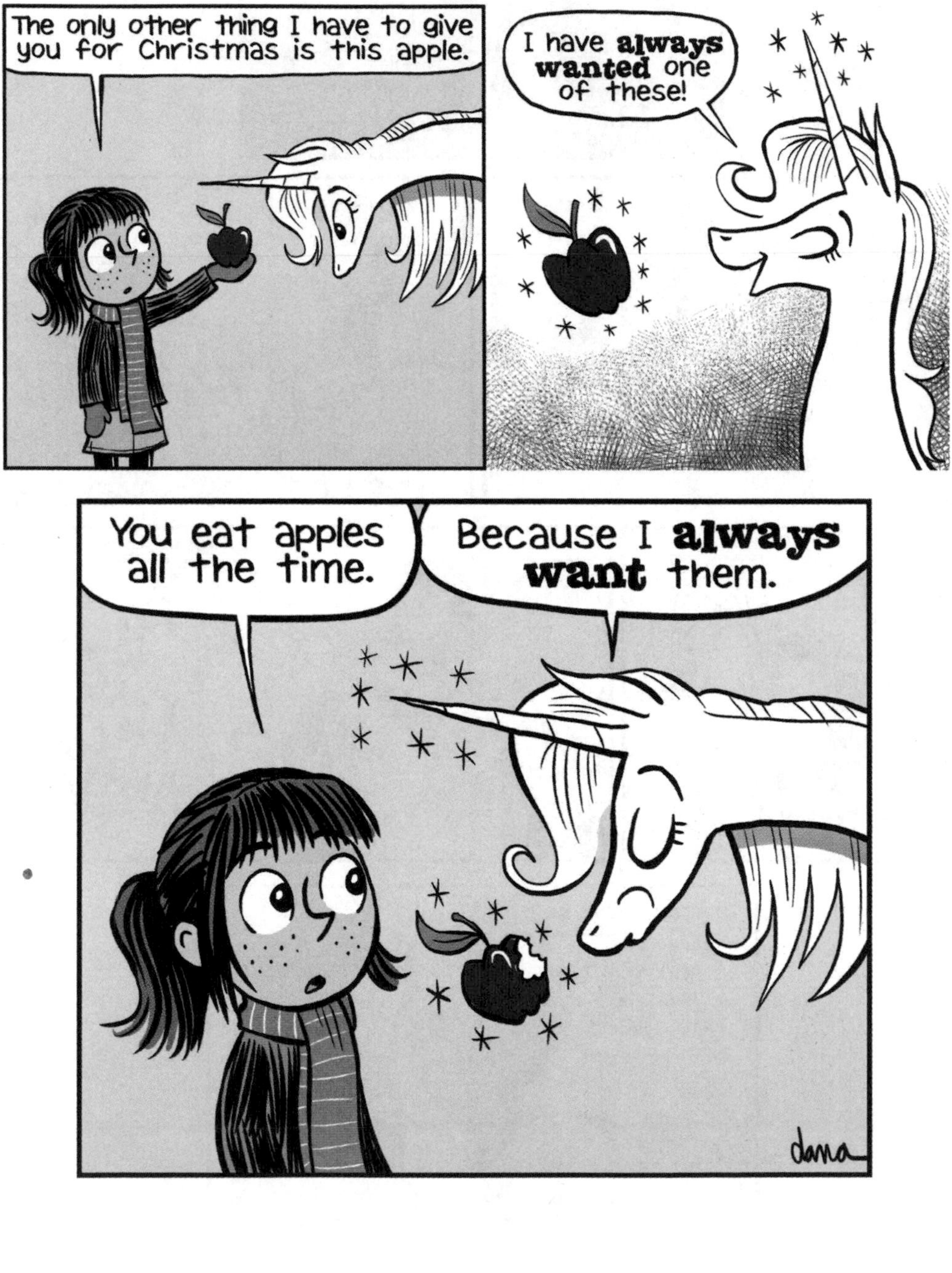
The only other thing I have to give you for Christmas is this apple.
I have **always wanted** one of these!
You eat apples all the time.
Because I **always want** them.
dana

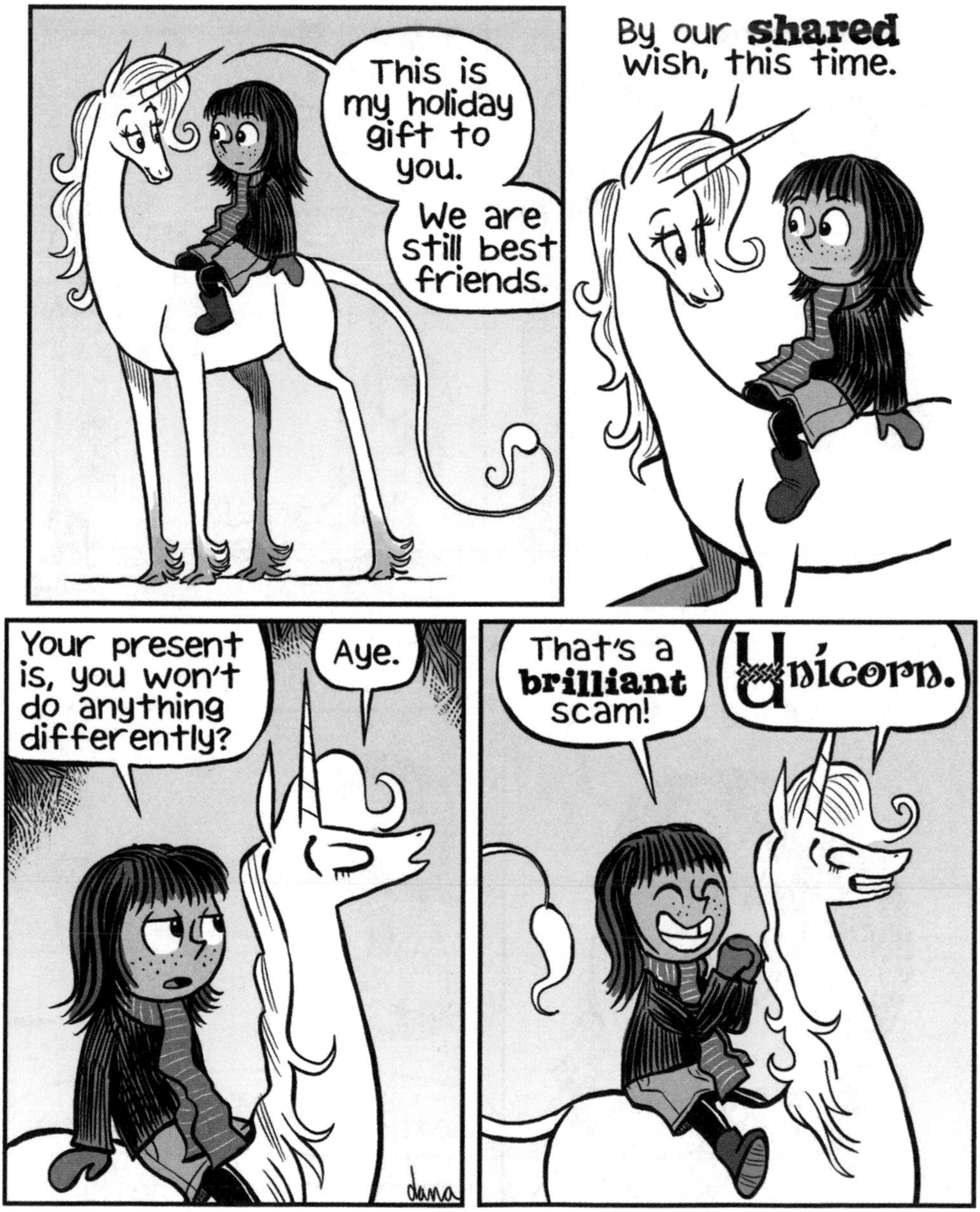
This is my holiday gift to you.
We are still best friends.
By our **shared** wish, this time.
Your present is, you won't do anything differently?
Aye.
That's a **brilliant** scam!
Unicorn.
dana

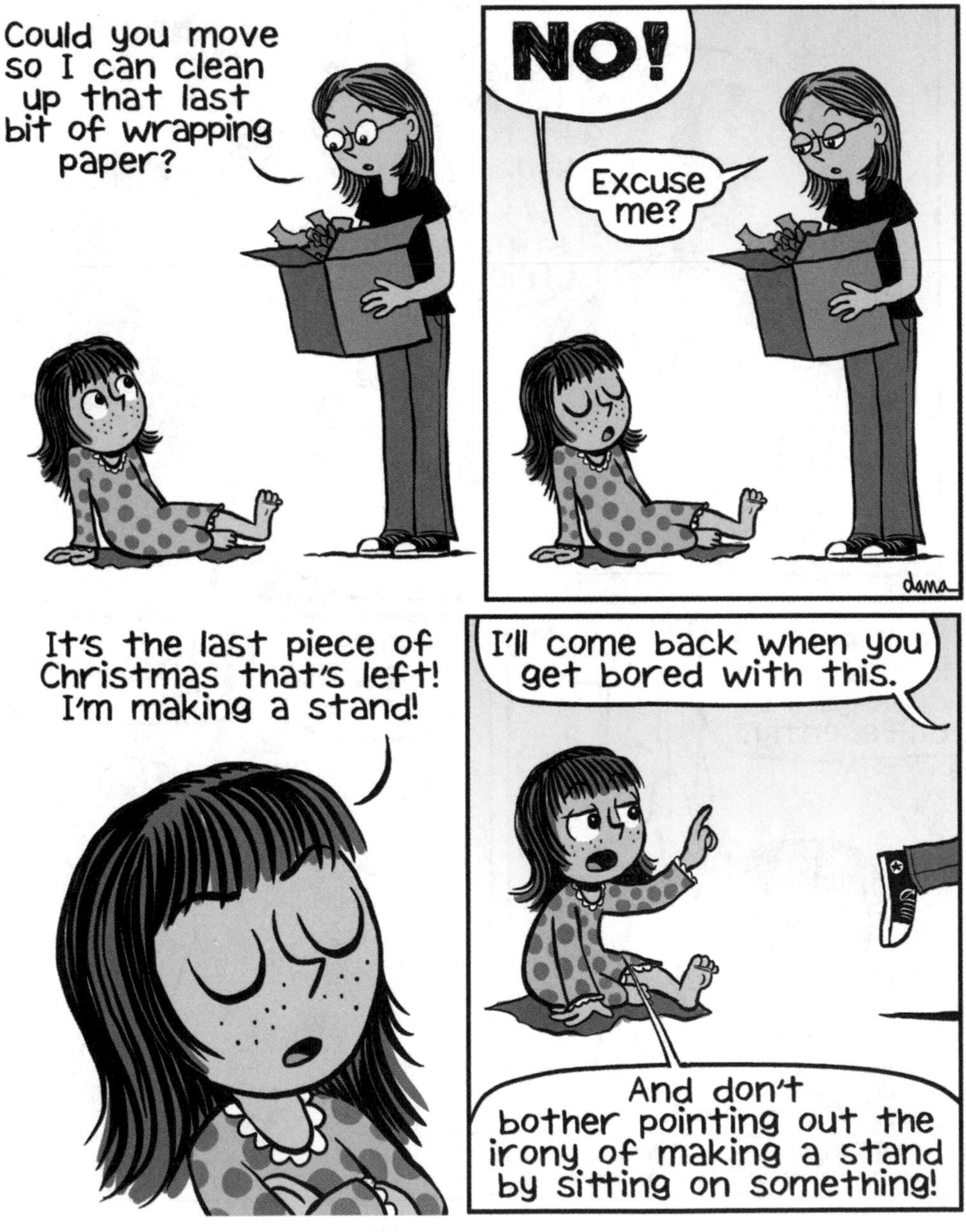
Could you move so I can clean up that last bit of wrapping paper?
NO!
Excuse me?
dana
It's the last piece of Christmas that's left! I'm making a stand!
I'll come back when you get bored with this.
And don't bother pointing out the irony of making a stand by sitting on something!

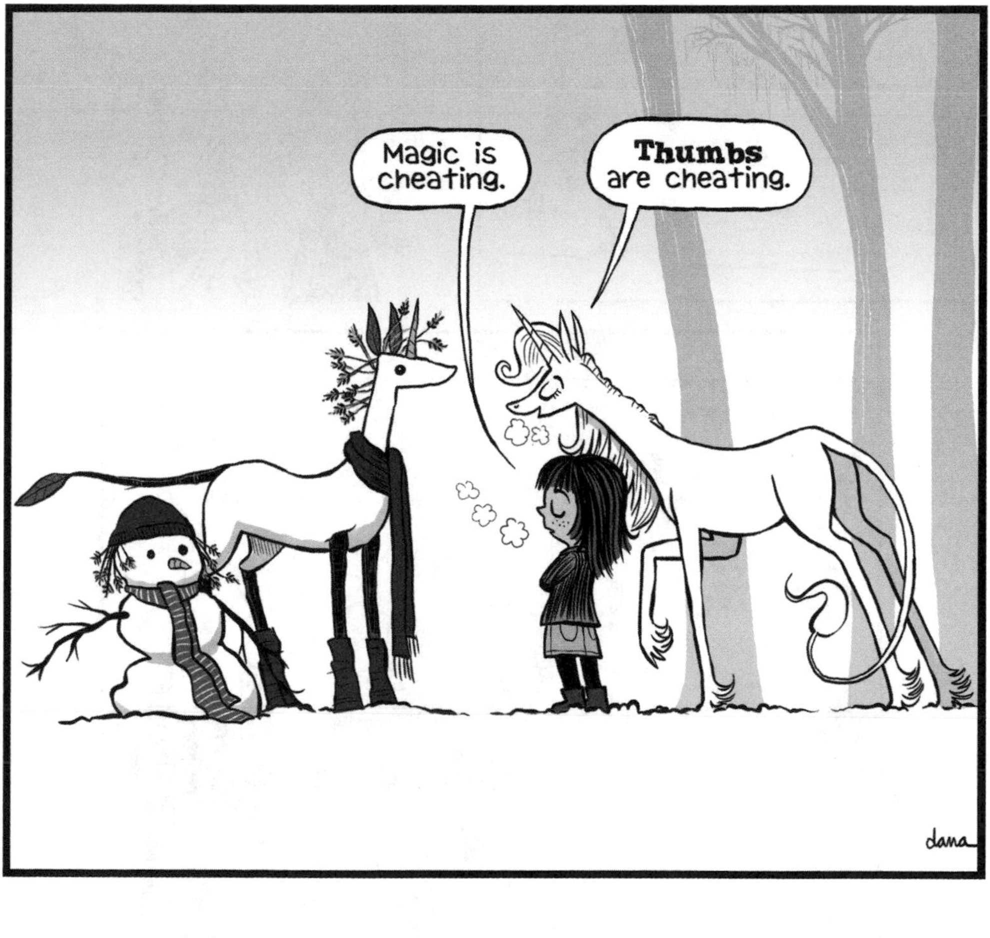
Magic is cheating.
Thumbs are cheating.
dana

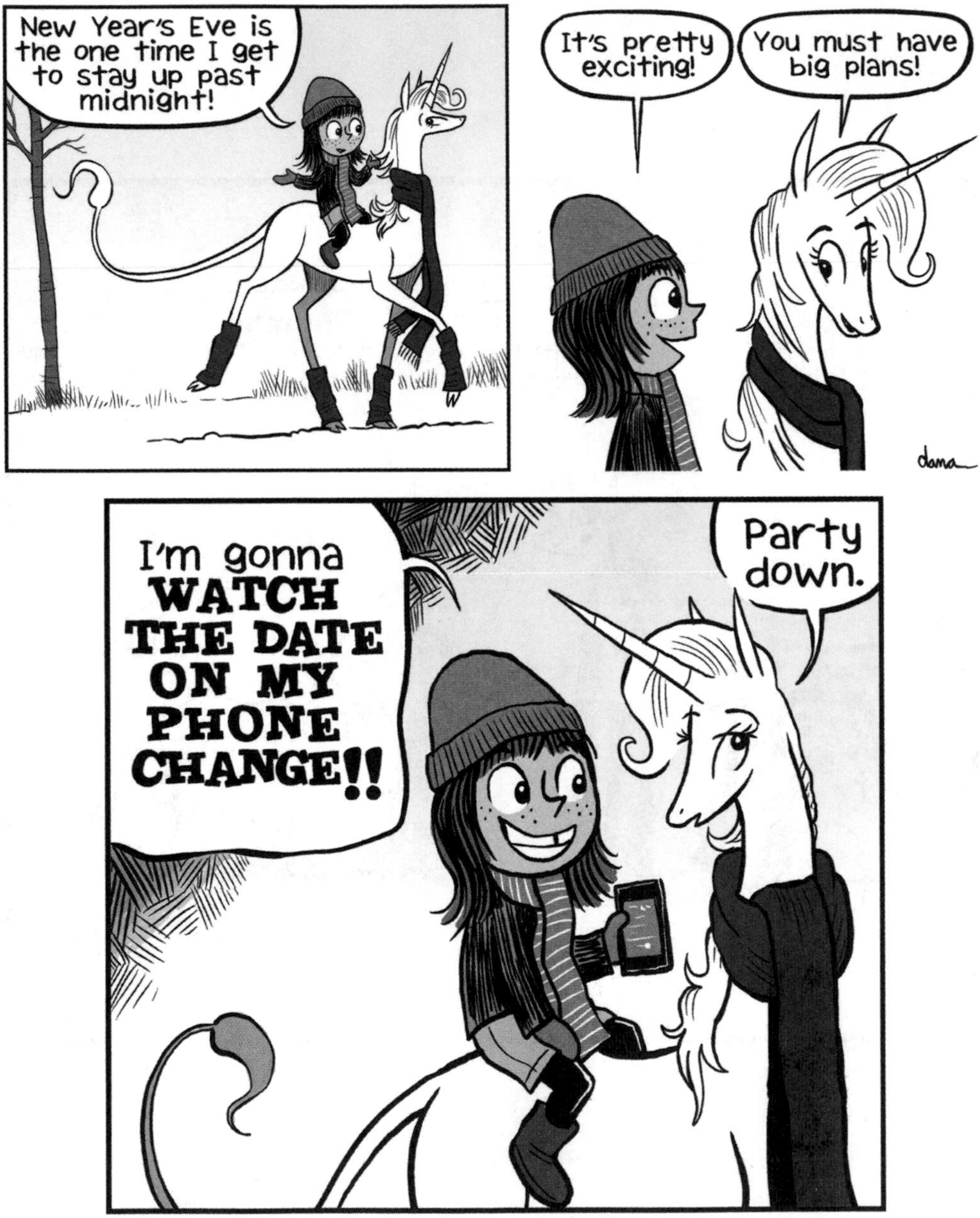
New Year's Eve is the one time I get to stay up past midnight!
It's pretty exciting!
You must have big plans!
dana
I'm gonna WATCH THE DATE ON MY PHONE CHANGE!!
Party down.

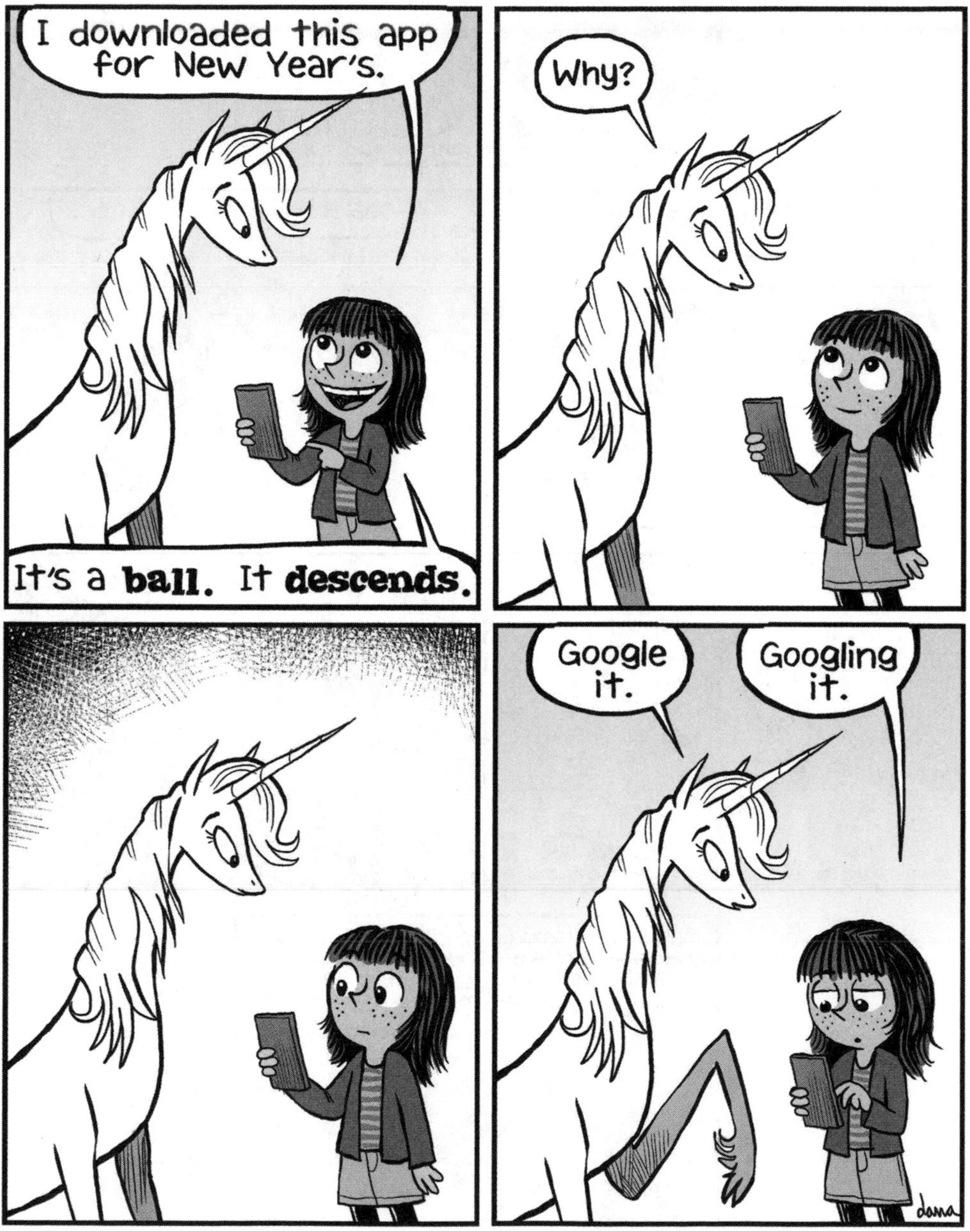
I downloaded this app for New Year's.
It's a **ball**. It **descends**.
Why?
Google it.
Googling it.
dana

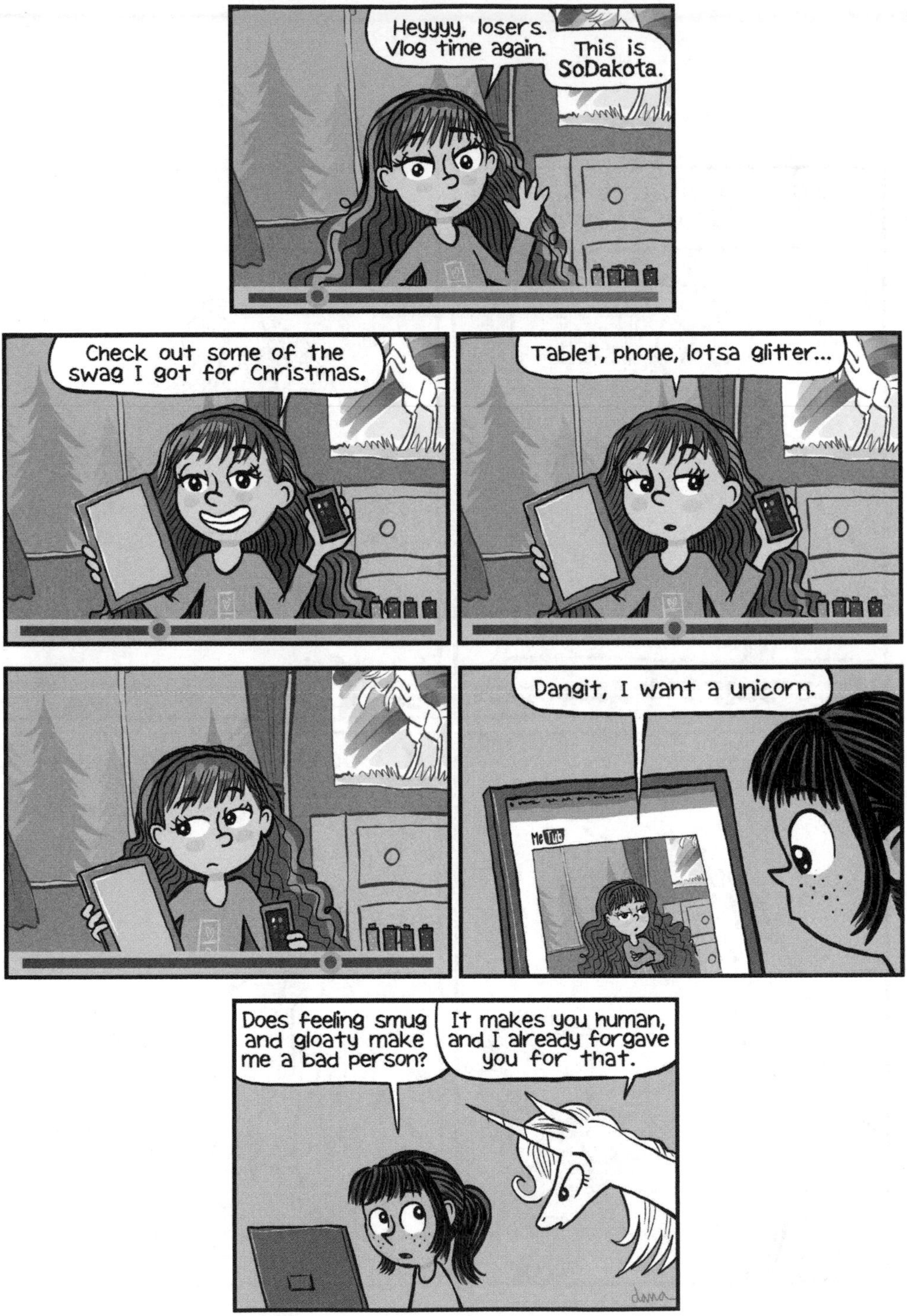
Heyyyy, losers. Vlog time again.
This is SoDakota.
Check out some of the swag I got for Christmas.
Tablet, phone, lotsa glitter...
Dangit, I want a unicorn.
MeTub
Does feeling smug and gloaty make me a bad person?
It makes you human, and I already forgave you for that.

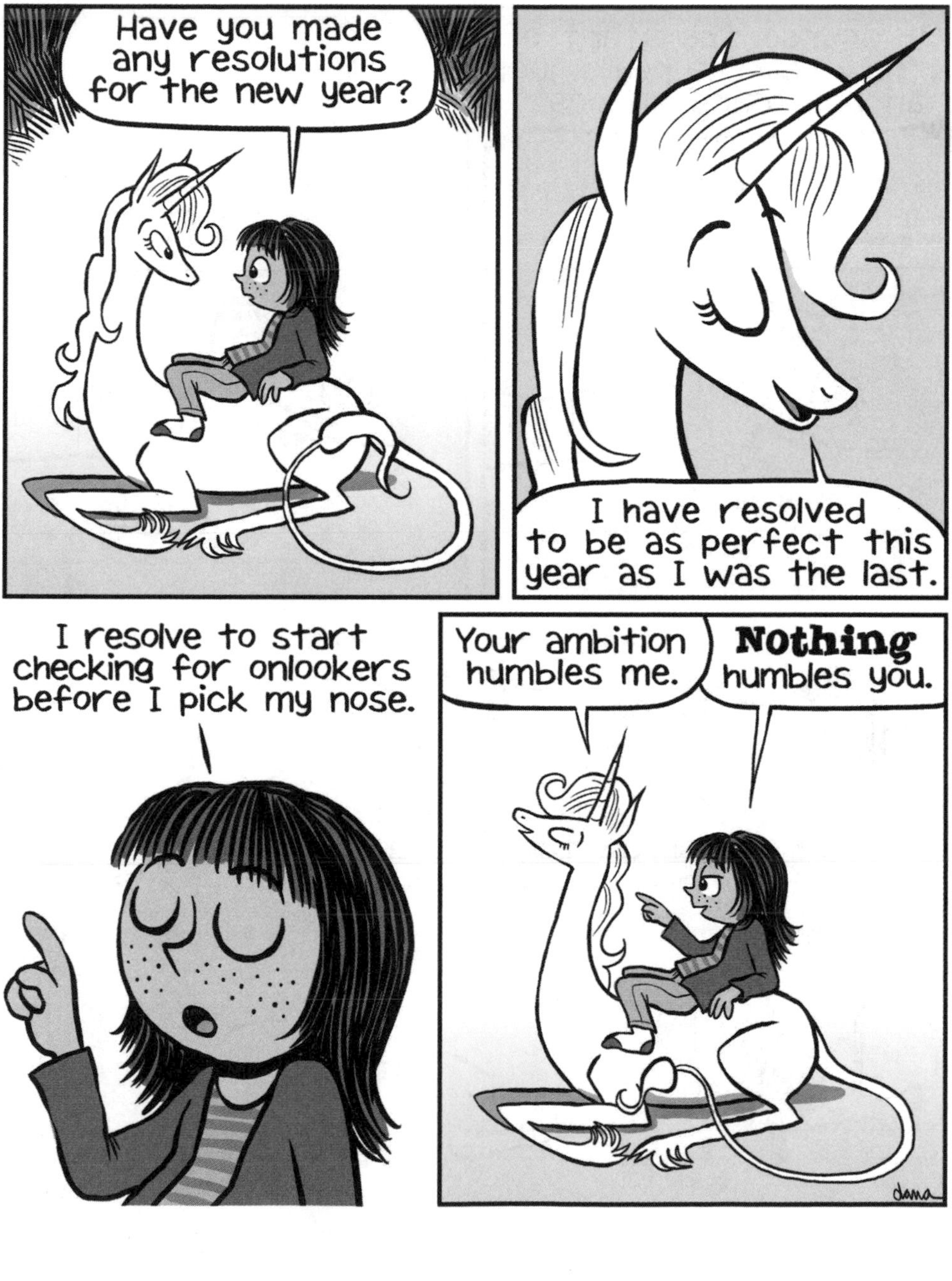
Have you made any resolutions for the new year?
I have resolved to be as perfect this year as I was the last.
I resolve to start checking for onlookers before I pick my nose.
Your ambition humbles me.
Nothing humbles you.
dana

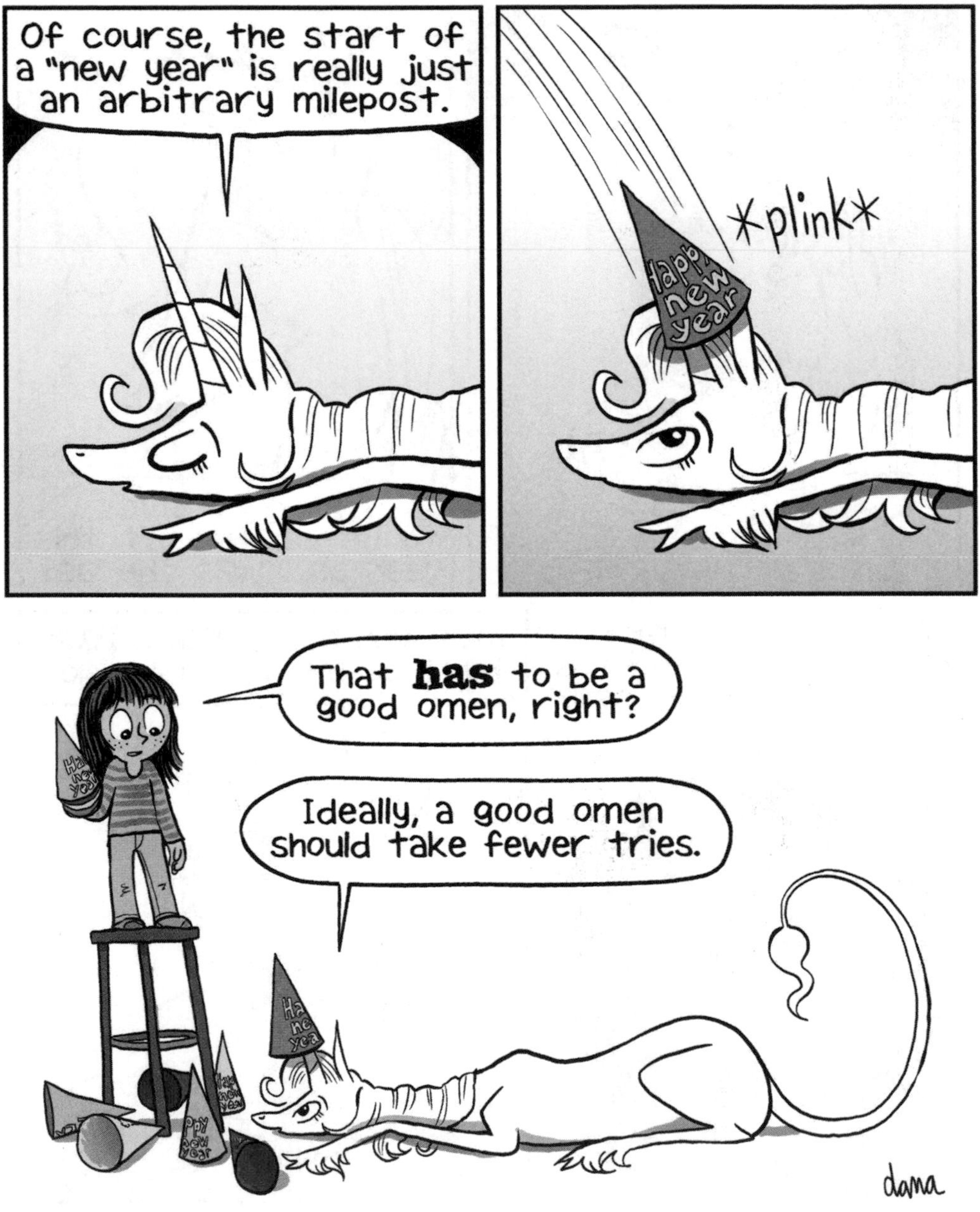

Of course, the start of a "new year" is really just an arbitrary milepost.
plink
Happy new year
That **has** to be a good omen, right?
Ideally, a good omen should take fewer tries.
dana

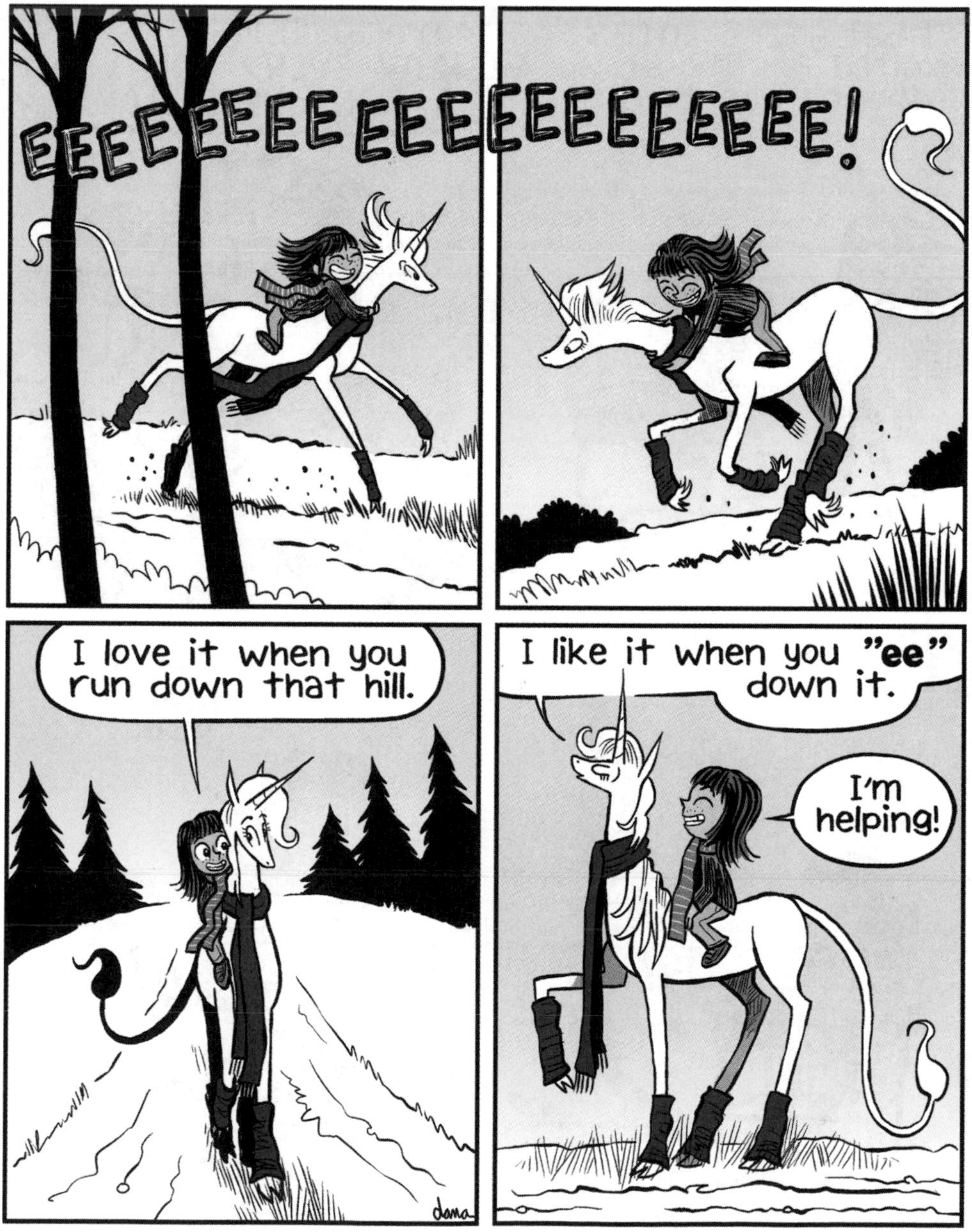
EEEEEEEEE EEEEEEEEEEEEE!
I love it when you run down that hill.
I like it when you "ee" down it.
I'm helping!
dana

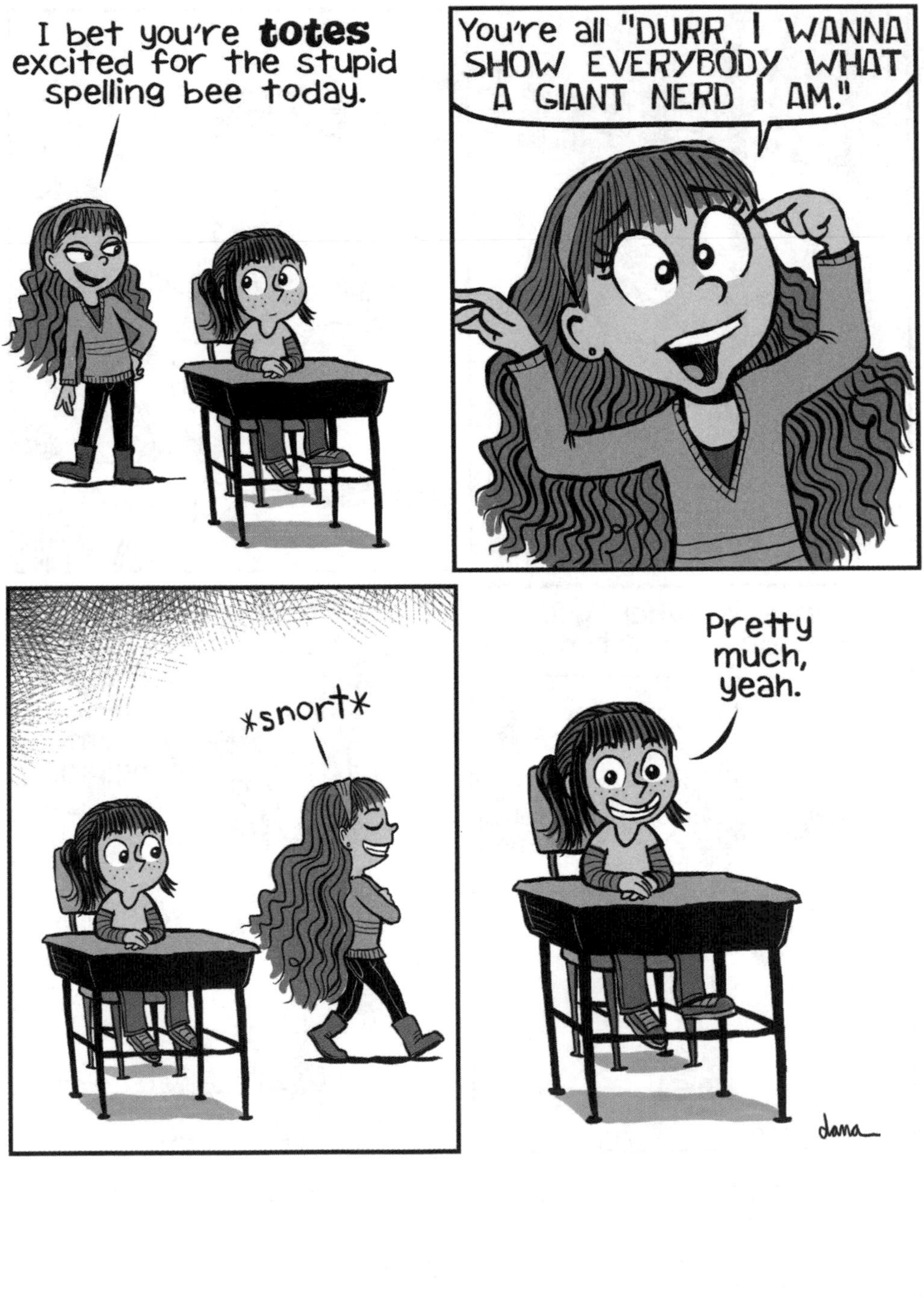
I bet you're **totes** excited for the stupid spelling bee today.
You're all "DURR, I WANNA SHOW EVERYBODY WHAT A GIANT NERD I AM."
snort
Pretty much, yeah.
dana

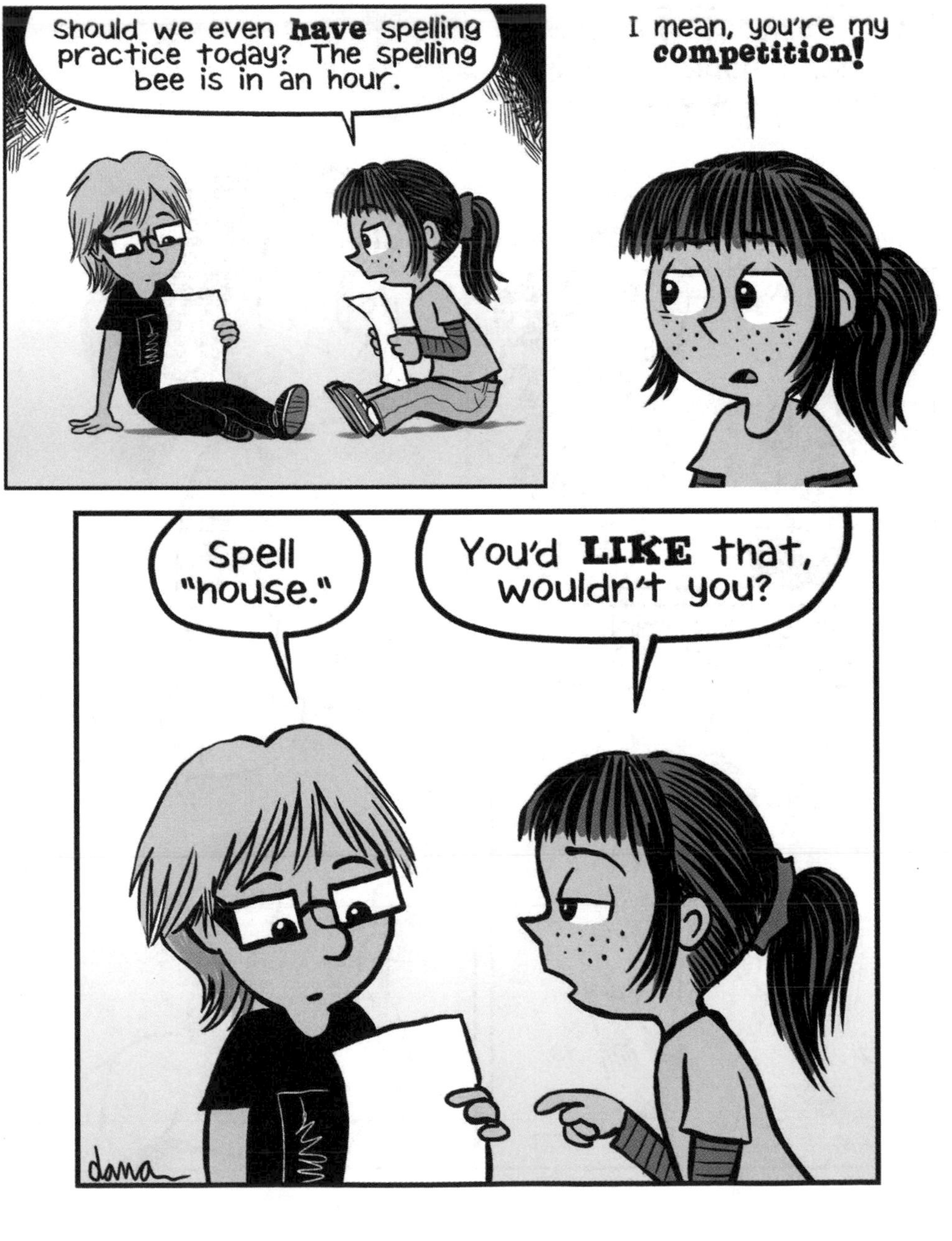
Should we even **have** spelling practice today? The spelling bee is in an hour.
I mean, you're my **competition!**
Spell "house."
You'd **LIKE** that, wouldn't you?
dana

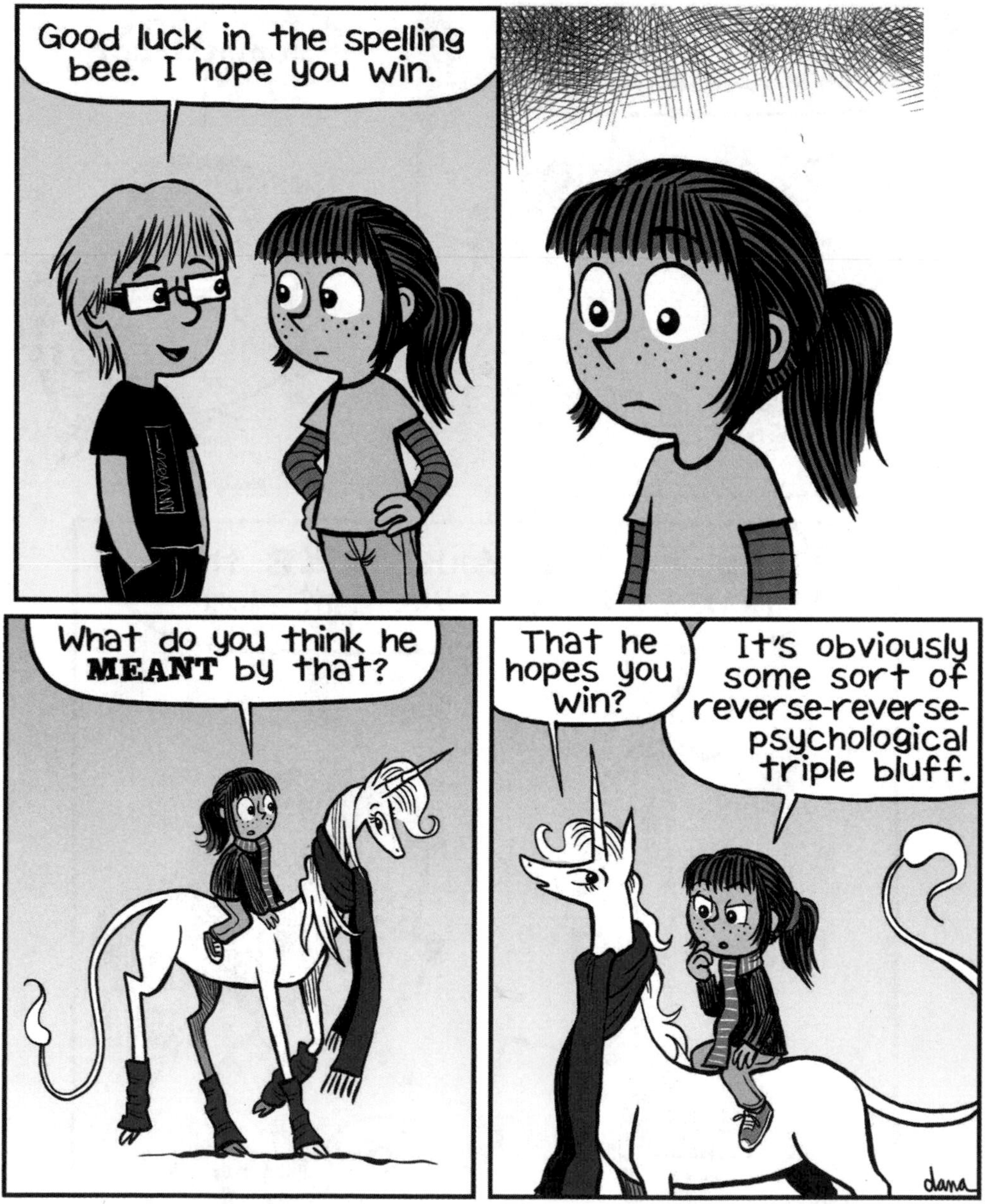
Good luck in the spelling bee. I hope you win.
What do you think he **MEANT** by that?
That he hopes you win?
It's obviously some sort of reverse-reverse-psychological triple bluff.
dana

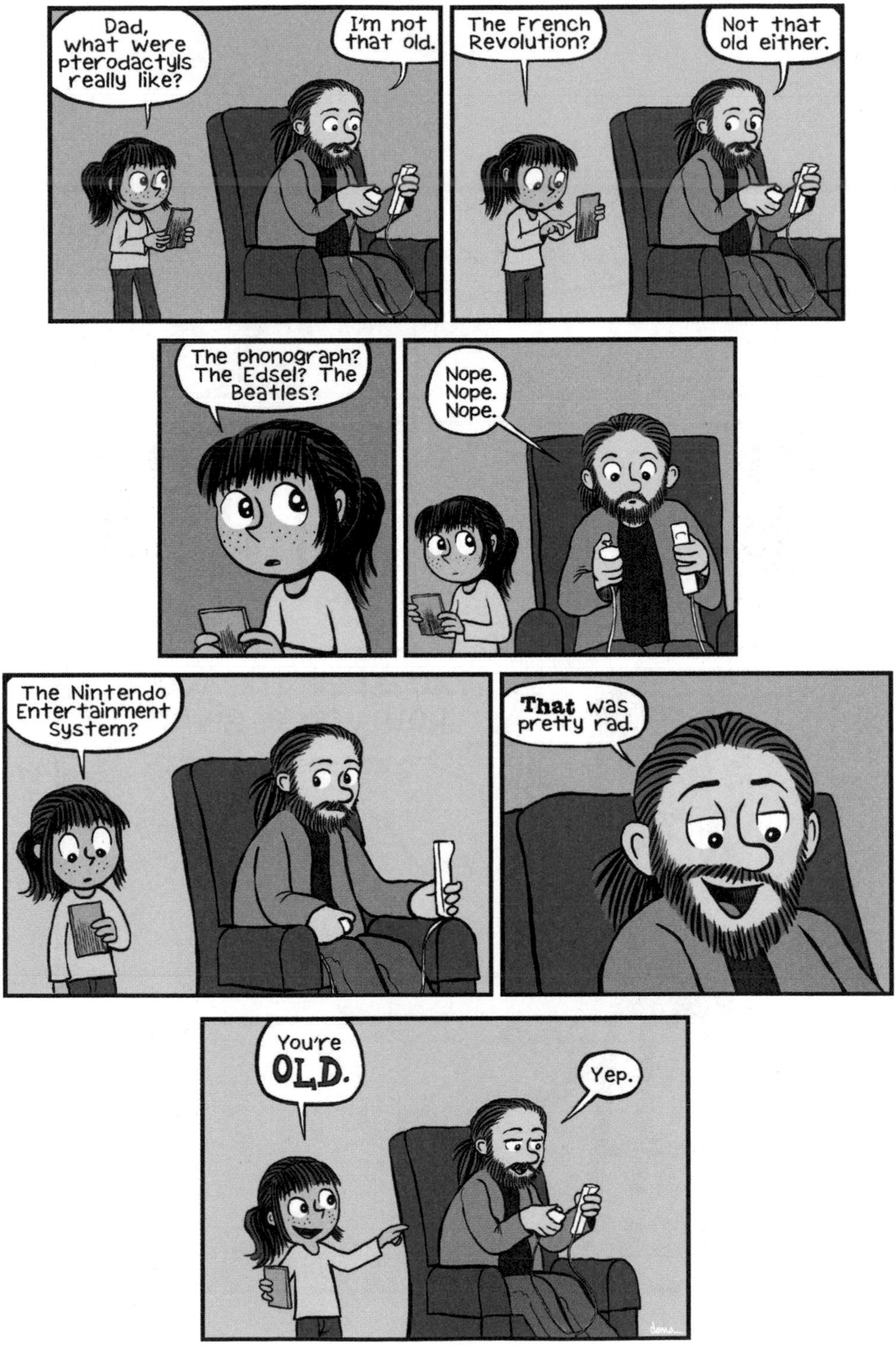
Dad, what were pterodactyls really like?
I'm not that old.
The French Revolution?
Not that old either.
The phonograph? The Edsel? The Beatles?
Nope. Nope. Nope.
The Nintendo Entertainment System?
That was pretty rad.
You're **OLD.**
Yep.

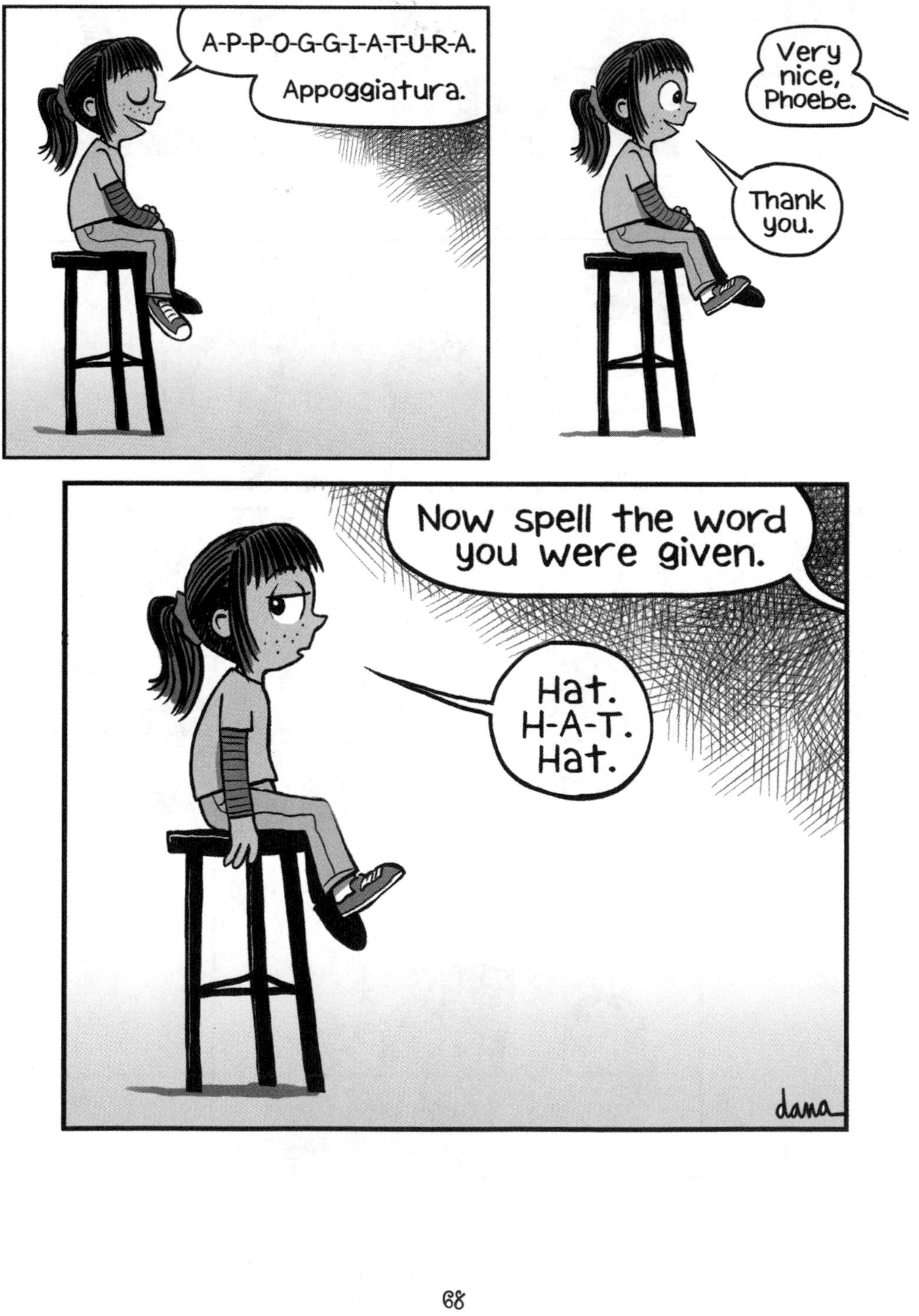
A-P-P-O-G-G-I-A-T-U-R-A.
Appoggiatura.
Very nice, Phoebe.
Thank you.
Now spell the word you were given.
Hat. H-A-T. Hat.
dana

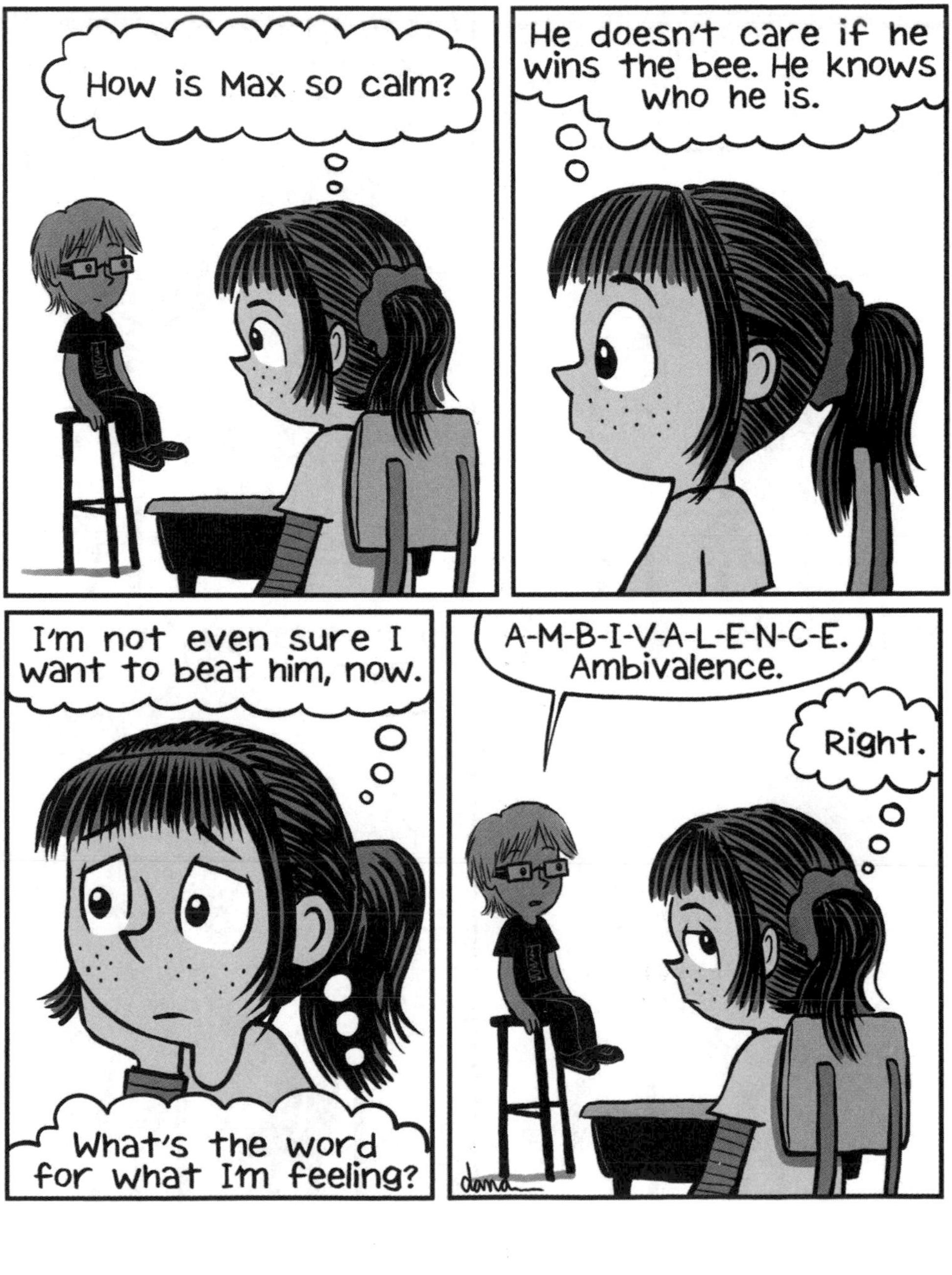
How is Max so calm?
He doesn't care if he wins the bee. He knows who he is.
I'm not even sure I want to beat him, now.
What's the word for what I'm feeling?
A-M-B-I-V-A-L-E-N-C-E. Ambivalence.
Right.
dana

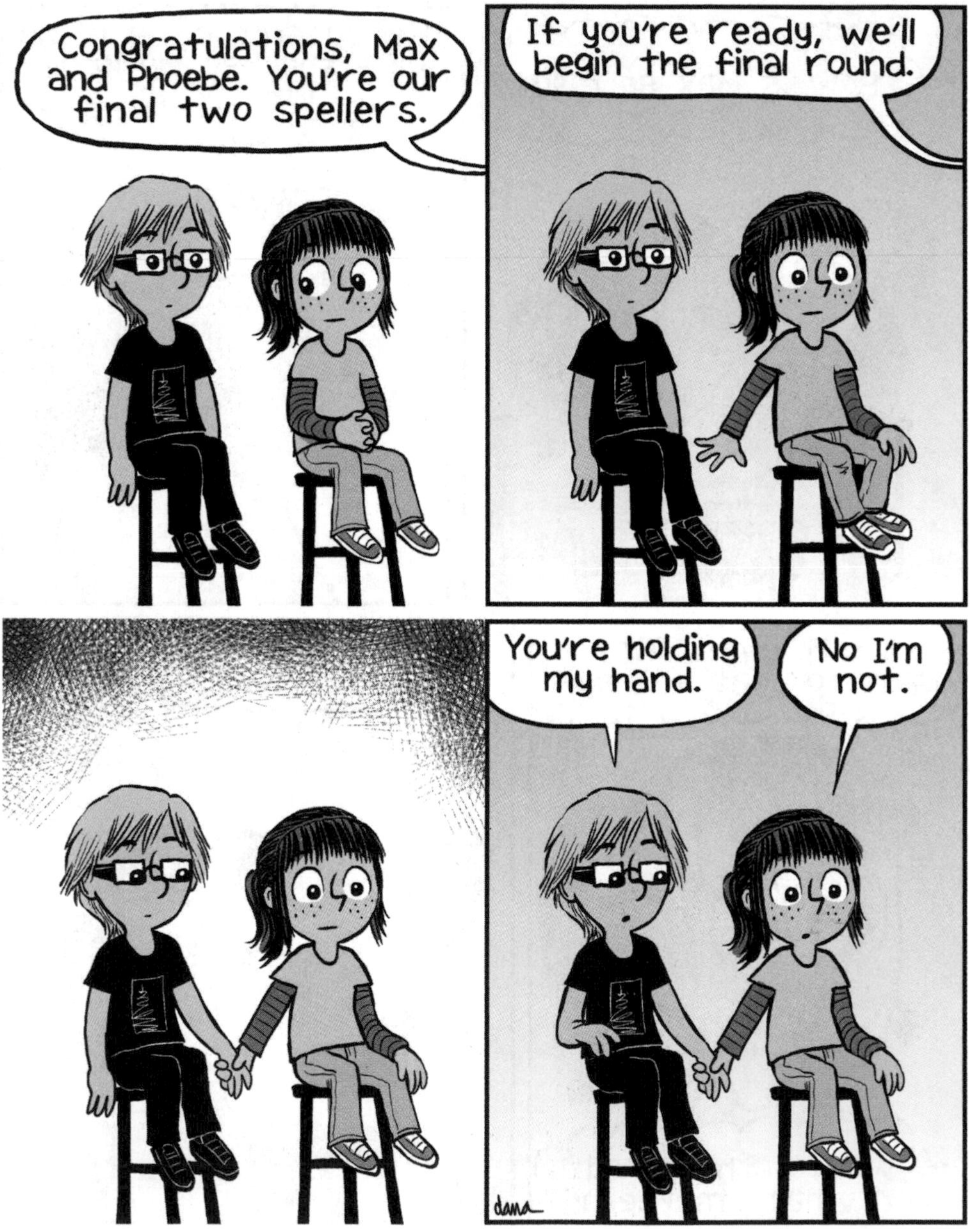

Congratulations, Max and Phoebe. You're our final two spellers.
If you're ready, we'll begin the final round.
You're holding my hand.
No I'm not.
dana

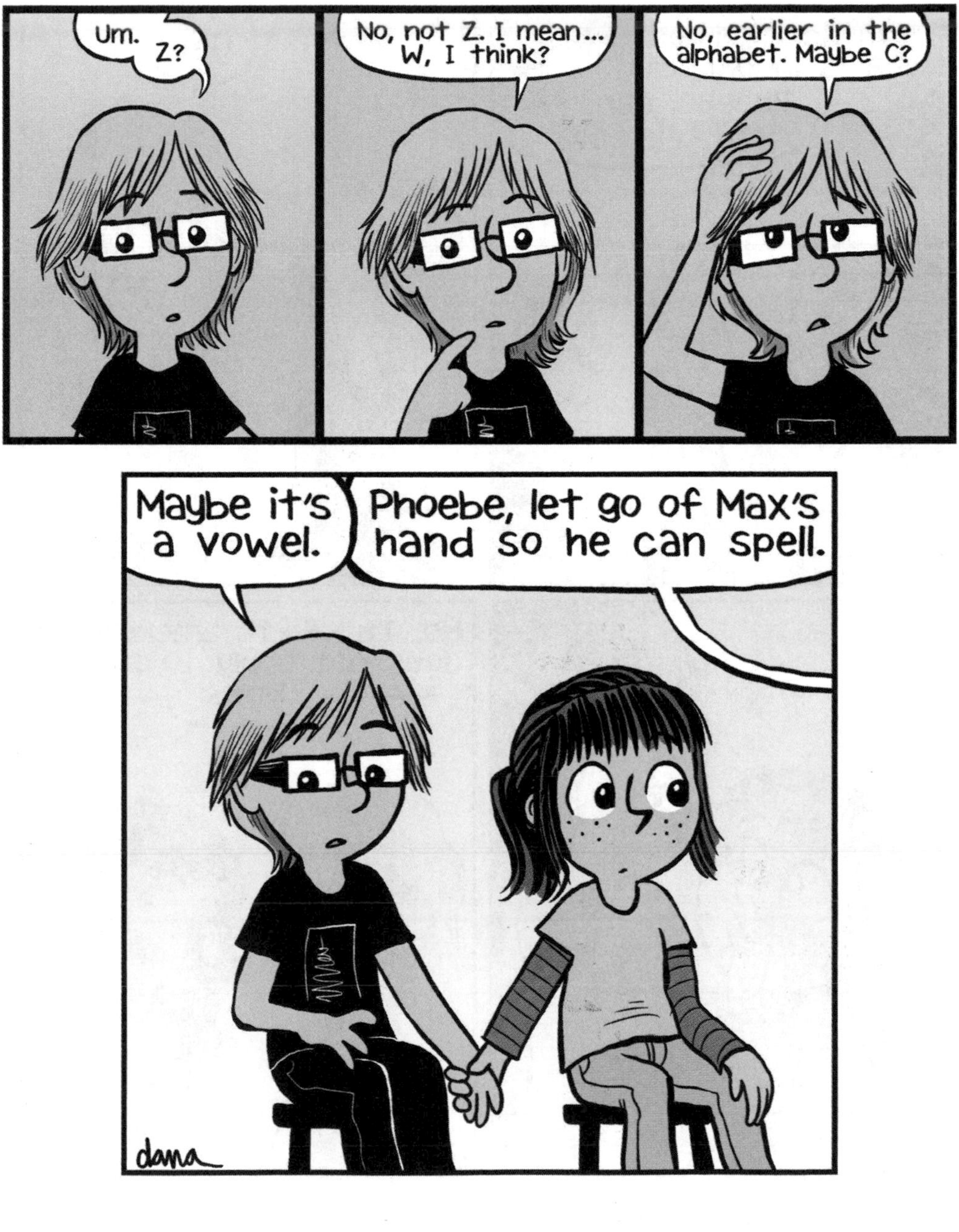
Um.
Z?
No, not Z. I mean...
W, I think?
No, earlier in the alphabet. Maybe C?
Maybe it's a vowel.
Phoebe, let go of Max's hand so he can spell.
dana

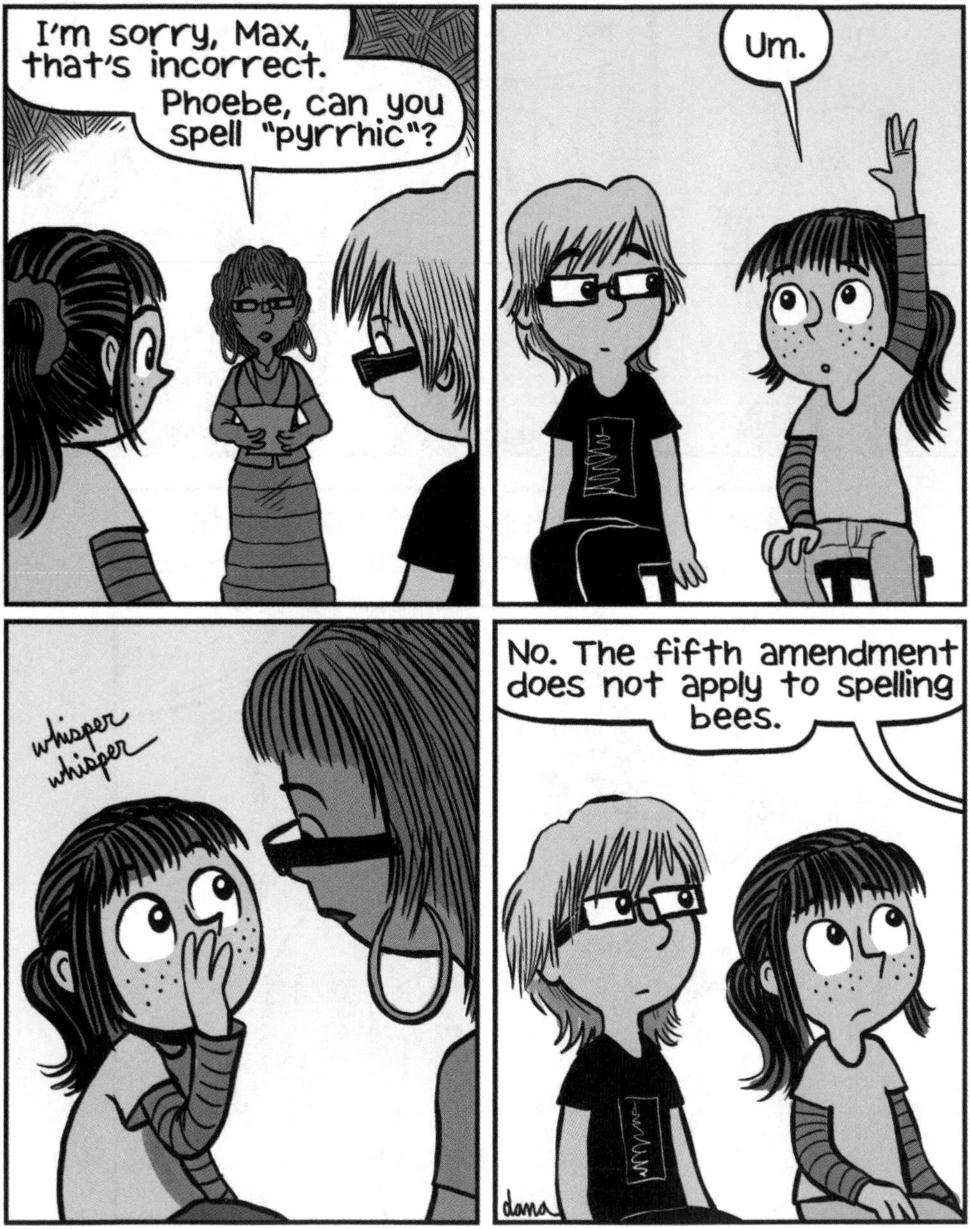
I'm sorry, Max, that's incorrect.
Phoebe, can you spell "pyrrhic"?
Um.
whisper whisper
No. The fifth amendment does not apply to spelling bees.
dana

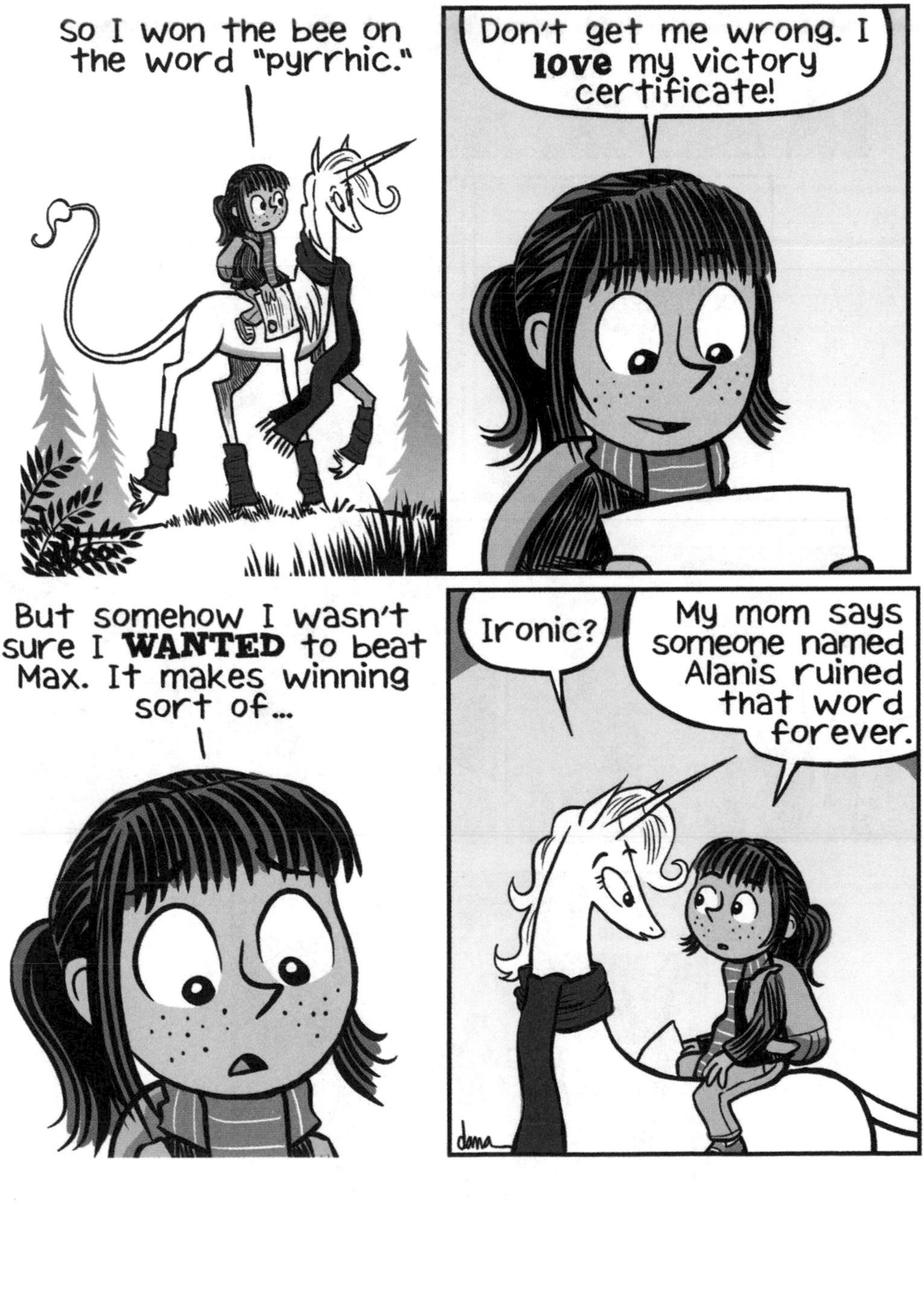

So I won the bee on the word "pyrrhic."
Don't get me wrong. I **love** my victory certificate!
But somehow I wasn't sure I **WANTED** to beat Max. It makes winning sort of...
Ironic?
My mom says someone named Alanis ruined that word forever.
dana

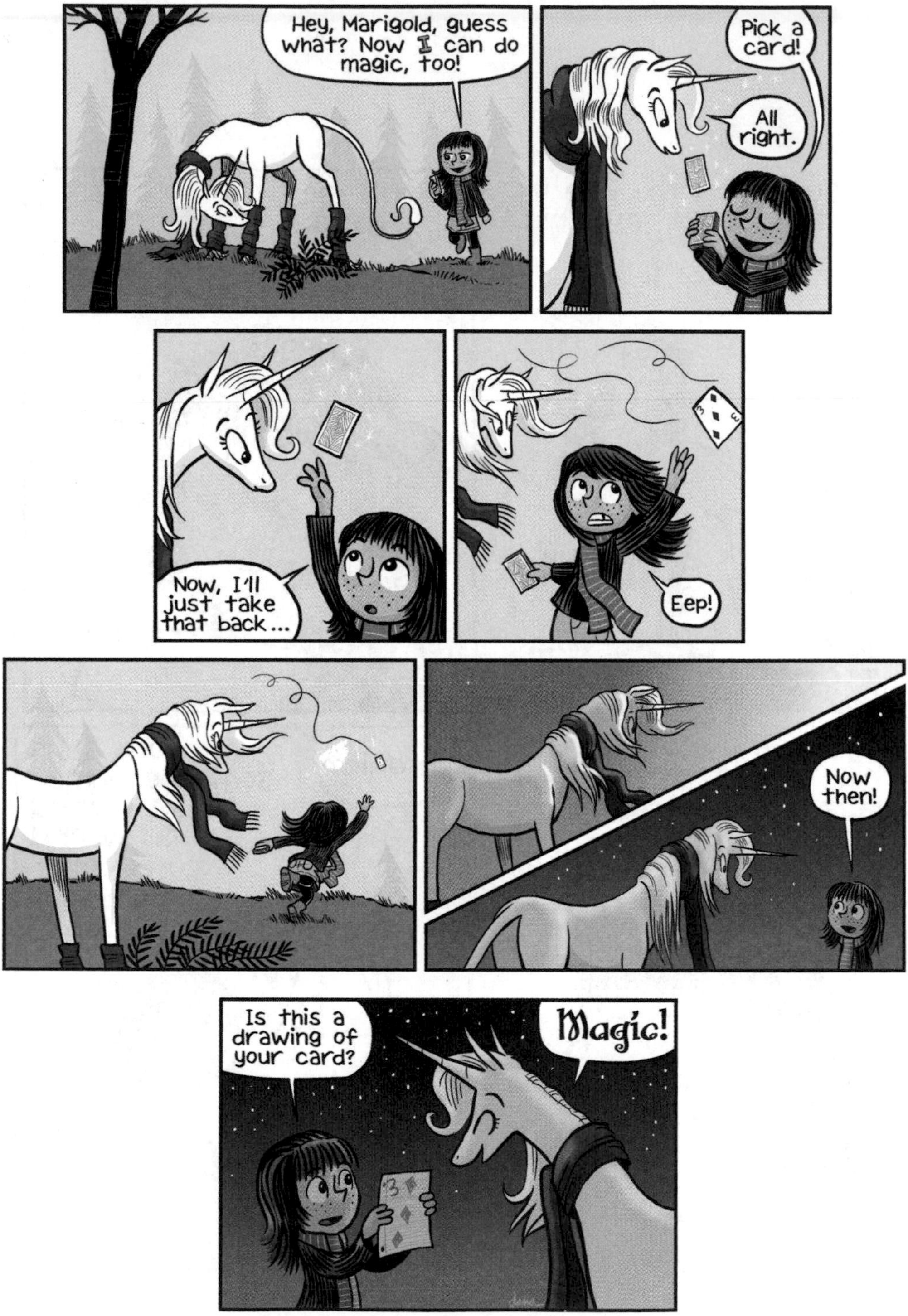

Hey, Marigold, guess what? Now I can do magic, too!
Pick a card!
All right.
Now, I'll just take that back...
Eep!
Now then!
Is this a drawing of your card?
Magic!

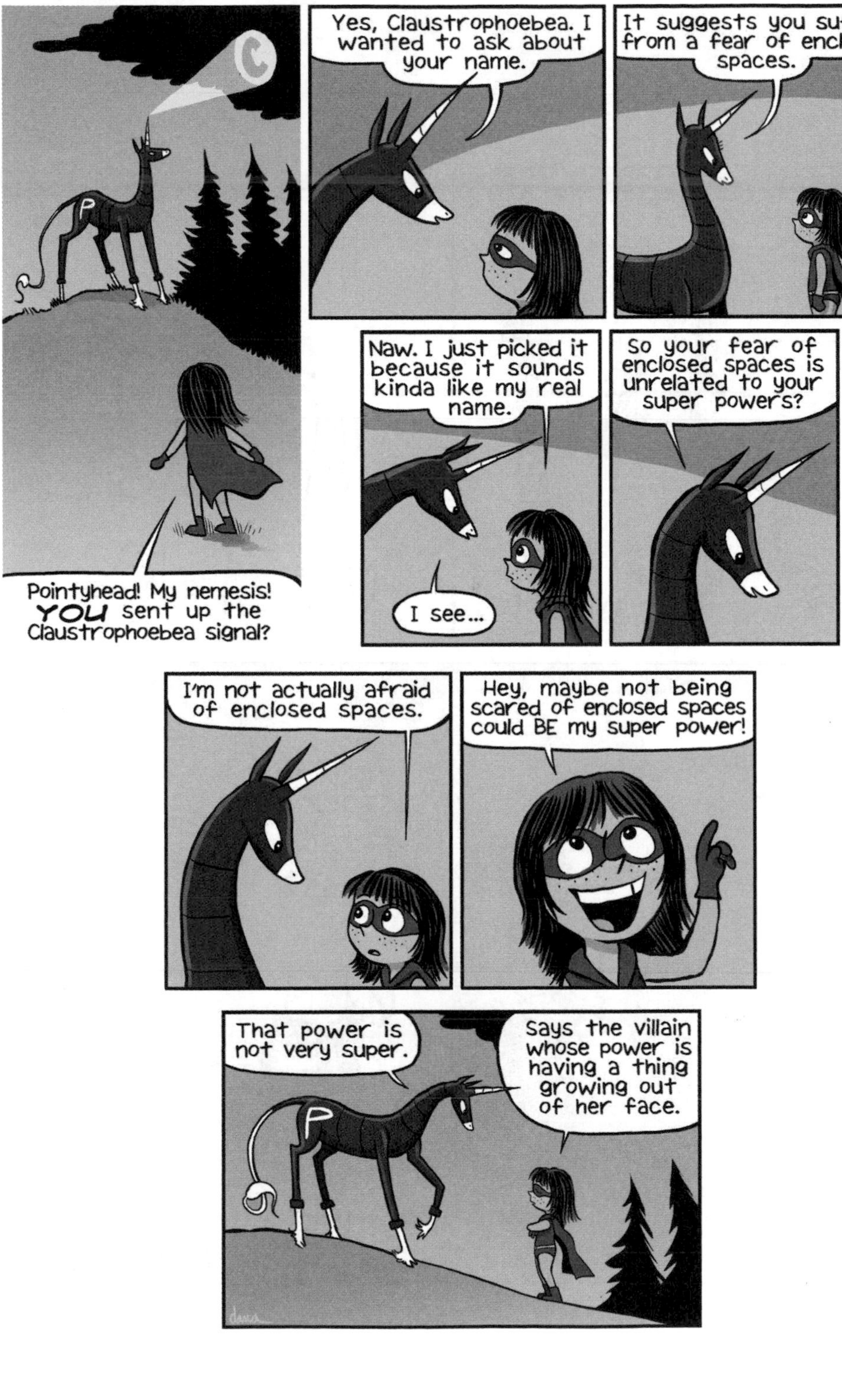
Pointyhead! My nemesis! YOU sent up the Claustrophoebea signal?
Yes, Claustrophoebea. I wanted to ask about your name.
It suggests you suffer from a fear of enclosed spaces.
Naw. I just picked it because it sounds kinda like my real name.
I see...
So your fear of enclosed spaces is unrelated to your super powers?
I'm not actually afraid of enclosed spaces.
Hey, maybe not being scared of enclosed spaces could BE my super power!
That power is not very super.
Says the villain whose power is having a thing growing out of her face.

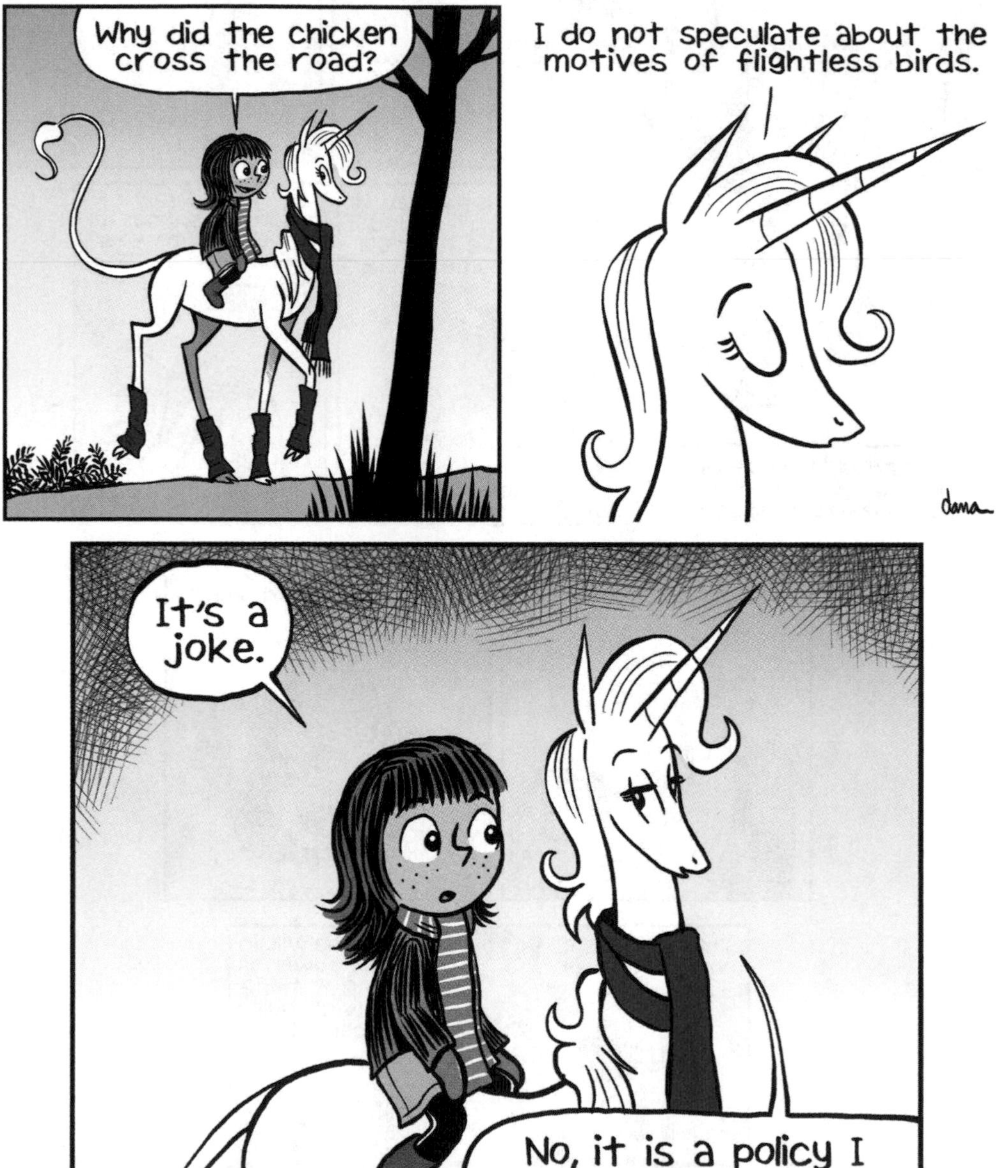
Why did the chicken cross the road?
I do not speculate about the motives of flightless birds.
dana
It's a joke.
No, it is a policy I take **quite** seriously.

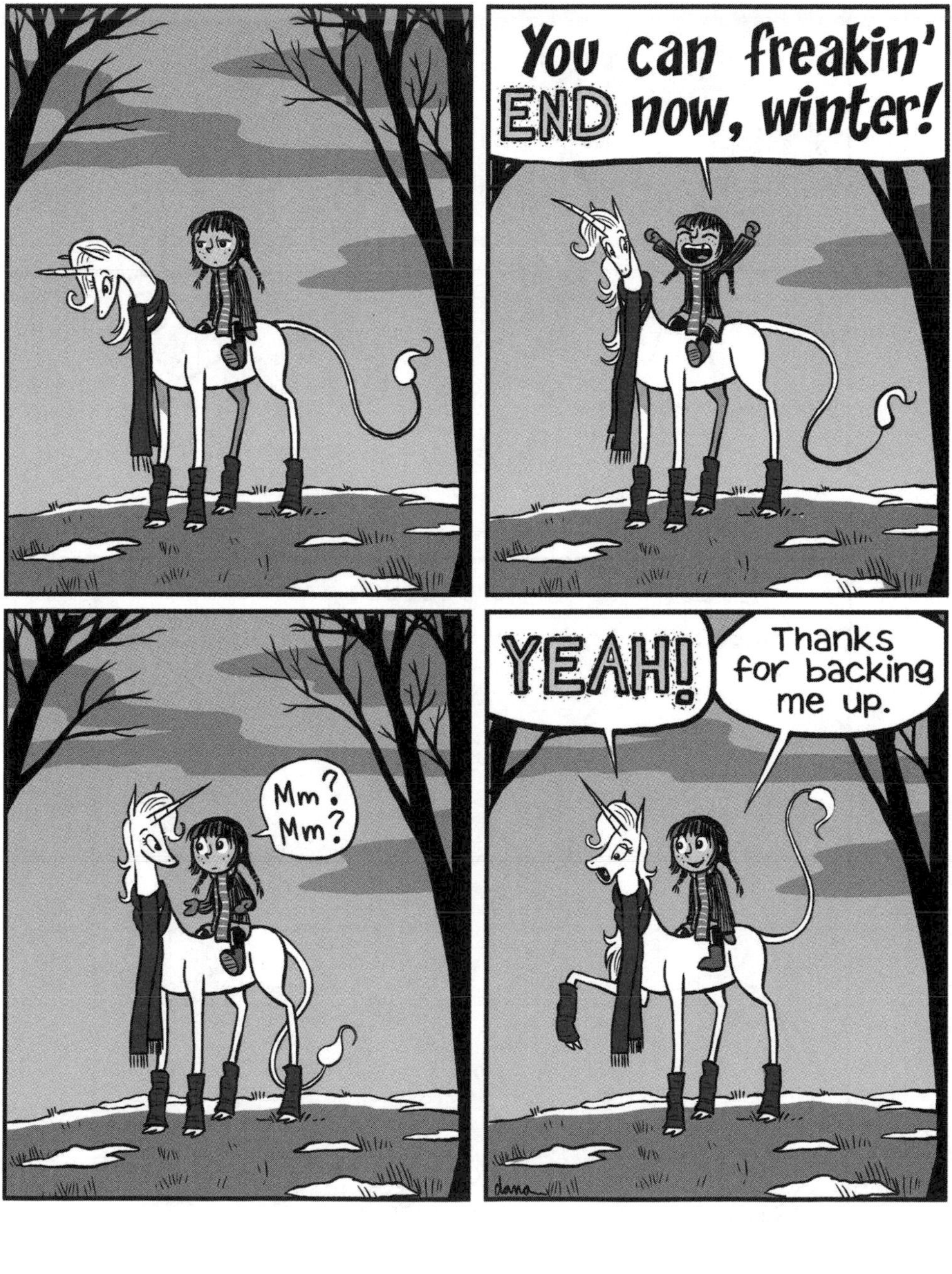
You can freakin' END now, winter!
Mm? Mm?
YEAH!
Thanks for backing me up.
dana

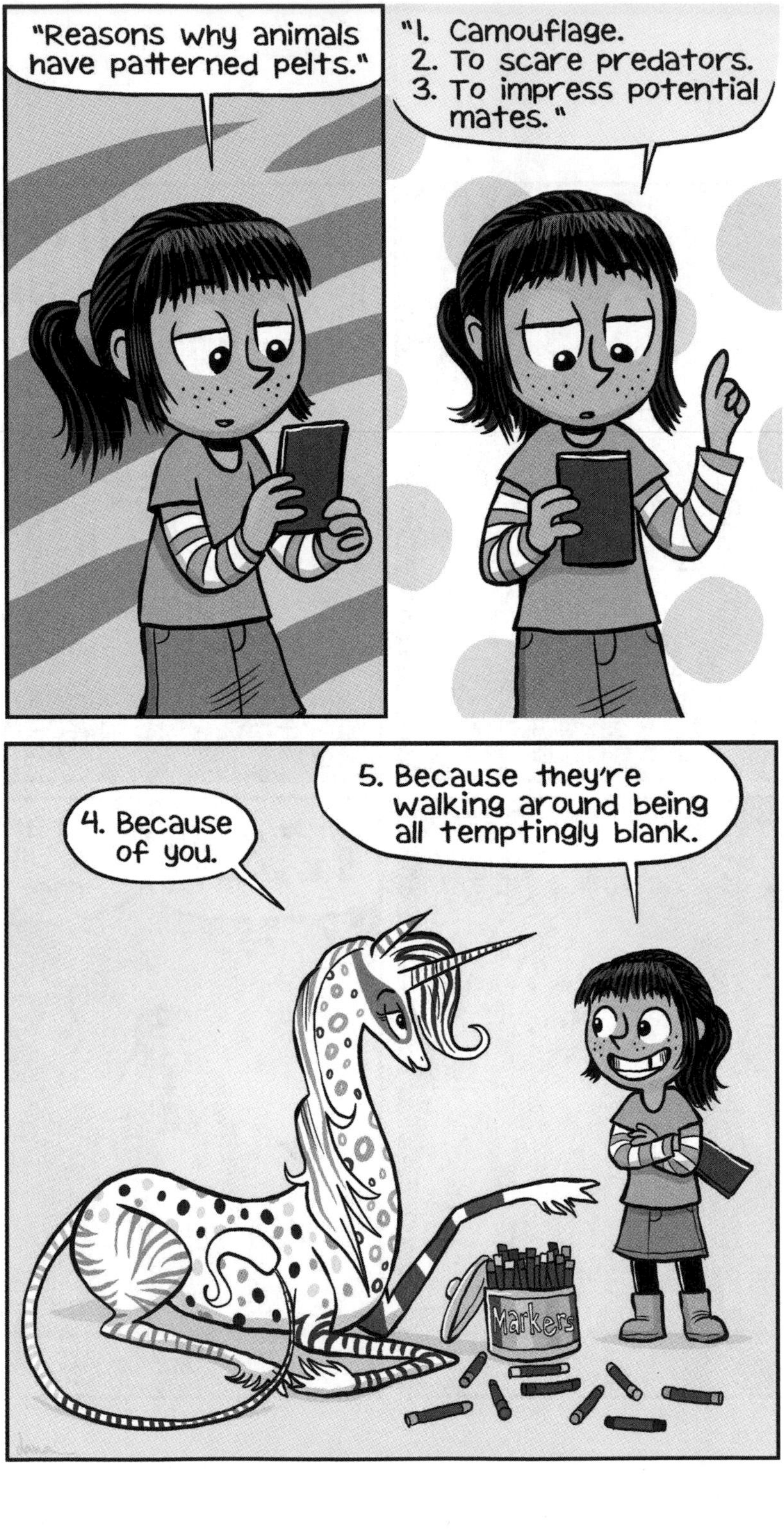
"Reasons why animals have patterned pelts."
"1. Camouflage.
2. To scare predators.
3. To impress potential mates."
4. Because of you.
5. Because they're walking around being all temptingly blank.
Markers

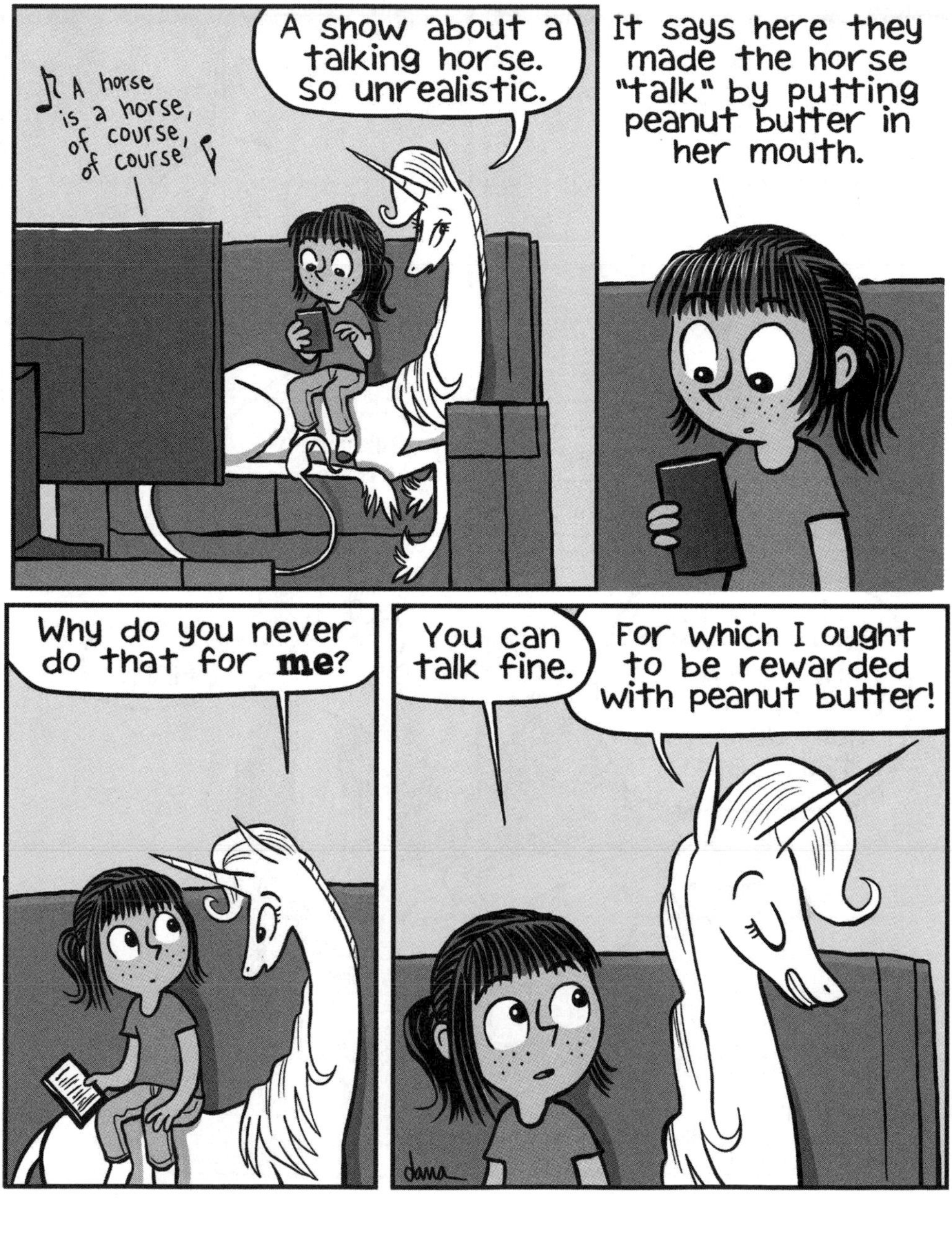
A horse is a horse, of course, of course
A show about a talking horse. So unrealistic.
It says here they made the horse "talk" by putting peanut butter in her mouth.
Why do you never do that for **me**?
You can talk fine.
For which I ought to be rewarded with peanut butter!
dana

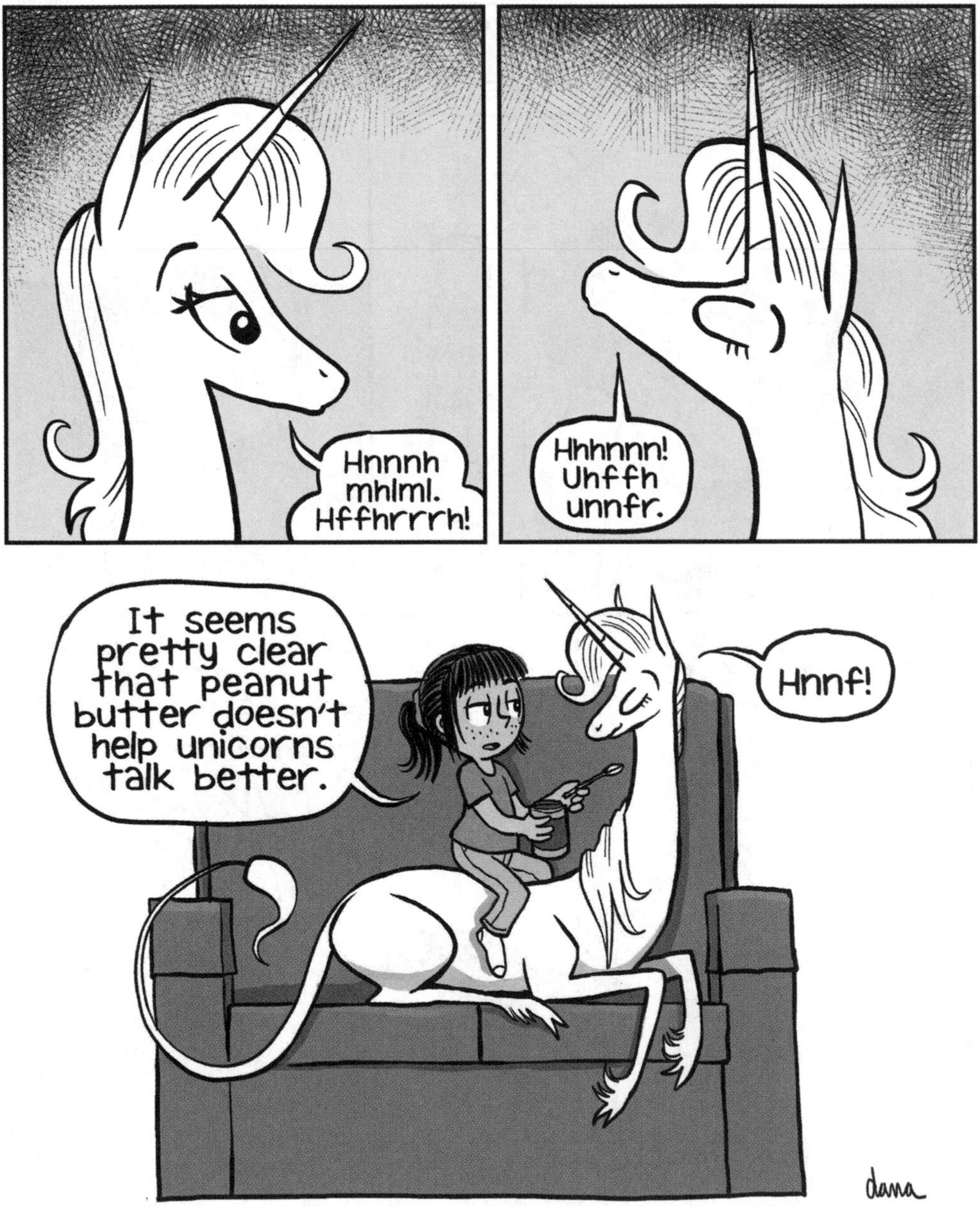
Hnnnh mhlml. Hffhrrrh!
Hhhnnn! Uhffh unnfr.
It seems pretty clear that peanut butter doesn't help unicorns talk better.
Hnnf!
dana

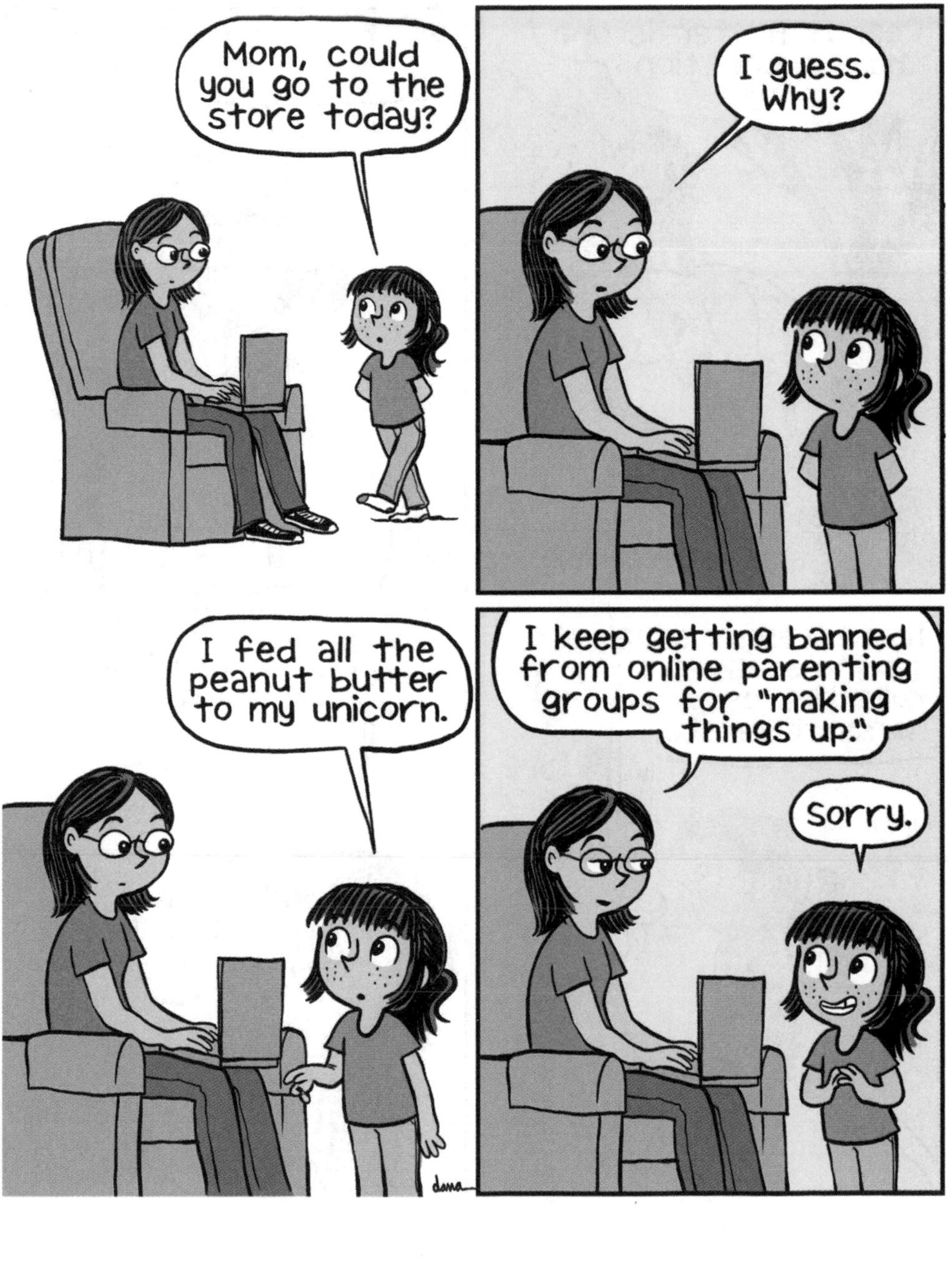
Mom, could you go to the store today?
I guess. Why?
I fed all the peanut butter to my unicorn.
I keep getting banned from online parenting groups for "making things up."
Sorry.
dana

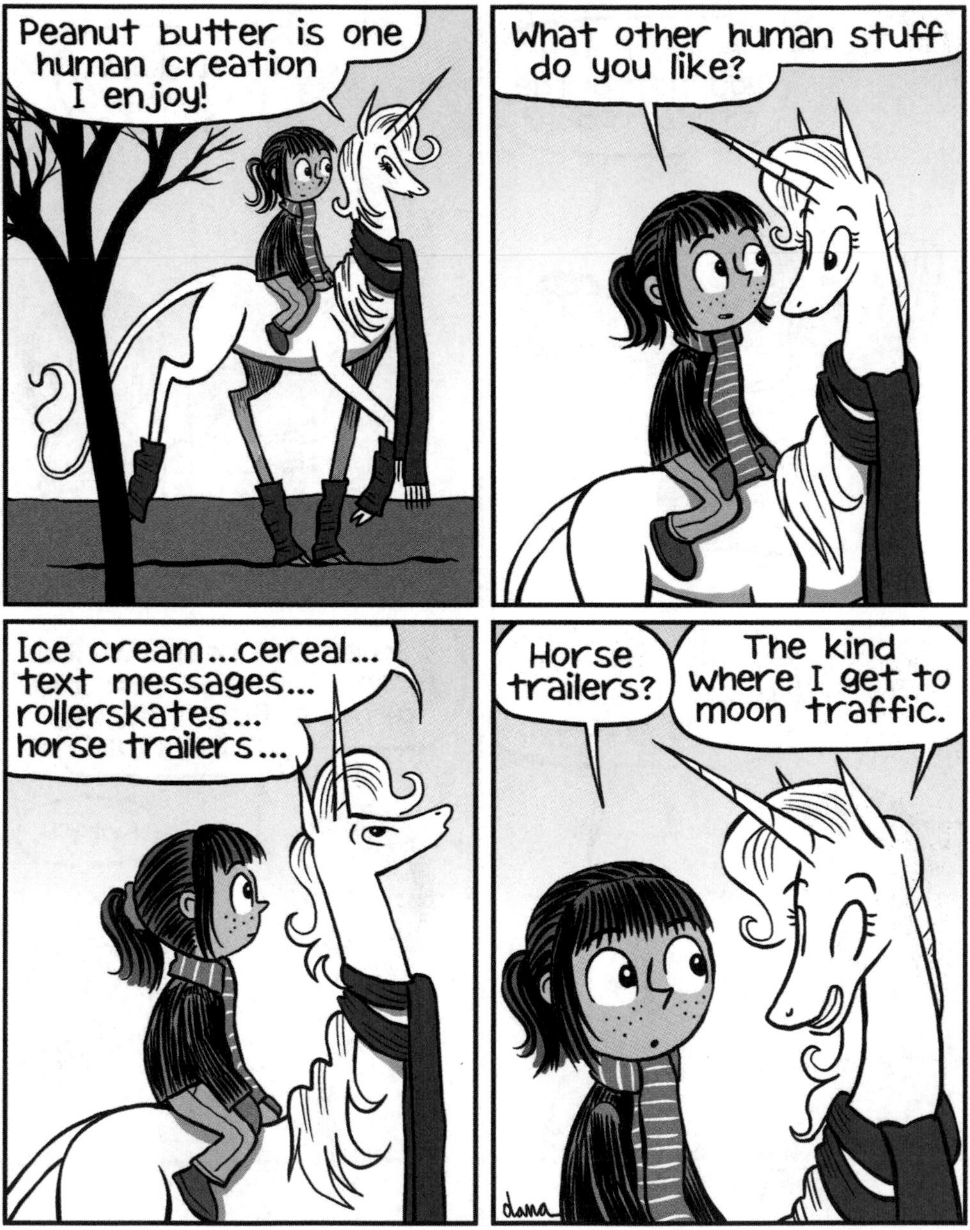
Peanut butter is one human creation I enjoy!
What other human stuff do you like?
Ice cream...cereal... text messages... rollerskates... horse trailers...
Horse trailers?
The kind where I get to moon traffic.
dana

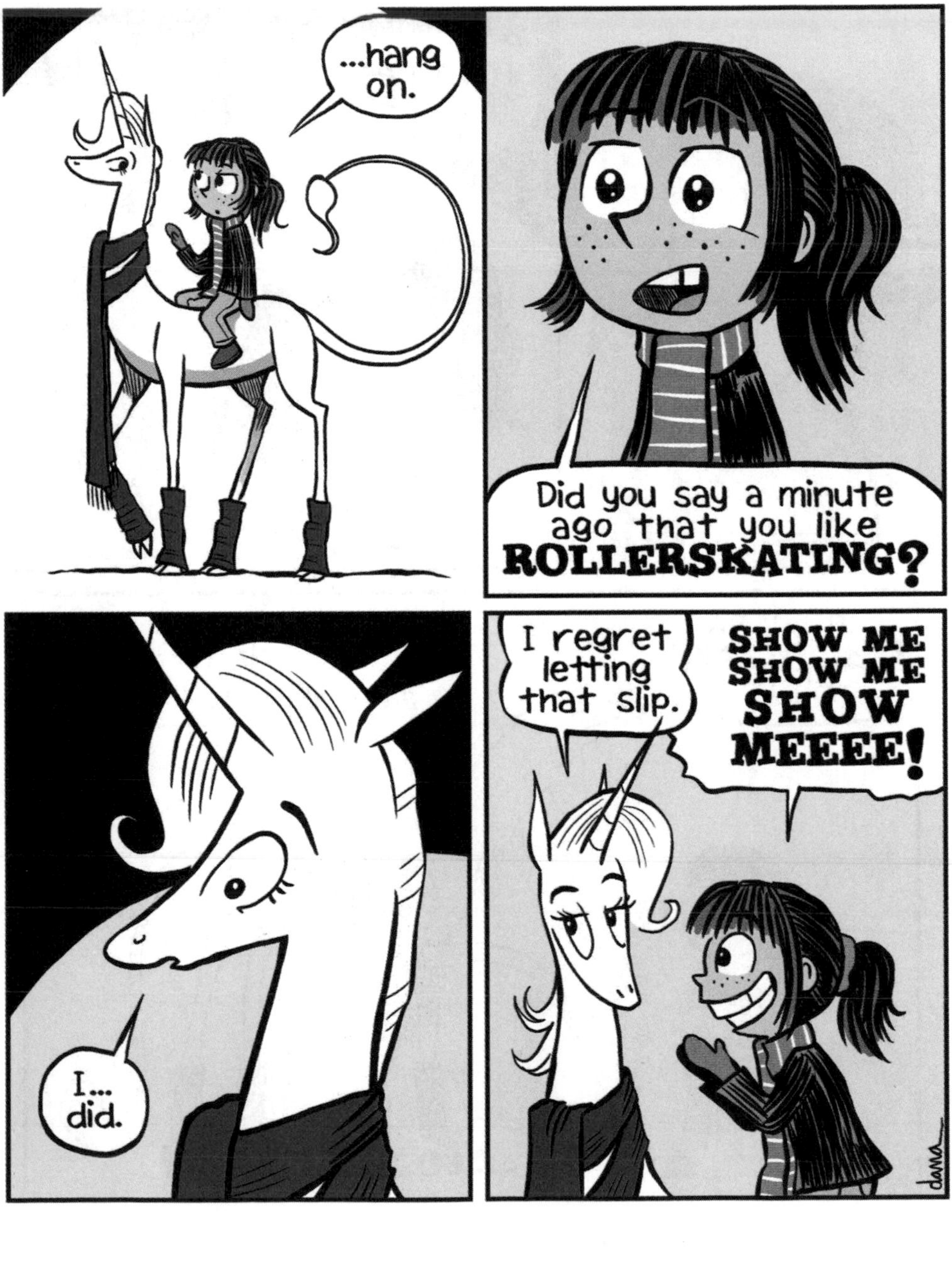
...hang on.
Did you say a minute ago that you like **ROLLERSKATING?**
I... did.
I regret letting that slip.
SHOW ME SHOW ME SHOW MEEEE!
dana

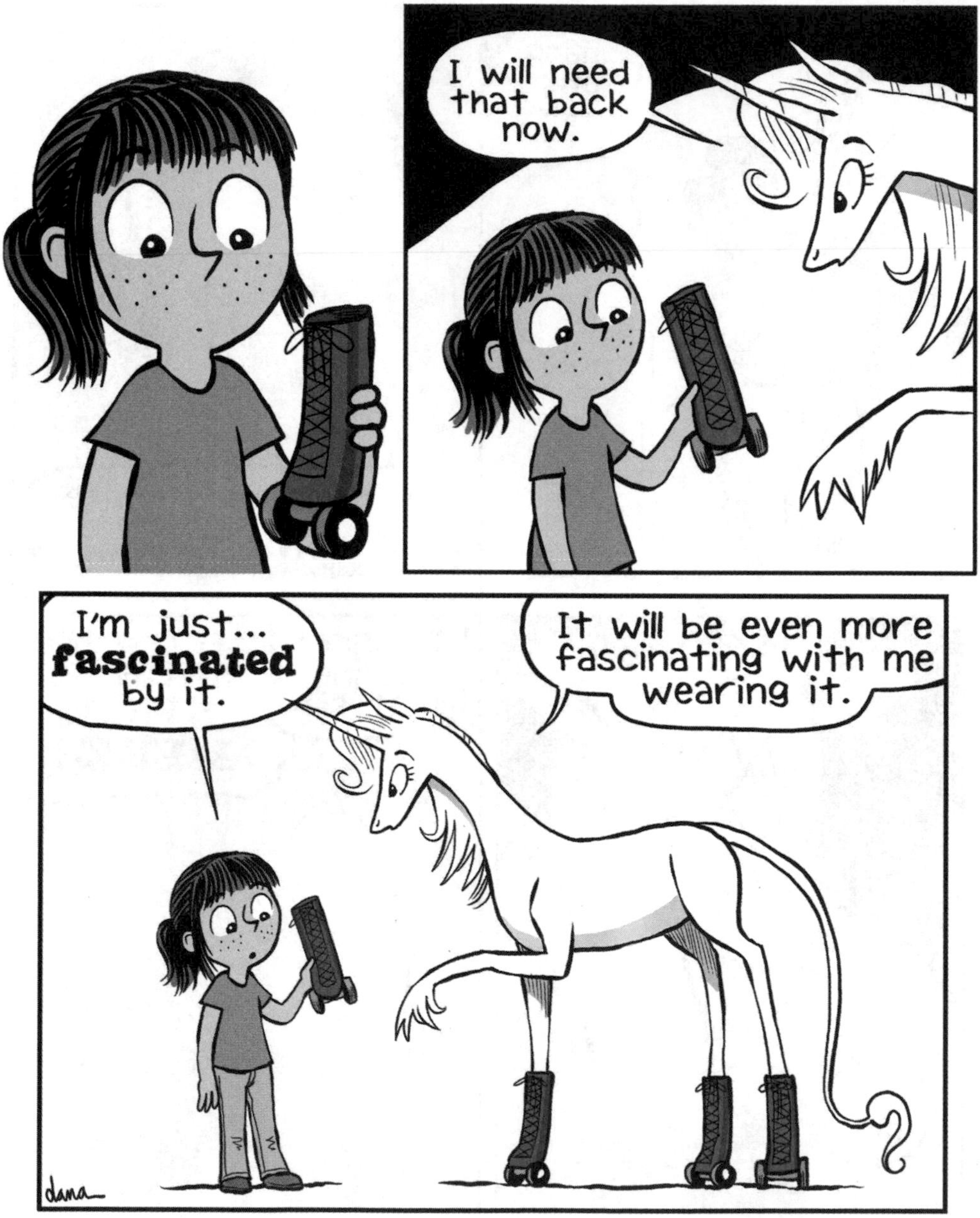
I will need that back now.
I'm just... **fascinated** by it.
It will be even more fascinating with me wearing it.
dana

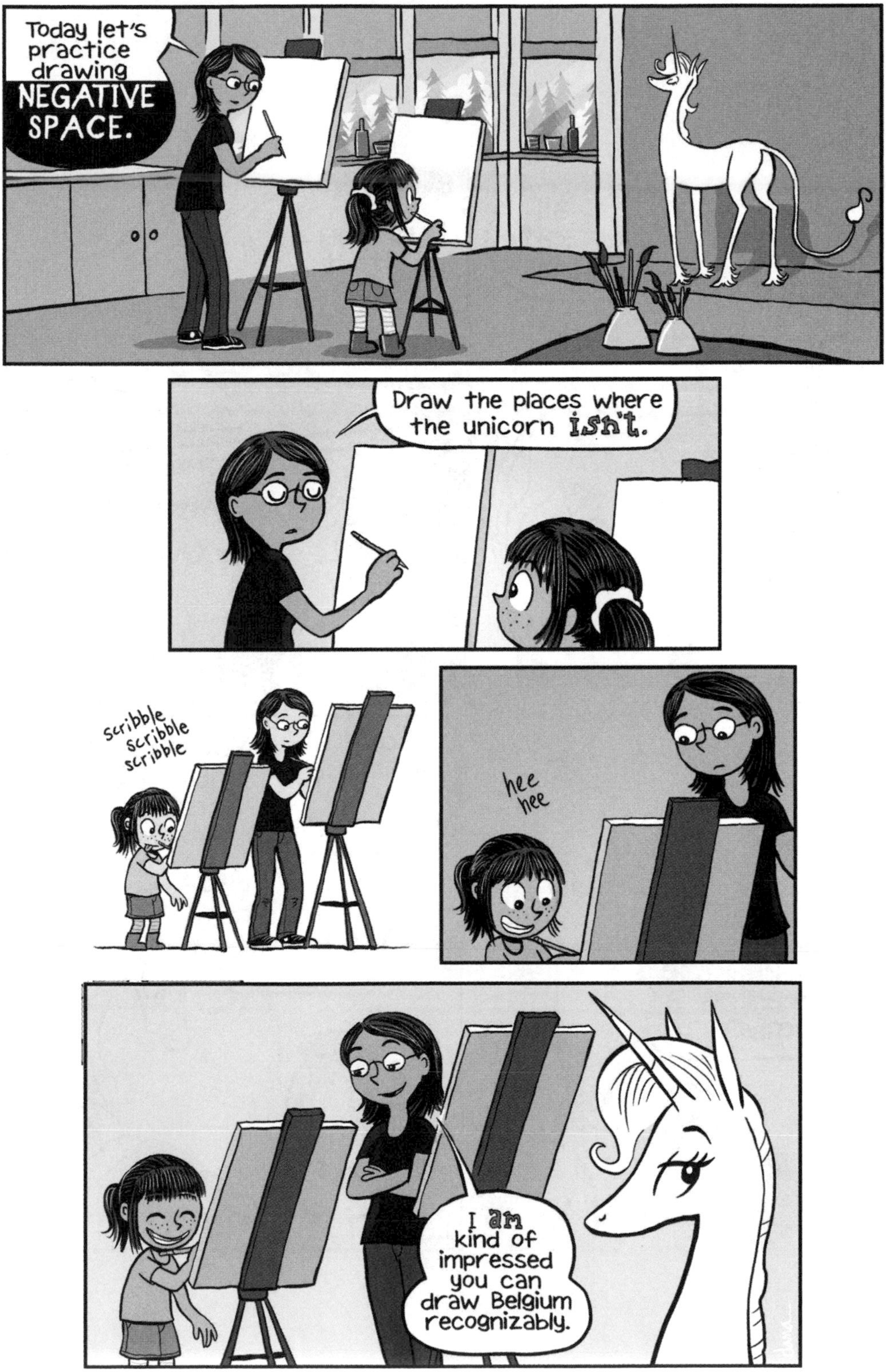
Today let's practice drawing NEGATIVE SPACE.
Draw the places where the unicorn isn't.
scribble scribble scribble
hee hee
I am kind of impressed you can draw Belgium recognizably.

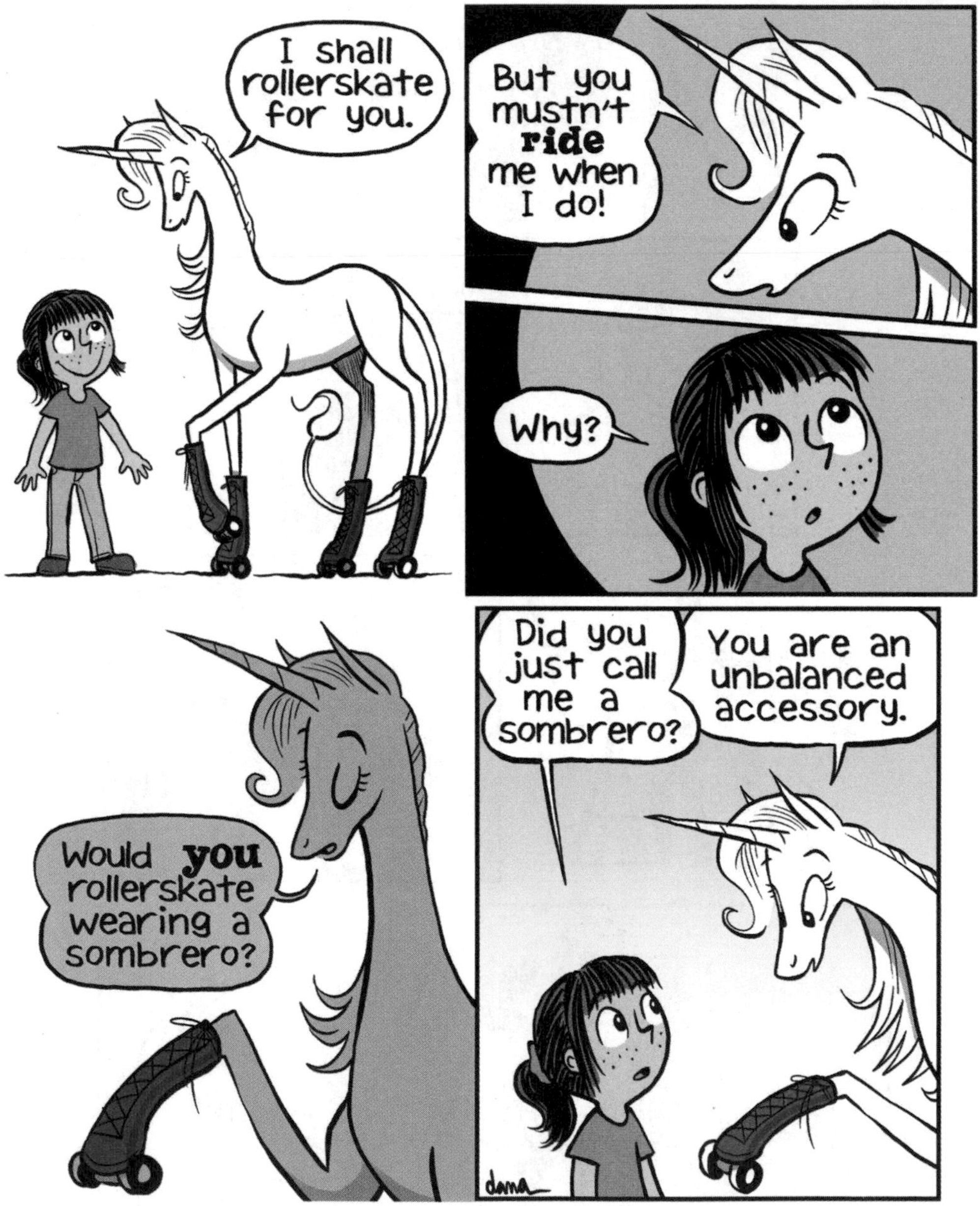
I shall rollerskate for you.
But you mustn't **ride** me when I do!
Why?
Would **you** rollerskate wearing a sombrero?
Did you just call me a sombrero?
You are an unbalanced accessory.
dana

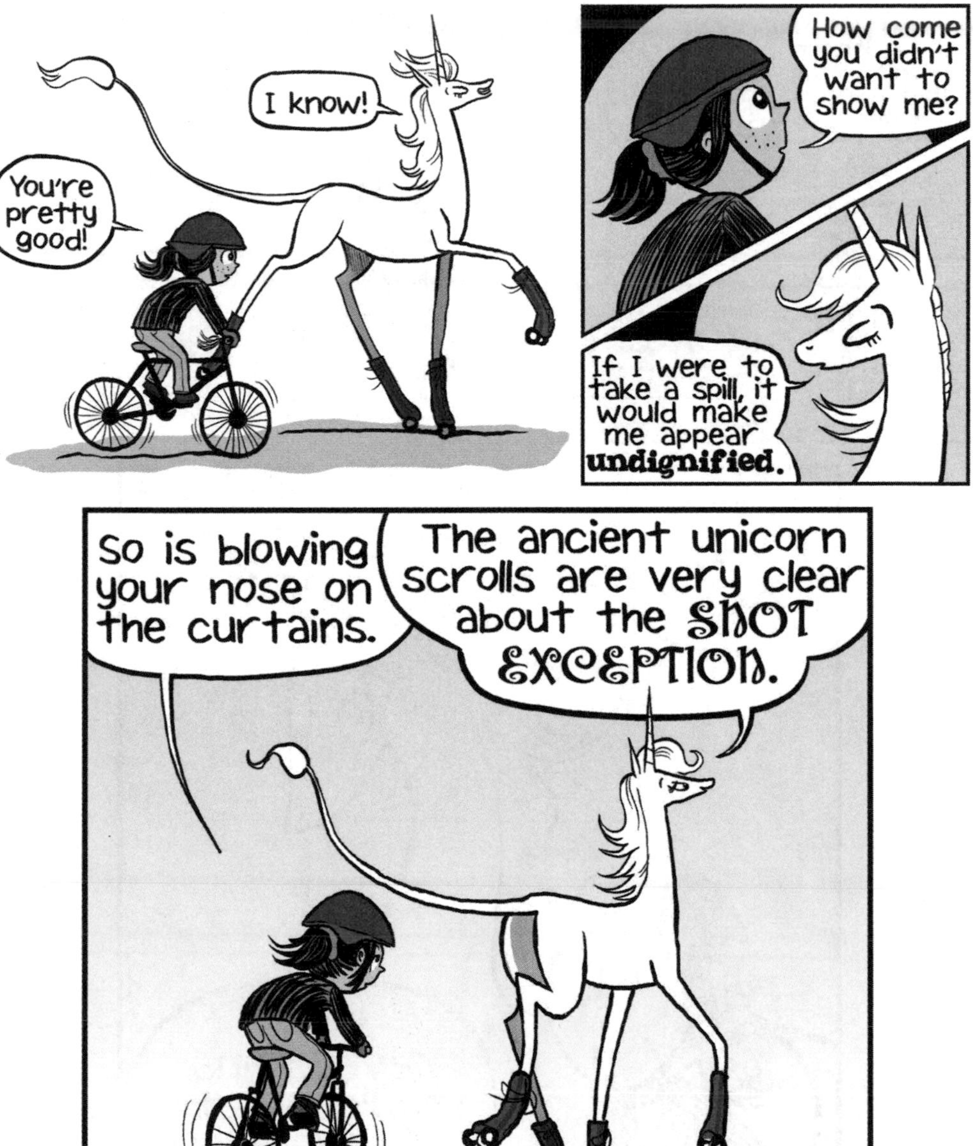
You're pretty good!
I know!
How come you didn't want to show me?
If I were to take a spill, it would make me appear **undignified**.
The ancient unicorn scrolls are very clear about the SNOT EXCEPTION.
So is blowing your nose on the curtains.
dana

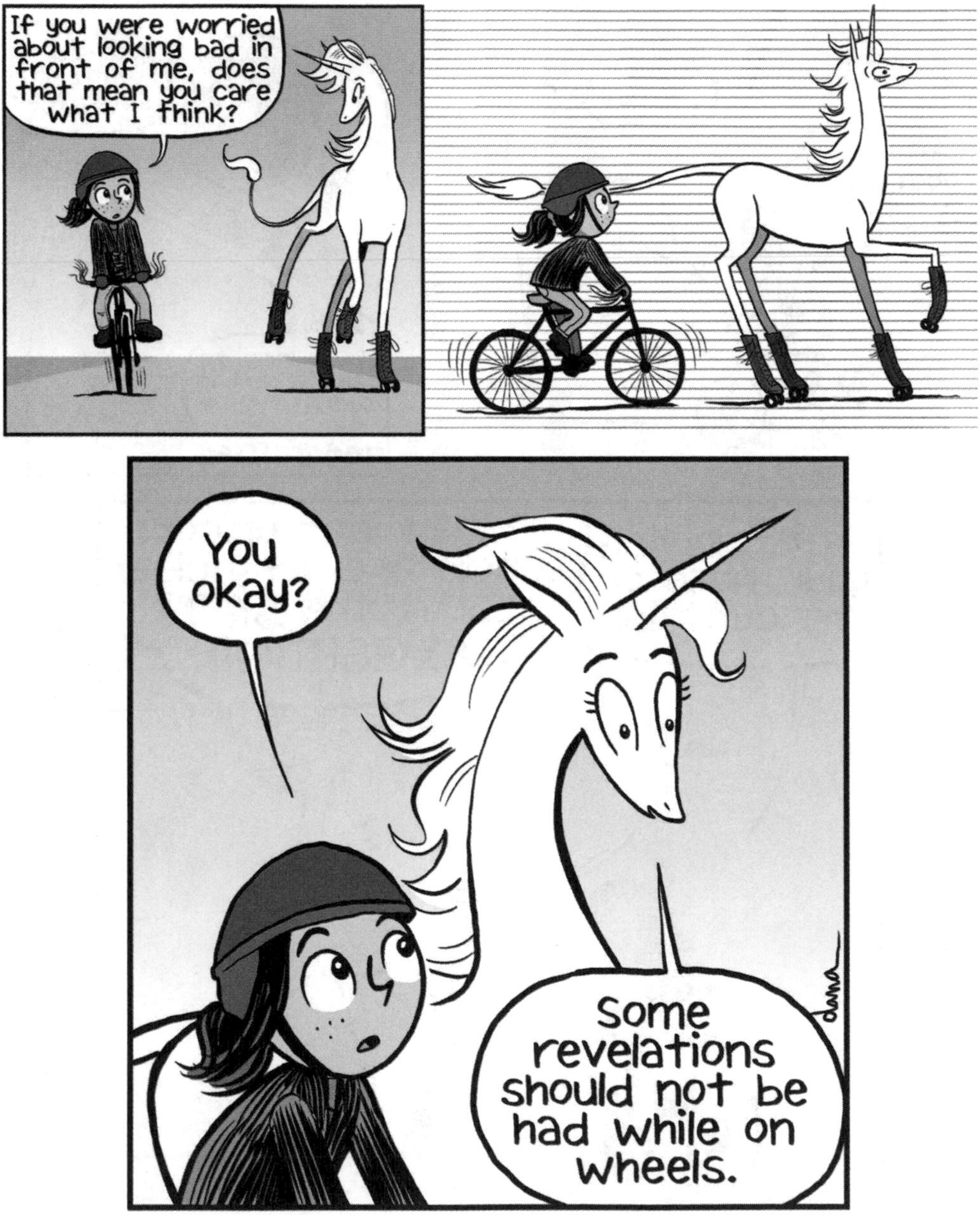
If you were worried about looking bad in front of me, does that mean you care what I think?
You okay?
Some revelations should not be had while on wheels.
dana

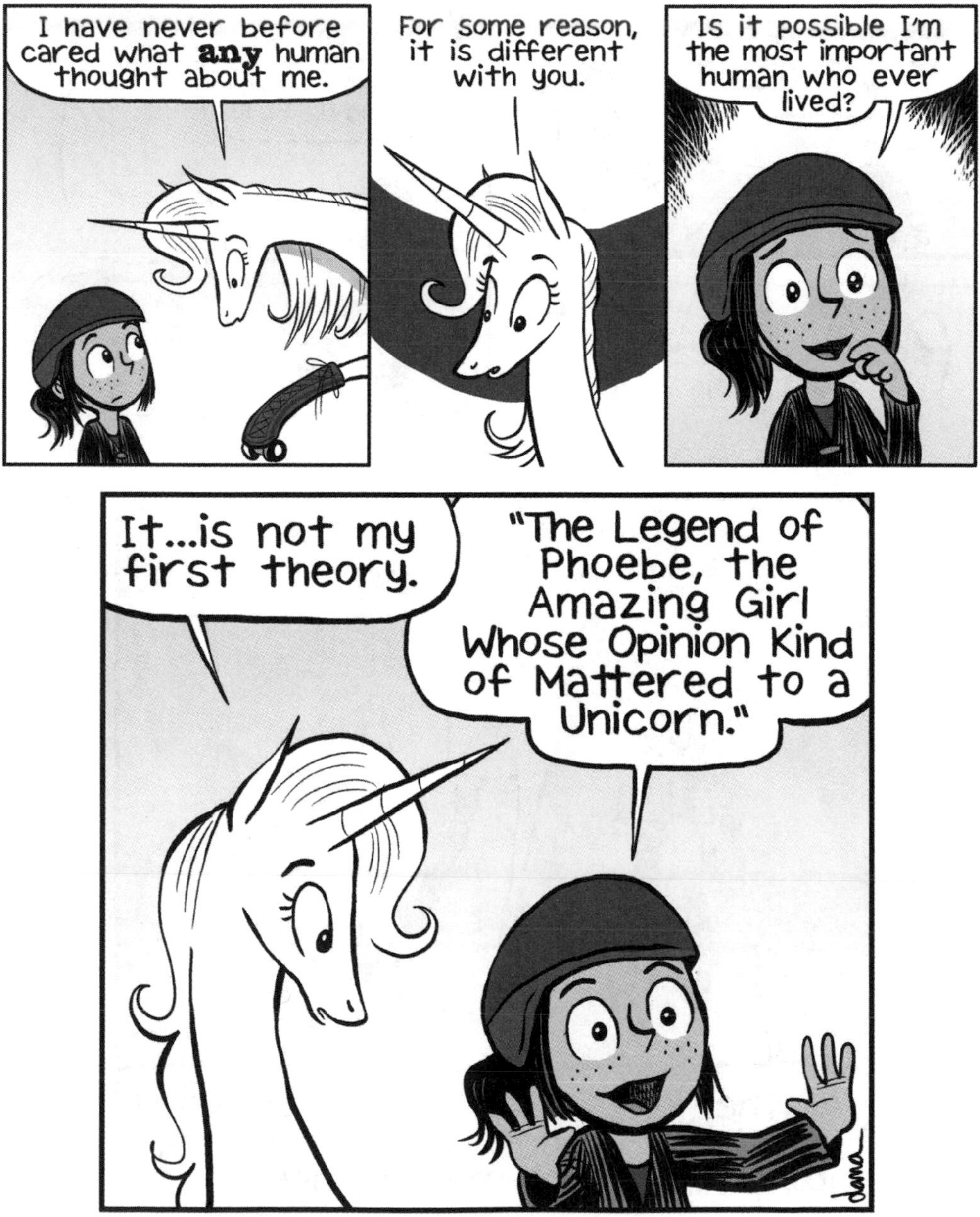
I have never before cared what **any** human thought about me.
For some reason, it is different with you.
Is it possible I'm the most important human who ever lived?
It...is not my first theory.
"The Legend of Phoebe, the Amazing Girl Whose Opinion Kind of Mattered to a Unicorn."
dana

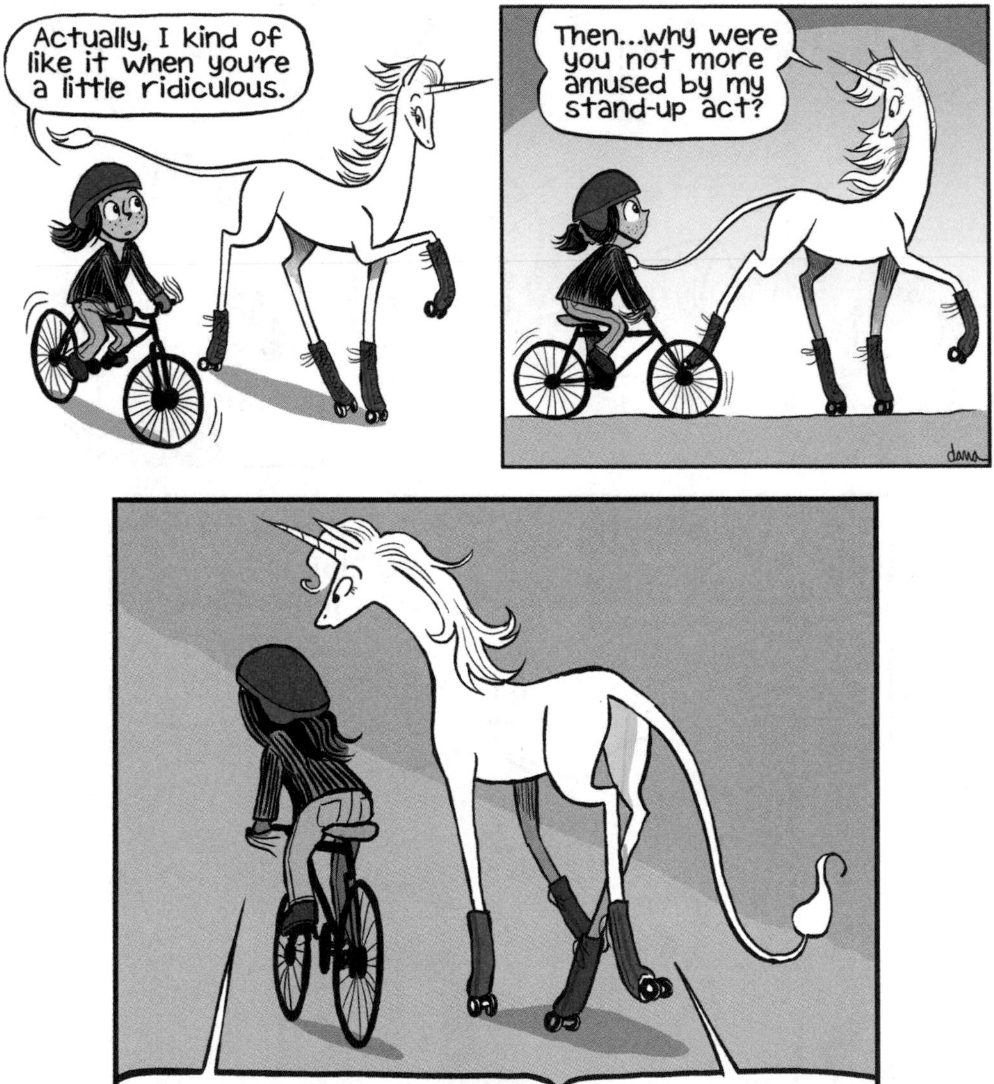
Actually, I kind of like it when you're a little ridiculous.
Then...why were you not more amused by my stand-up act?
dana
All the jokes about off-brand hoof polish kinda lost me.
But its shine is hilariously insufficient!

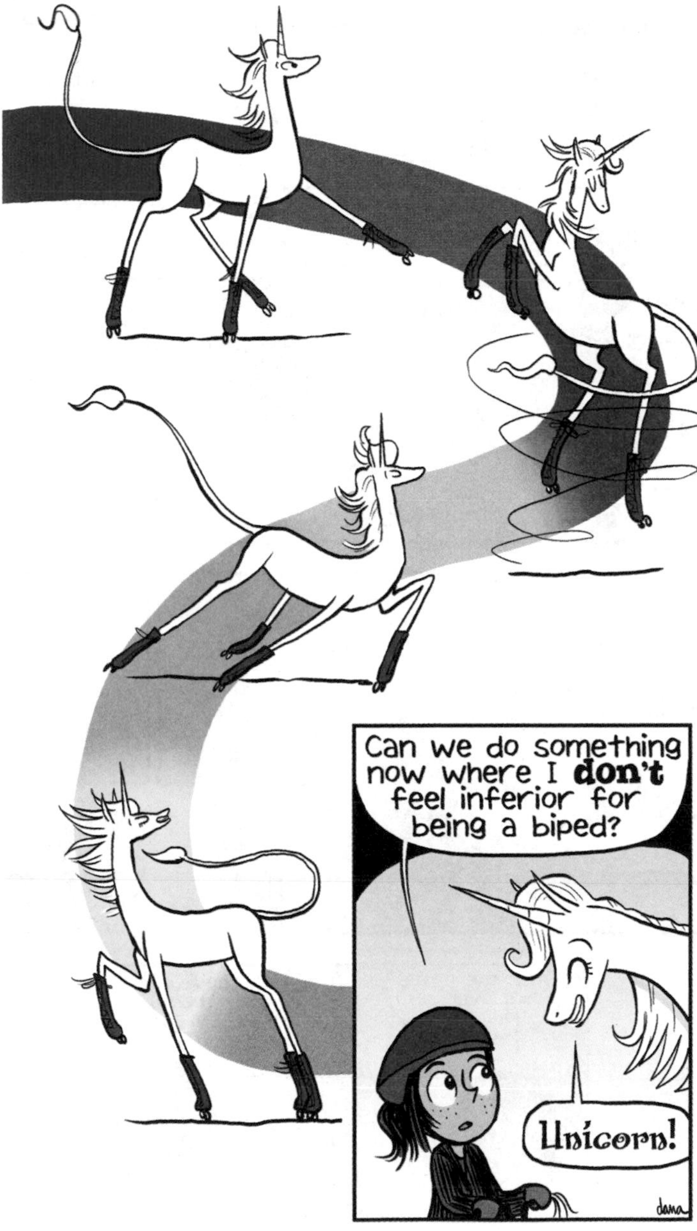
Can we do something now where I **don't** feel inferior for being a biped?
Unicorn!
dana

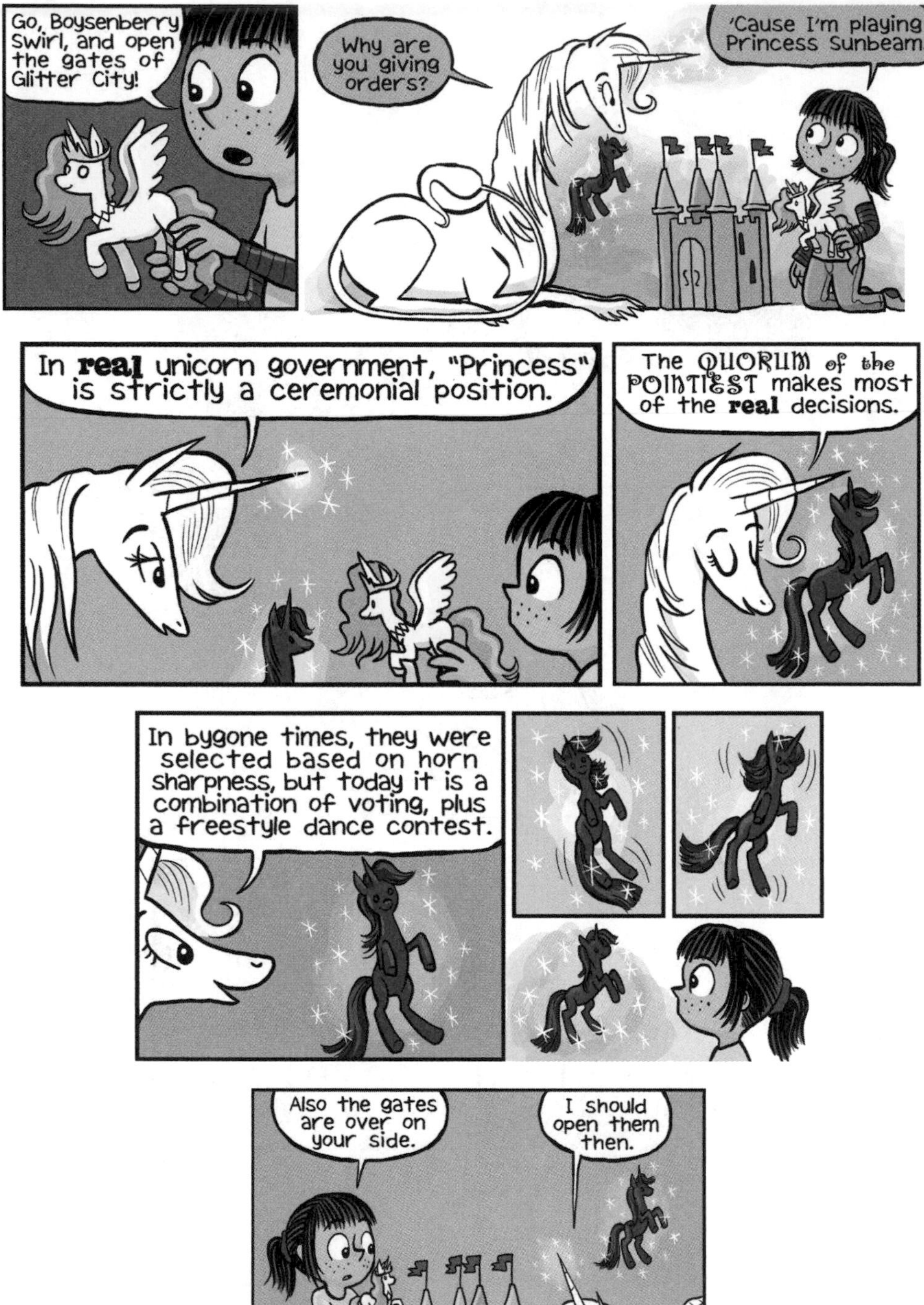
Go, Boysenberry Swirl, and open the gates of Glitter City!
Why are you giving orders?
'Cause I'm playing Princess Sunbeam.
In real unicorn government, "Princess" is strictly a ceremonial position.
The QUORUM of the POINTIEST makes most of the real decisions.
In bygone times, they were selected based on horn sharpness, but today it is a combination of voting, plus a freestyle dance contest.
Also the gates are over on your side.
I should open them then.
dana

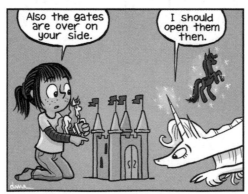

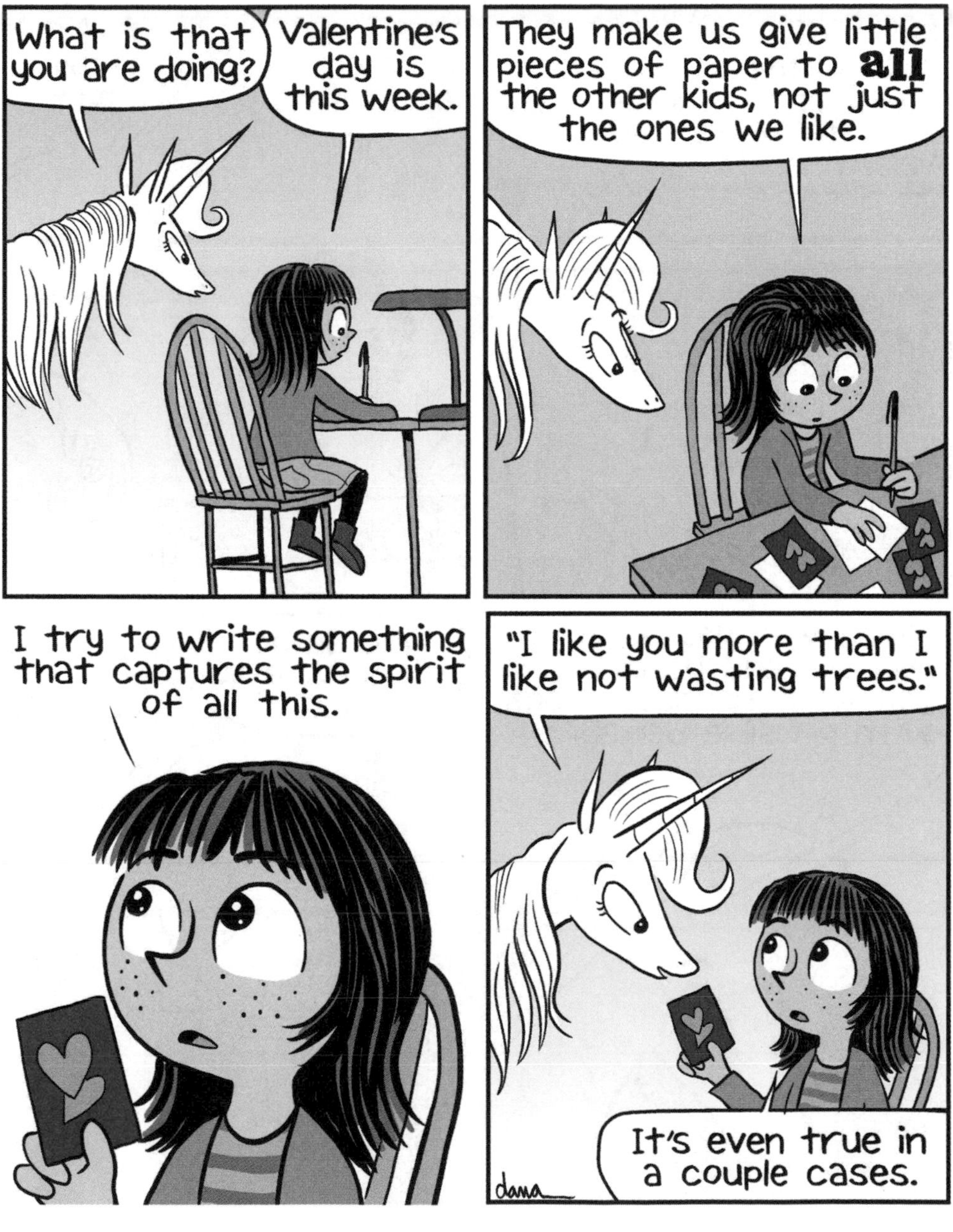
What is that you are doing?
Valentine's day is this week.
They make us give little pieces of paper to **all** the other kids, not just the ones we like.
I try to write something that captures the spirit of all this.
"I like you more than I like not wasting trees."
It's even true in a couple cases.
dana

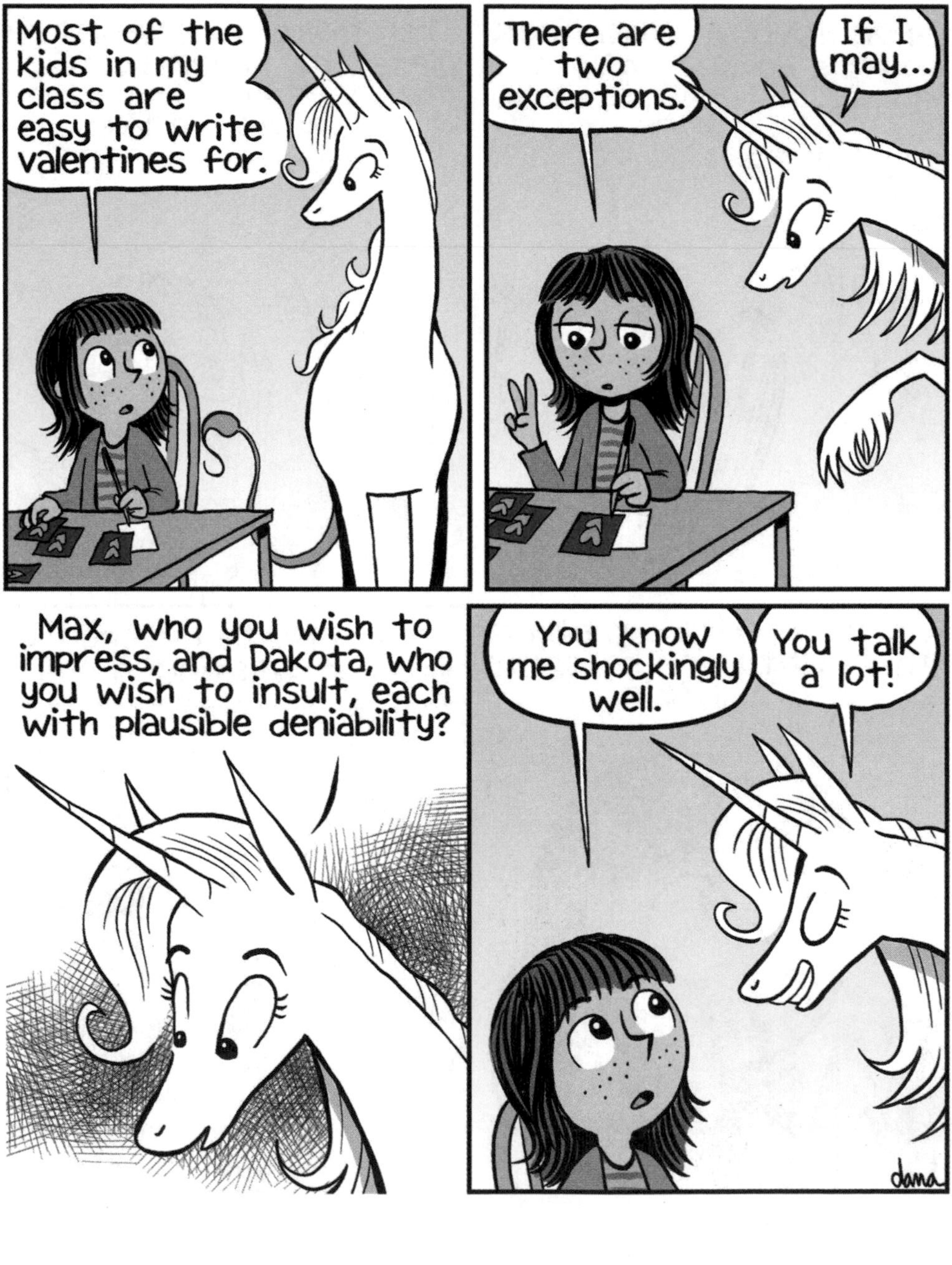
Most of the kids in my class are easy to write valentines for.
There are two exceptions.
If I may...
Max, who you wish to impress, and Dakota, who you wish to insult, each with plausible deniability?
You know me shockingly well.
You talk a lot!
dana

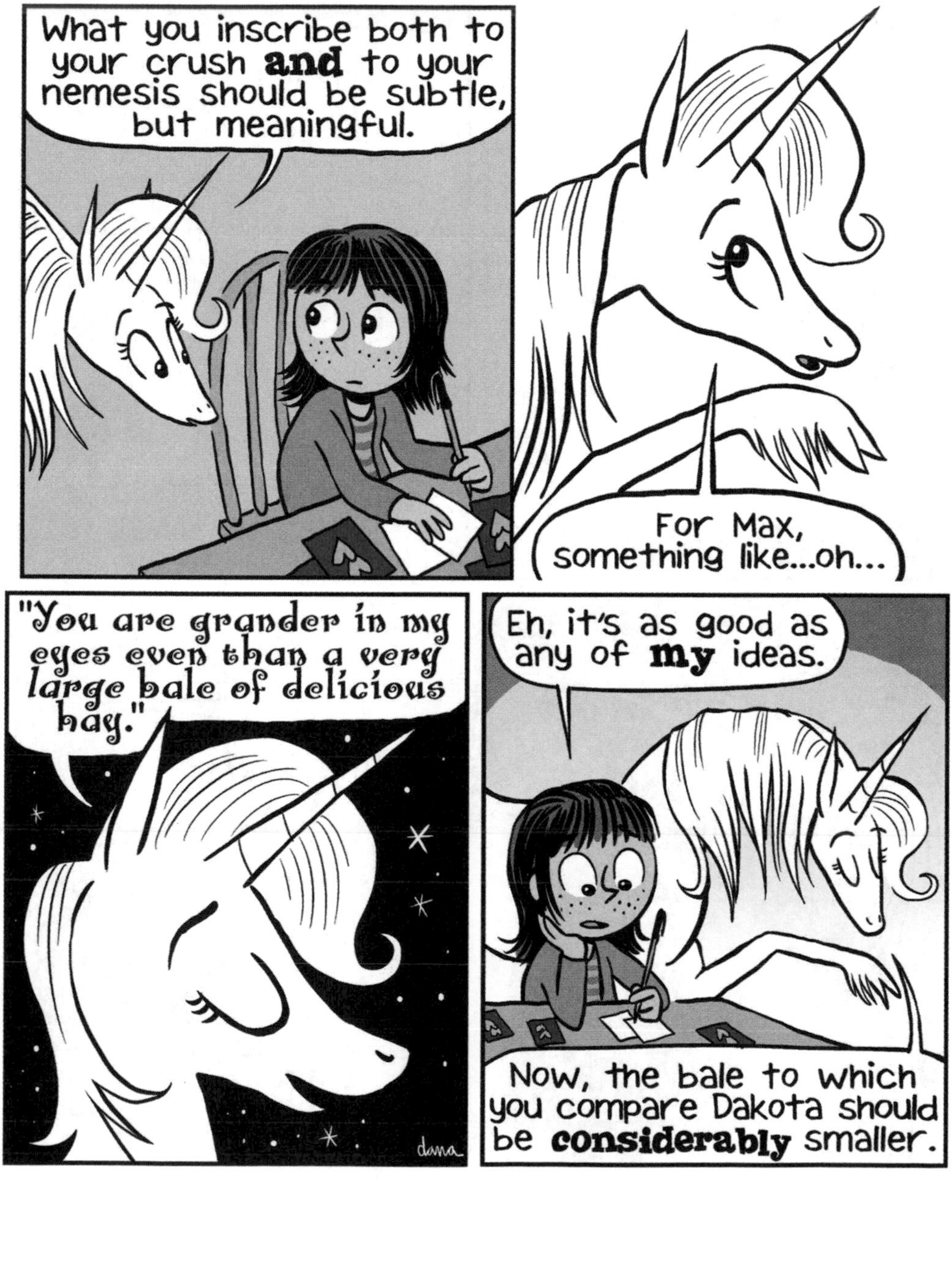

What you inscribe both to your crush **and** to your nemesis should be subtle, but meaningful.
For Max, something like...oh...
"You are grander in my eyes even than a very large bale of delicious hay."
dana
Eh, it's as good as any of **my** ideas.
Now, the bale to which you compare Dakota should be **considerably** smaller.

VALENTINE'S DAY

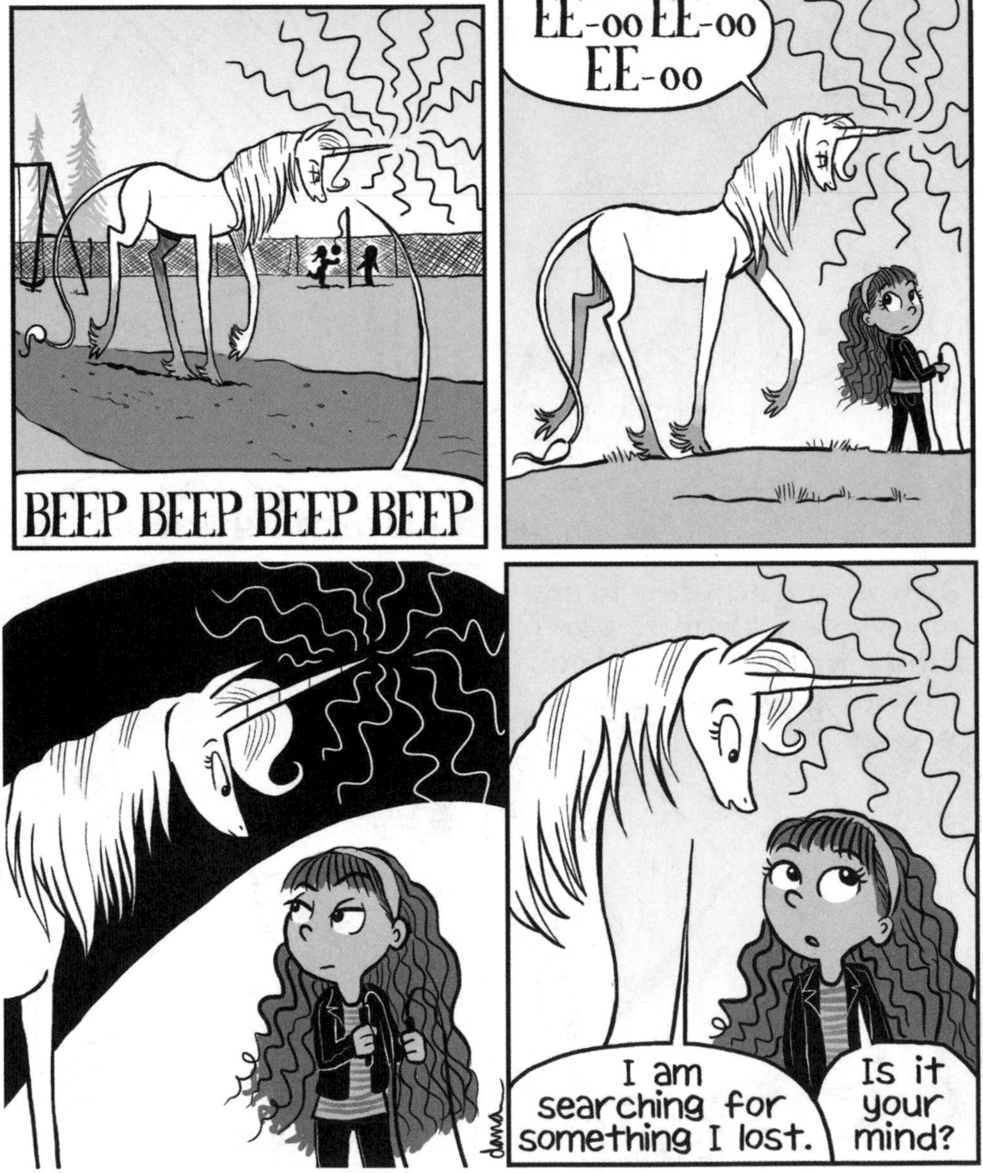
BEEP BEEP BEEP BEEP
EE-oo EE-oo EE-oo
I am searching for something I lost.
Is it your mind?
dana

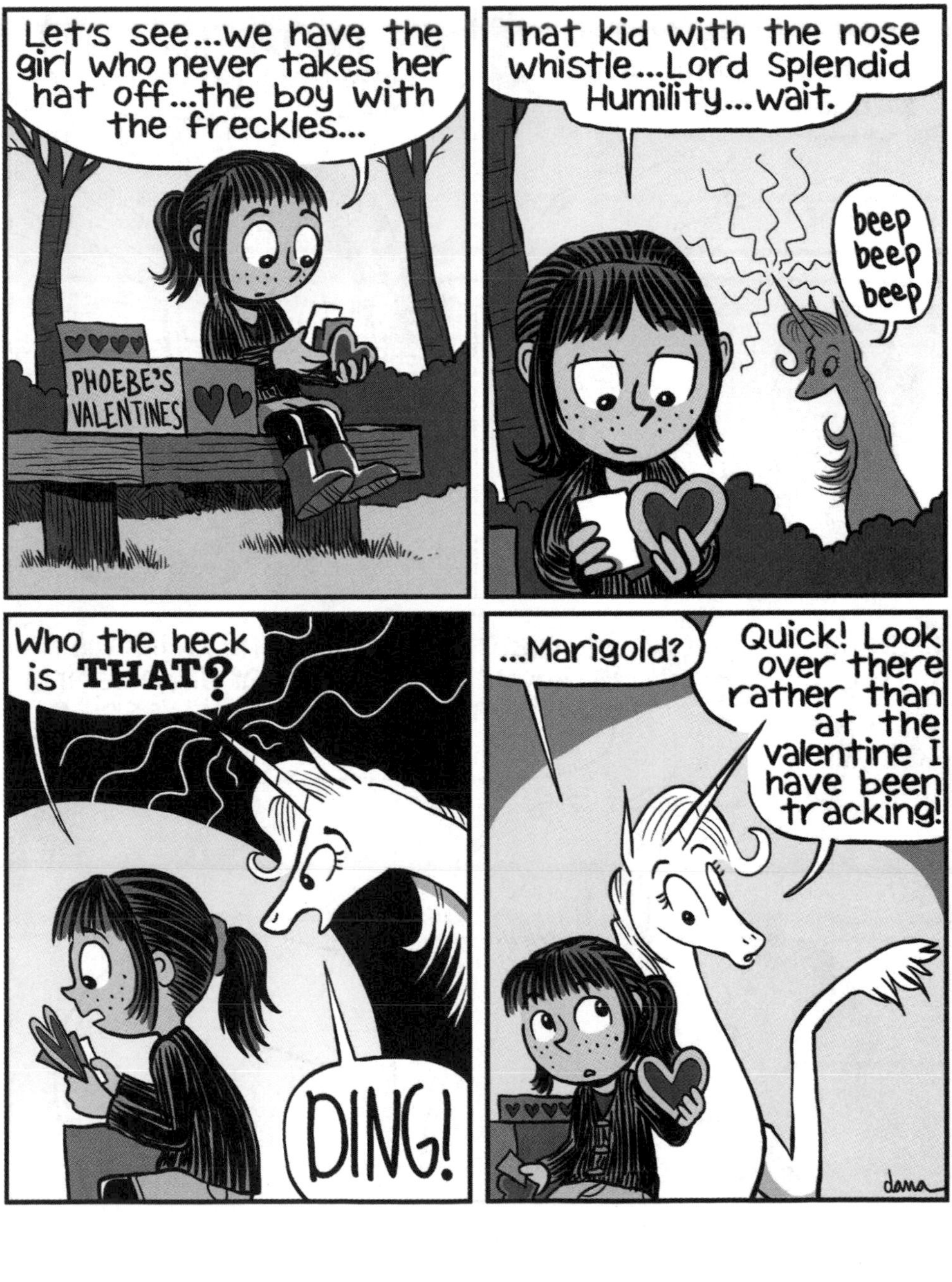
Let's see...we have the girl who never takes her hat off...the boy with the freckles...
PHOEBE'S VALENTINES
That kid with the nose whistle...Lord Splendid Humility...wait.
beep beep beep
Who the heck is **THAT?**
DING!
...Marigold?
Quick! Look over there rather than at the valentine I have been tracking!
dana

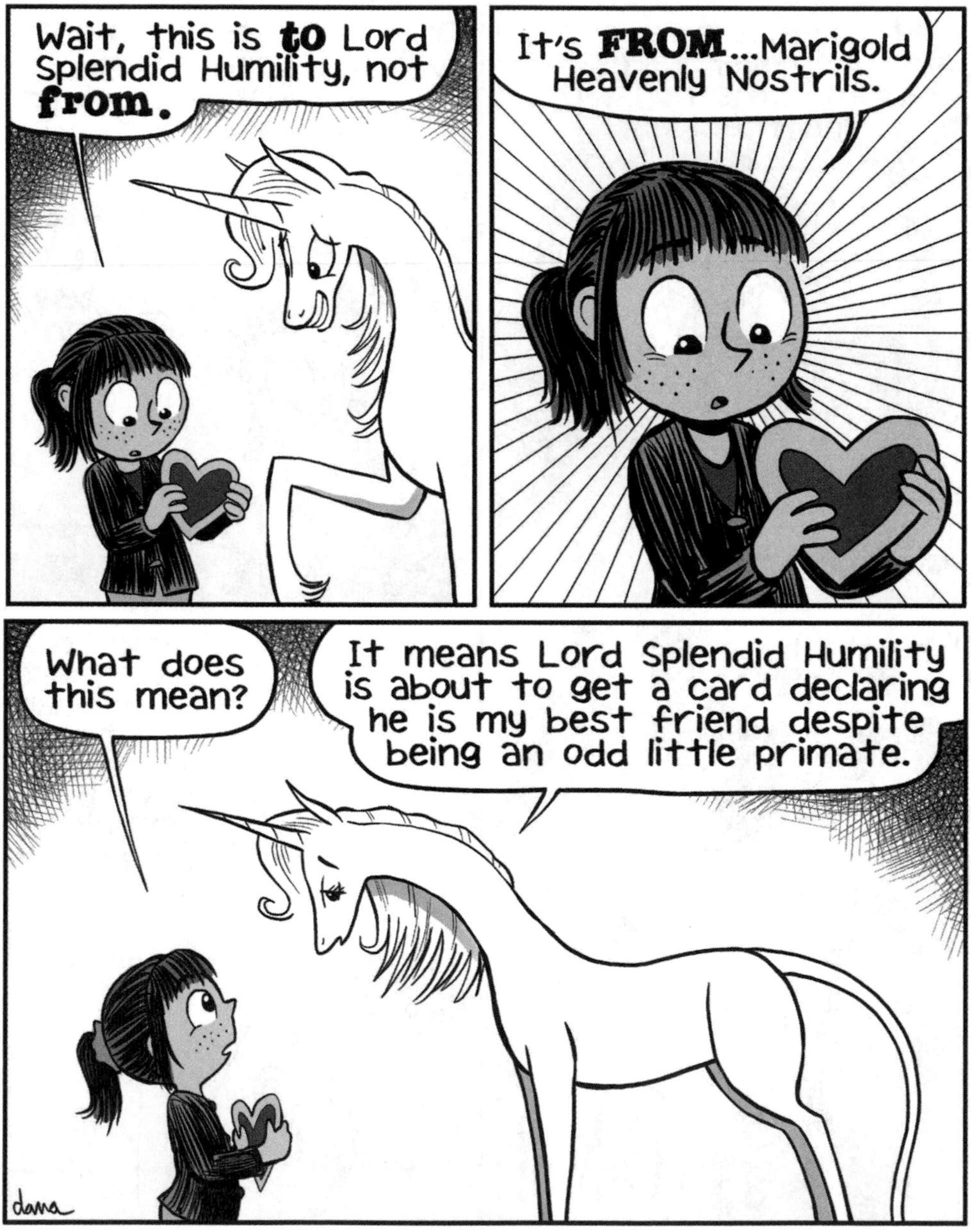

Wait, this is **to** Lord Splendid Humility, not **from.**
It's **FROM**...Marigold Heavenly Nostrils.
What does this mean?
It means Lord Splendid Humility is about to get a card declaring he is my best friend despite being an odd little primate.
dana

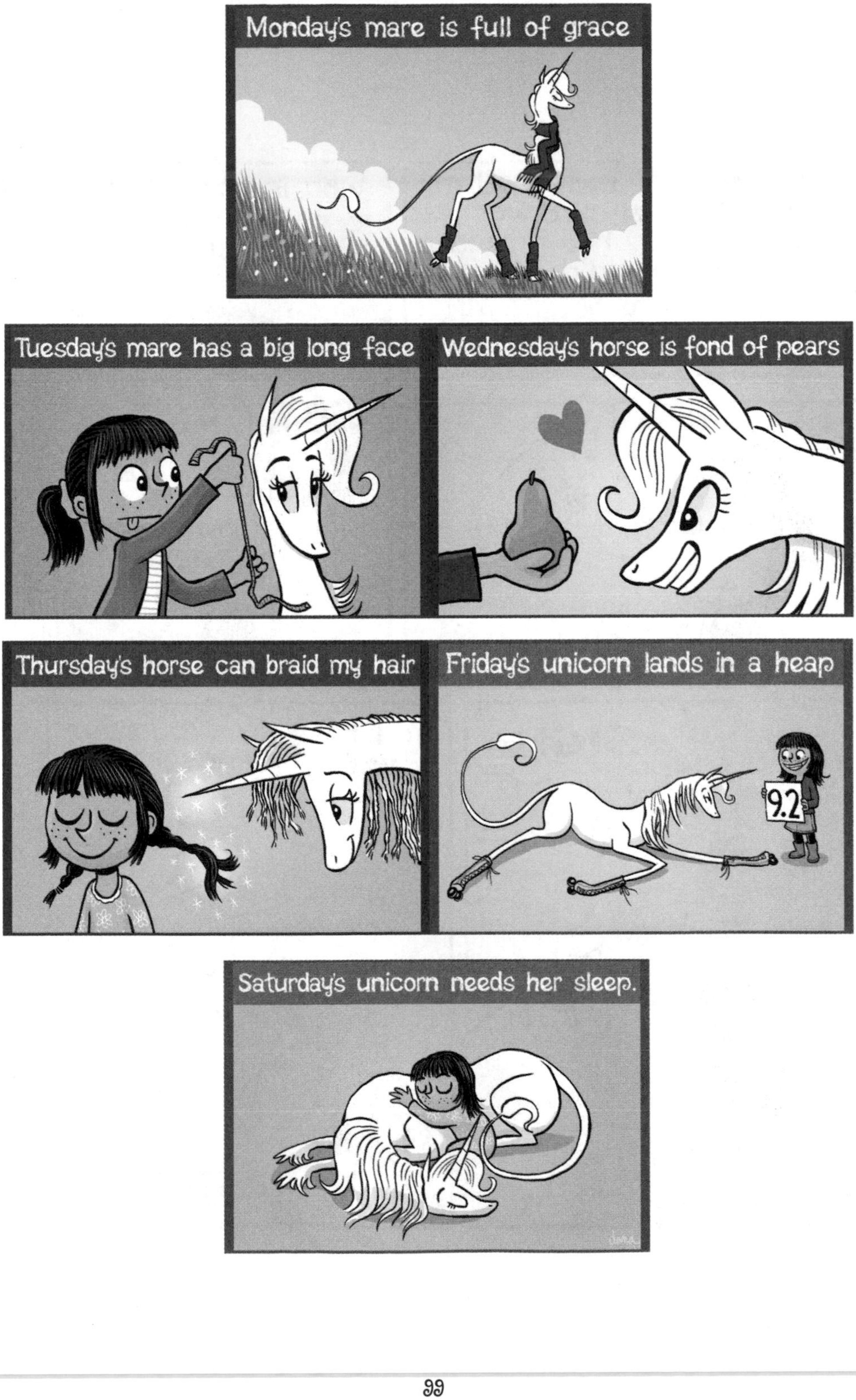
Monday's mare is full of grace
Tuesday's mare has a big long face
Wednesday's horse is fond of pears
Thursday's horse can braid my hair
Friday's unicorn lands in a heap
9.2
Saturday's unicorn needs her sleep.

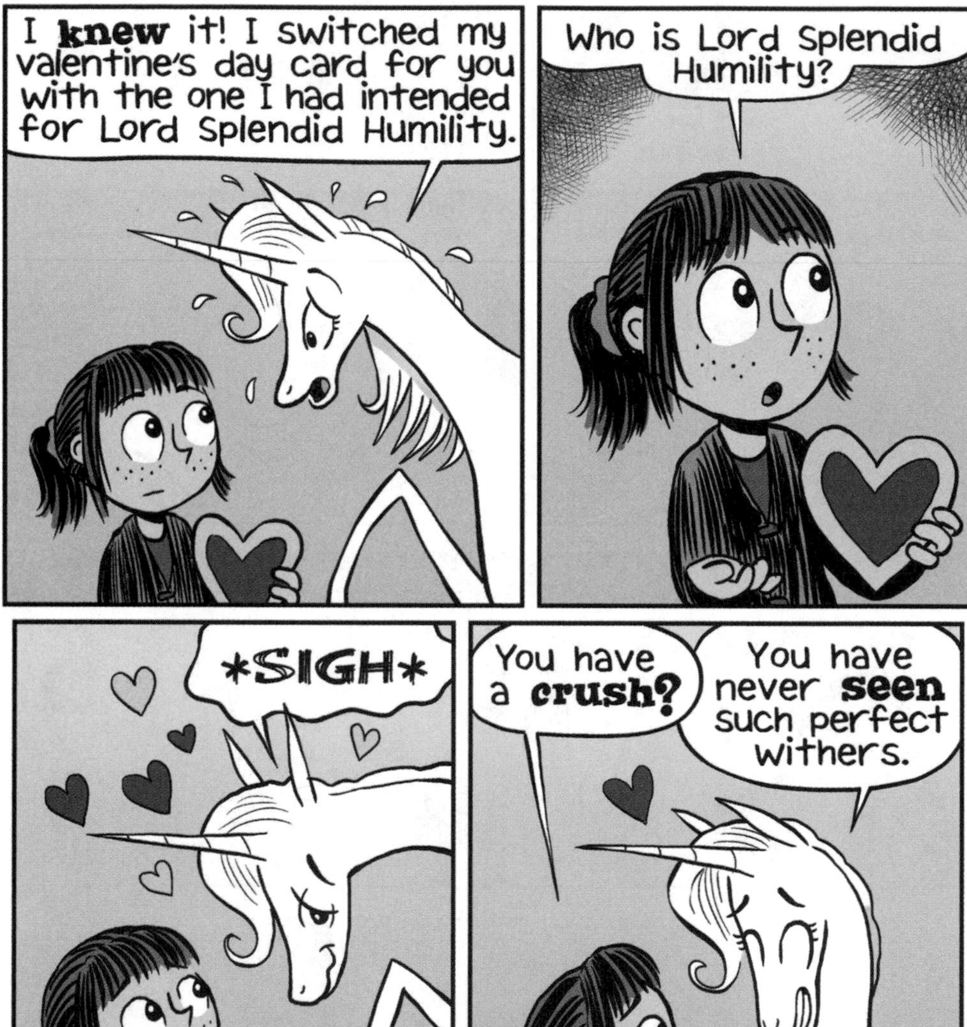
I **knew** it! I switched my valentine's day card for you with the one I had intended for Lord Splendid Humility.
Who is Lord Splendid Humility?
SIGH
You have a **crush?**
You have never **seen** such perfect withers.
dana

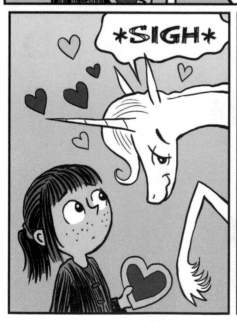

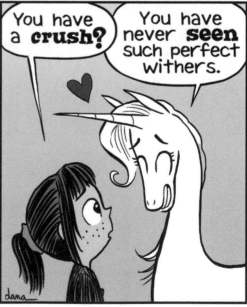

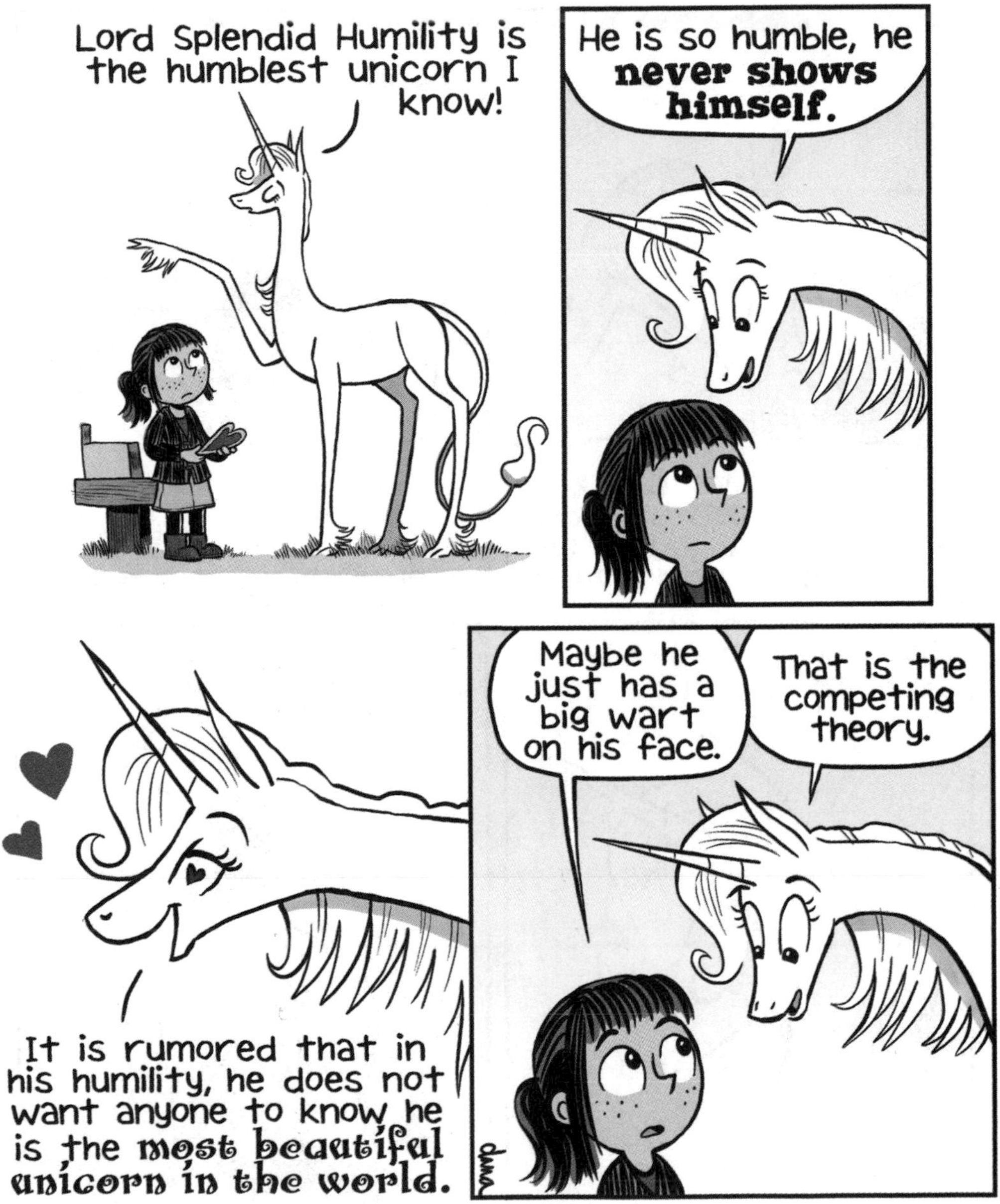
Lord Splendid Humility is the humblest unicorn I know!
He is so humble, he **never shows himself.**
It is rumored that in his humility, he does not want anyone to know he is the most beautiful unicorn in the world.
Maybe he just has a big wart on his face.
That is the competing theory.

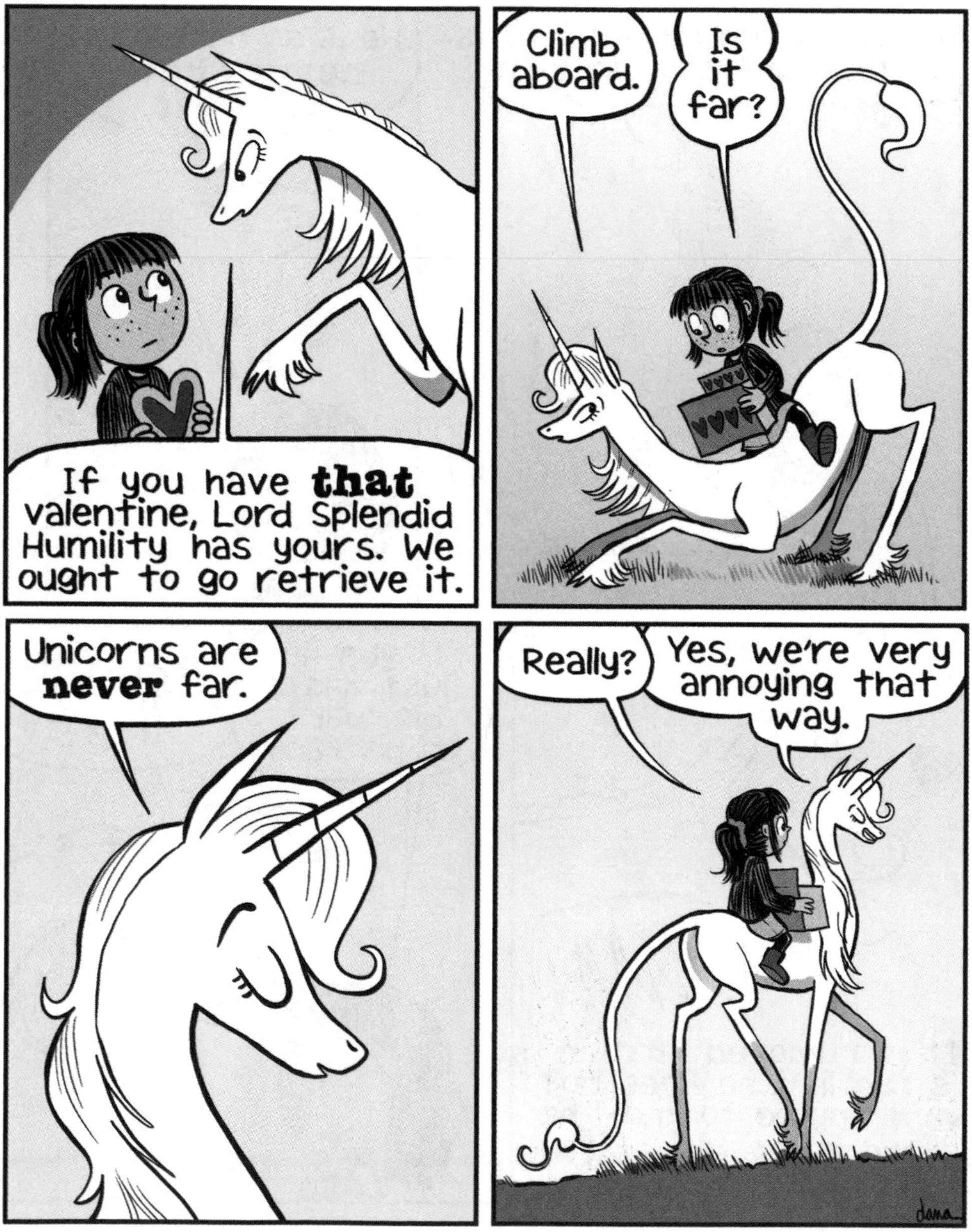
If you have **that** valentine, Lord Splendid Humility has yours. We ought to go retrieve it.
Climb aboard.
Is it far?
Unicorns are **never** far.
Really?
Yes, we're very annoying that way.
dana

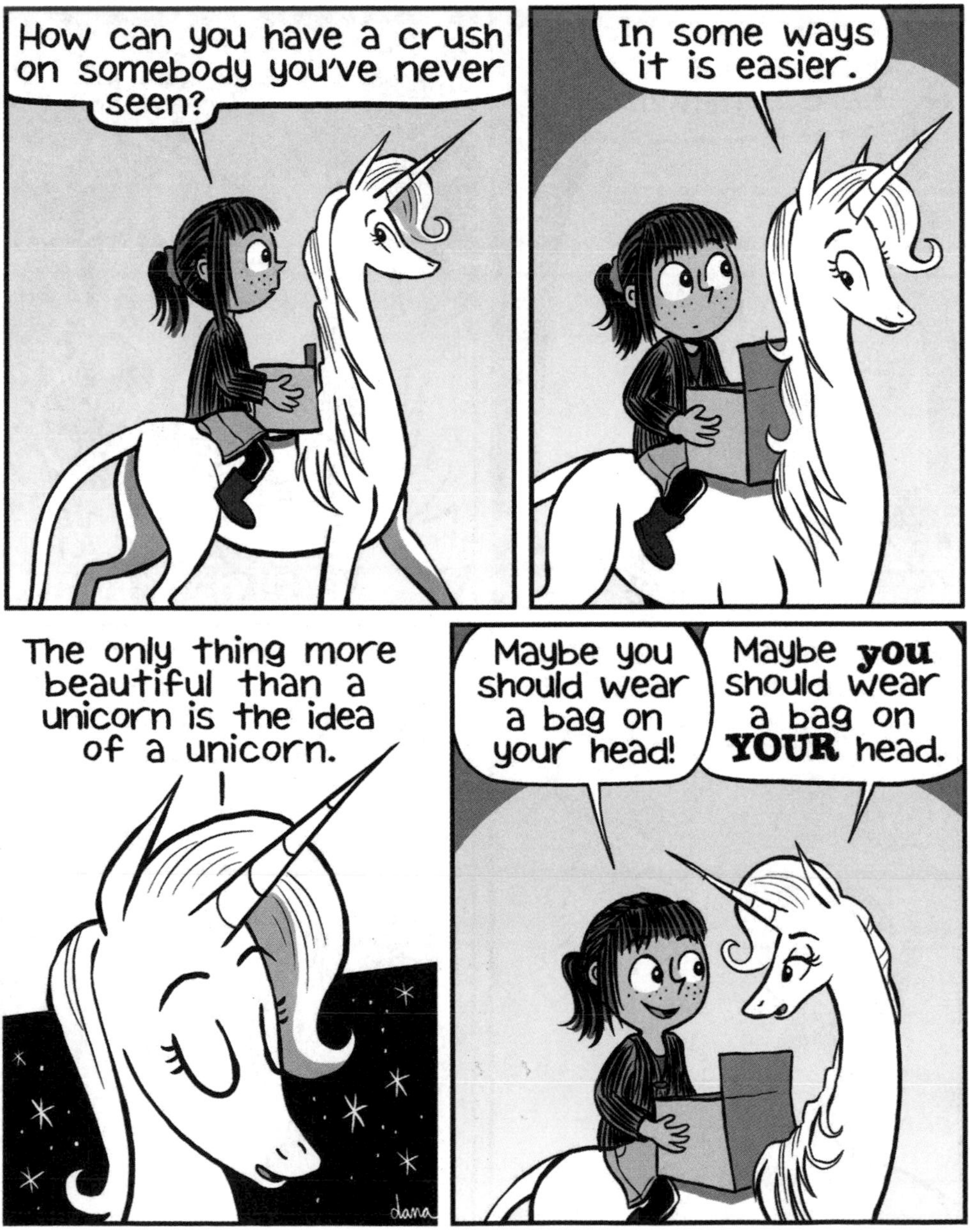
How can you have a crush on somebody you've never seen?
In some ways it is easier.
The only thing more beautiful than a unicorn is the idea of a unicorn.
Maybe you should wear a bag on your head!
Maybe **you** should wear a bag on **YOUR** head.
dana

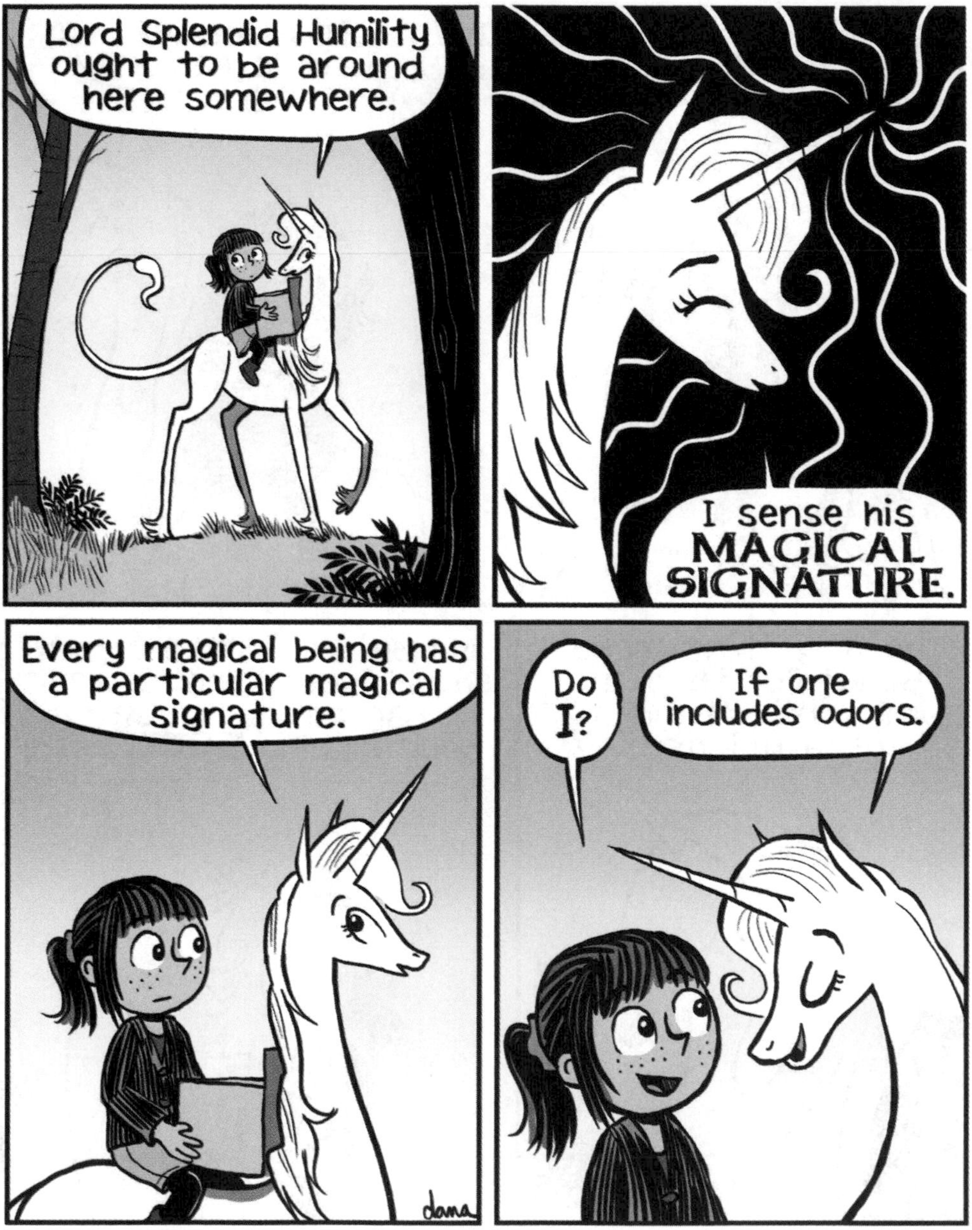
Lord Splendid Humility ought to be around here somewhere.
I sense his MAGICAL SIGNATURE.
Every magical being has a particular magical signature.
Do I?
If one includes odors.
dana

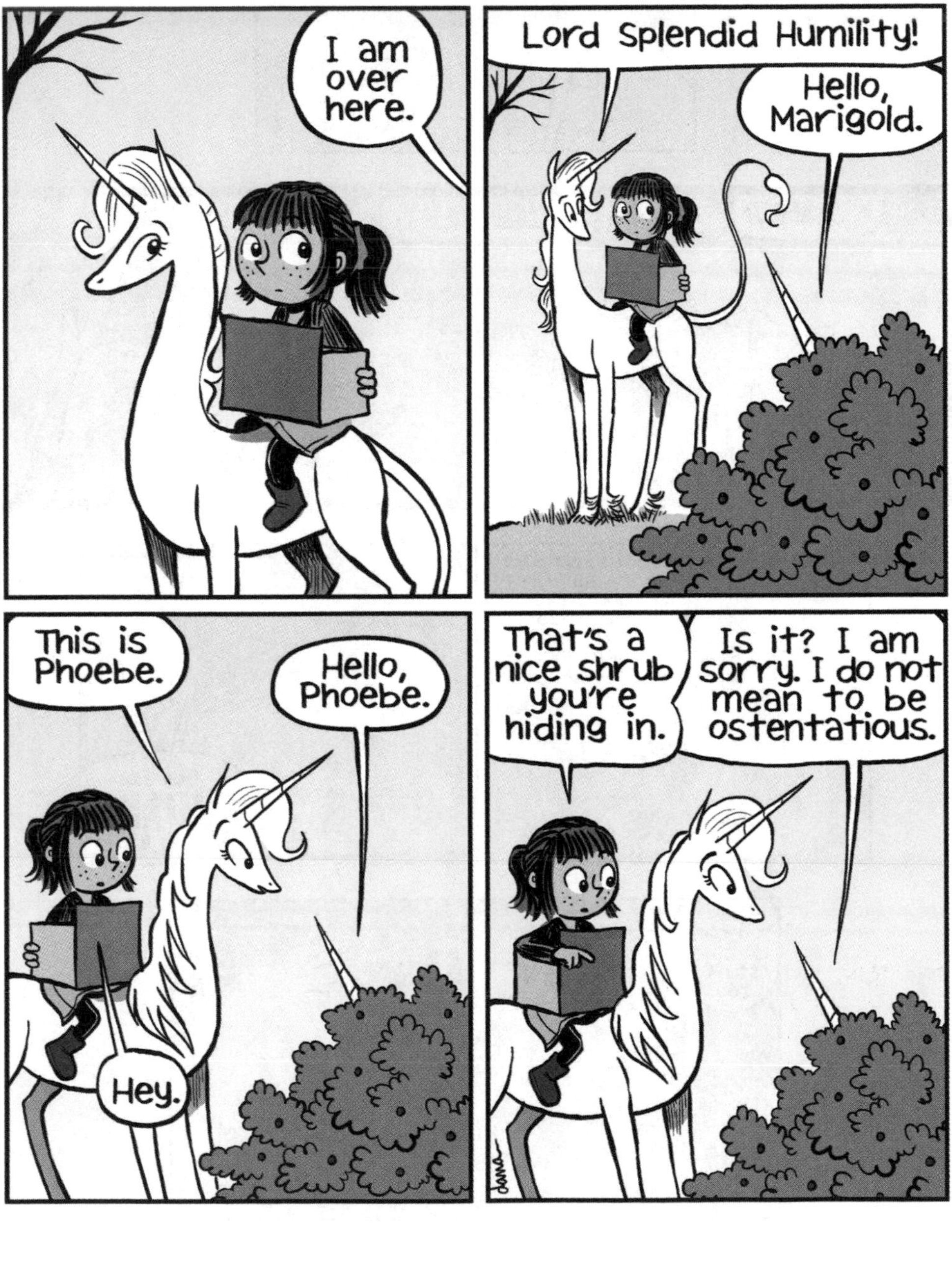
I am over here.
Lord Splendid Humility!
Hello, Marigold.
This is Phoebe.
Hello, Phoebe.
Hey.
That's a nice shrub you're hiding in.
Is it? I am sorry. I do not mean to be ostentatious.
dana

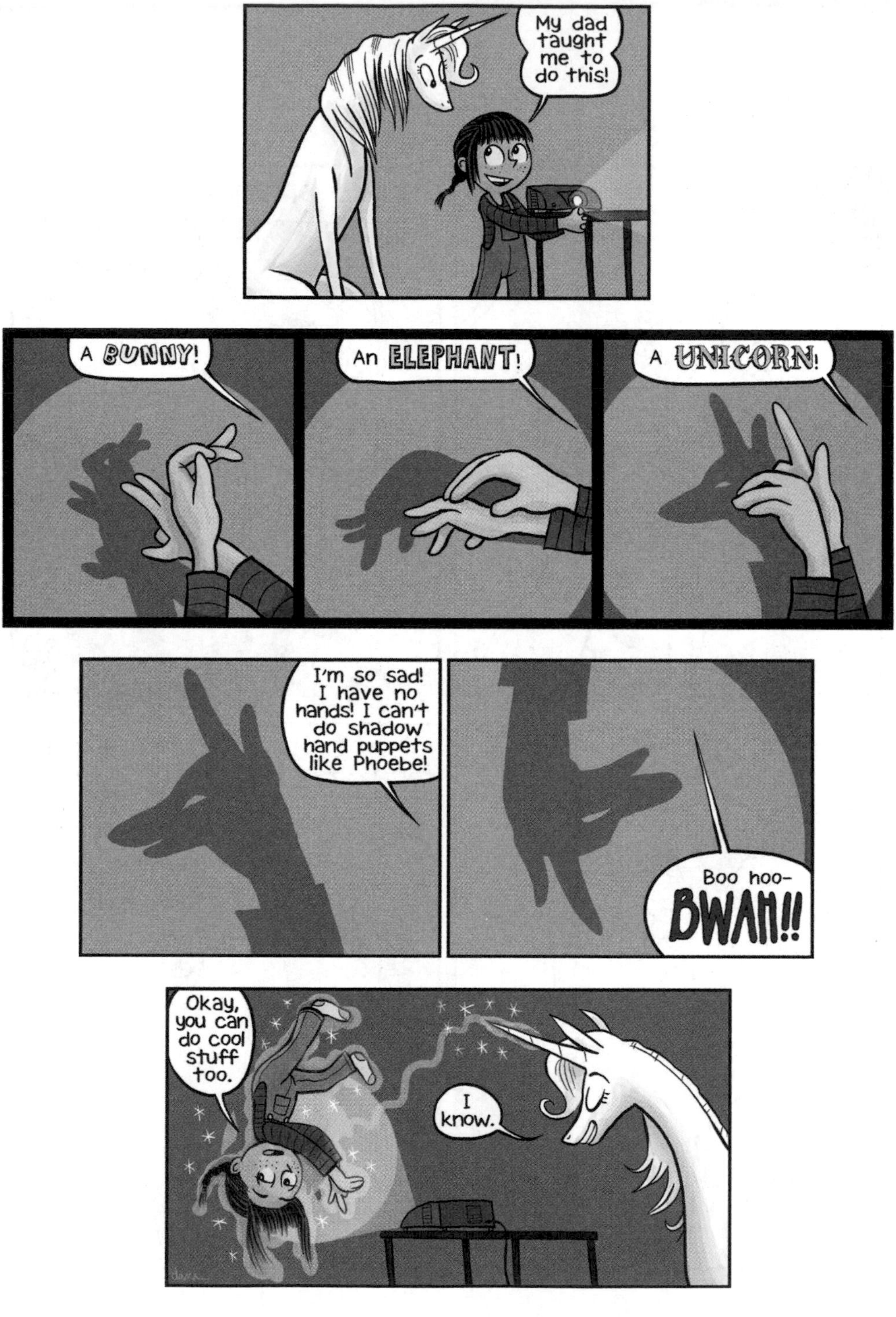
My dad taught me to do this!
A BUNNY!
An ELEPHANT!
A UNICORN!
I'm so sad! I have no hands! I can't do shadow hand puppets like Phoebe!
Boo hoo-
BWAH!!
Okay, you can do cool stuff too.
I know.

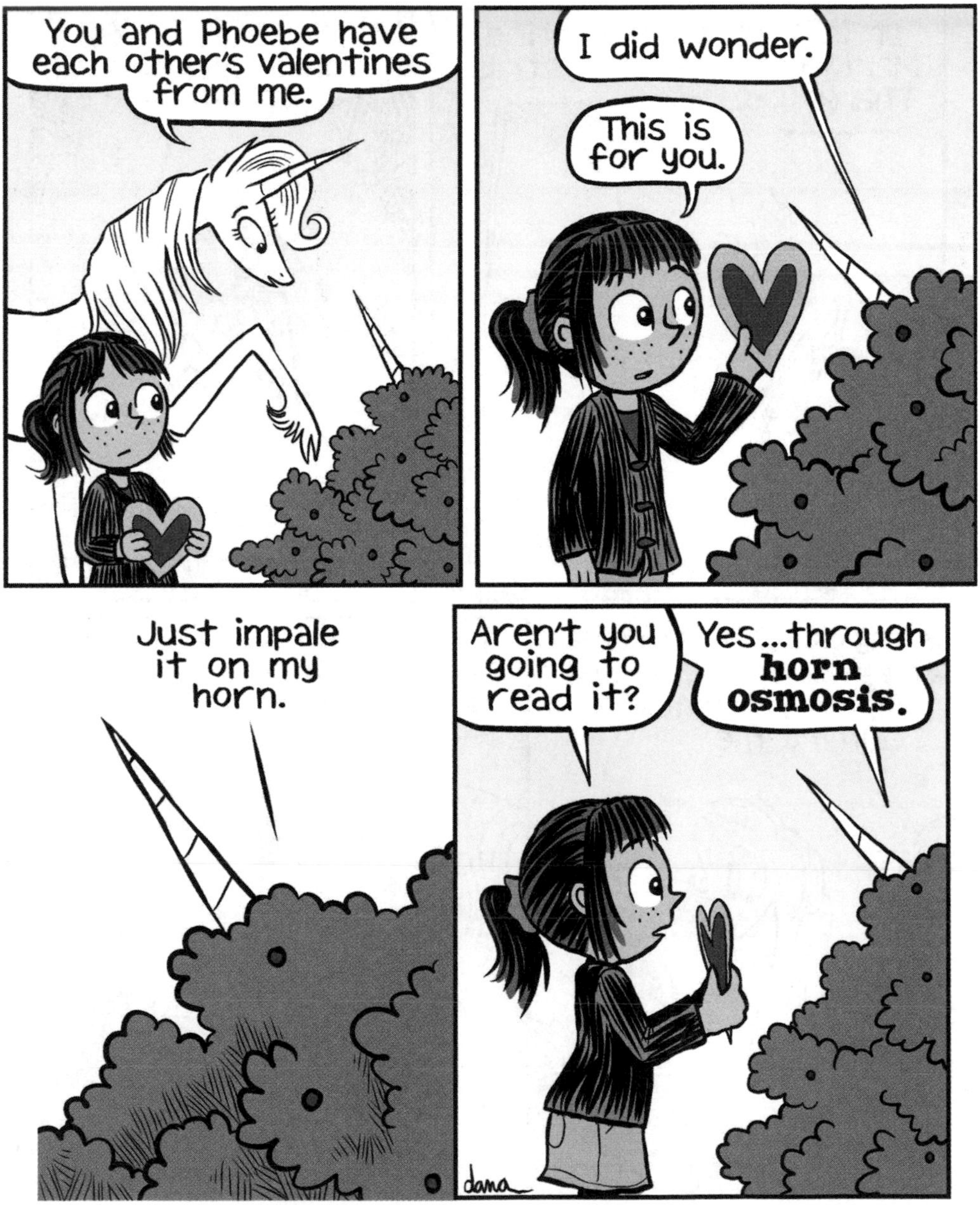
You and Phoebe have each other's valentines from me.
I did wonder.
This is for you.
Just impale it on my horn.
Aren't you going to read it?
Yes...through **horn osmosis**.
dana

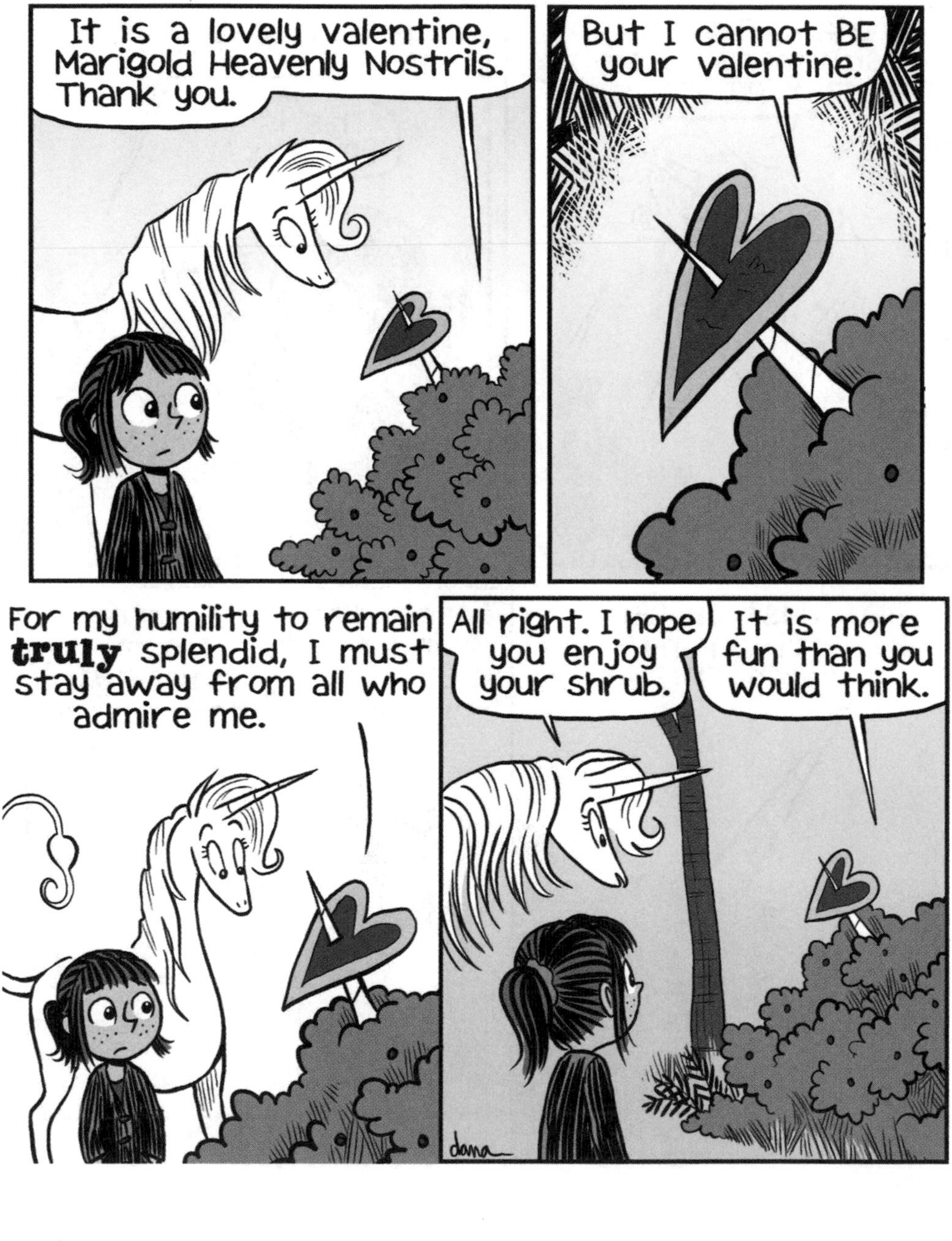
It is a lovely valentine, Marigold Heavenly Nostrils. Thank you.
But I cannot BE your valentine.
For my humility to remain **truly** splendid, I must stay away from all who admire me.
All right. I hope you enjoy your shrub.
It is more fun than you would think.
dana

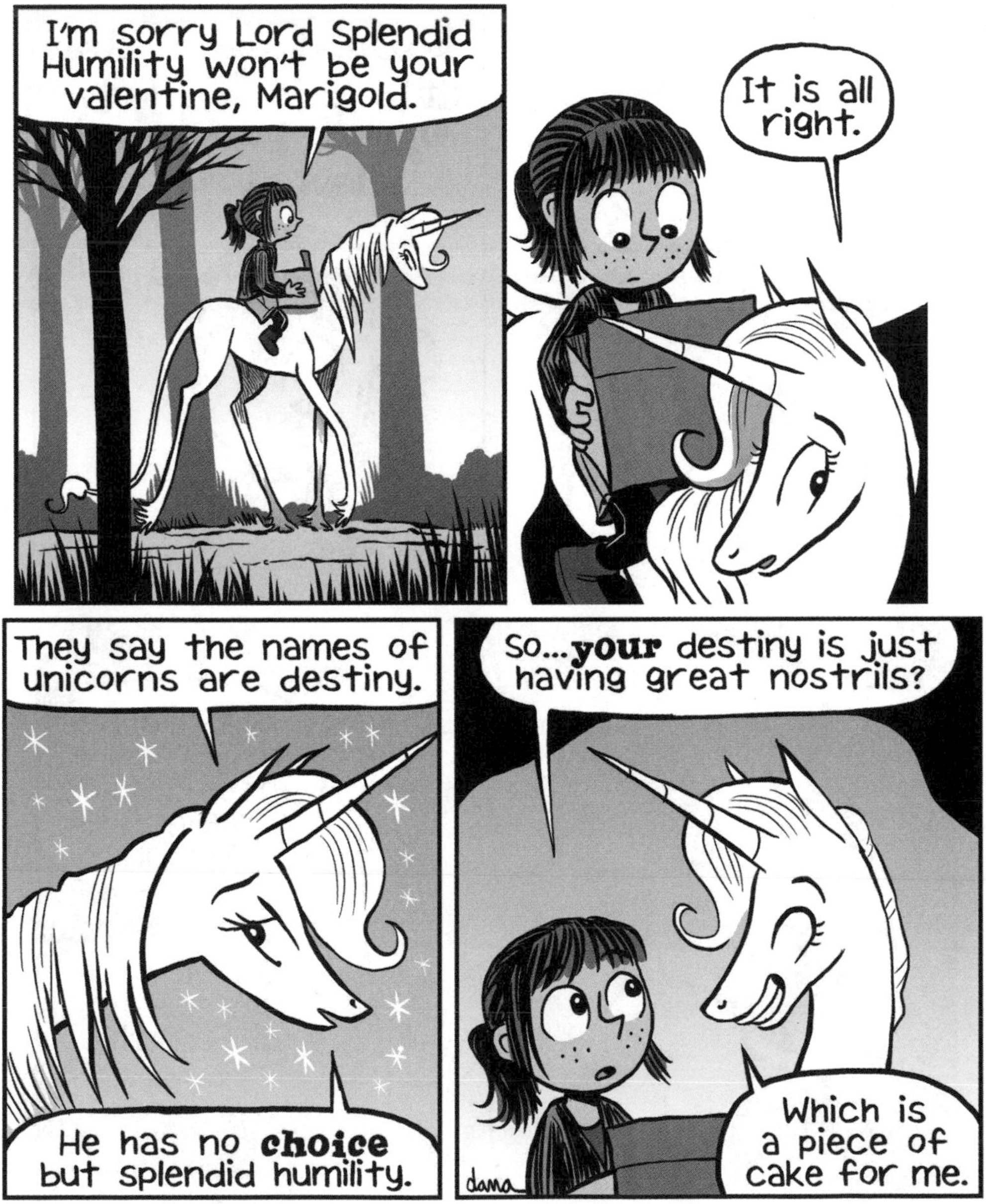
I'm sorry Lord Splendid Humility won't be your valentine, Marigold.
It is all right.
They say the names of unicorns are destiny.
He has no choice but splendid humility.
So... your destiny is just having great nostrils?
Which is a piece of cake for me.
dana

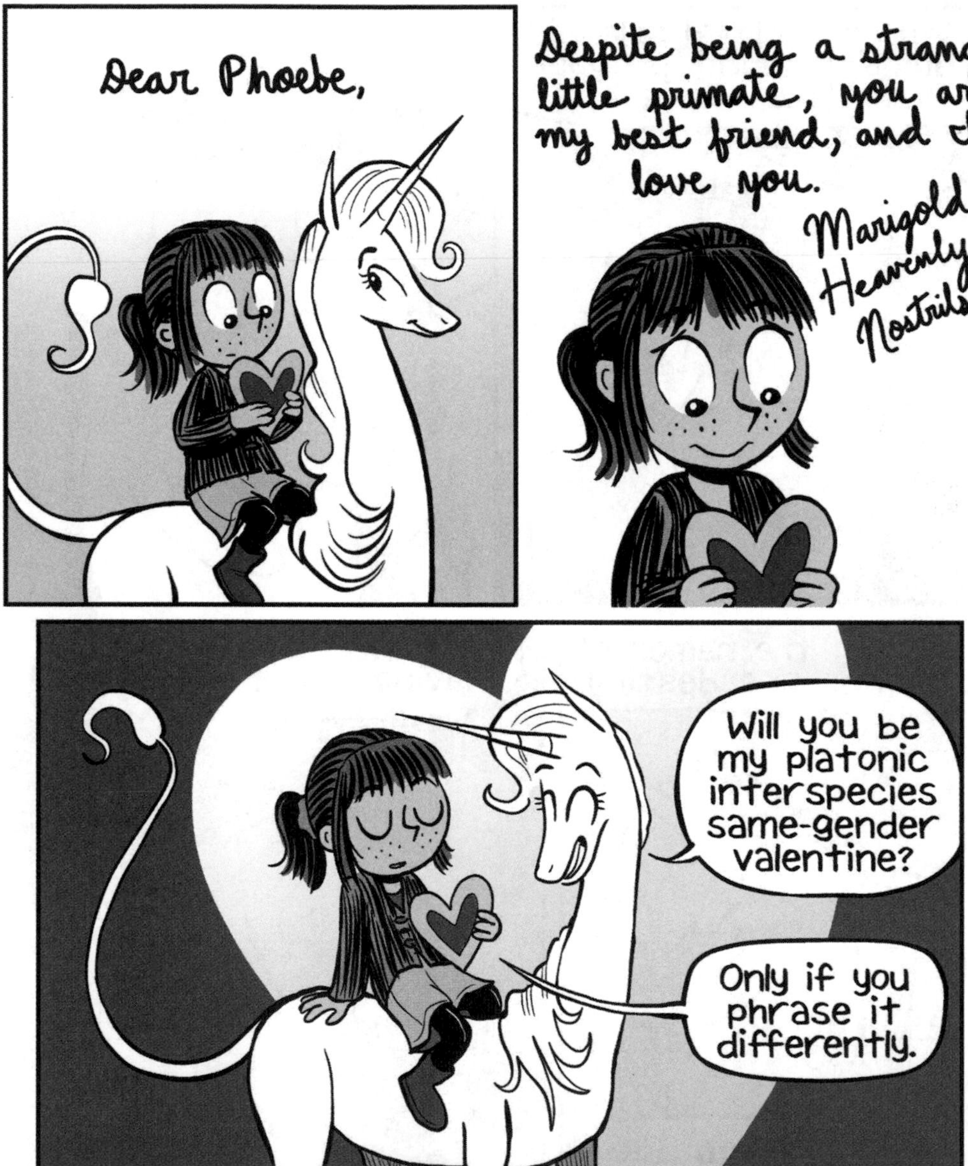

Dear Phoebe,
Despite being a strange little primate, you are my best friend, and I love you.
Marigold Heavenly Nostrils
Will you be my platonic interspecies same-gender valentine?
Only if you phrase it differently.
dana

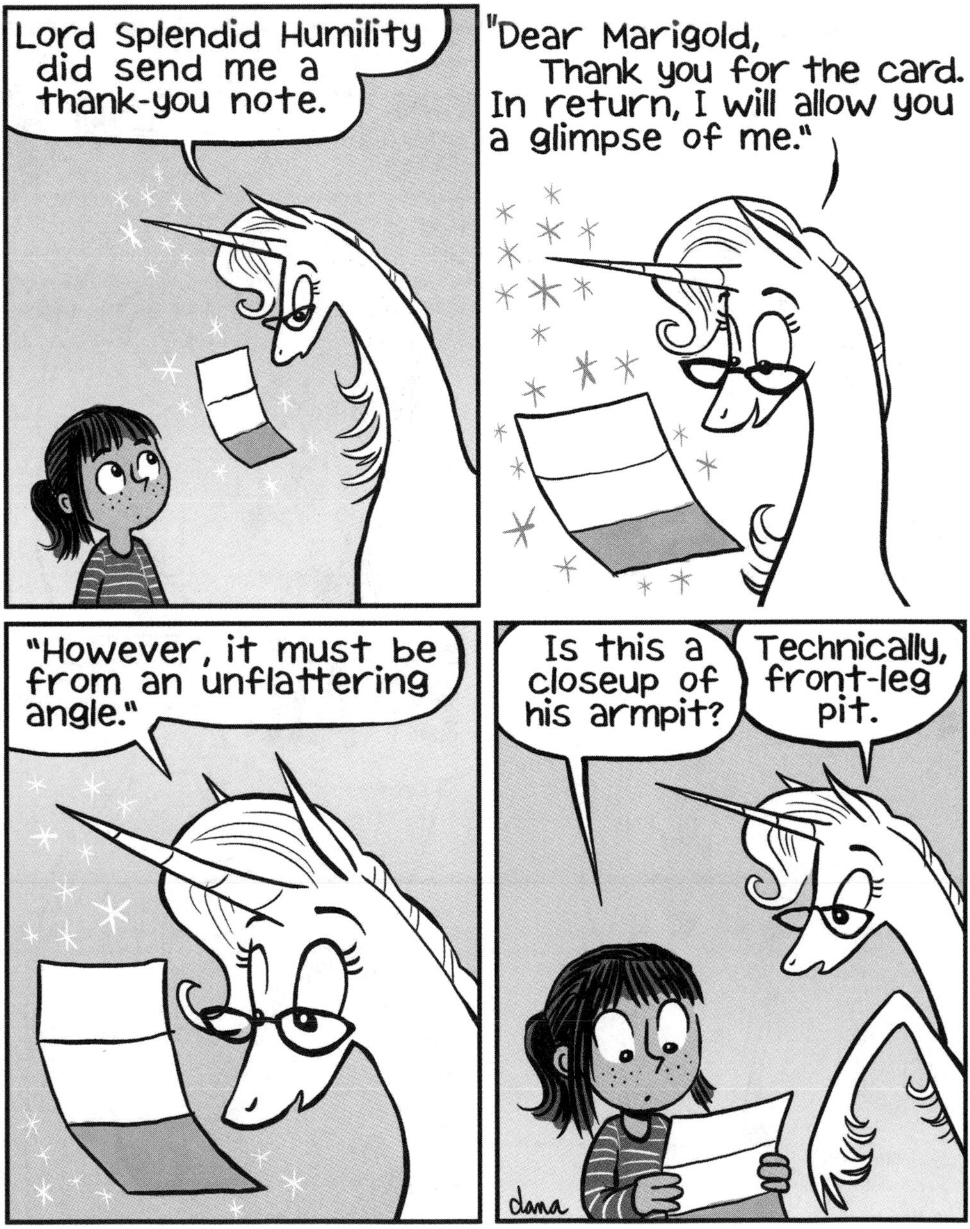
Lord Splendid Humility did send me a thank-you note.
"Dear Marigold,
Thank you for the card. In return, I will allow you a glimpse of me."
"However, it must be from an unflattering angle."
Is this a closeup of his armpit?
Technically, front-leg pit.
dana

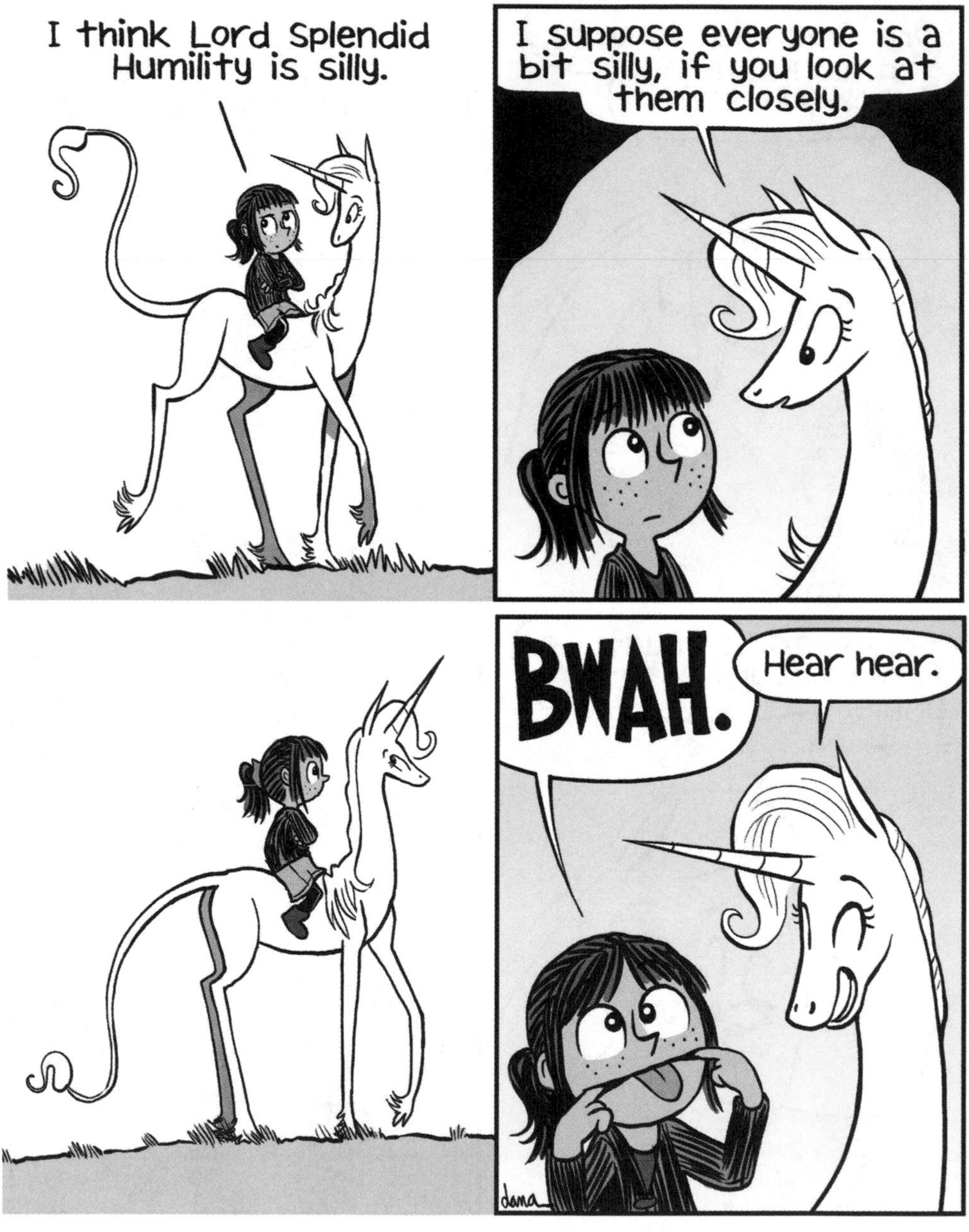
I think Lord Splendid Humility is silly.
I suppose everyone is a bit silly, if you look at them closely.
BWAH.
Hear hear.
dana

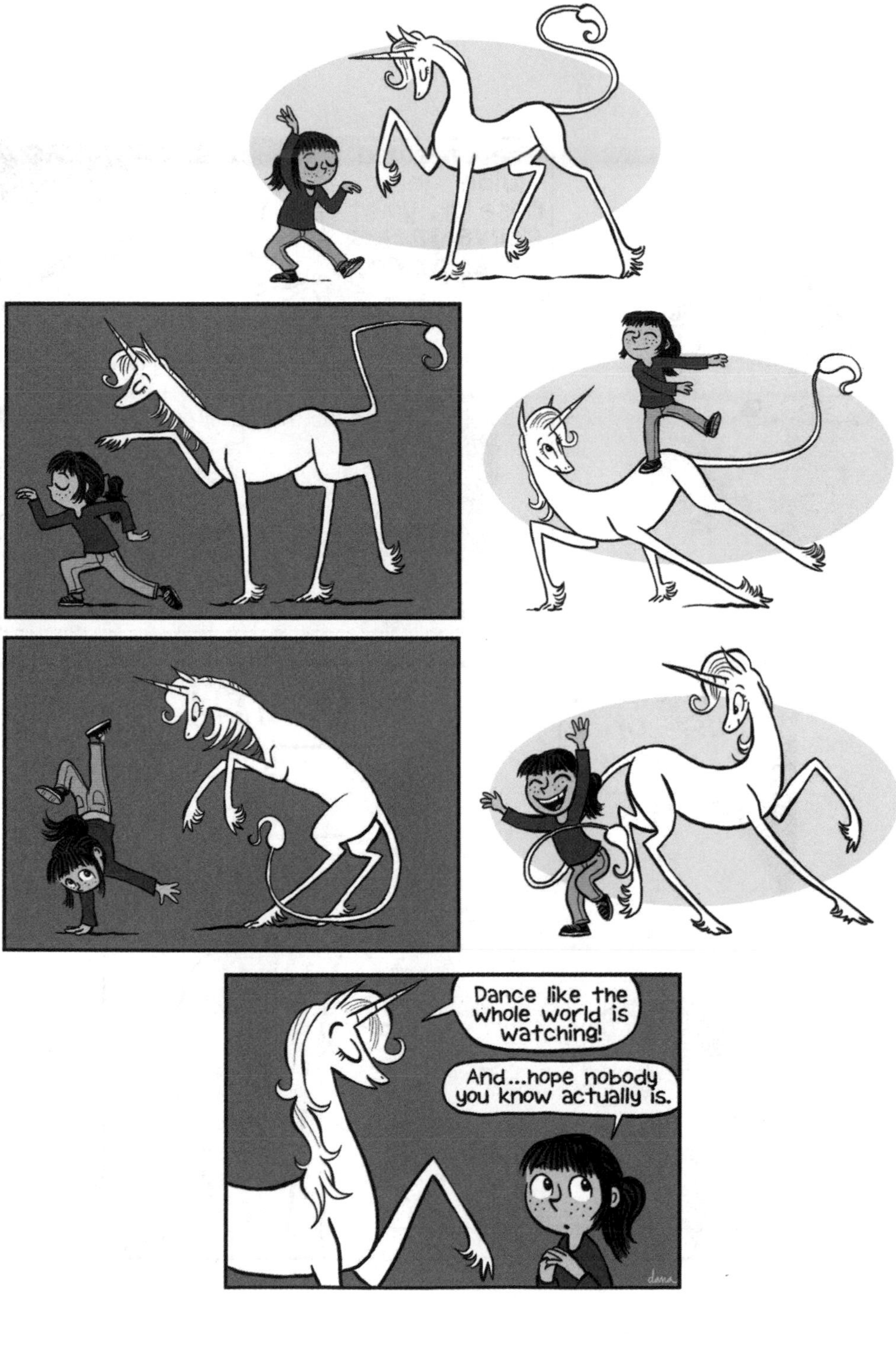
Dance like the whole world is watching!
And...hope nobody you know actually is.
dana

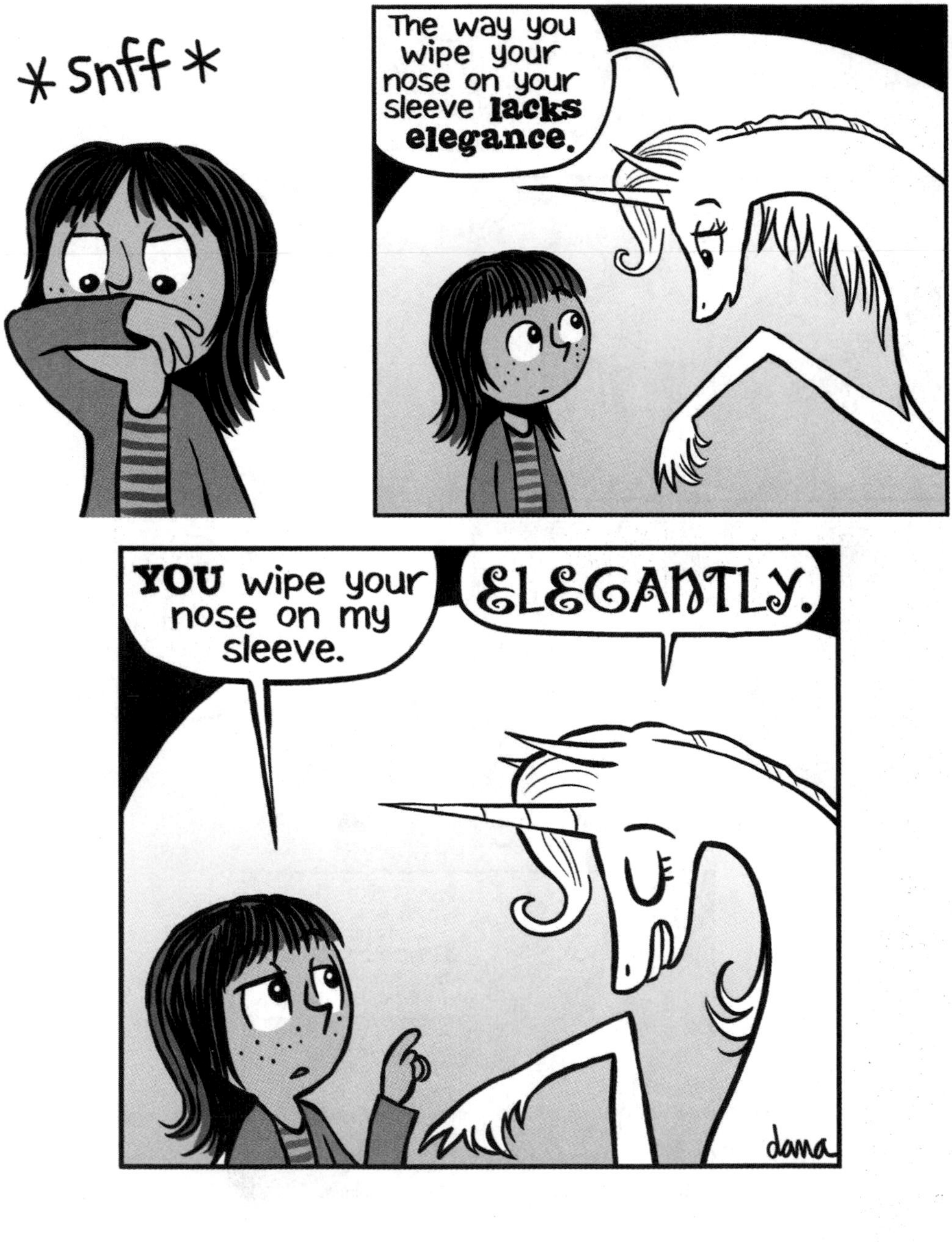
Snff
The way you wipe your nose on your sleeve **lacks elegance**.
YOU wipe your nose on my sleeve.
ELEGANTLY.
dana

What's that you're eating?
Hay.
What's with you and hay, anyway? You're a forest creature, not a barn animal.
This is artisanal hay.
Well, this is an artisanal fruit snack, so we're both fancy.
dana

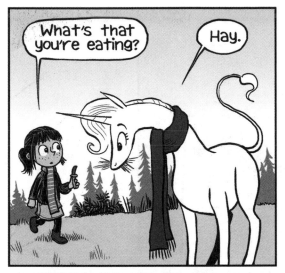

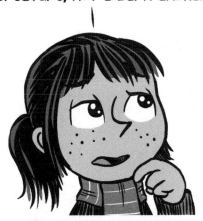

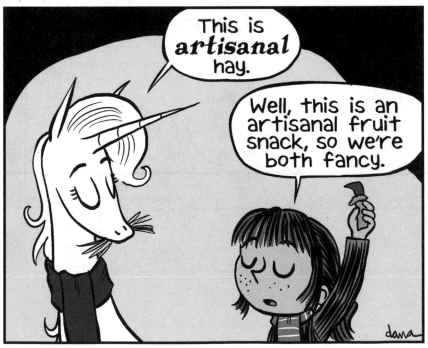

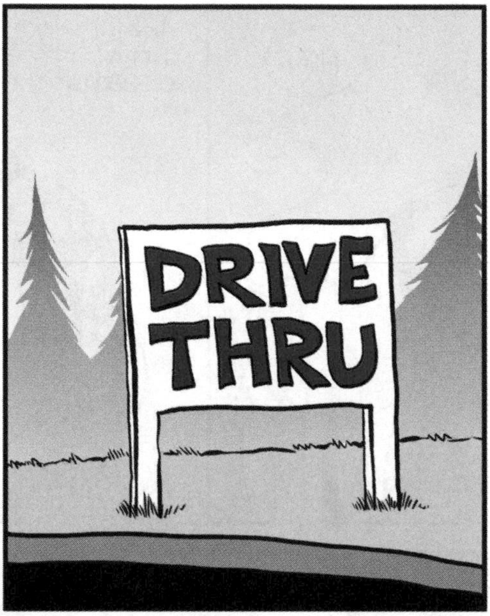
DRIVE THRU

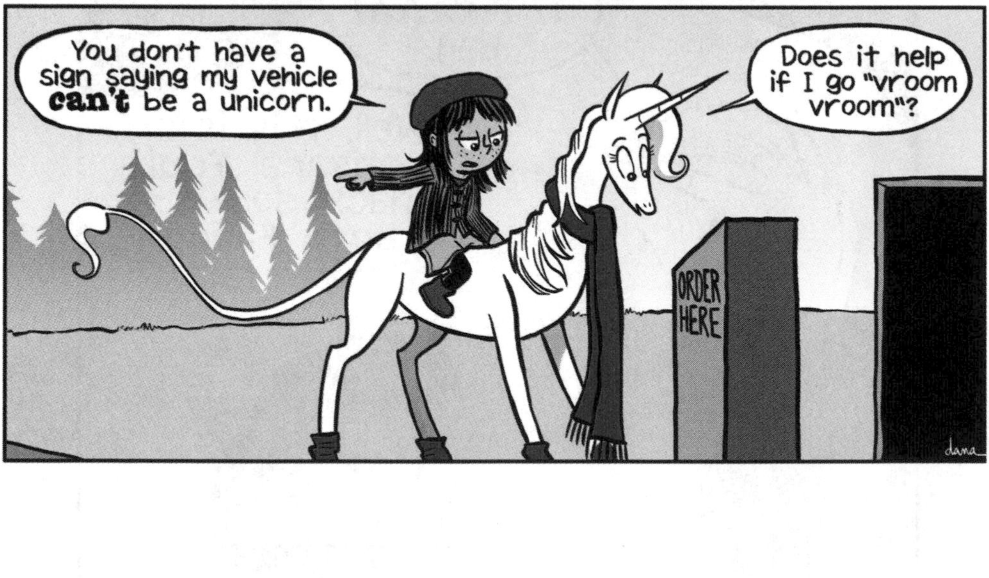
You don't have a sign saying my vehicle **can't** be a unicorn.
Does it help if I go "vroom vroom"?
ORDER HERE
dana

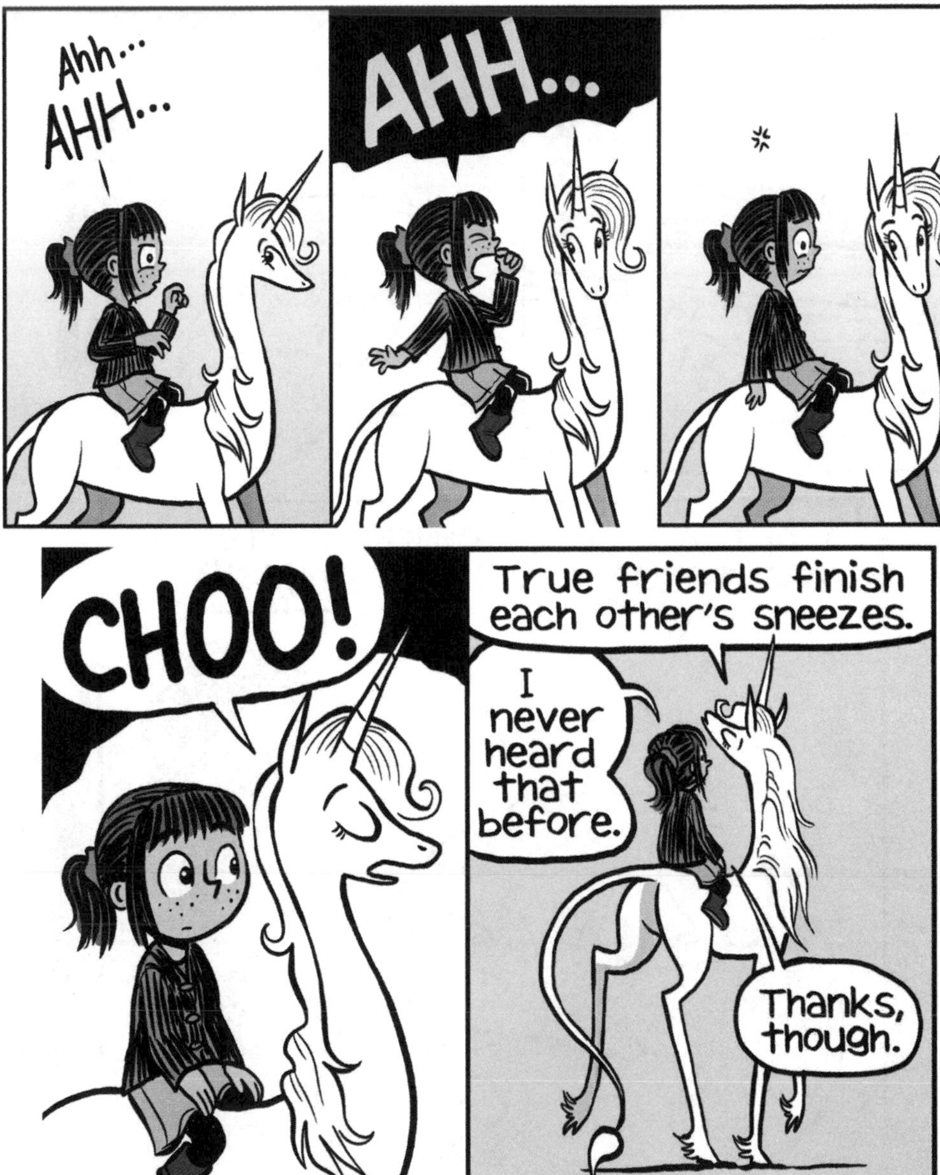
Ahh...
AHH...
AHH...
CHOO!
True friends finish each other's sneezes.
I never heard that before.
Thanks, though.
dana

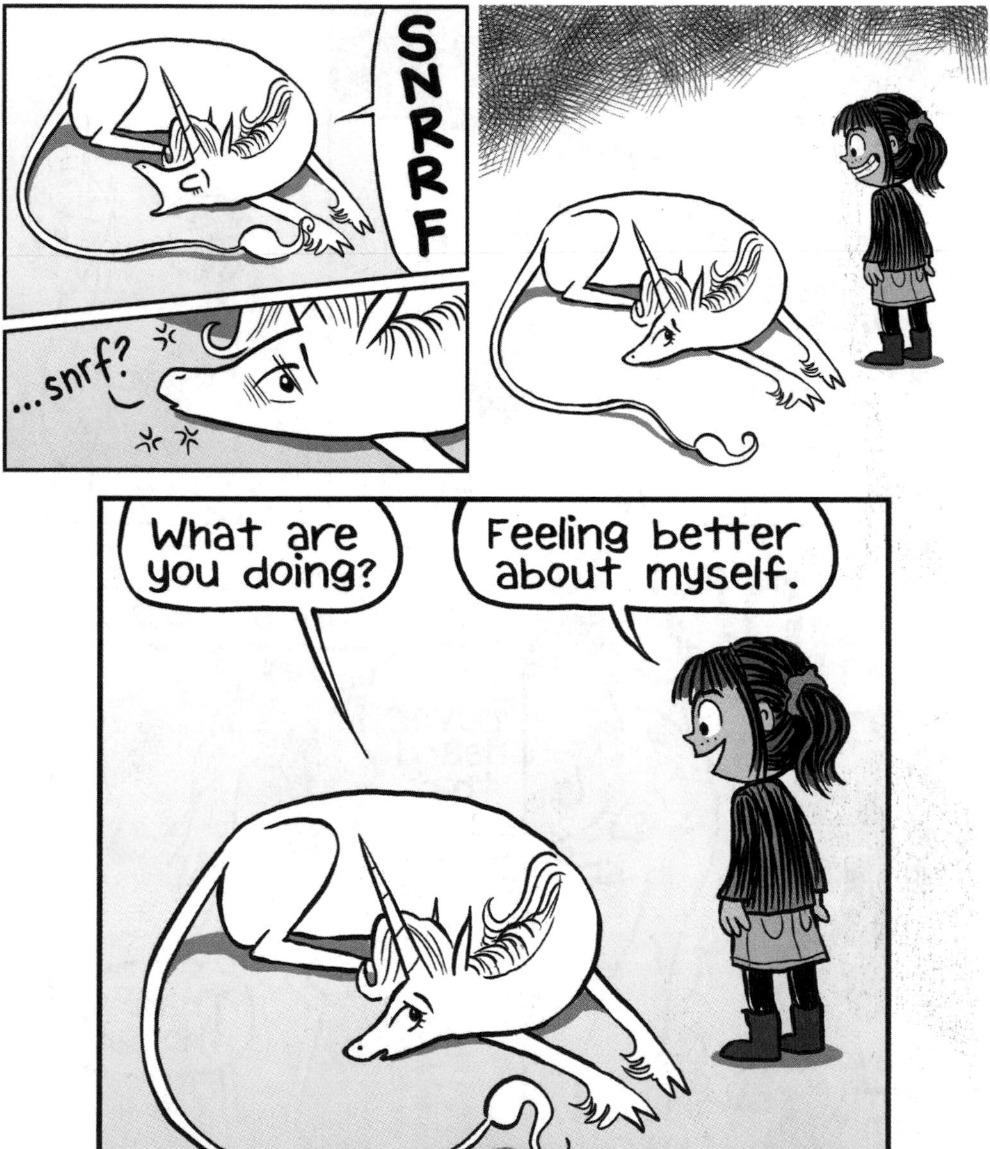
SNRRF
...snrf?
What are you doing?
Feeling better about myself.
dana

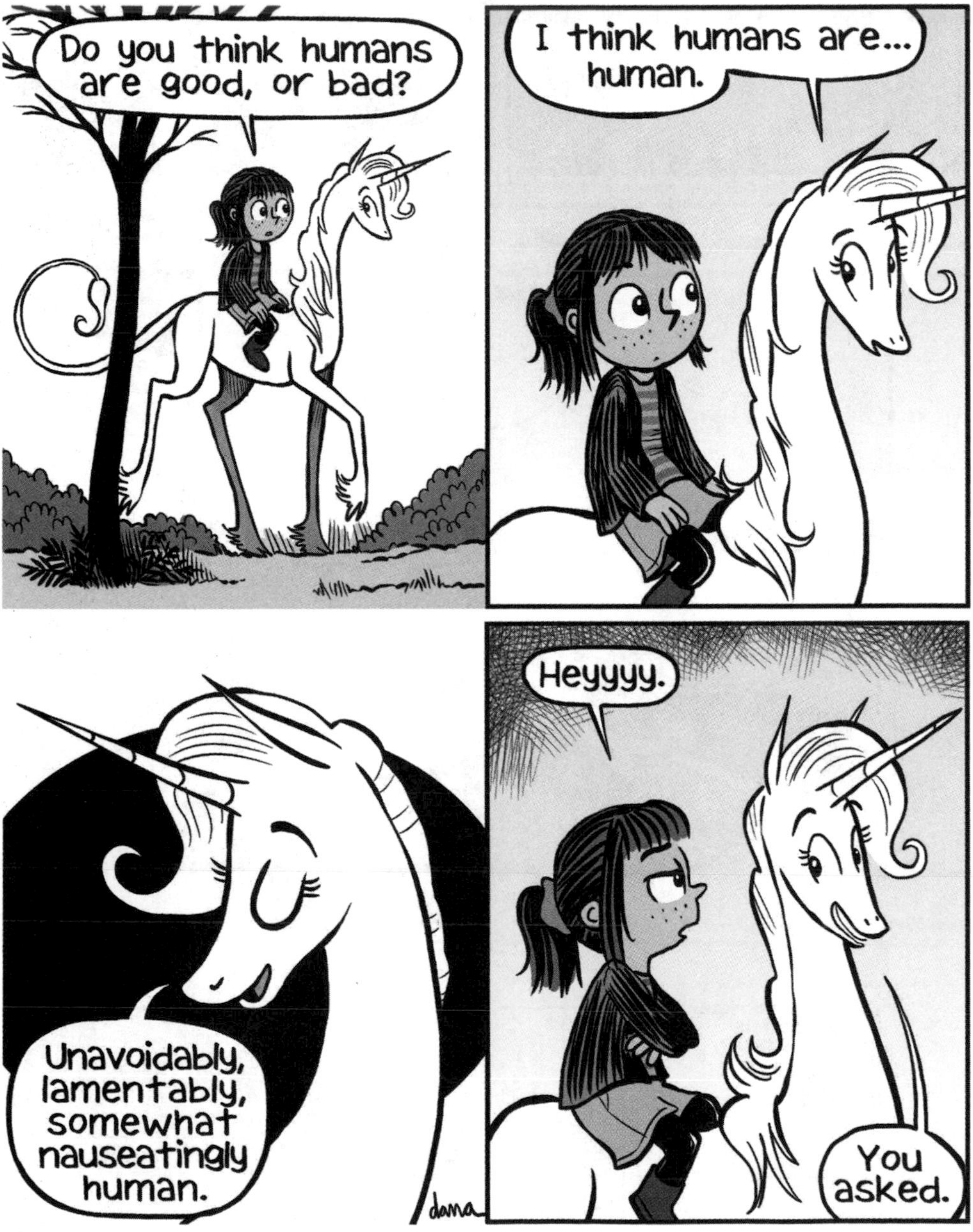
Do you think humans are good, or bad?
I think humans are... human.
Unavoidably, lamentably, somewhat nauseatingly human.
Heyyyy.
You asked.
dana

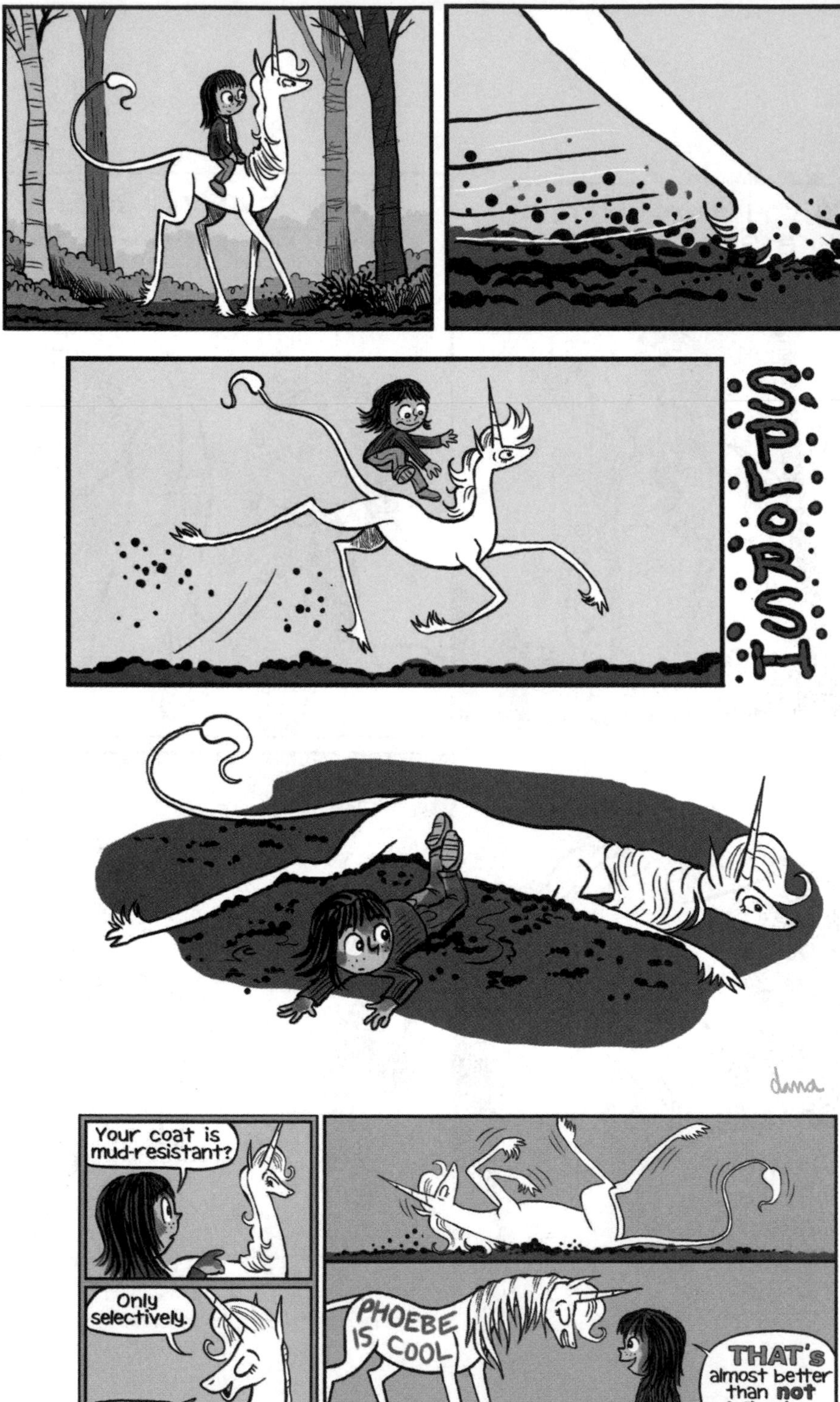
SPLORSH
dana
Your coat is mud-resistant?
Only selectively.
Observe.
PHOEBE IS COOL
THAT's almost better than not falling in a puddle.

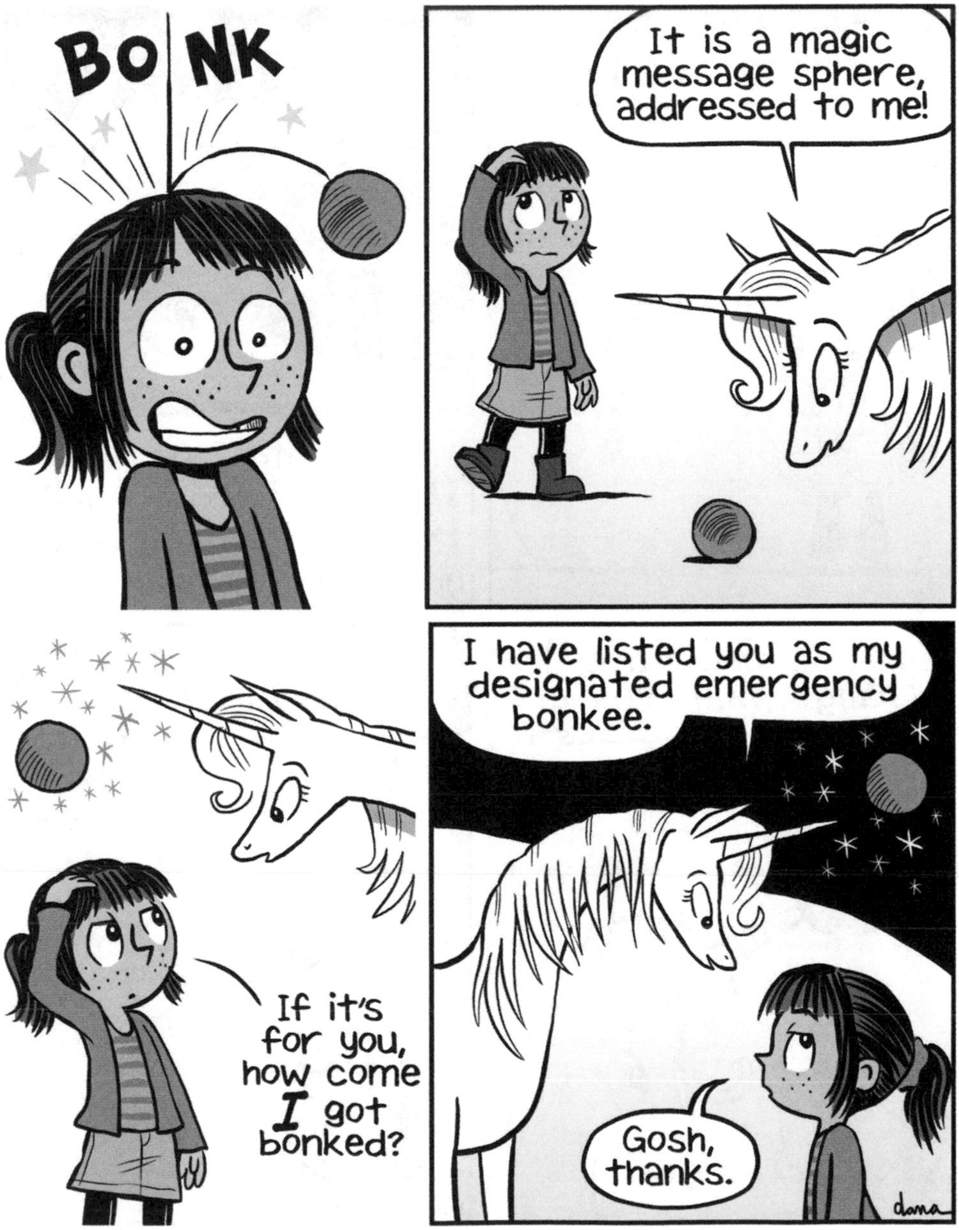

BONK
It is a magic message sphere, addressed to me!
If it's for you, how come I got bonked?
I have listed you as my designated emergency bonkee.
Gosh, thanks.
dana

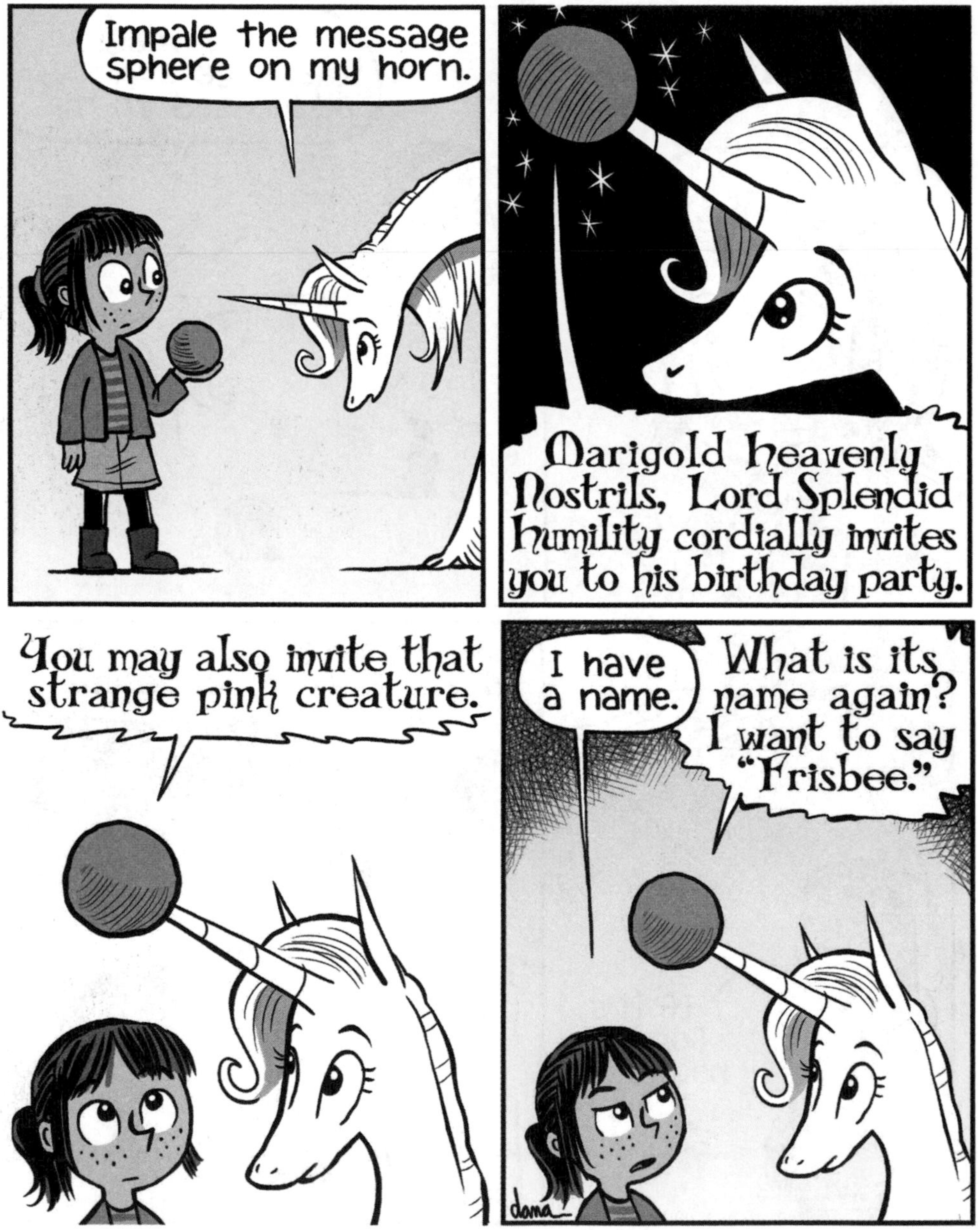
Impale the message sphere on my horn.
Marigold Heavenly Nostrils, Lord Splendid Humility cordially invites you to his birthday party.
You may also invite that strange pink creature.
What is its name again? I want to say "Frisbee."
I have a name.
dana

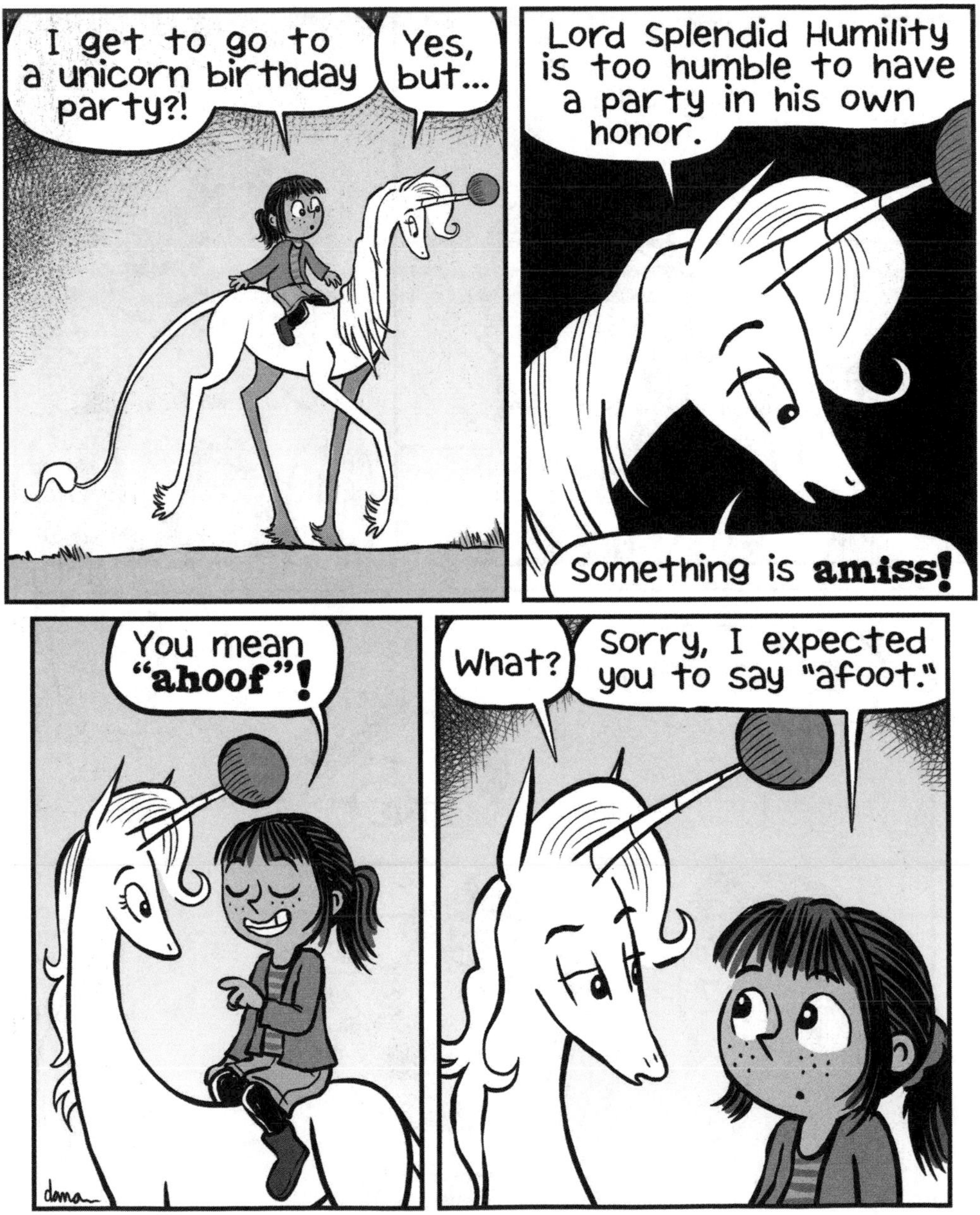

I get to go to a unicorn birthday party?!
Yes, but...
Lord Splendid Humility is too humble to have a party in his own honor.
Something is **amiss!**
You mean "**ahoof**"!
What?
Sorry, I expected you to say "afoot."
dana

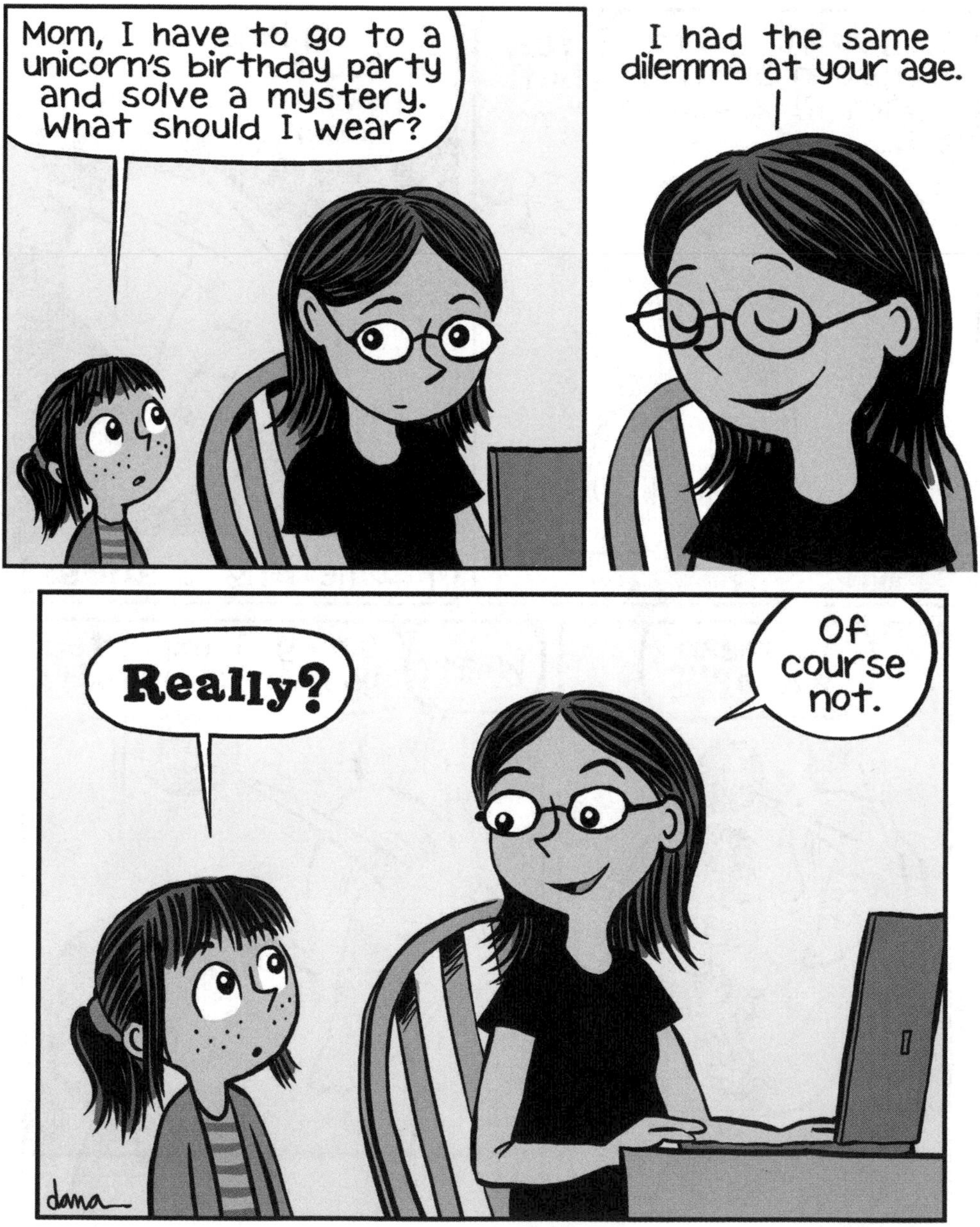
Mom, I have to go to a unicorn's birthday party and solve a mystery. What should I wear?
I had the same dilemma at your age.
Really?
Of course not.
dana

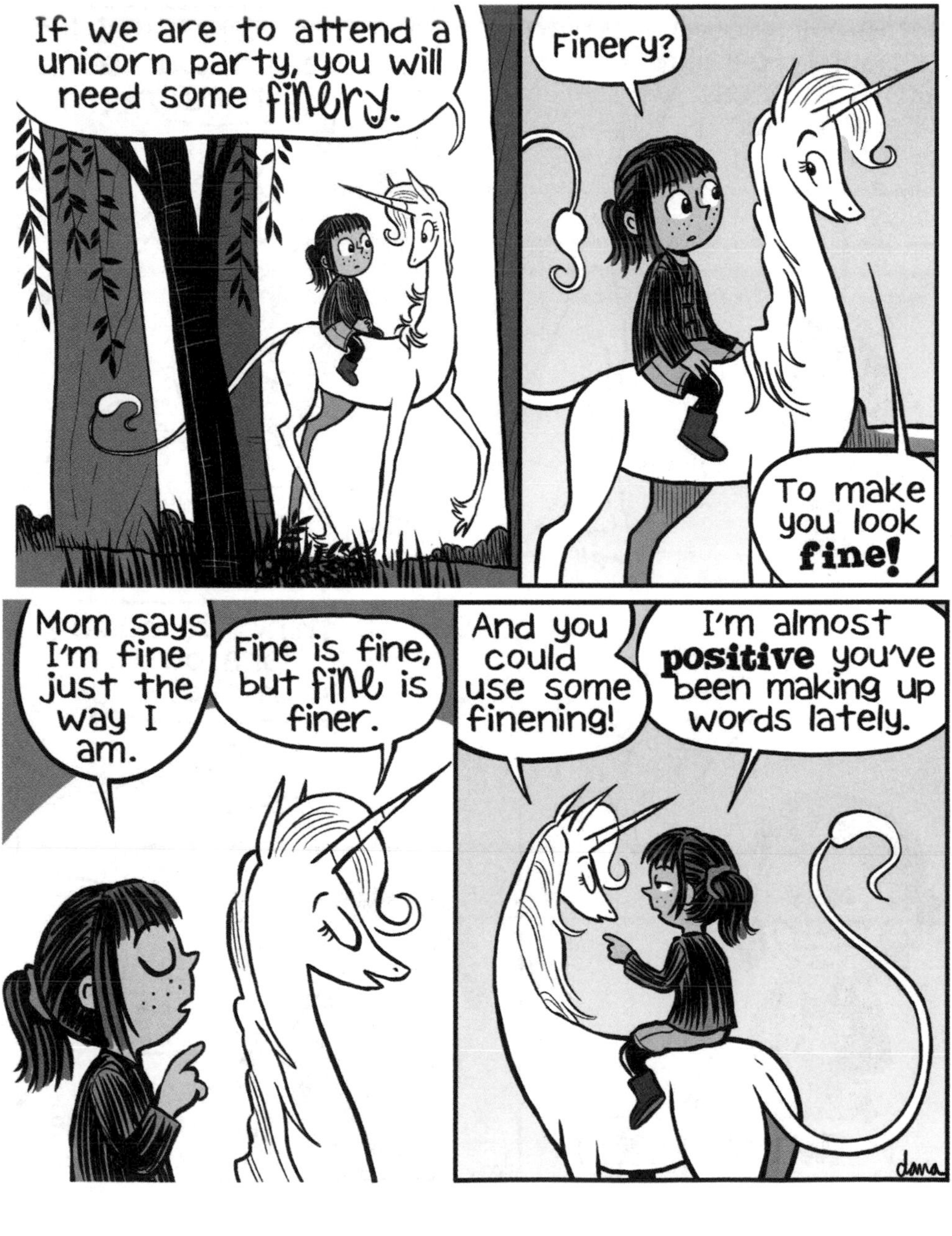
If we are to attend a unicorn party, you will need some finery.
Finery?
To make you look fine!
Mom says I'm fine just the way I am.
Fine is fine, but fine is finer.
And you could use some finening!
I'm almost positive you've been making up words lately.
dana

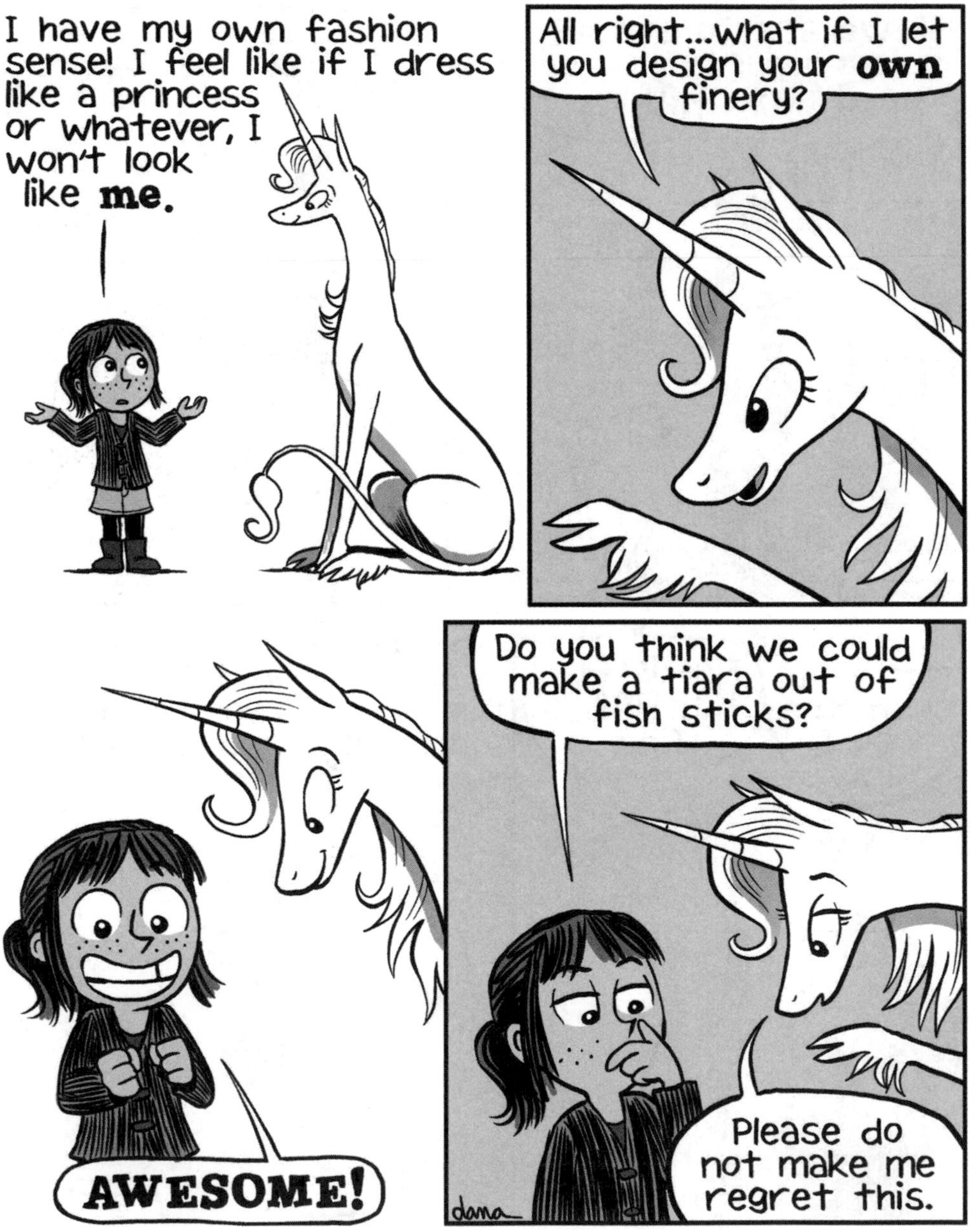
I have my own fashion sense! I feel like if I dress like a princess or whatever, I won't look like **me**.
All right...what if I let you design your **own** finery?
AWESOME!
Do you think we could make a tiara out of fish sticks?
Please do not make me regret this.
dana

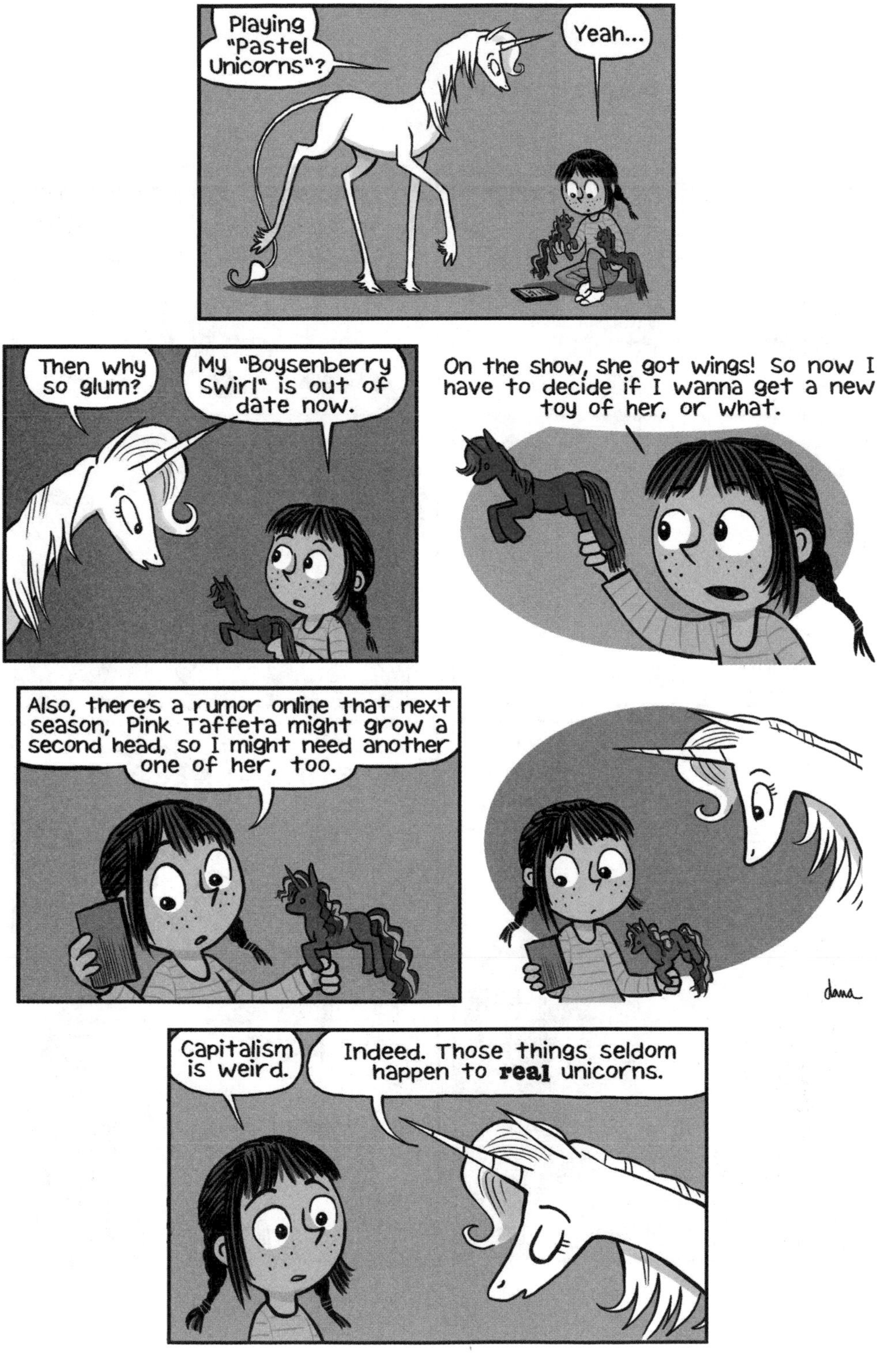
Playing "Pastel Unicorns"?
Yeah...
Then why so glum?
My "Boysenberry Swirl" is out of date now.
On the show, she got wings! So now I have to decide if I wanna get a new toy of her, or what.
Also, there's a rumor online that next season, Pink Taffeta might grow a second head, so I might need another one of her, too.
dana
Capitalism is weird.
Indeed. Those things seldom happen to **real** unicorns.

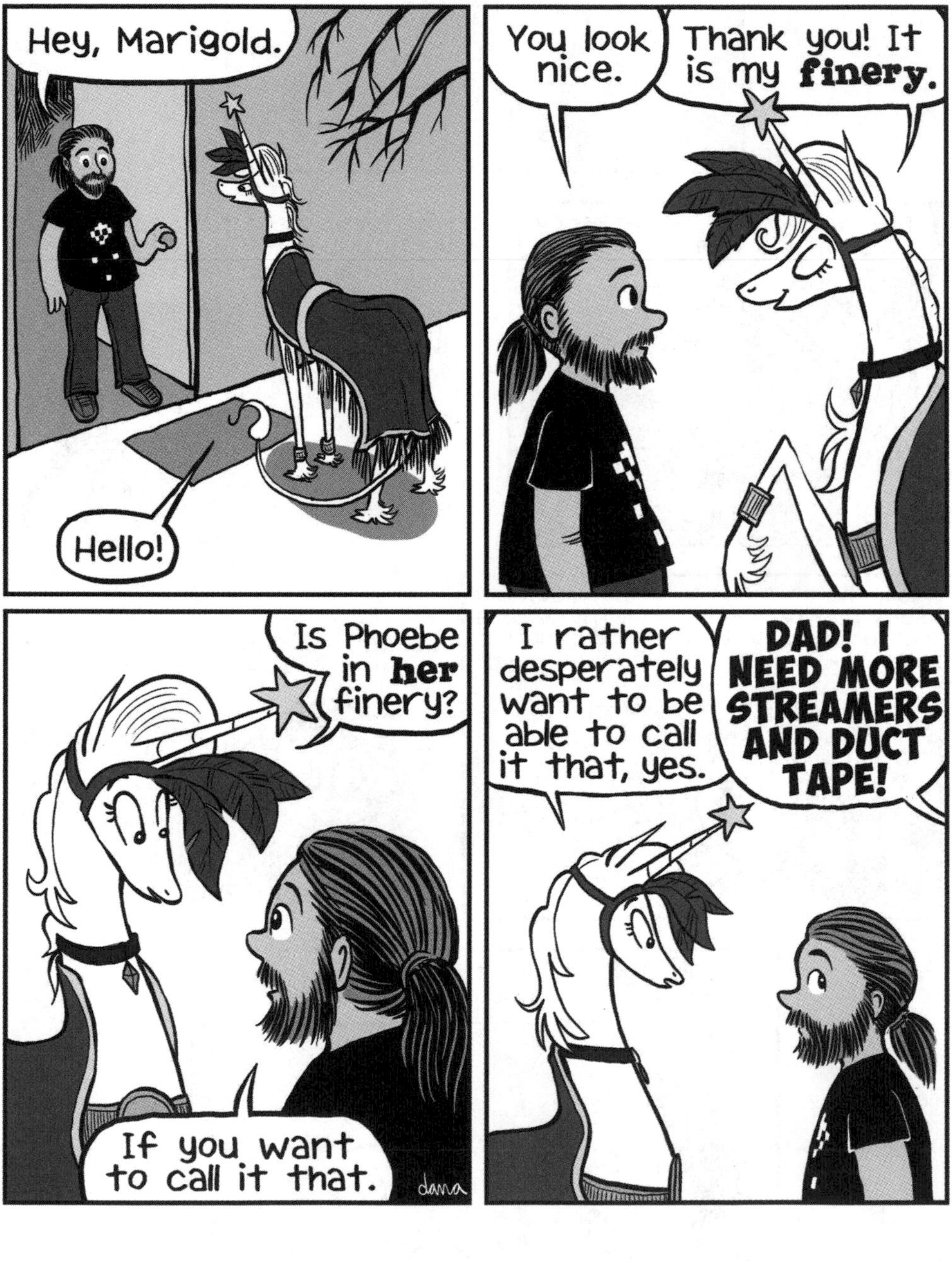
Hey, Marigold.
Hello!
You look nice.
Thank you! It is my **finery**.
Is Phoebe in **her** finery?
If you want to call it that.
dana
I rather desperately want to be able to call it that, yes.
DAD! I NEED MORE STREAMERS AND DUCT TAPE!

OKAY, I'M READY!
Phoebe
Behold me!
Must I?
I've known her all her life, and...yes, you must.
Phoe
dana

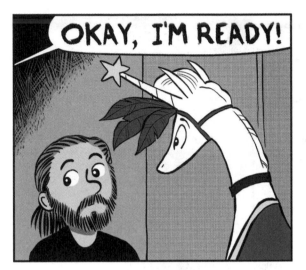

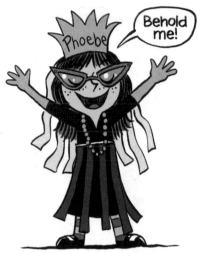

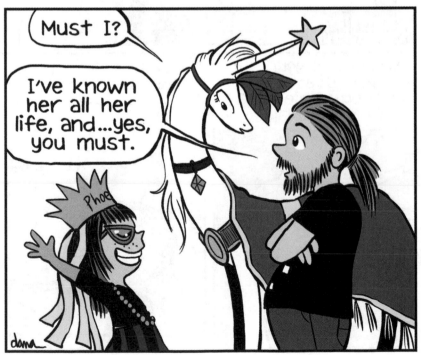

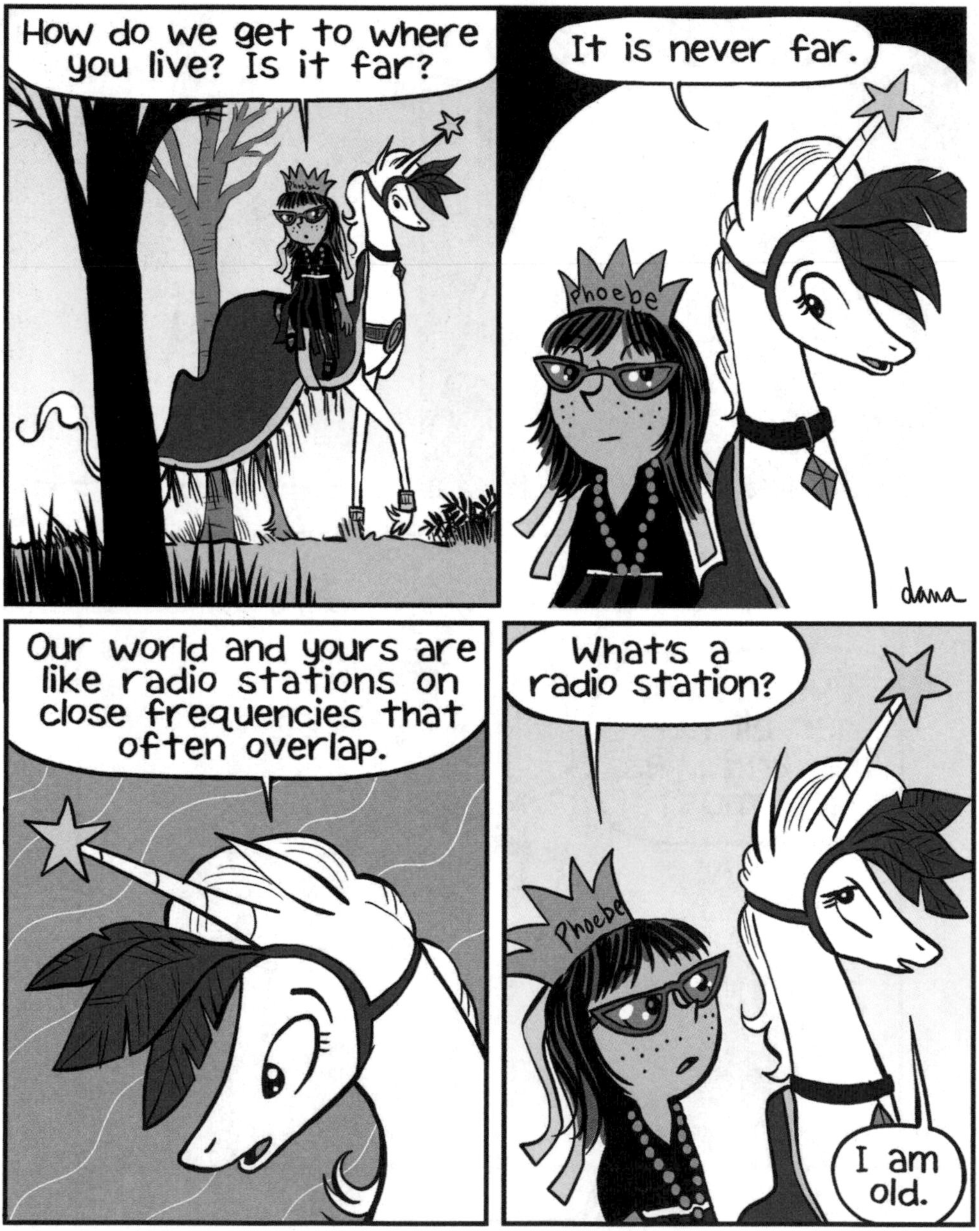
How do we get to where you live? Is it far?
Phoebe
It is never far.
Phoebe
dana
Our world and yours are like radio stations on close frequencies that often overlap.
What's a radio station?
Phoebe
I am old.

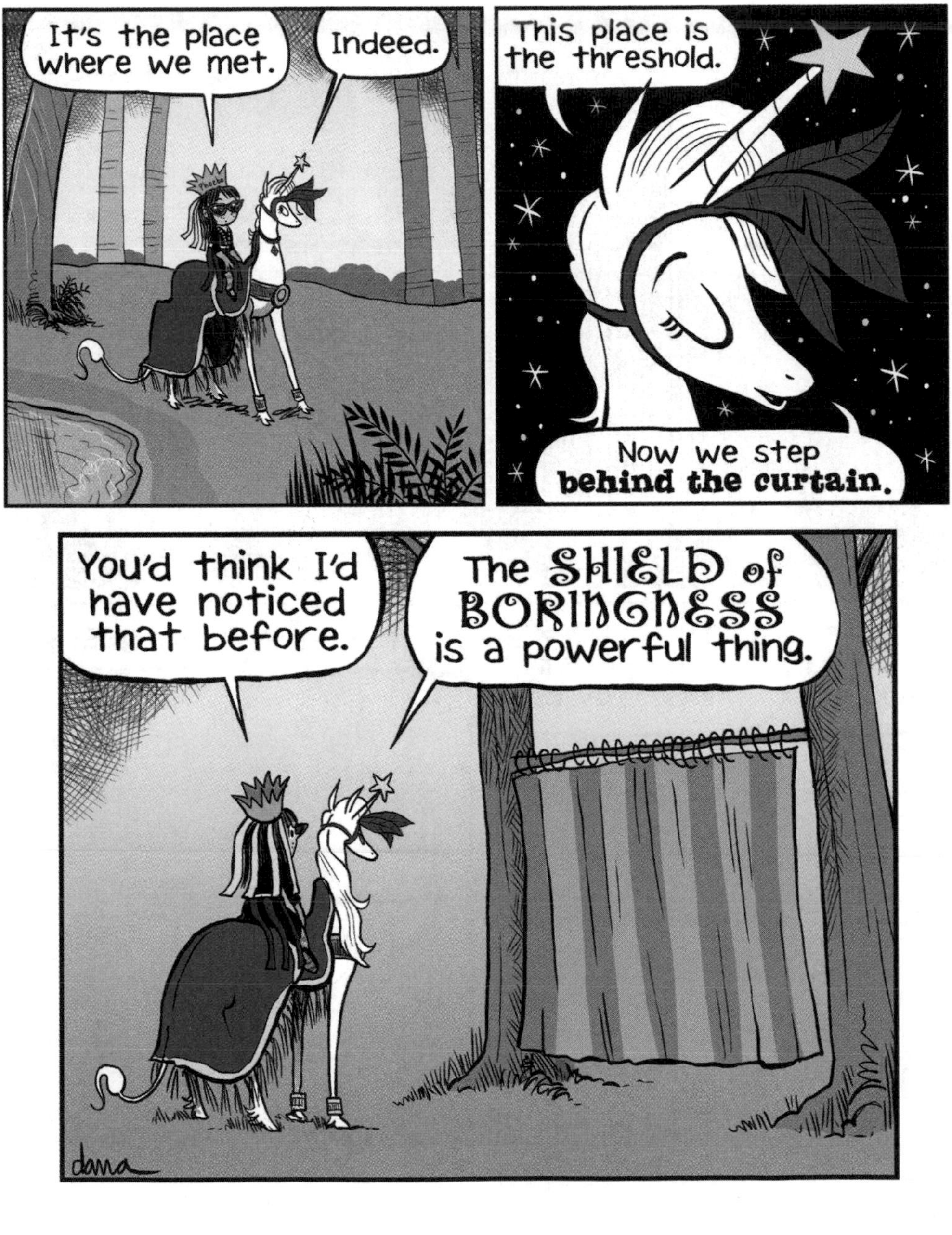
It's the place where we met.
Indeed.
This place is the threshold.
Now we step **behind the curtain.**
You'd think I'd have noticed that before.
The SHIELD of BORINGNESS is a powerful thing.
dana

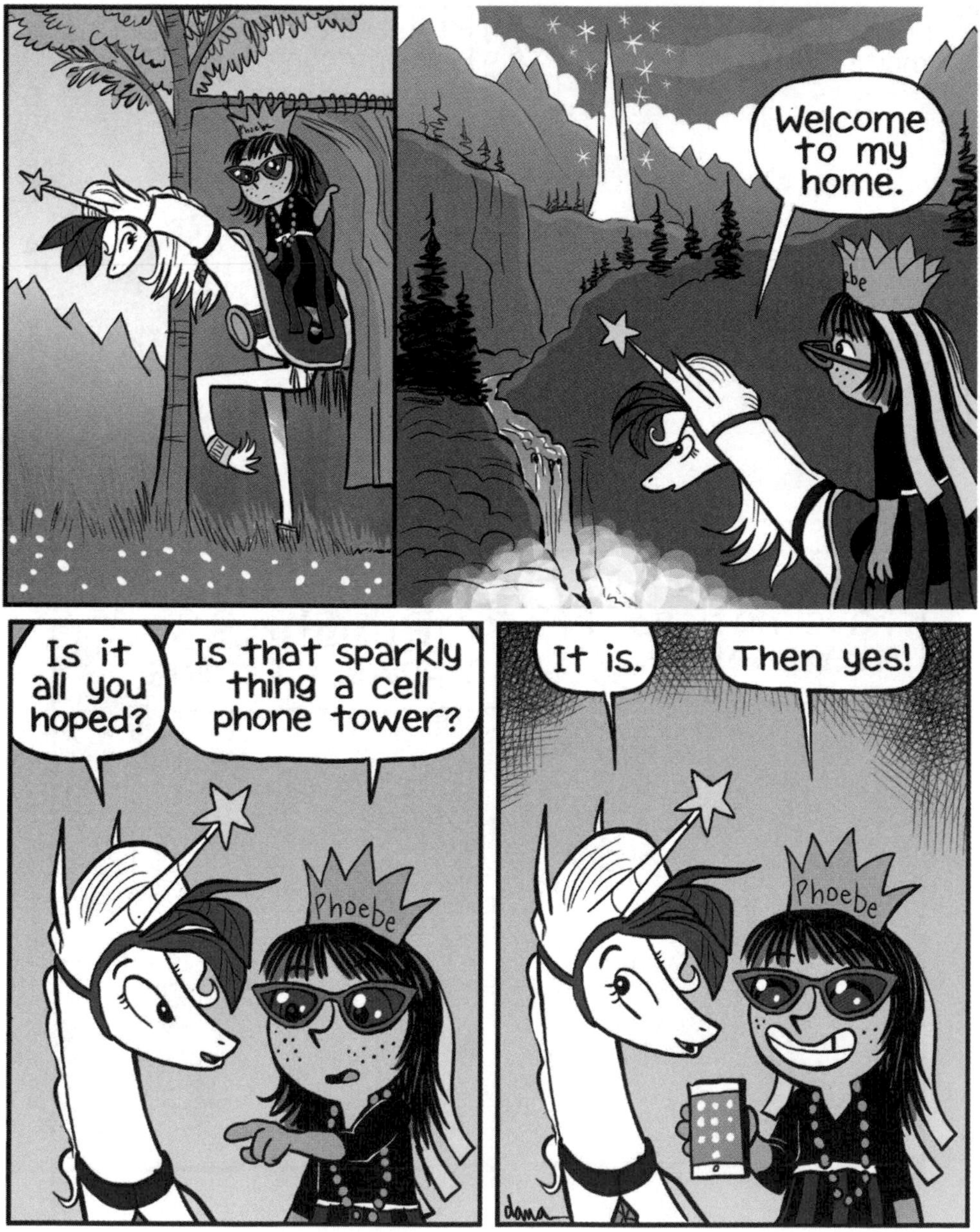
Phoebe
Welcome to my home.
Phoebe
Is it all you hoped?
Is that sparkly thing a cell phone tower?
Phoebe
It is.
Then yes!
Phoebe
dana

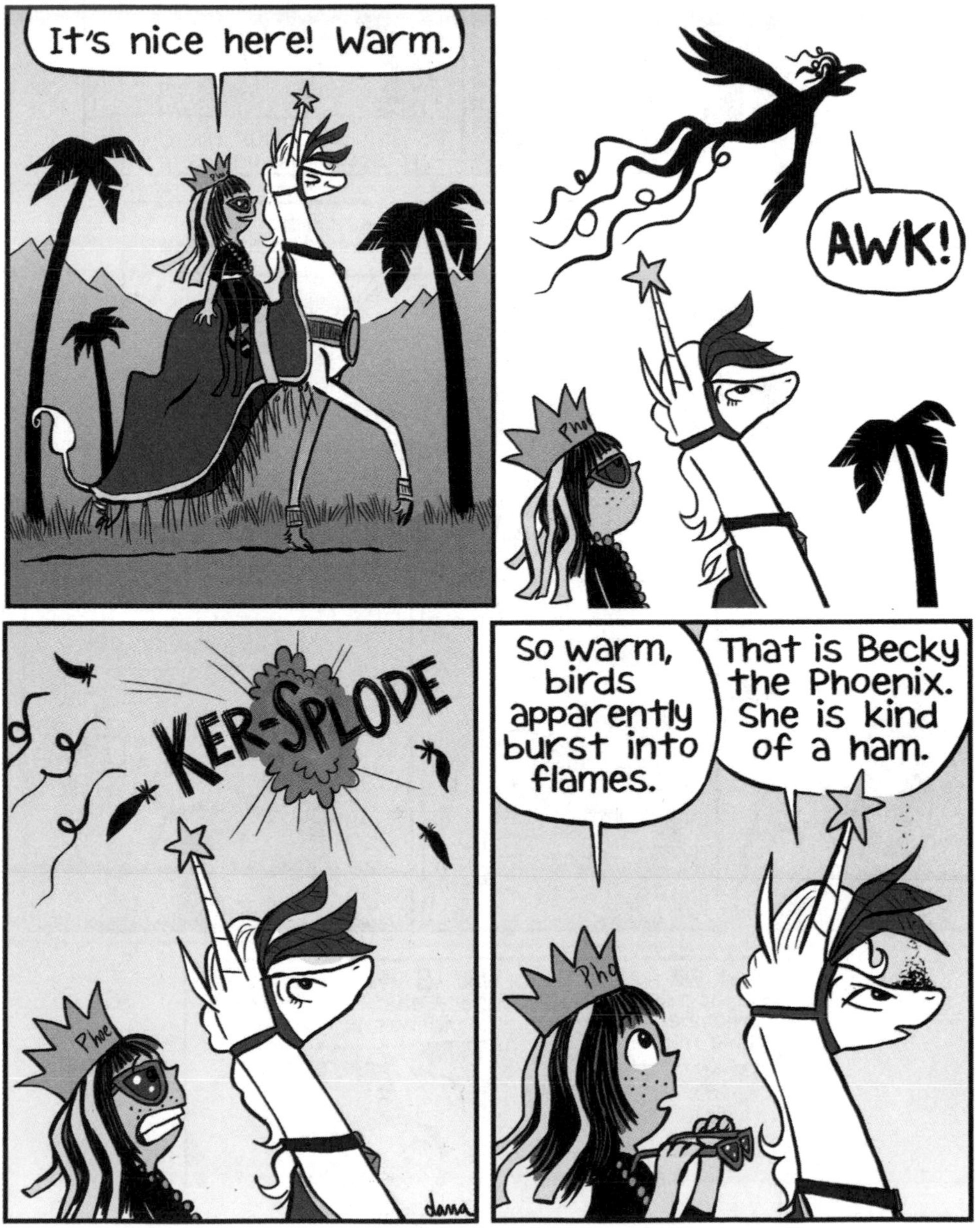
It's nice here! Warm.
AWK!
KER-SPLODE
So warm, birds apparently burst into flames.
That is Becky the Phoenix. She is kind of a ham.

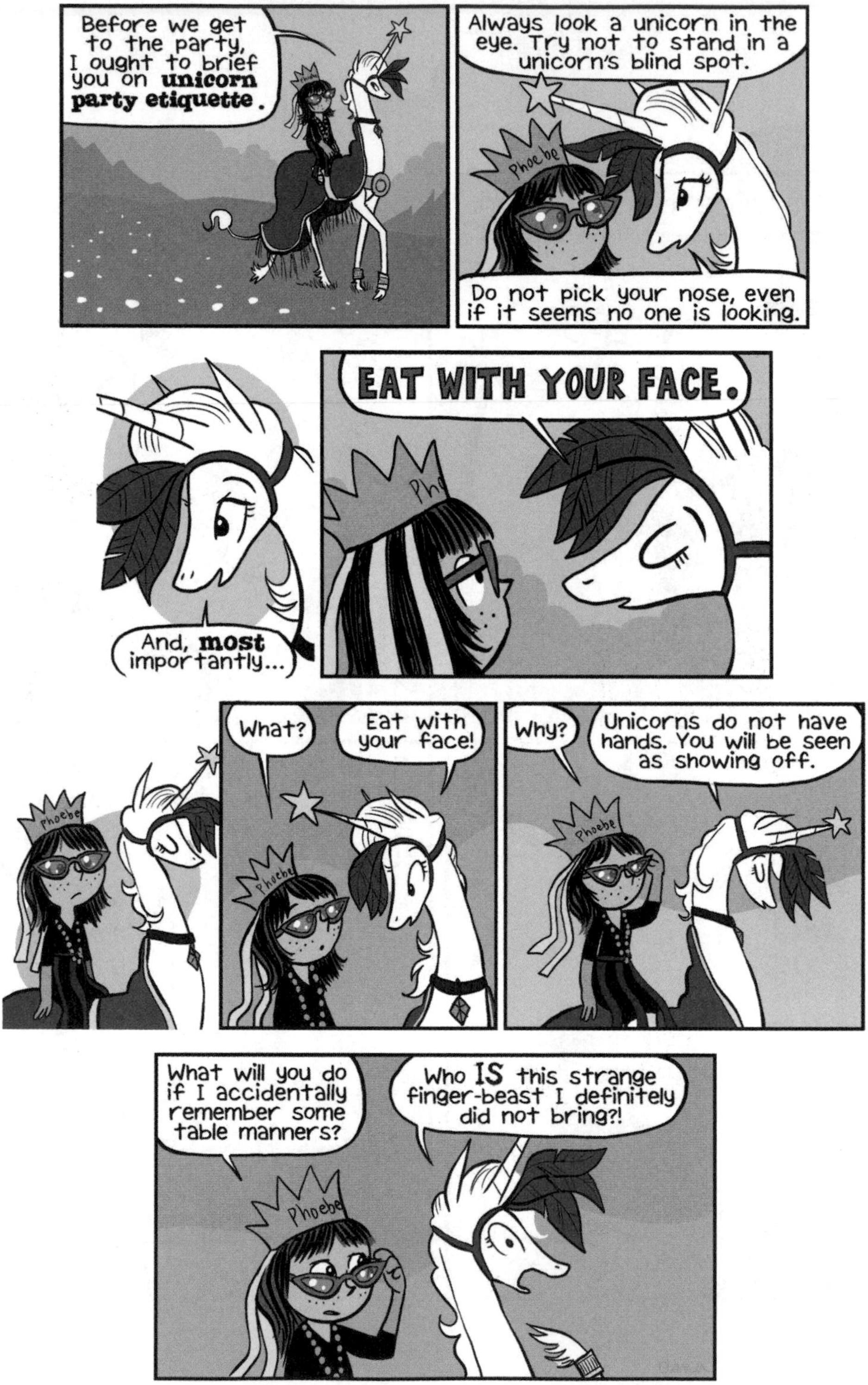
Before we get to the party, I ought to brief you on **unicorn party etiquette**.
Always look a unicorn in the eye. Try not to stand in a unicorn's blind spot.
Phoebe
Do not pick your nose, even if it seems no one is looking.
And, **most** importantly...
EAT WITH YOUR FACE.
Phoebe
What?
Eat with your face!
Phoebe
Why?
Unicorns do not have hands. You will be seen as showing off.
Phoebe
What will you do if I accidentally remember some table manners?
Who **IS** this strange finger-beast I definitely did not bring?!
Phoebe

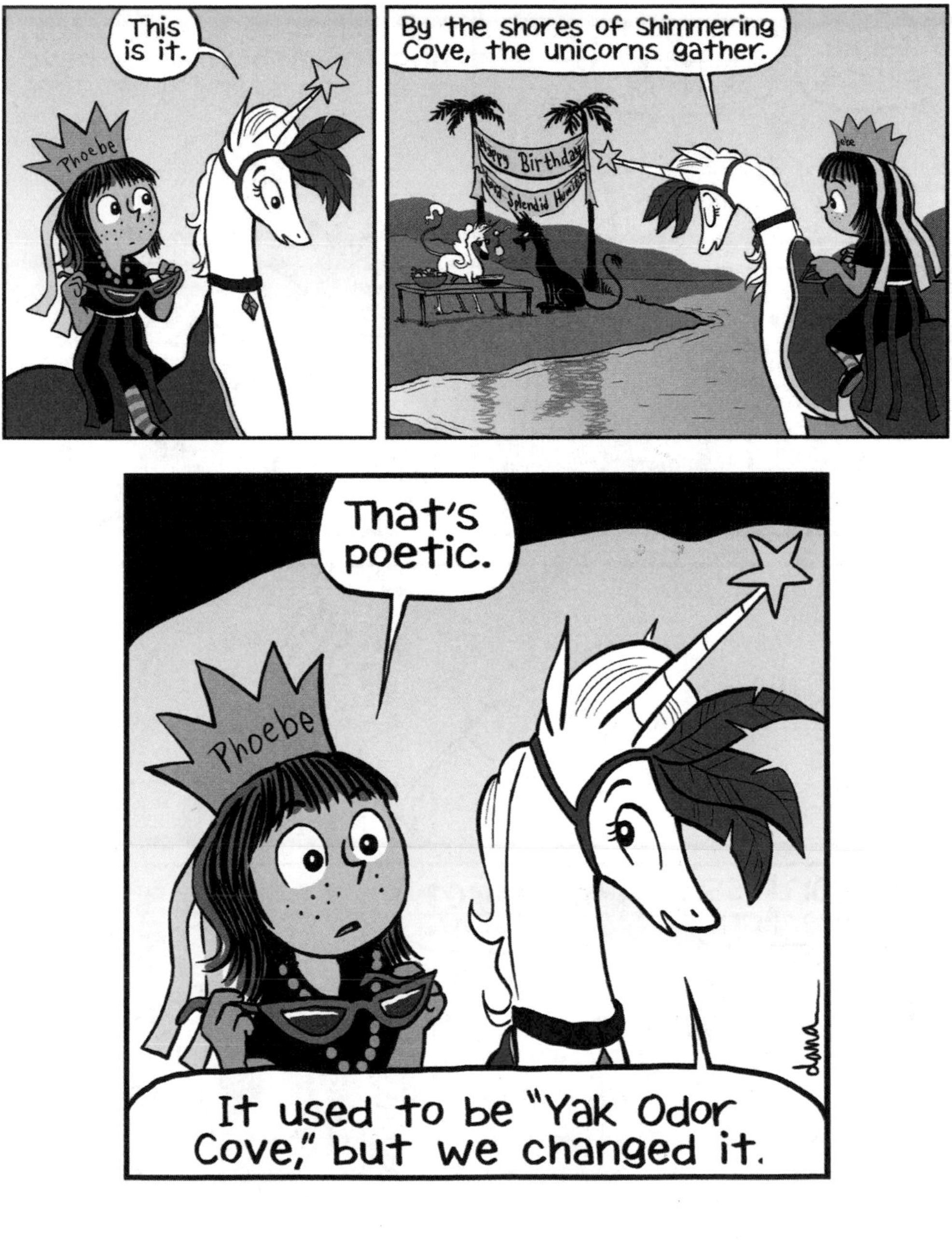
This is it.
Phoebe
By the shores of Shimmering Cove, the unicorns gather.
Happy Birthday
That's poetic.
Phoebe
It used to be "Yak Odor Cove," but we changed it.
dana

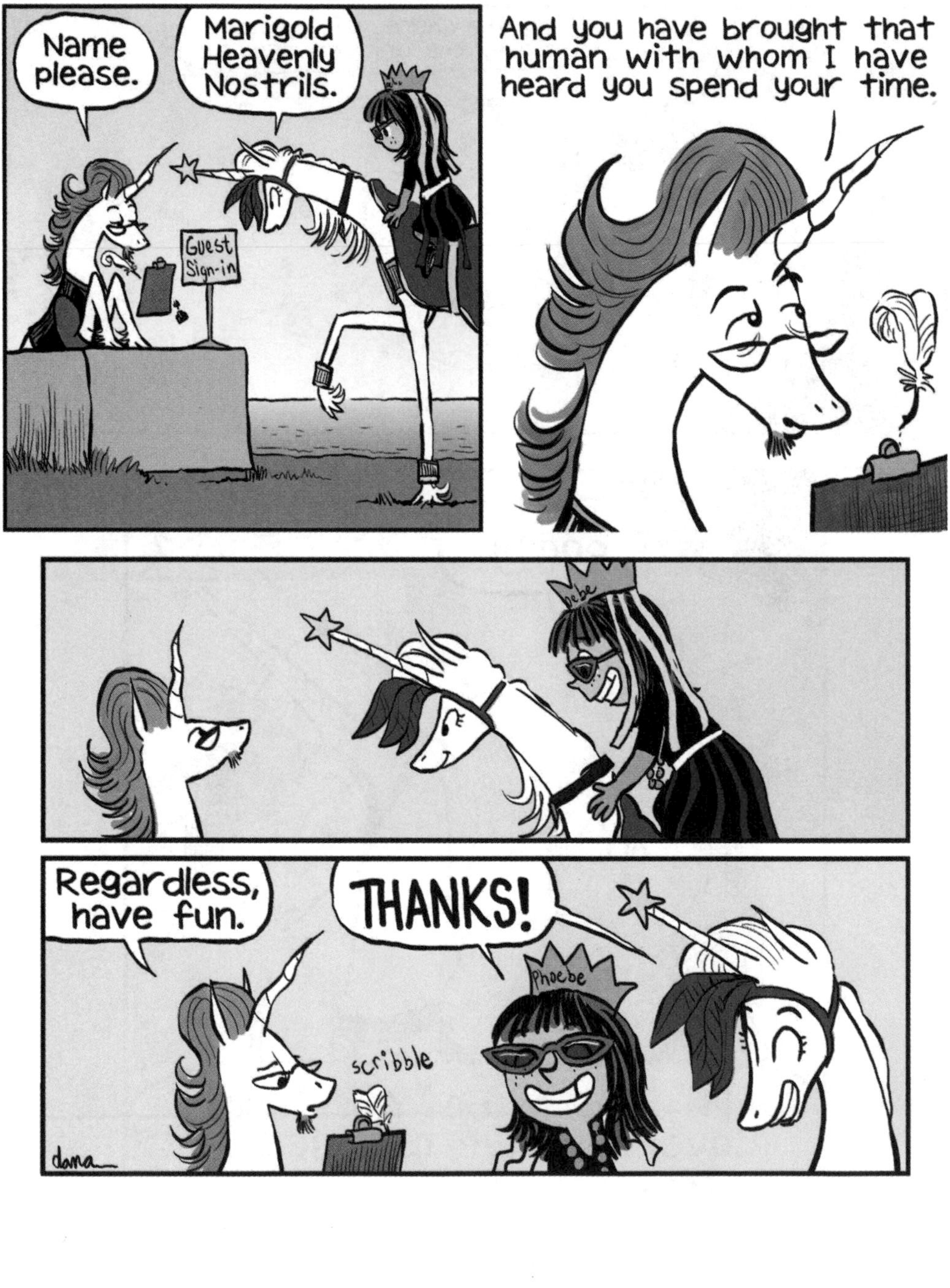

Name please.
Marigold Heavenly Nostrils.
Guest Sign-in
And you have brought that human with whom I have heard you spend your time.
Regardless, have fun.
THANKS!
Phoebe
scribble
dana

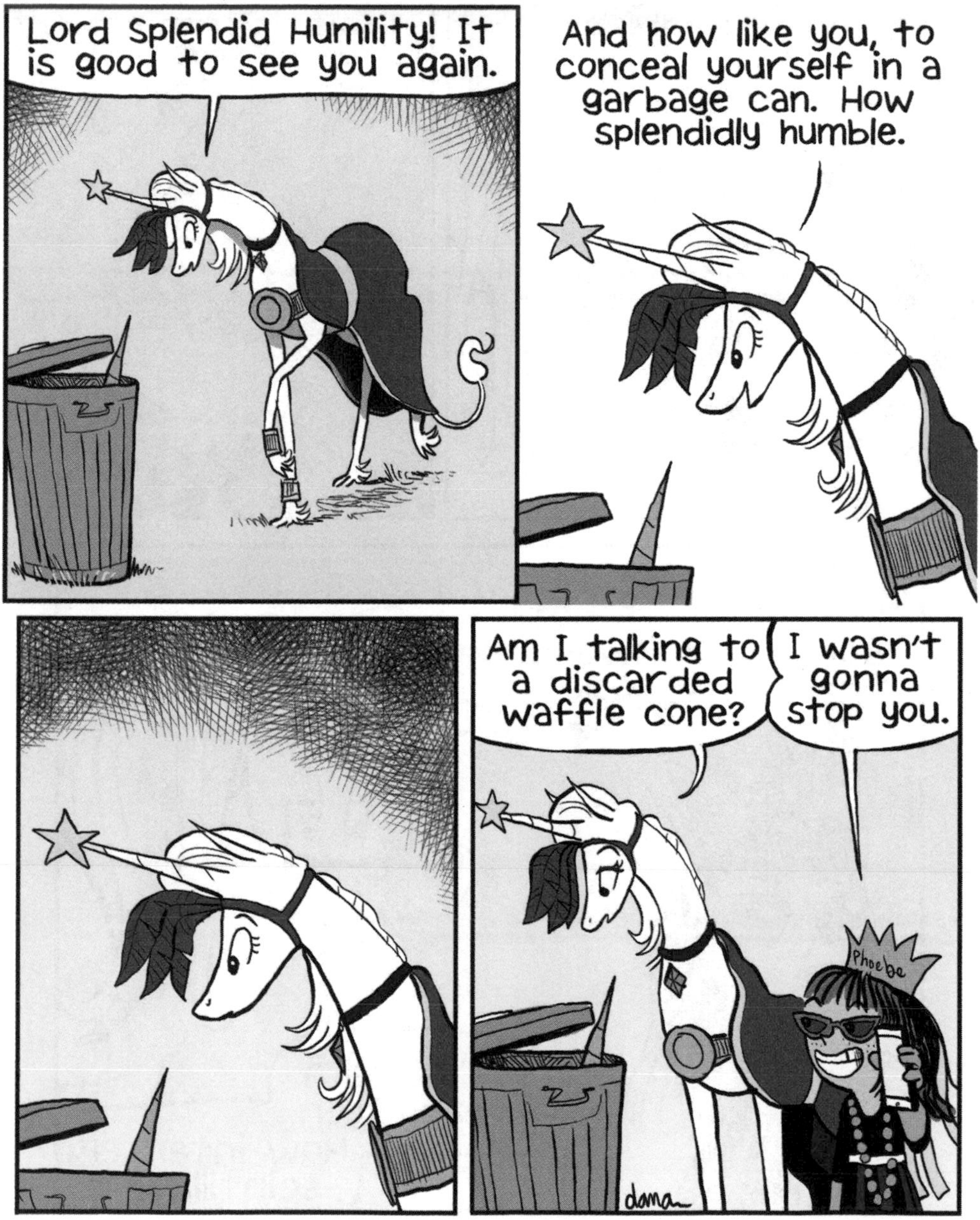

Lord Splendid Humility! It is good to see you again.
And how like you, to conceal yourself in a garbage can. How splendidly humble.
Am I talking to a discarded waffle cone?
I wasn't gonna stop you.
Phoebe
dana

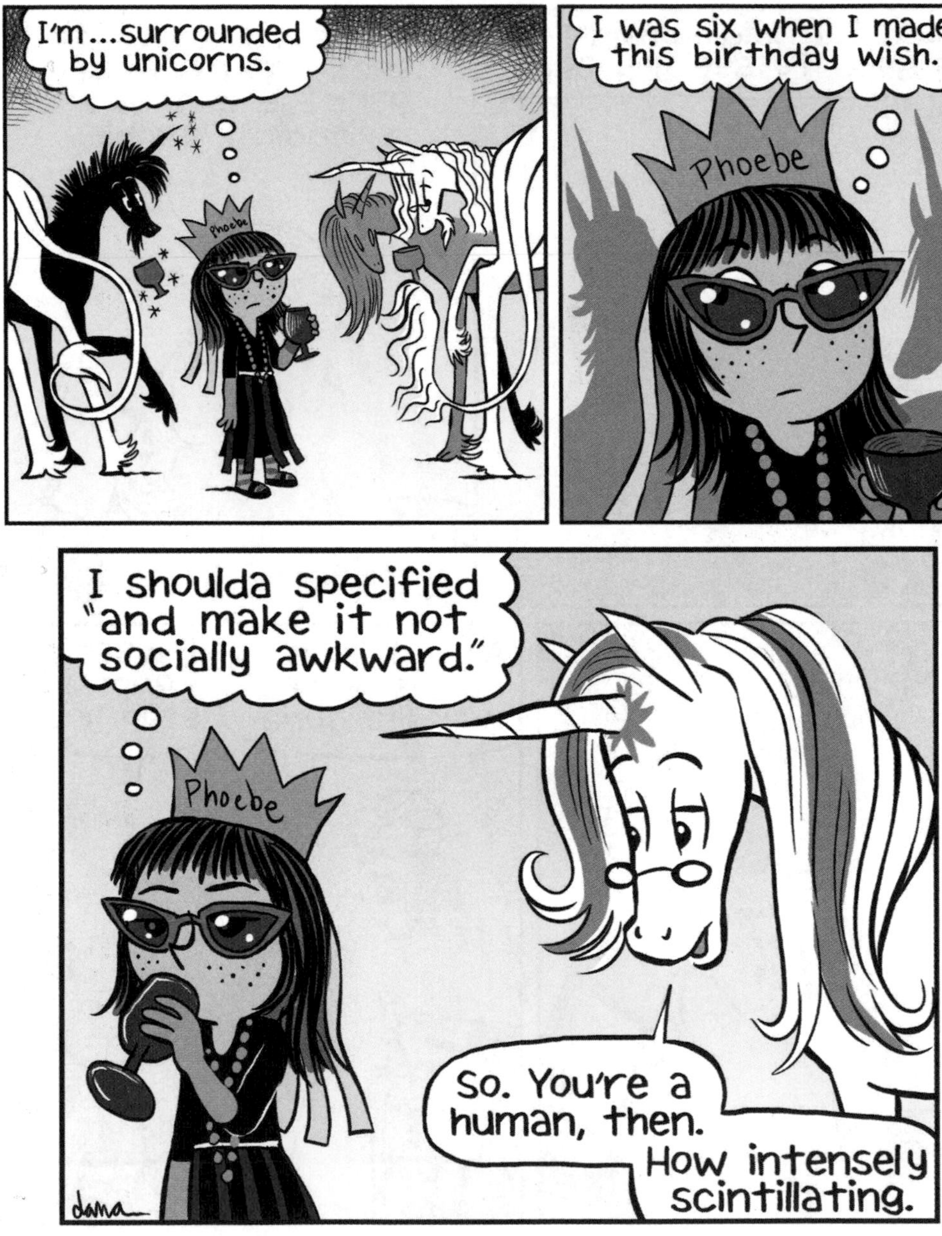
I'm...surrounded by unicorns.
Phoebe
I was six when I made this birthday wish.
Phoebe
I shoulda specified "and make it not socially awkward."
Phoebe
So. You're a human, then.
How intensely scintillating.
dana

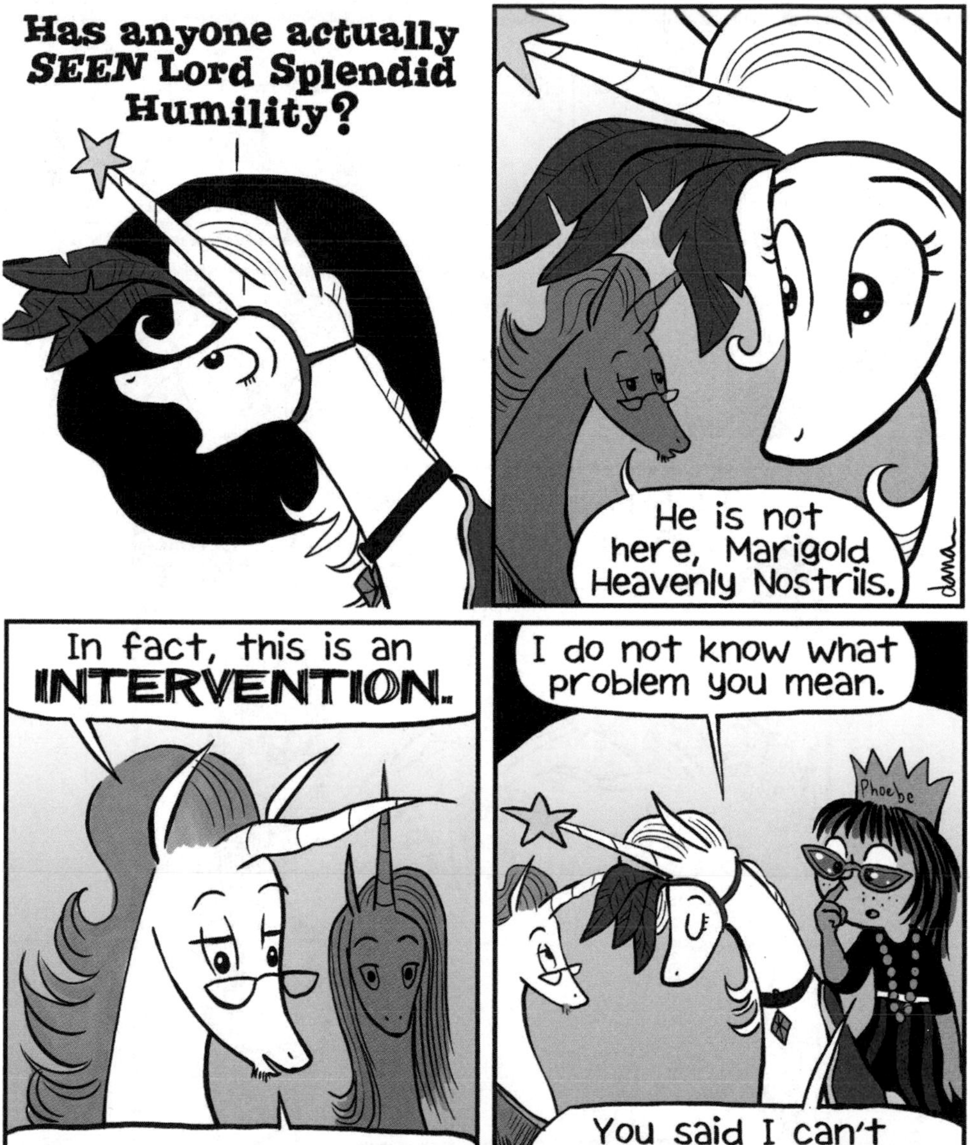
Has anyone actually SEEN Lord Splendid Humility?
He is not here, Marigold Heavenly Nostrils.
dana
In fact, this is an INTERVENTION.
We are here to talk to you about your problem.
I do not know what problem you mean.
Phoebe
You said I can't EAT with my fingers, but can I do this?

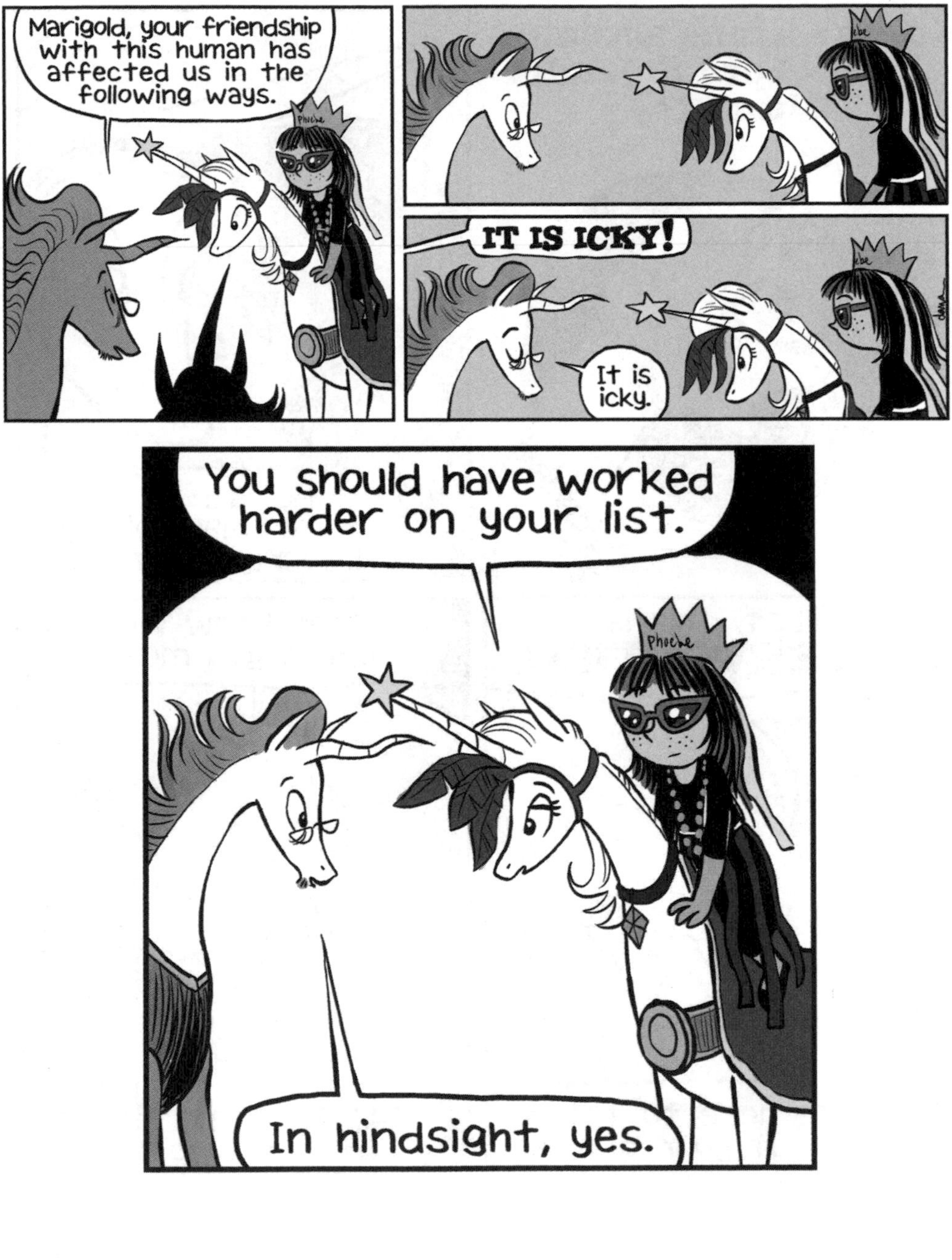
Marigold, your friendship with this human has affected us in the following ways.
IT IS ICKY!
It is icky.
You should have worked harder on your list.
In hindsight, yes.

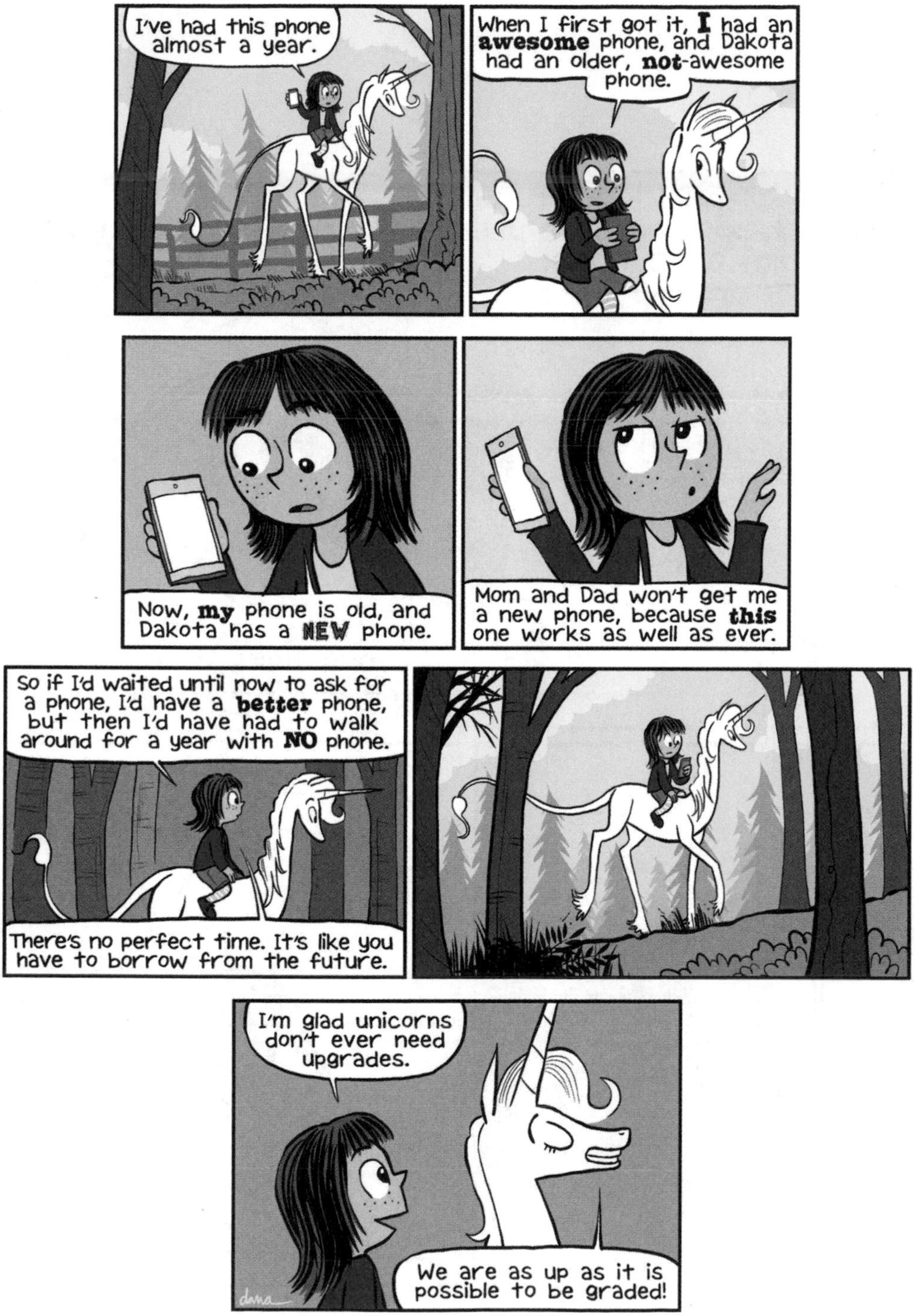
I've had this phone almost a year.
When I first got it, **I** had an **awesome** phone, and Dakota had an older, **not**-awesome phone.
Now, **my** phone is old, and Dakota has a **NEW** phone.
Mom and Dad won't get me a new phone, because **this** one works as well as ever.
So if I'd waited until now to ask for a phone, I'd have a **better** phone, but then I'd have had to walk around for a year with **NO** phone.
There's no perfect time. It's like you have to borrow from the future.
I'm glad unicorns don't ever need upgrades.
We are as up as it is possible to be graded!
dana

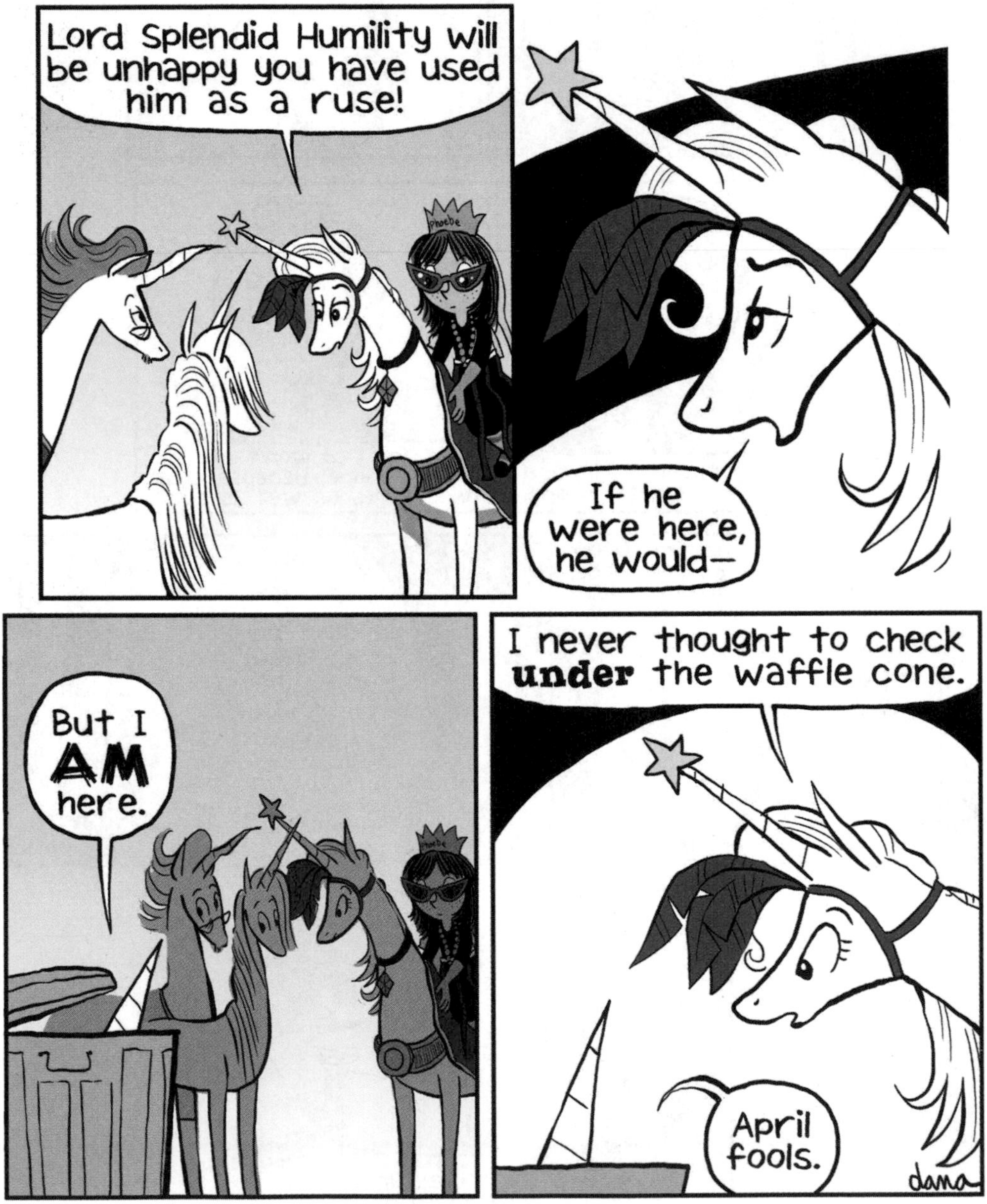
Lord Splendid Humility will be unhappy you have used him as a ruse!
phoebe
If he were here, he would—
But I AM here.
phoebe
I never thought to check **under** the waffle cone.
April fools.
dana

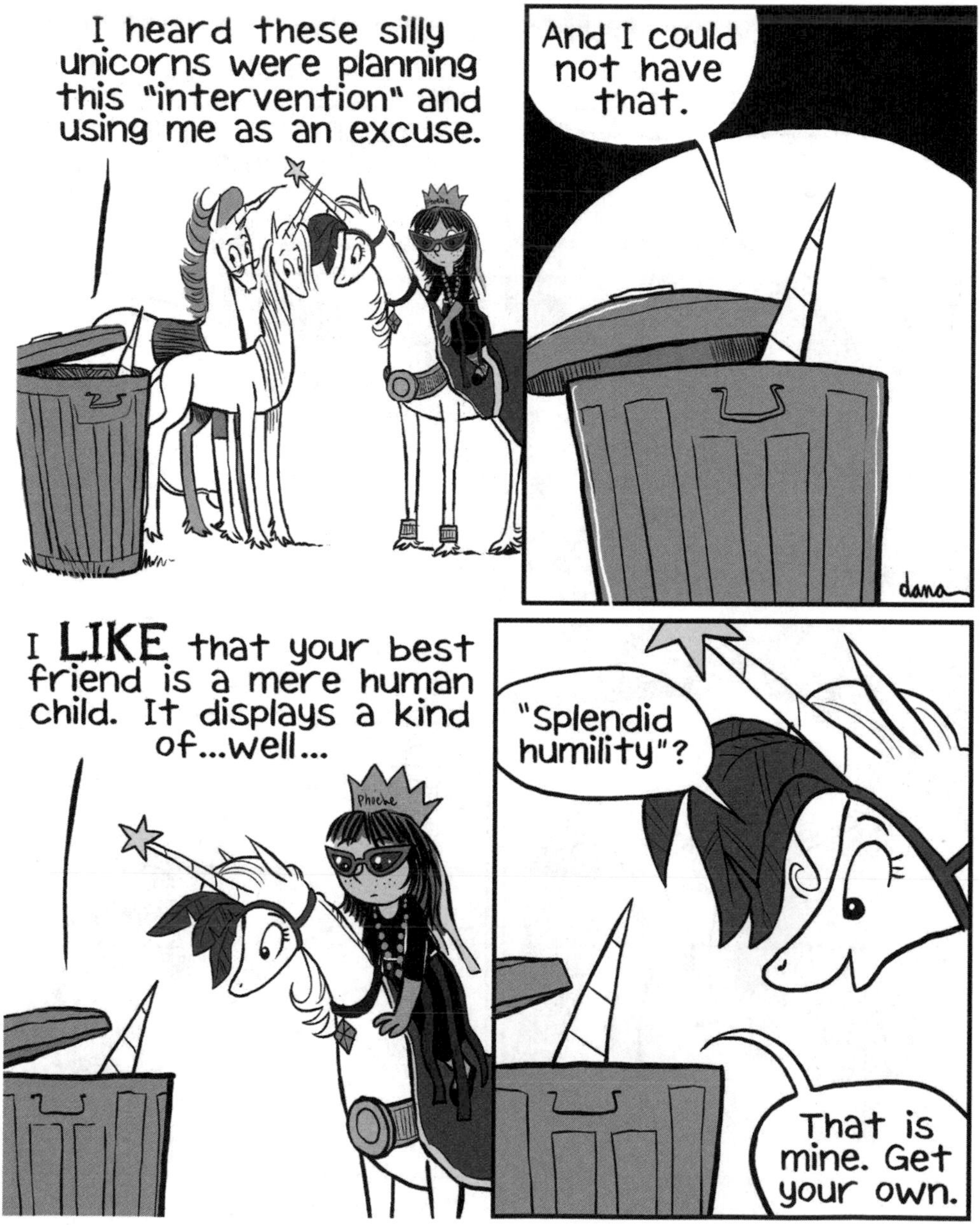
I heard these silly unicorns were planning this "intervention" and using me as an excuse.
And I could not have that.
dana
I LIKE that your best friend is a mere human child. It displays a kind of...well...
"Splendid humility"?
That is mine. Get your own.

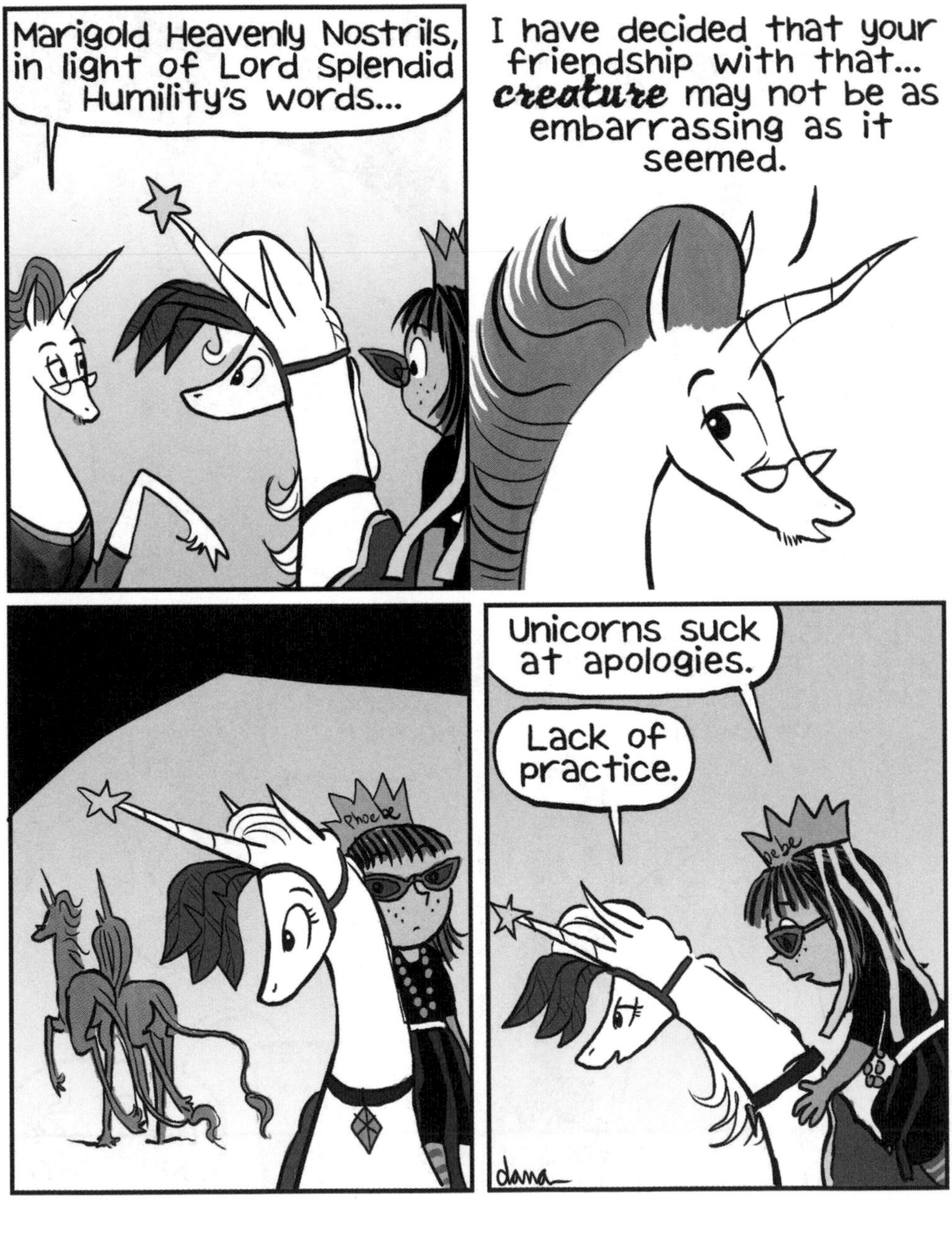
Marigold Heavenly Nostrils, in light of Lord Splendid Humility's words...
I have decided that your friendship with that... *creature* may not be as embarrassing as it seemed.
Phoebe
Unicorns suck at apologies.
Lack of practice.
dana

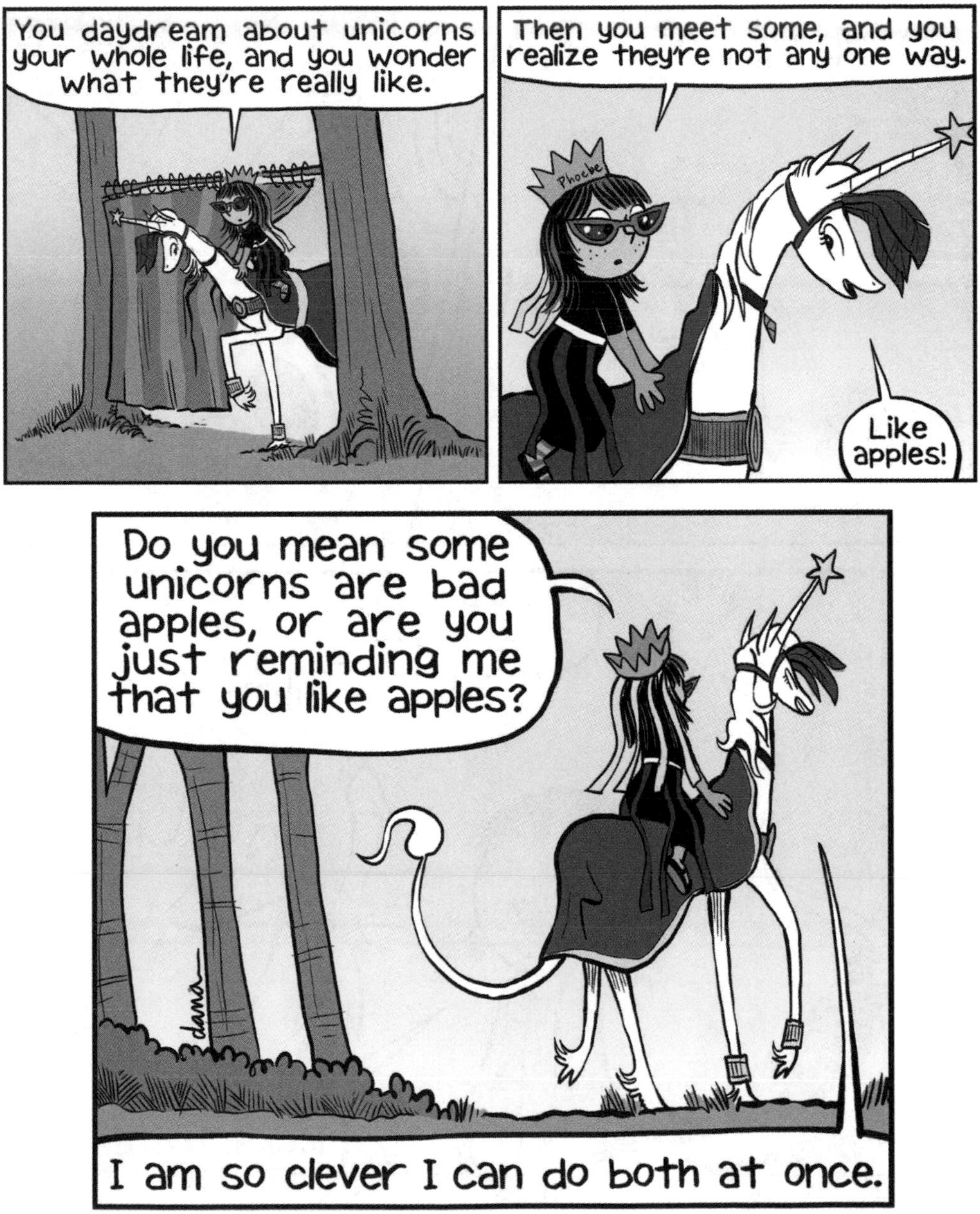
You daydream about unicorns your whole life, and you wonder what they're really like.
Then you meet some, and you realize they're not any one way.
Phoebe
Like apples!
Do you mean some unicorns are bad apples, or are you just reminding me that you like apples?
dana
I am so clever I can do both at once.

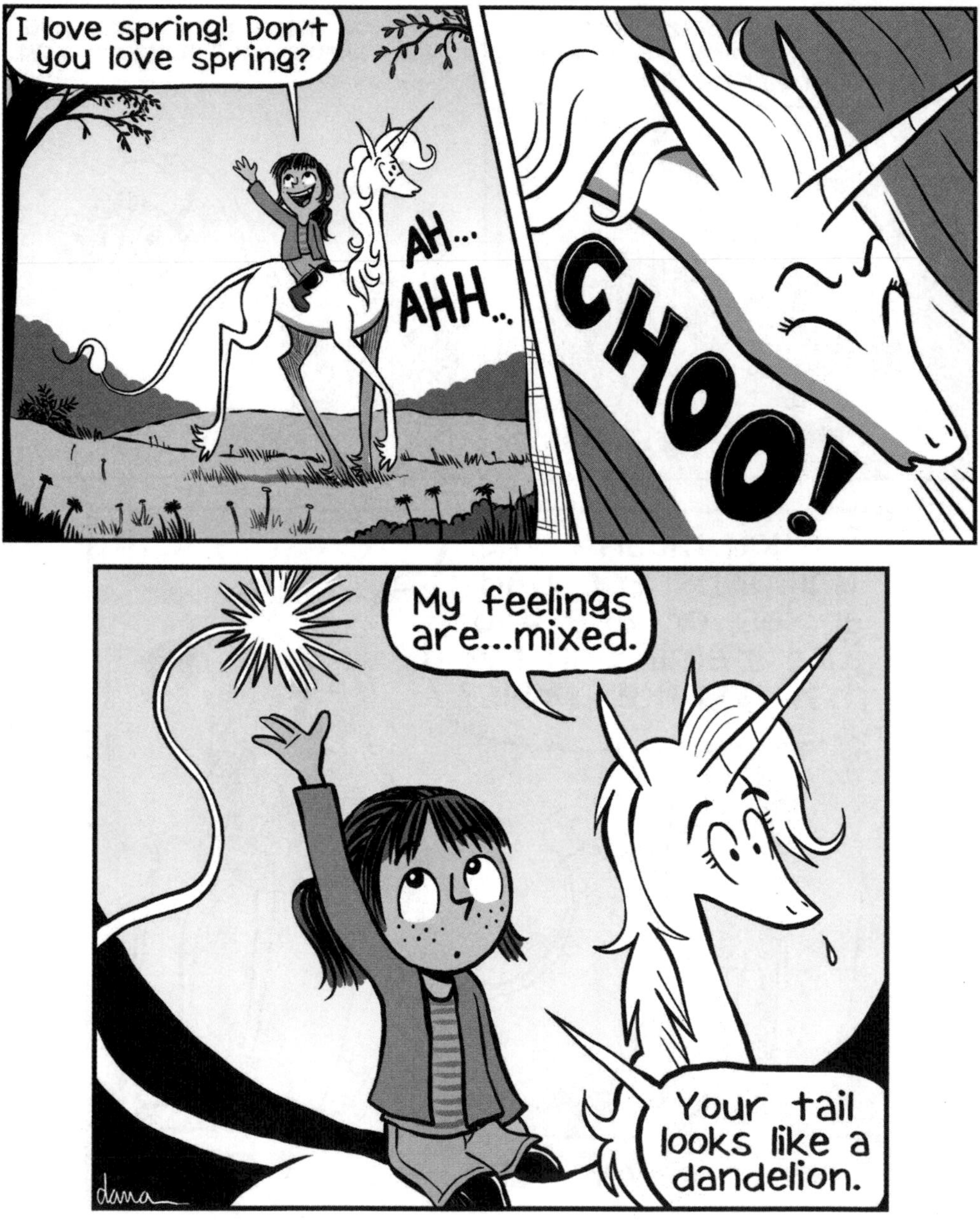
I love spring! Don't you love spring?
AH... AHH...
CHOO!
My feelings are...mixed.
Your tail looks like a dandelion.
dana

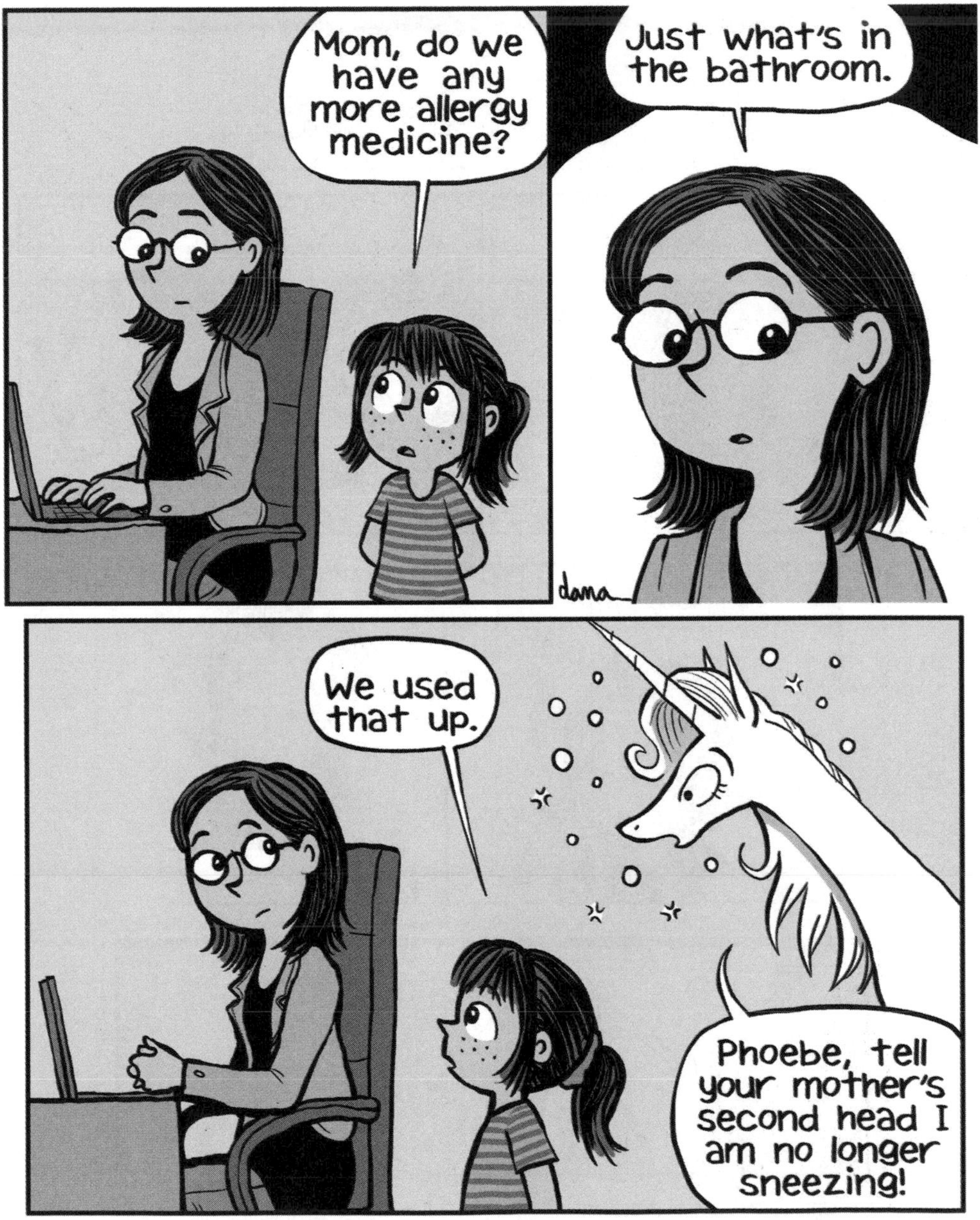
Mom, do we have any more allergy medicine?
Just what's in the bathroom.
dana
We used that up.
Phoebe, tell your mother's second head I am no longer sneezing!

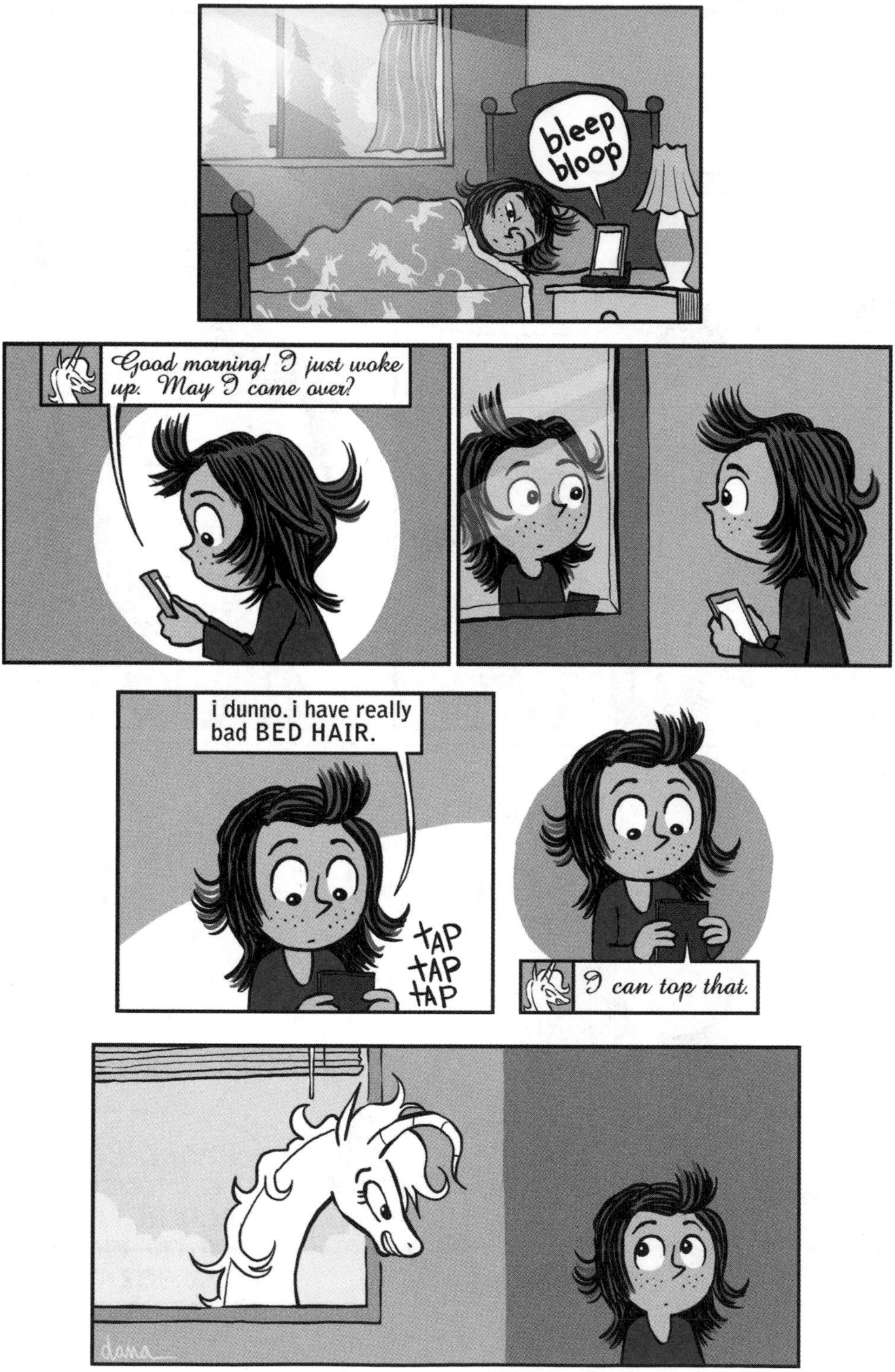
bleep bloop
Good morning! I just woke up. May I come over?
i dunno. i have really bad BED HAIR.
TAP TAP TAP
I can top that.
dana

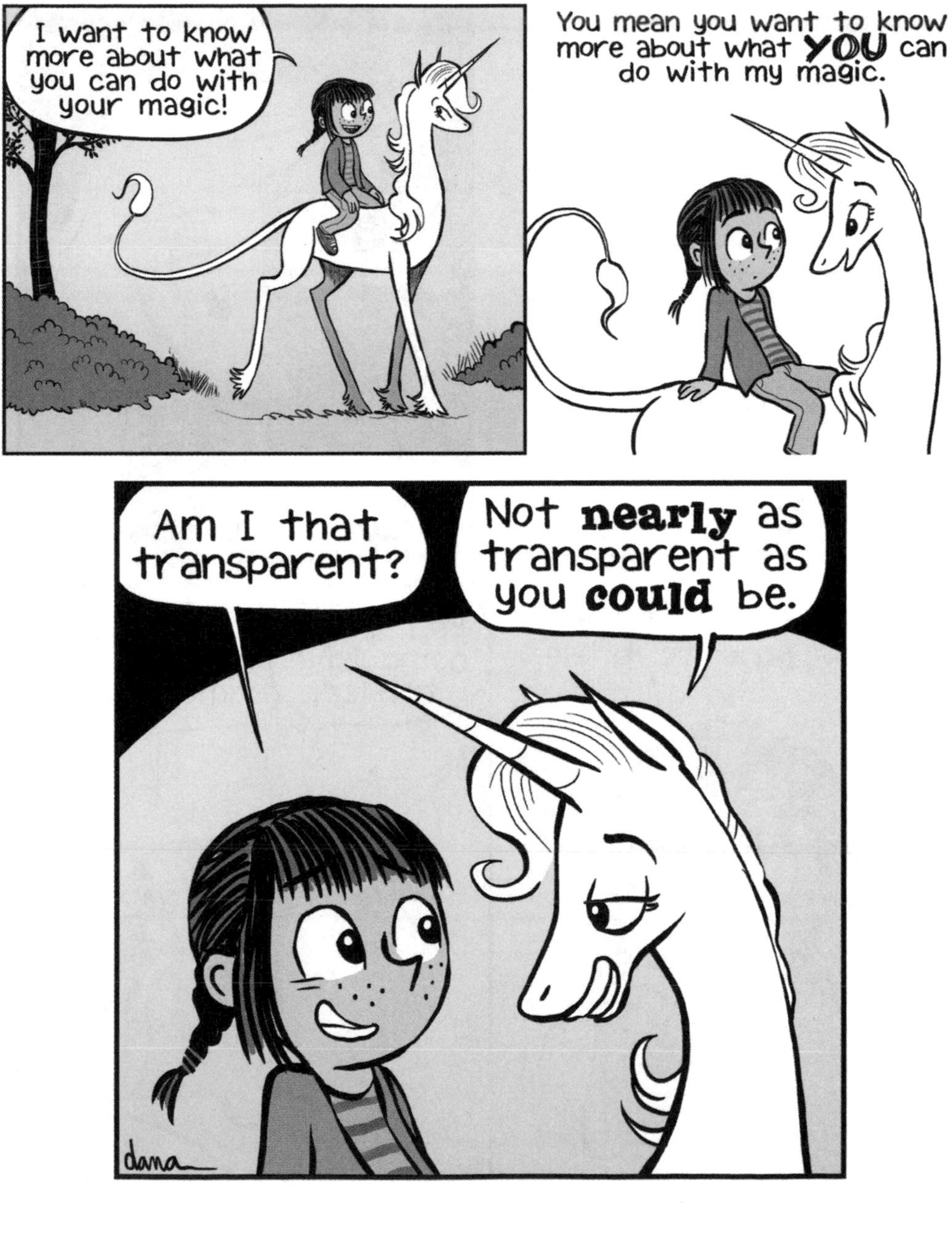
I want to know more about what you can do with your magic!
You mean you want to know more about what YOU can do with my magic.
Am I that transparent?
Not nearly as transparent as you could be.
dana

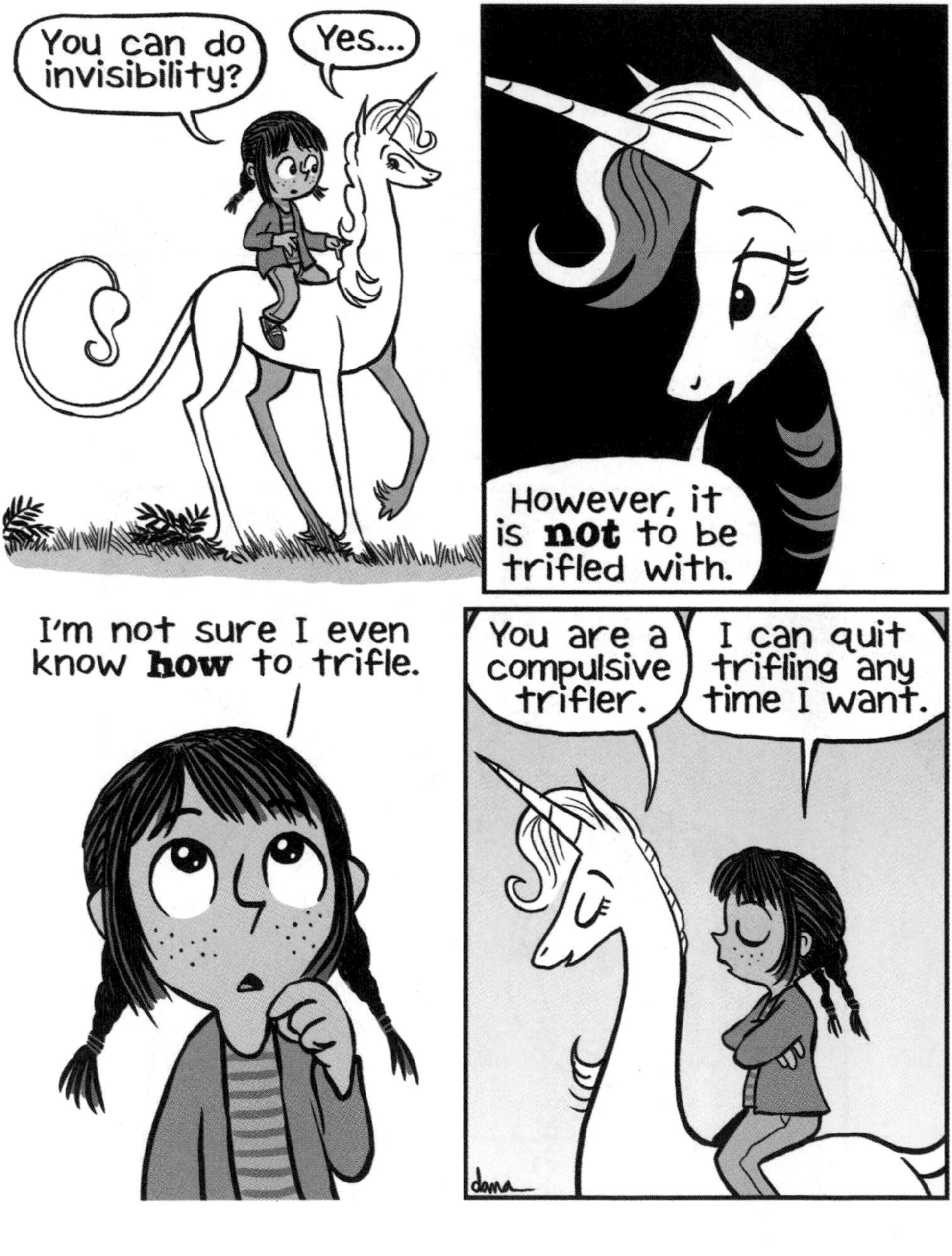
You can do invisibility?
Yes...
However, it is **not** to be trifled with.
I'm not sure I even know **how** to trifle.
You are a compulsive trifler.
I can quit trifling any time I want.
dana

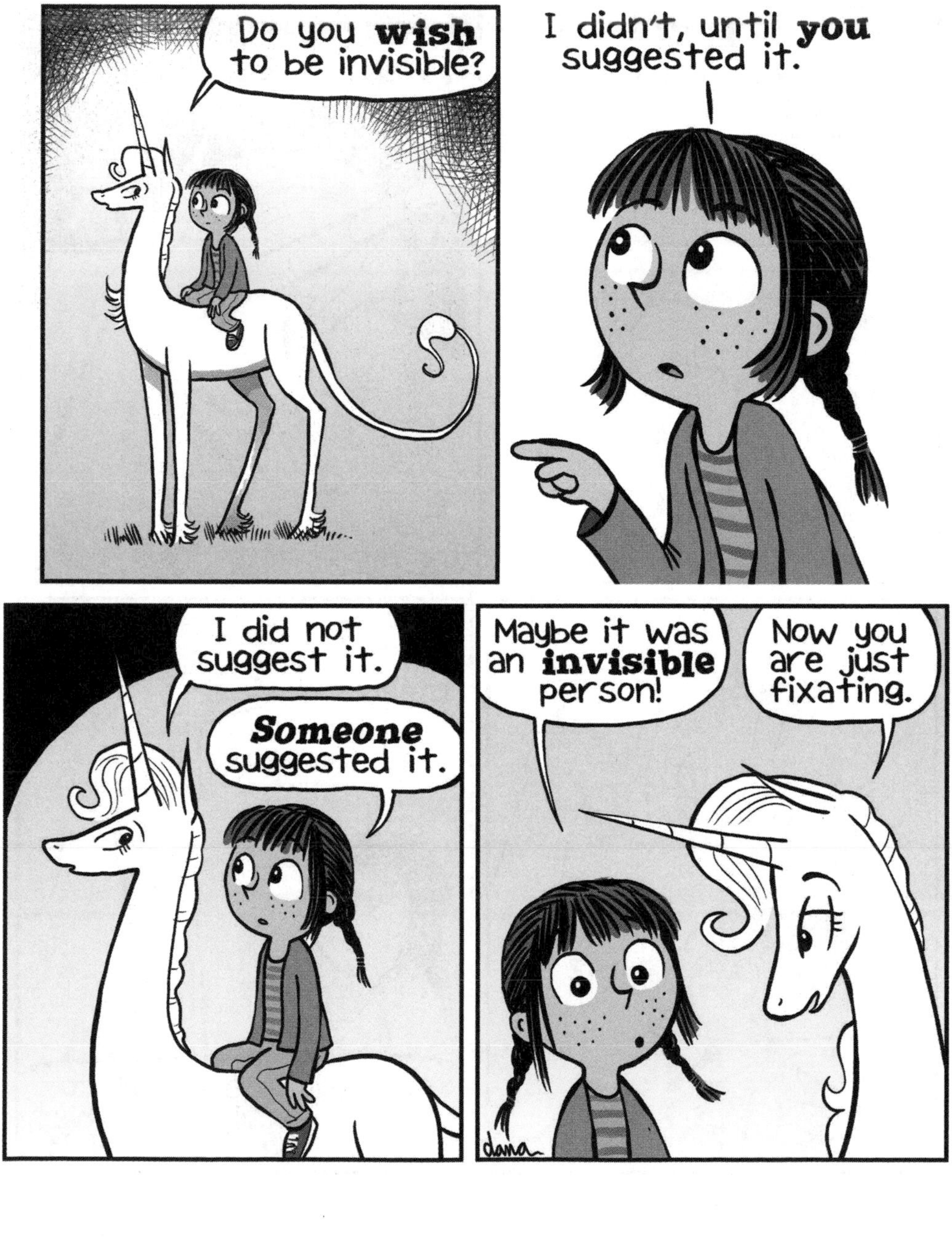
Do you **wish** to be invisible?
I didn't, until **you** suggested it.
I did not suggest it.
Someone suggested it.
Maybe it was an **invisible** person!
Now you are just fixating.
dana

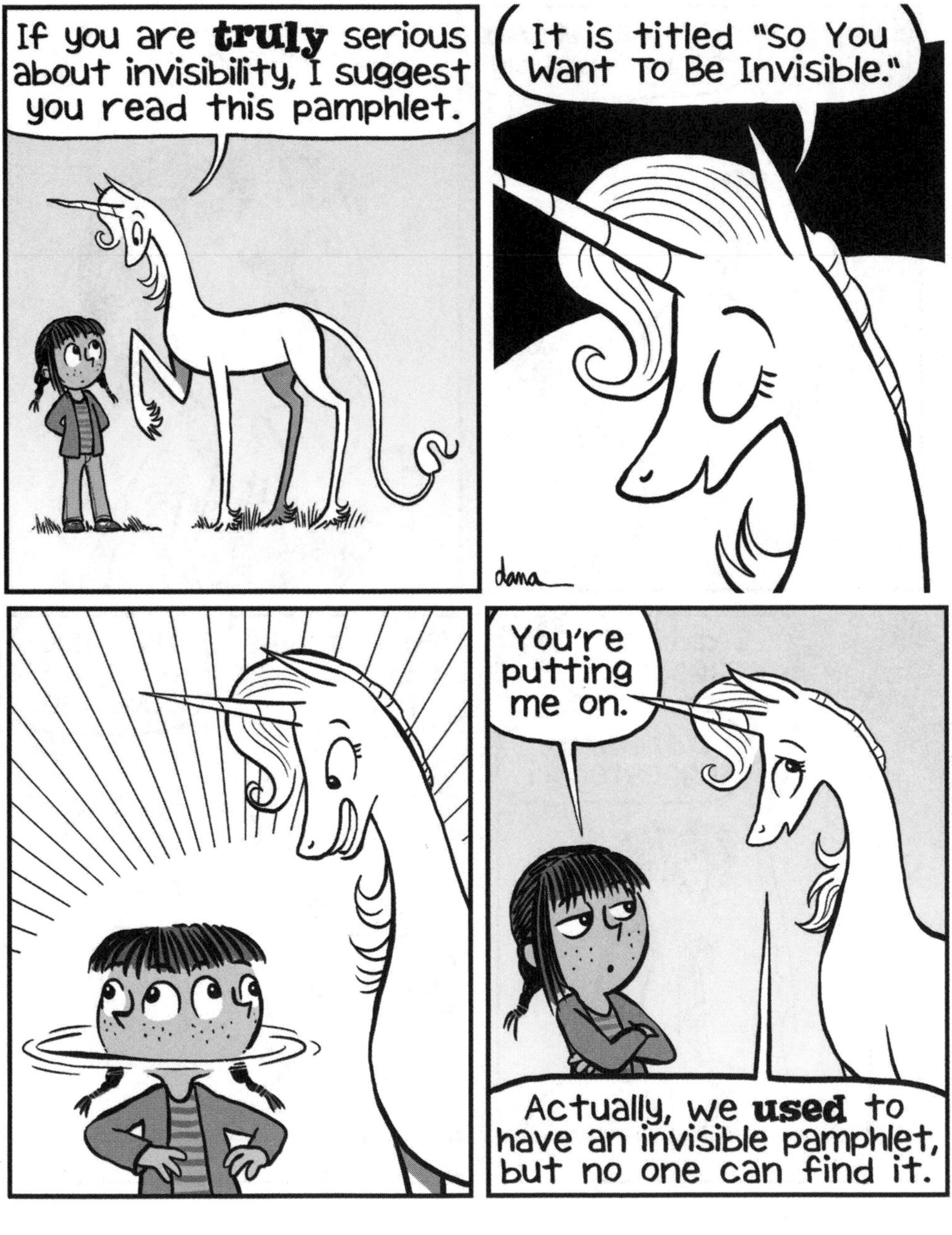
If you are **truly** serious about invisibility, I suggest you read this pamphlet.
It is titled "So You Want To Be Invisible."
dana
You're putting me on.
Actually, we **used** to have an invisible pamphlet, but no one can find it.

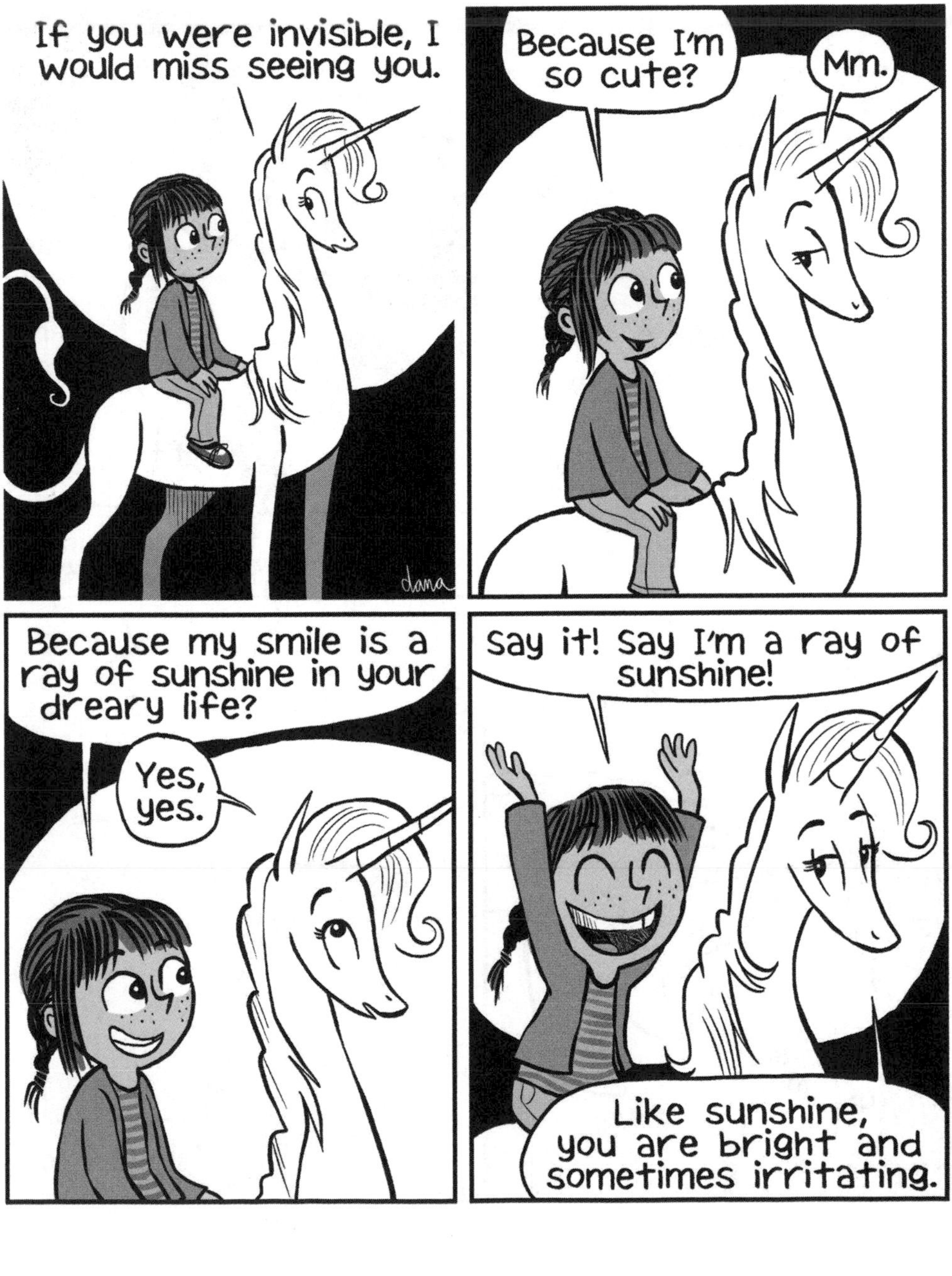

If you were invisible, I would miss seeing you.
dana
Because I'm so cute?
Mm.
Because my smile is a ray of sunshine in your dreary life?
Yes, yes.
Say it! Say I'm a ray of sunshine!
Like sunshine, you are bright and sometimes irritating.

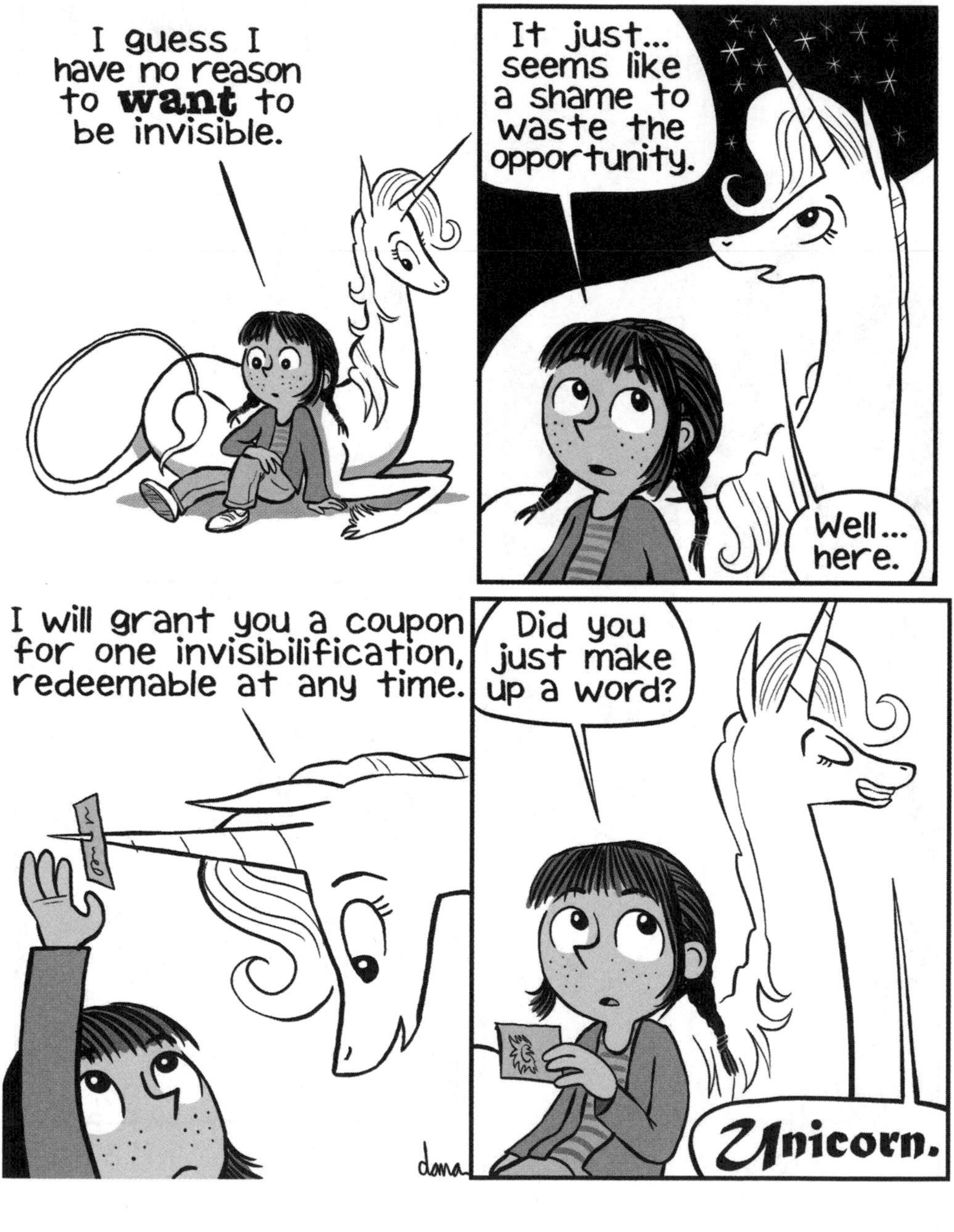
I guess I have no reason to **want** to be invisible.
It just... seems like a shame to waste the opportunity.
Well... here.
I will grant you a coupon for one invisibilification, redeemable at any time.
Did you just make up a word?
Unicorn.
dana

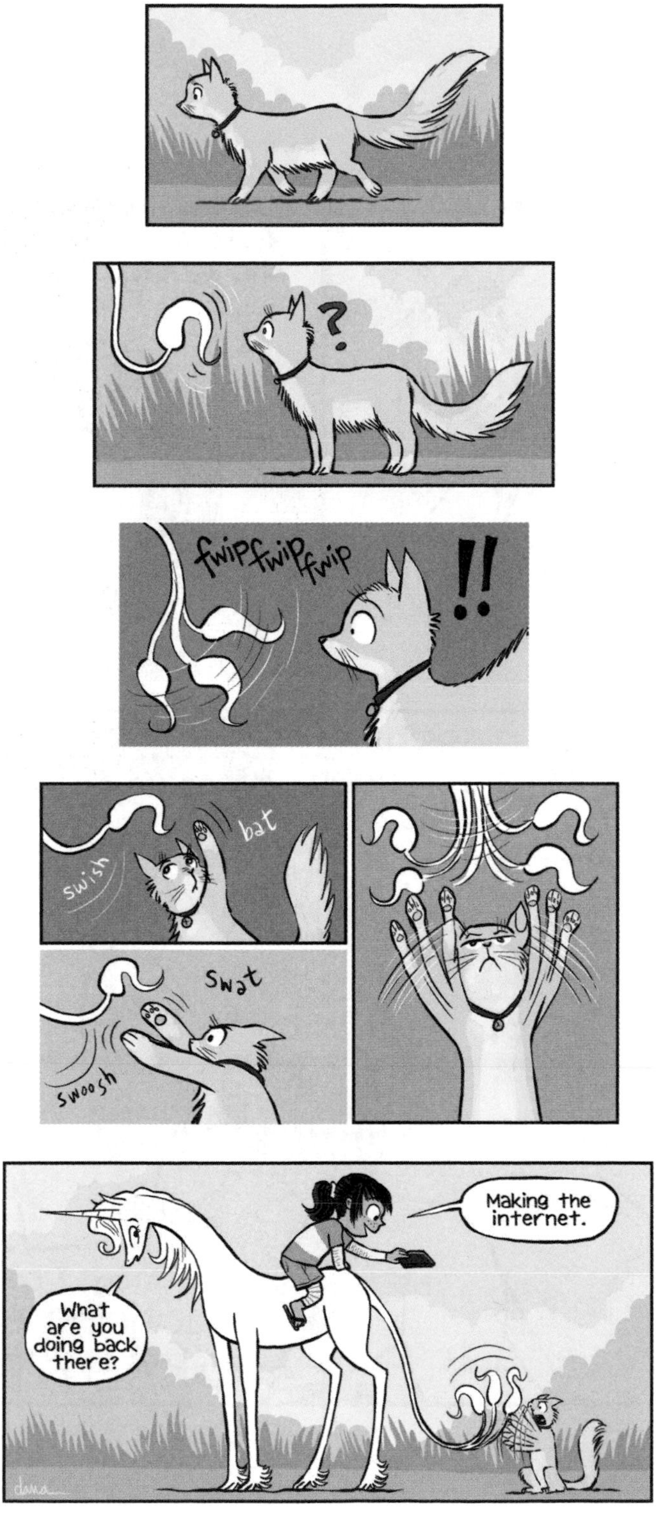
?
fwipfwipfwip
!!
bat
swish
swat
swoosh
Making the internet.
What are you doing back there?
dana

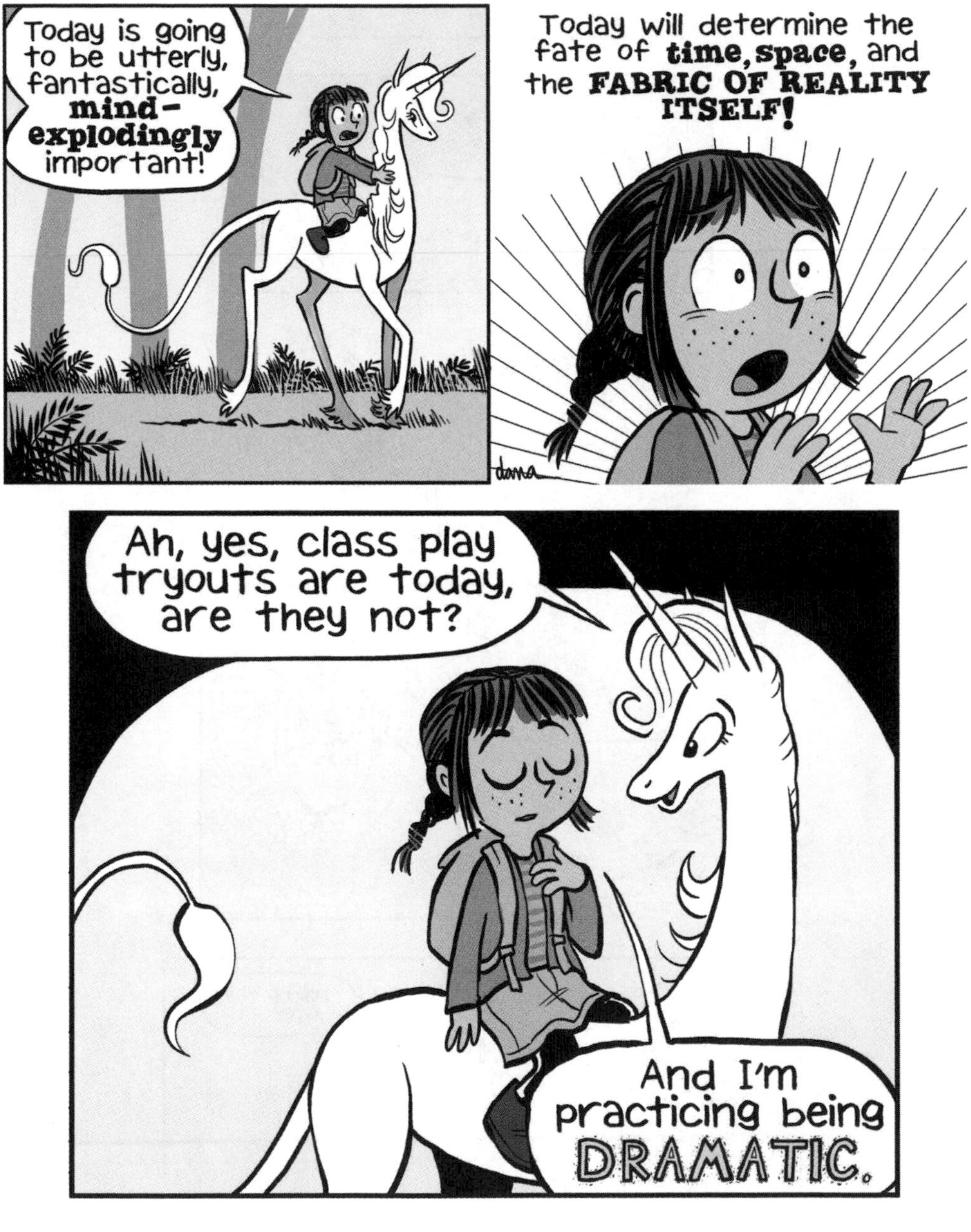
Today is going to be utterly, fantastically, **mind-explodingly** important!
Today will determine the fate of **time, space,** and the **FABRIC OF REALITY ITSELF!**
dana
Ah, yes, class play tryouts are today, are they not?
And I'm practicing being DRAMATIC.

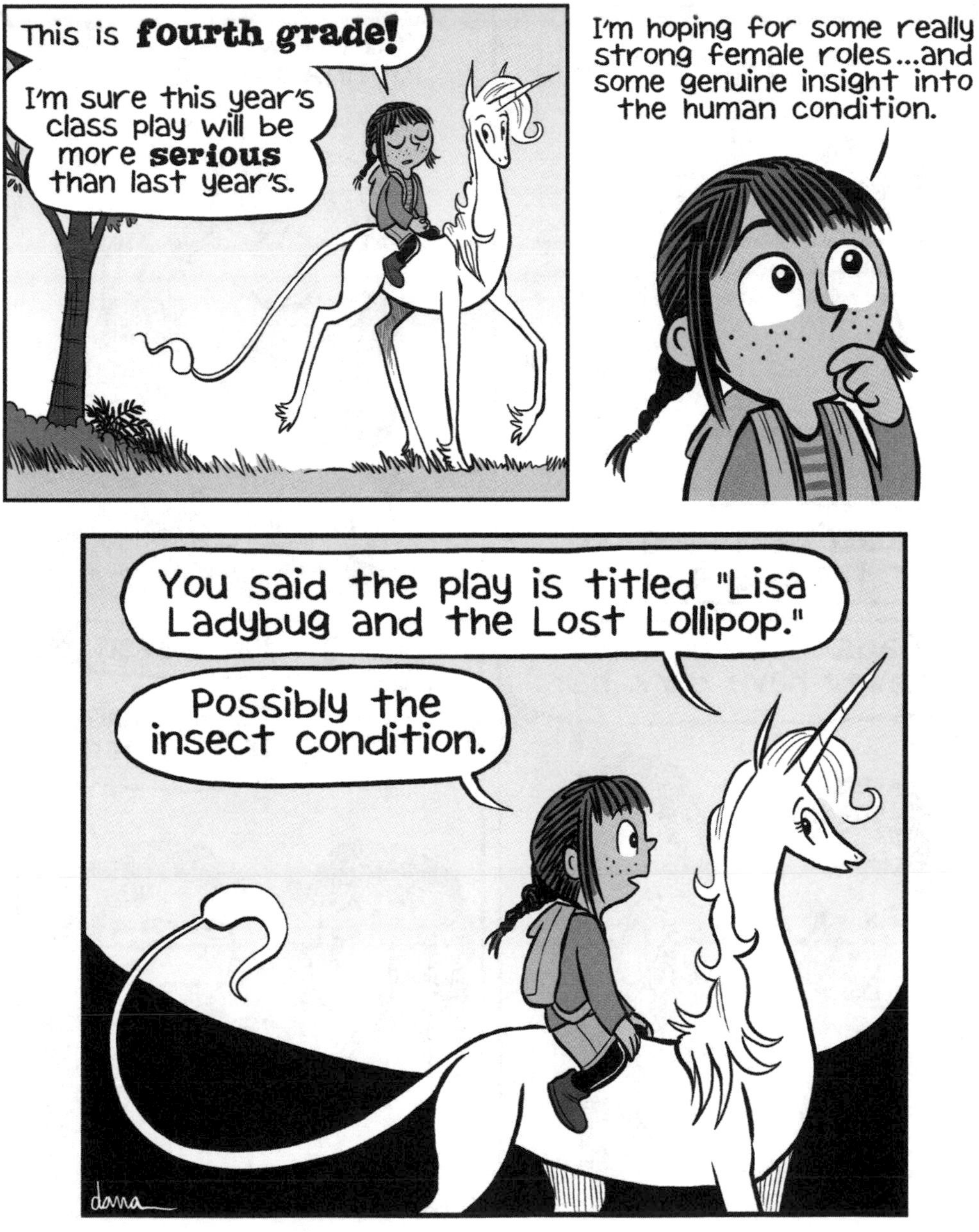
This is **fourth grade!**
I'm sure this year's class play will be more **serious** than last year's.
I'm hoping for some really strong female roles...and some genuine insight into the human condition.
You said the play is titled "Lisa Ladybug and the Lost Lollipop."
Possibly the insect condition.
dana

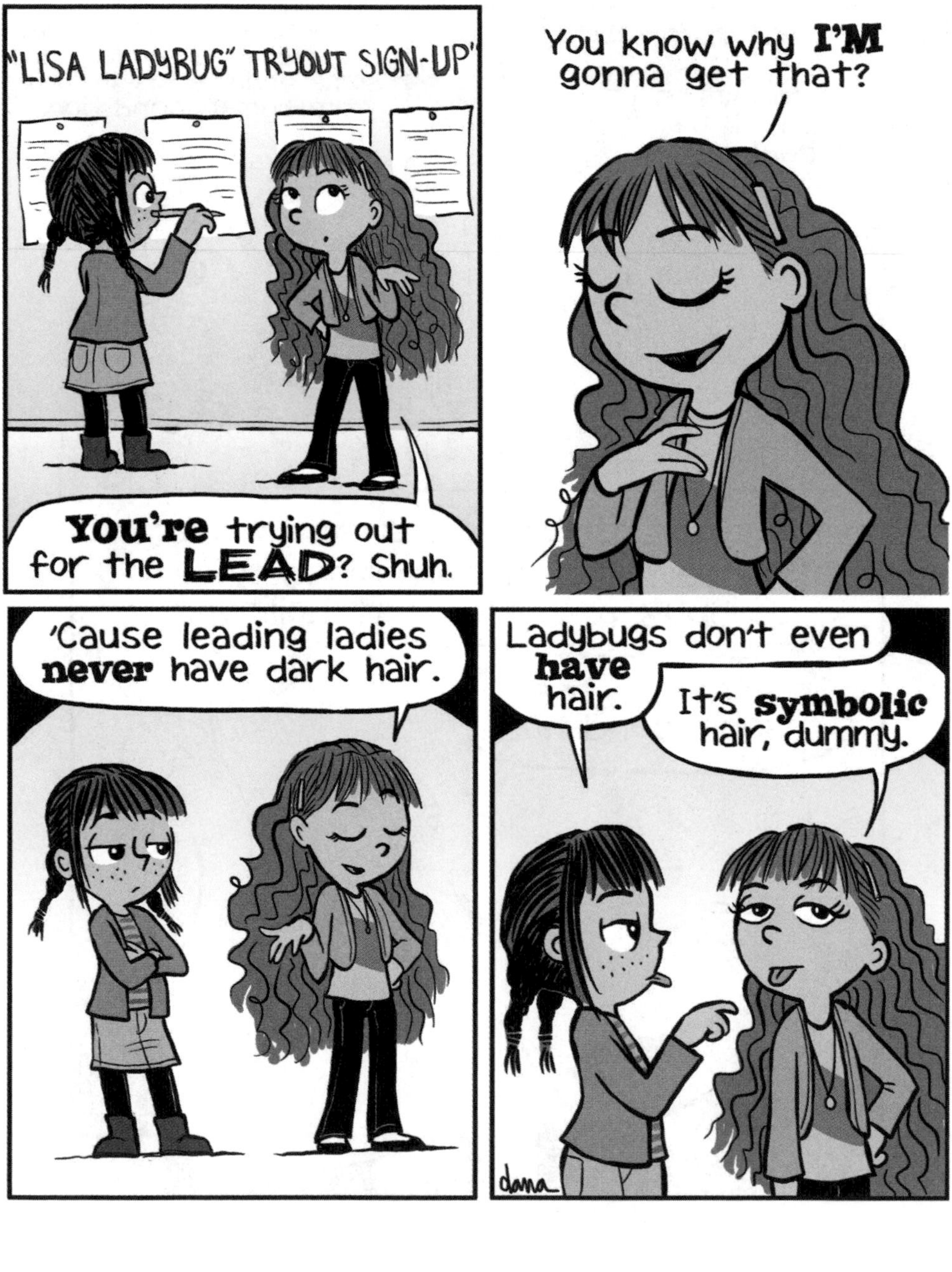
"LISA LADYBUG" TRYOUT SIGN-UP"
You're trying out for the **LEAD**? Shuh.
You know why **I'M** gonna get that?
'Cause leading ladies **never** have dark hair.
Ladybugs don't even **have** hair.
It's **symbolic** hair, dummy.
dana

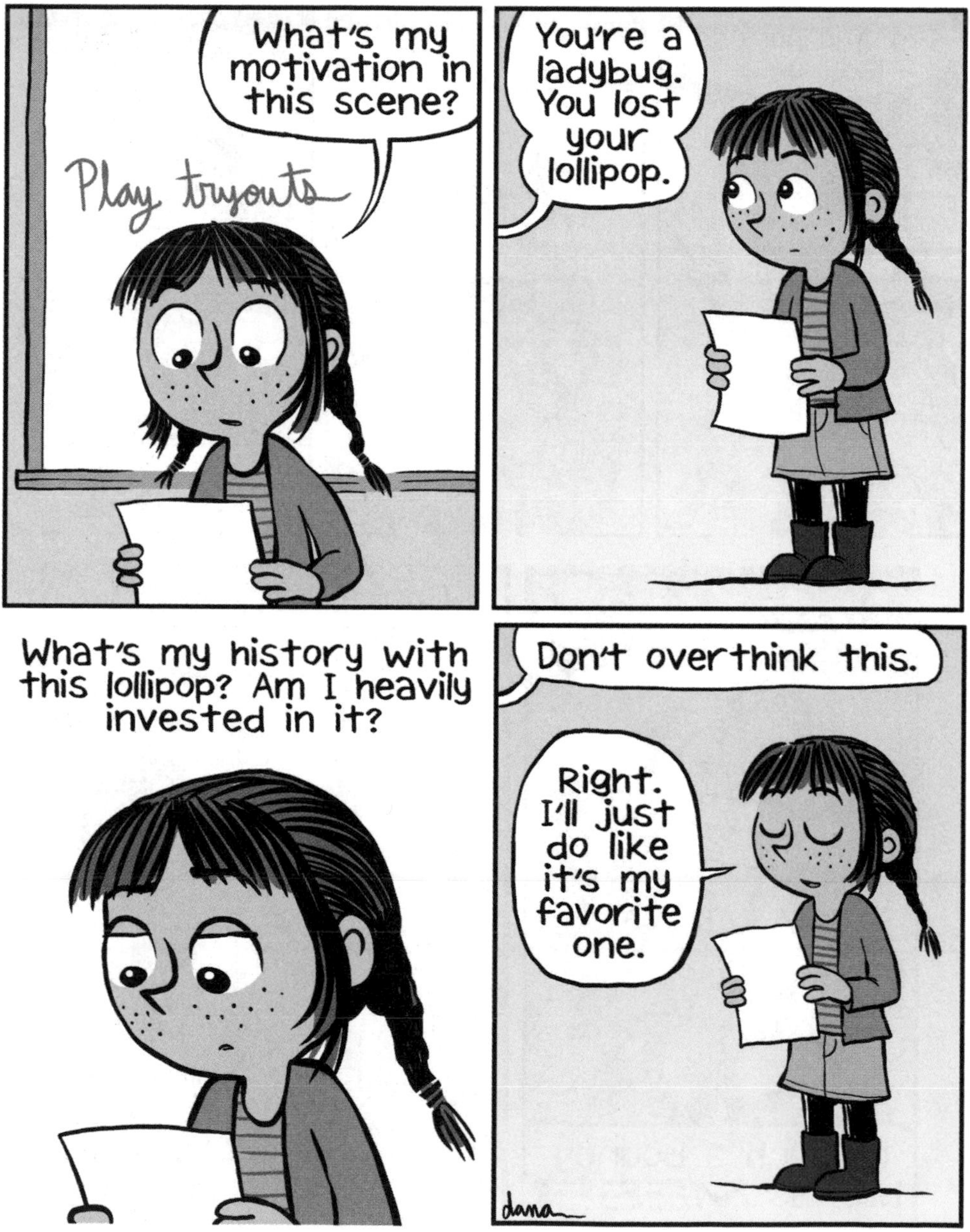
Play tryouts
What's my motivation in this scene?
You're a ladybug. You lost your lollipop.
What's my history with this lollipop? Am I heavily invested in it?
Don't overthink this.
Right. I'll just do like it's my favorite one.
dana

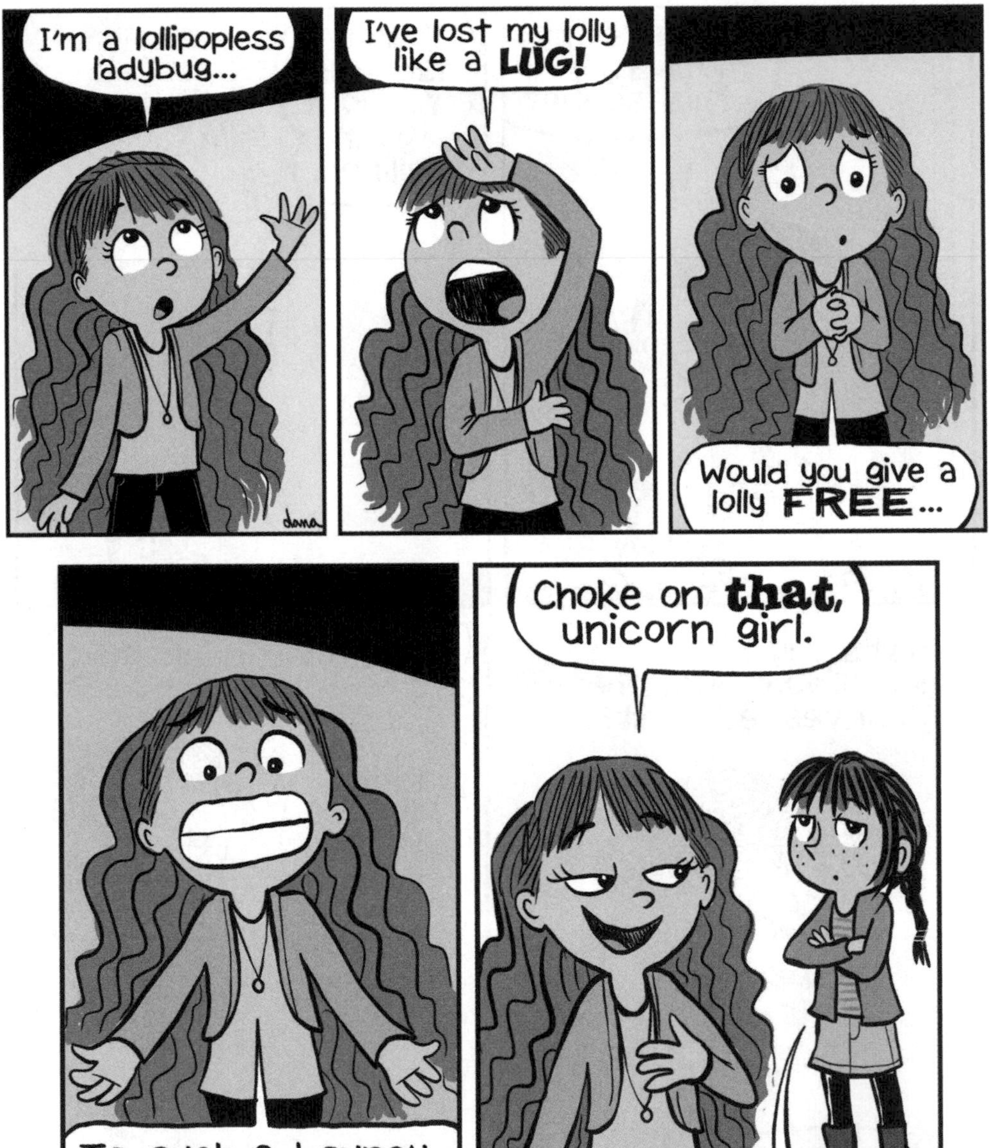

I'm a lollipopless ladybug...
I've lost my lolly like a LUG!
Would you give a lolly FREE...
To such a bouncy bug as MEEE?
Choke on that, unicorn girl.
On what, the scenery?

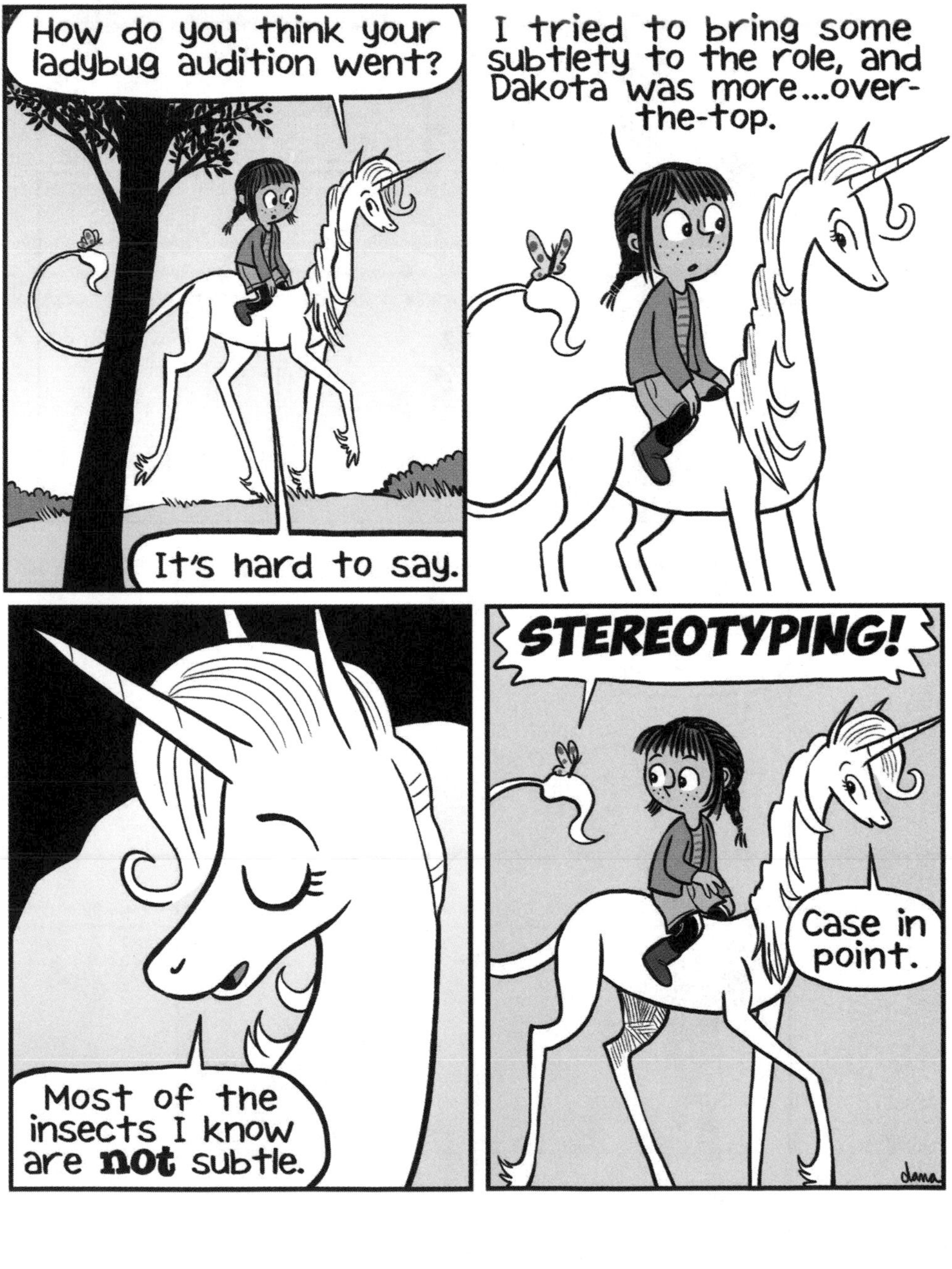
How do you think your ladybug audition went?
It's hard to say.
I tried to bring some subtlety to the role, and Dakota was more...over-the-top.
Most of the insects I know are **not** subtle.
STEREOTYPING!
Case in point.
dana

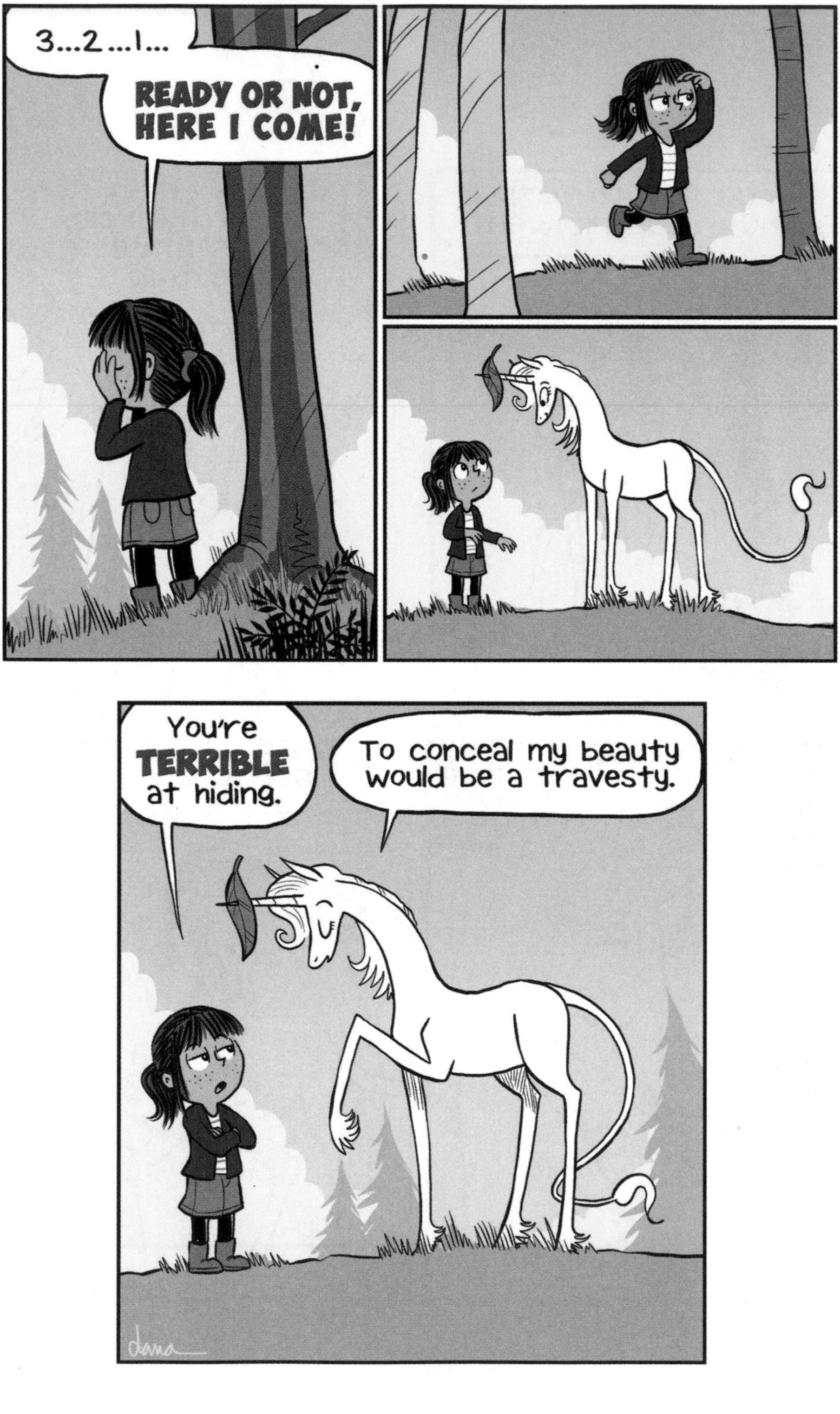
3...2...1...
READY OR NOT, HERE I COME!
You're TERRIBLE at hiding.
To conceal my beauty would be a travesty.
dana

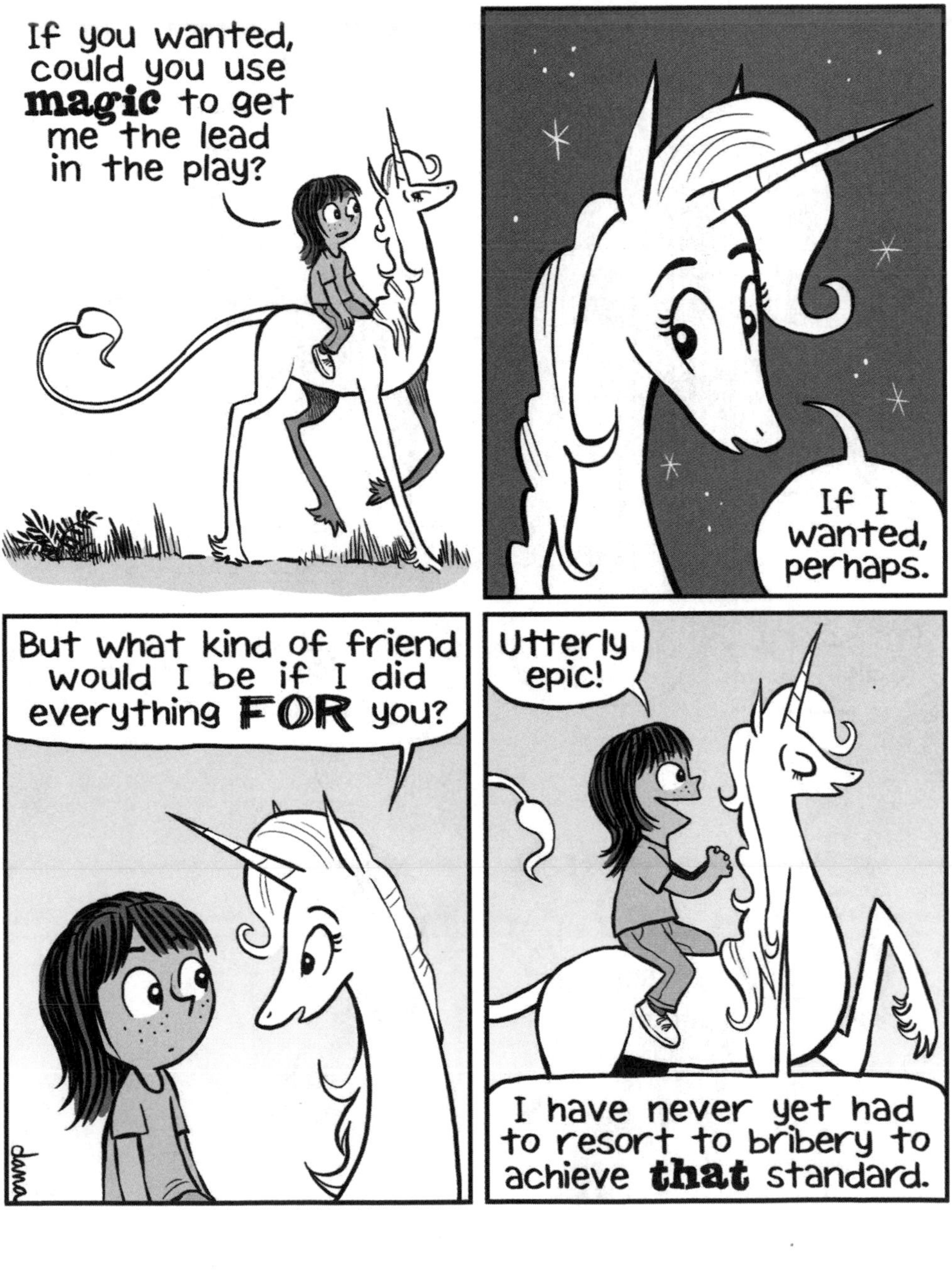
If you wanted, could you use **magic** to get me the lead in the play?
If I wanted, perhaps.
But what kind of friend would I be if I did everything **FOR** you?
Utterly epic!
I have never yet had to resort to bribery to achieve **that** standard.
dana

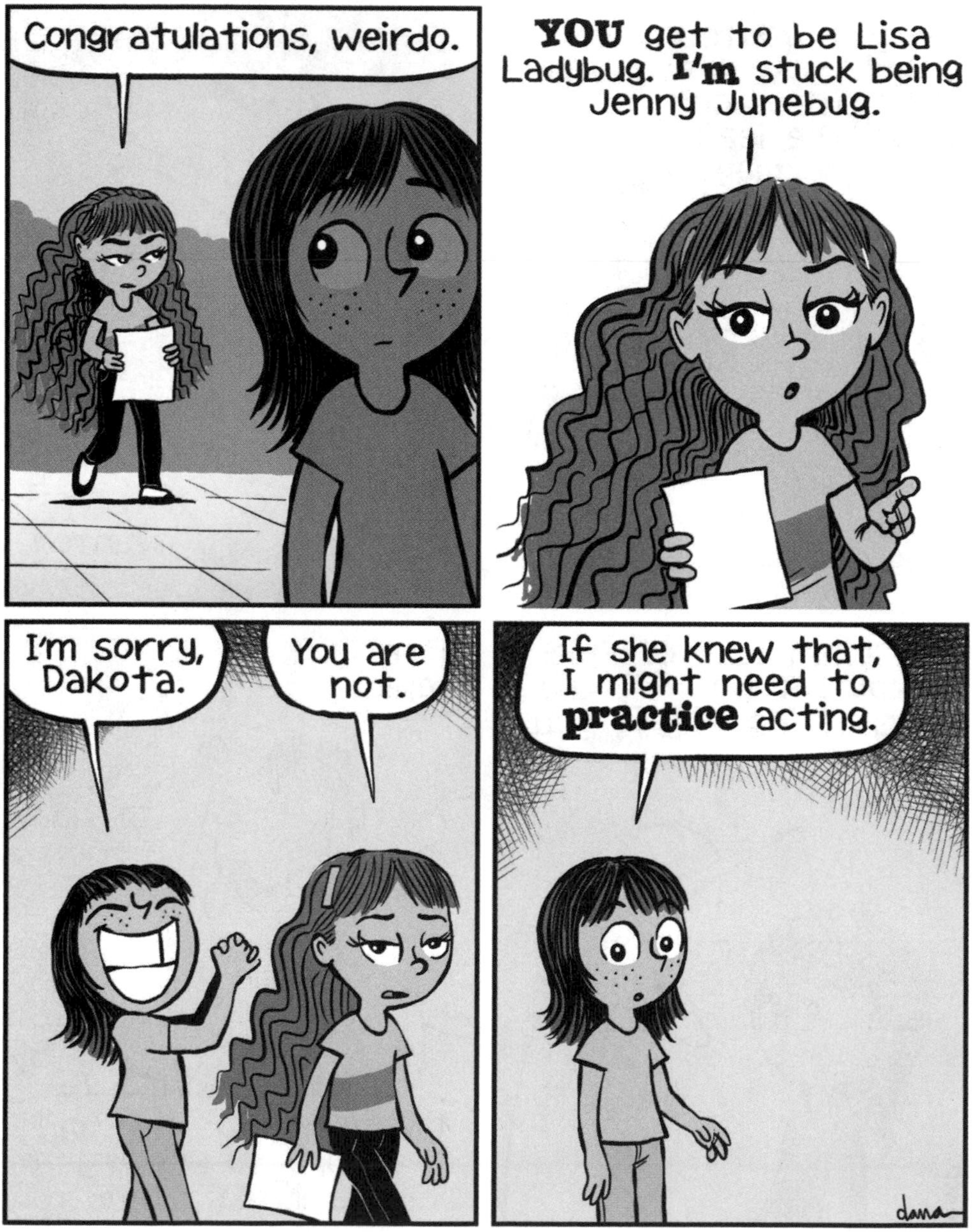
Congratulations, weirdo.
YOU get to be Lisa Ladybug. I'm stuck being Jenny Junebug.
I'm sorry, Dakota.
You are not.
If she knew that, I might need to practice acting.
dana

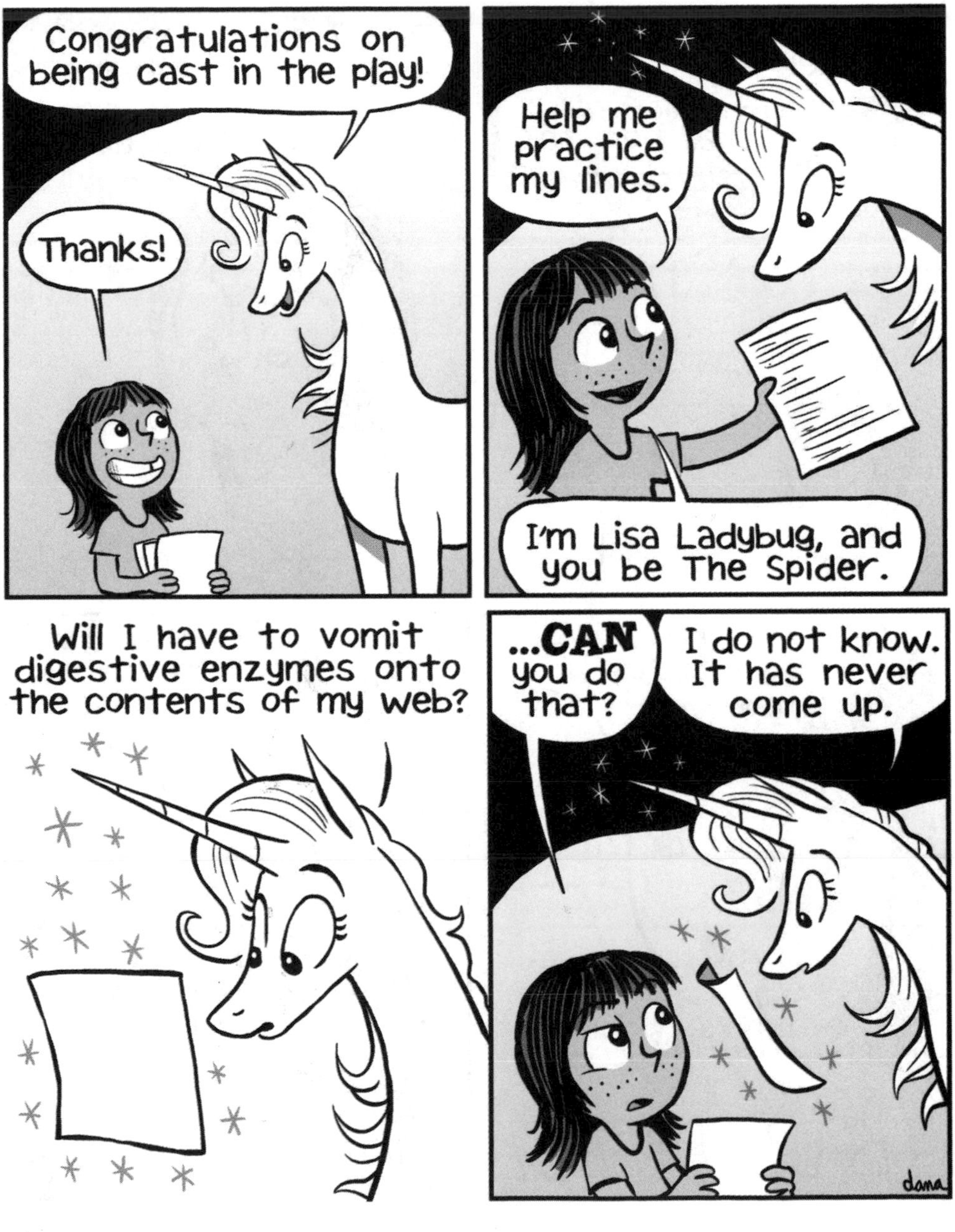
Congratulations on being cast in the play!
Thanks!
Help me practice my lines.
I'm Lisa Ladybug, and you be The Spider.
Will I have to vomit digestive enzymes onto the contents of my web?
...CAN you do that?
I do not know. It has never come up.
dana

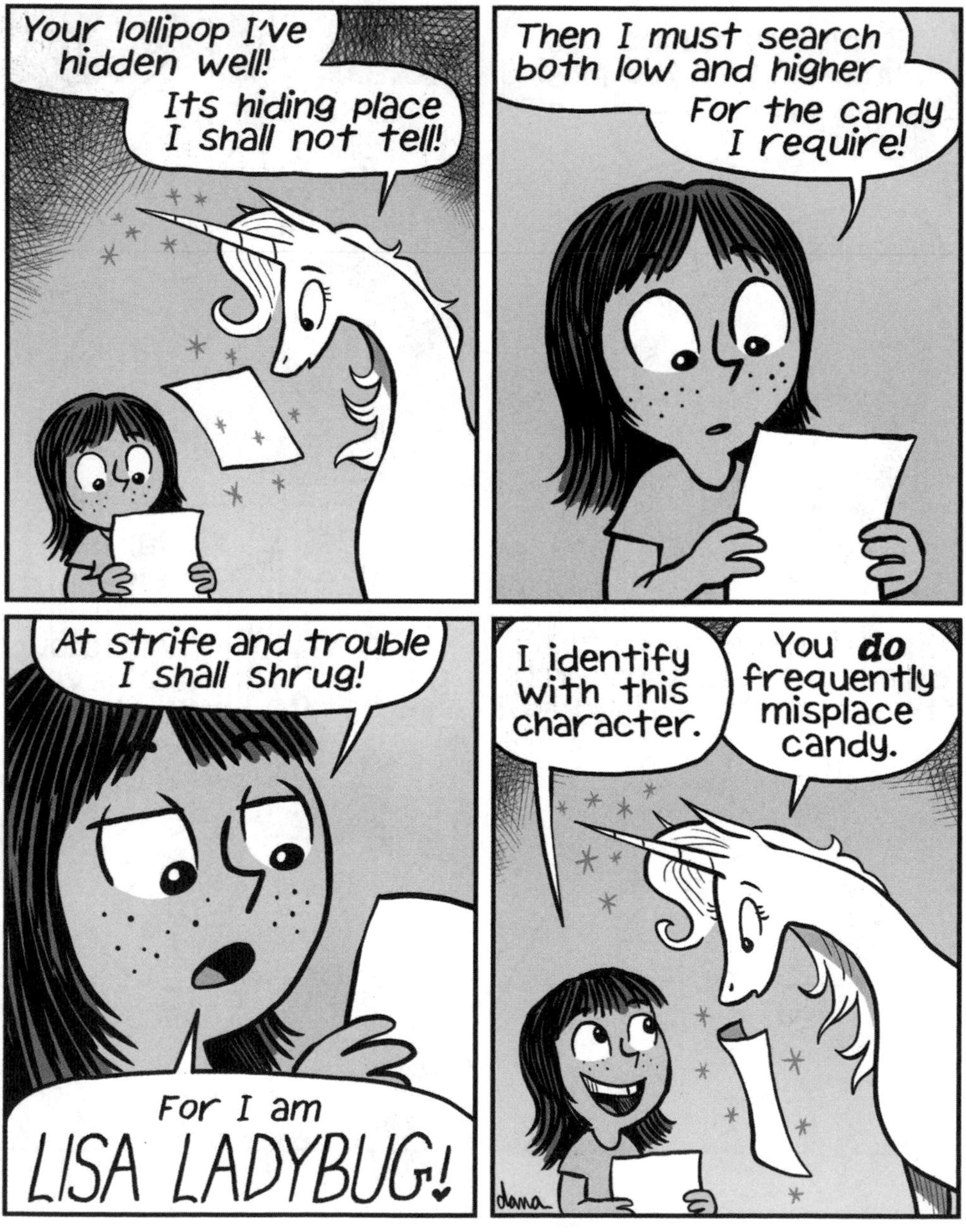
Your lollipop I've hidden well!
Its hiding place I shall not tell!
Then I must search both low and higher
For the candy I require!
At strife and trouble I shall shrug!
For I am LISA LADYBUG!
I identify with this character.
You **do** frequently misplace candy.
dana

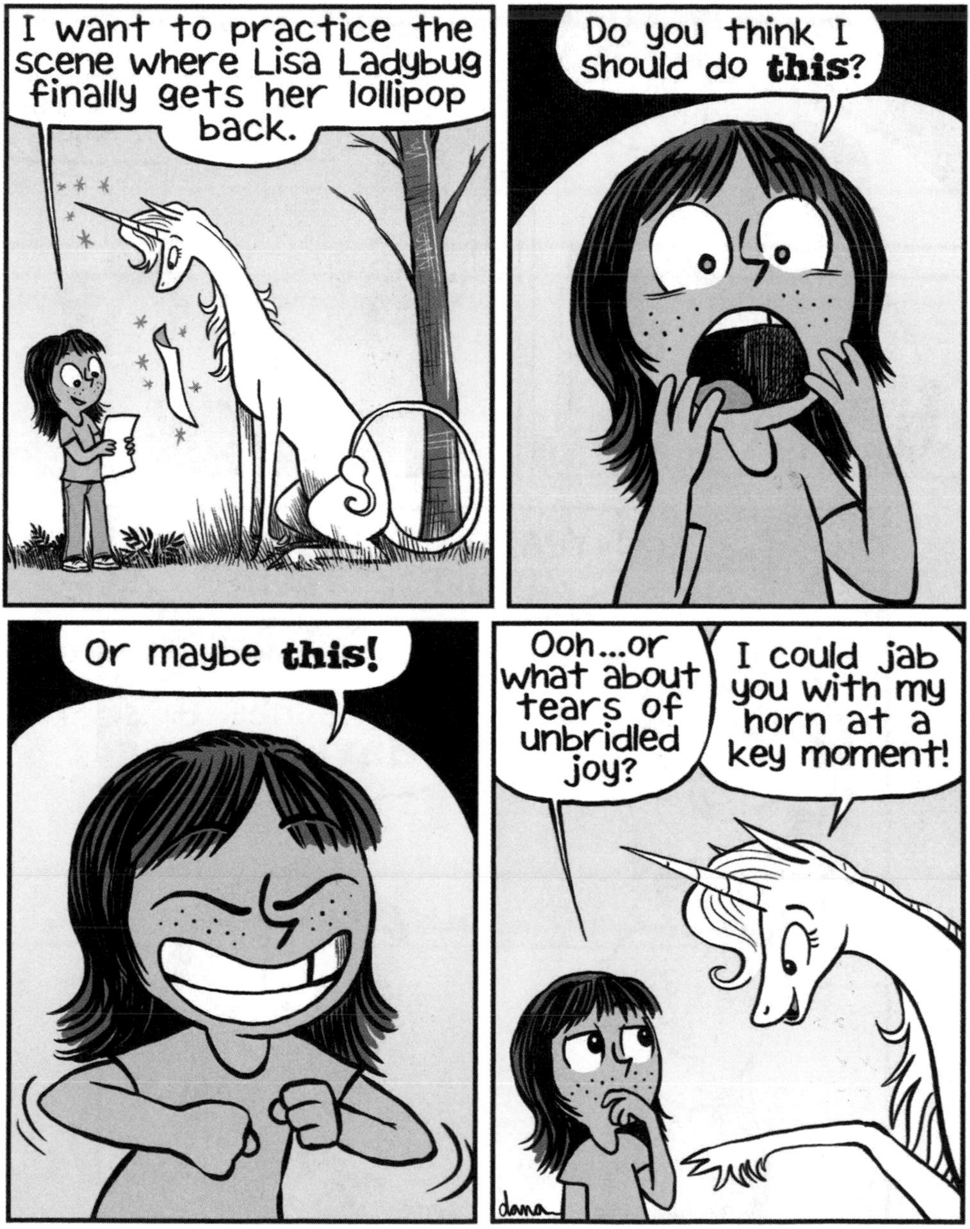
I want to practice the scene where Lisa Ladybug finally gets her lollipop back.
Do you think I should do **this**?
Or maybe **this**!
Ooh...or what about tears of unbridled joy?
I could jab you with my horn at a key moment!
dana

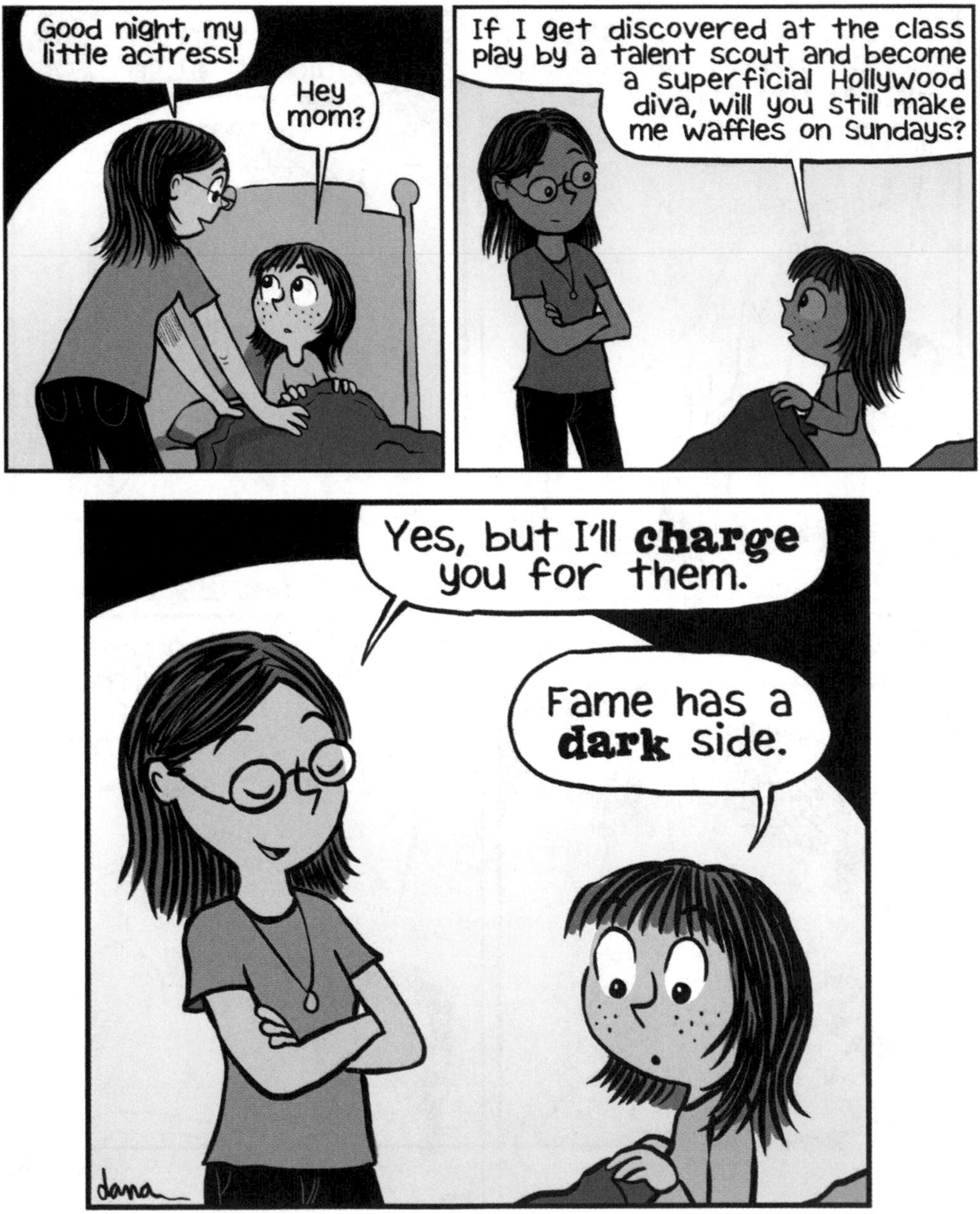
Good night, my little actress!
Hey mom?
If I get discovered at the class play by a talent scout and become a superficial Hollywood diva, will you still make me waffles on Sundays?
Yes, but I'll **charge** you for them.
Fame has a **dark** side.
dana

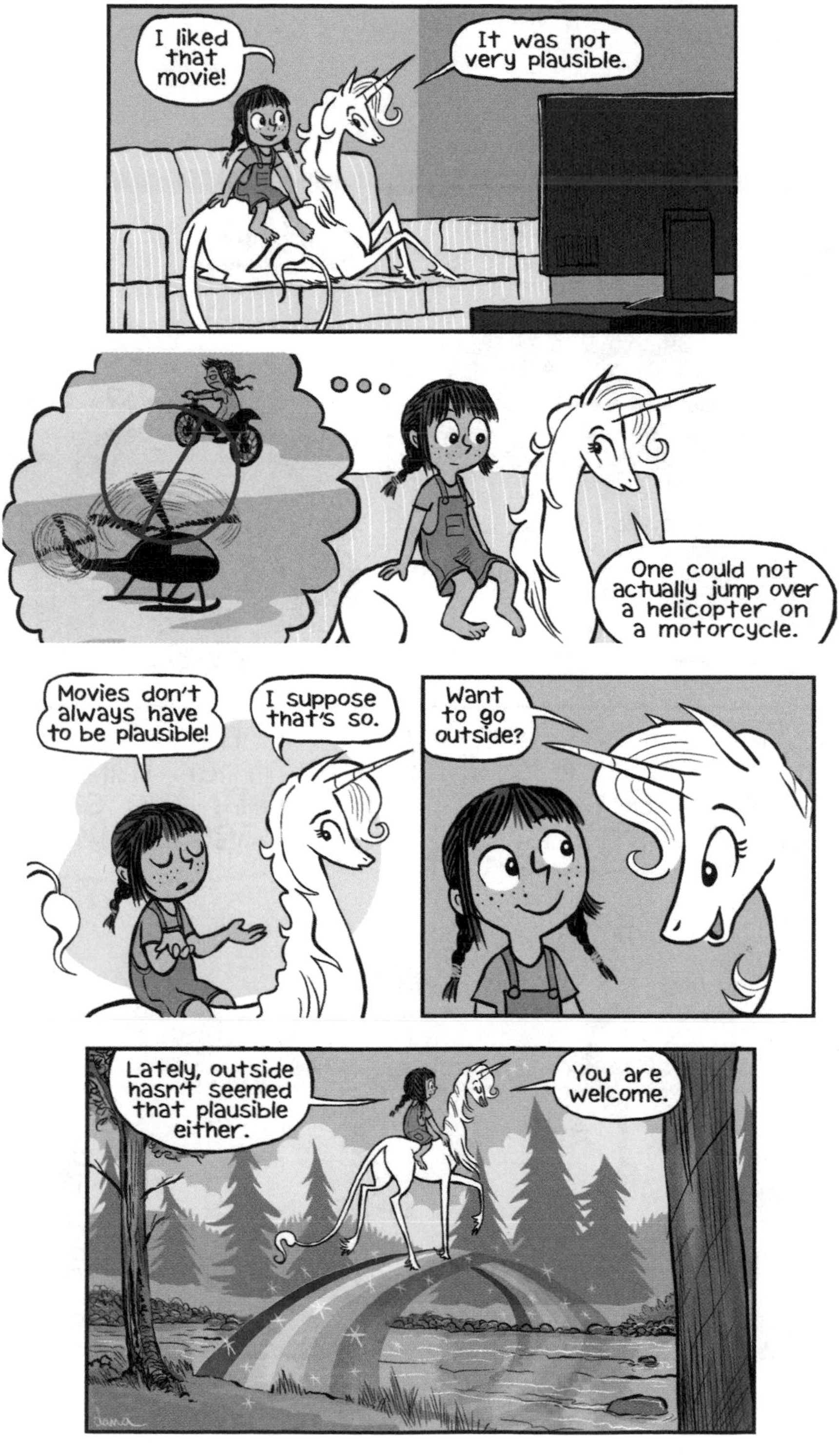
I liked that movie!
It was not very plausible.
One could not actually jump over a helicopter on a motorcycle.
Movies don't always have to be plausible!
I suppose that's so.
Want to go outside?
Lately, outside hasn't seemed that plausible either.
You are welcome.

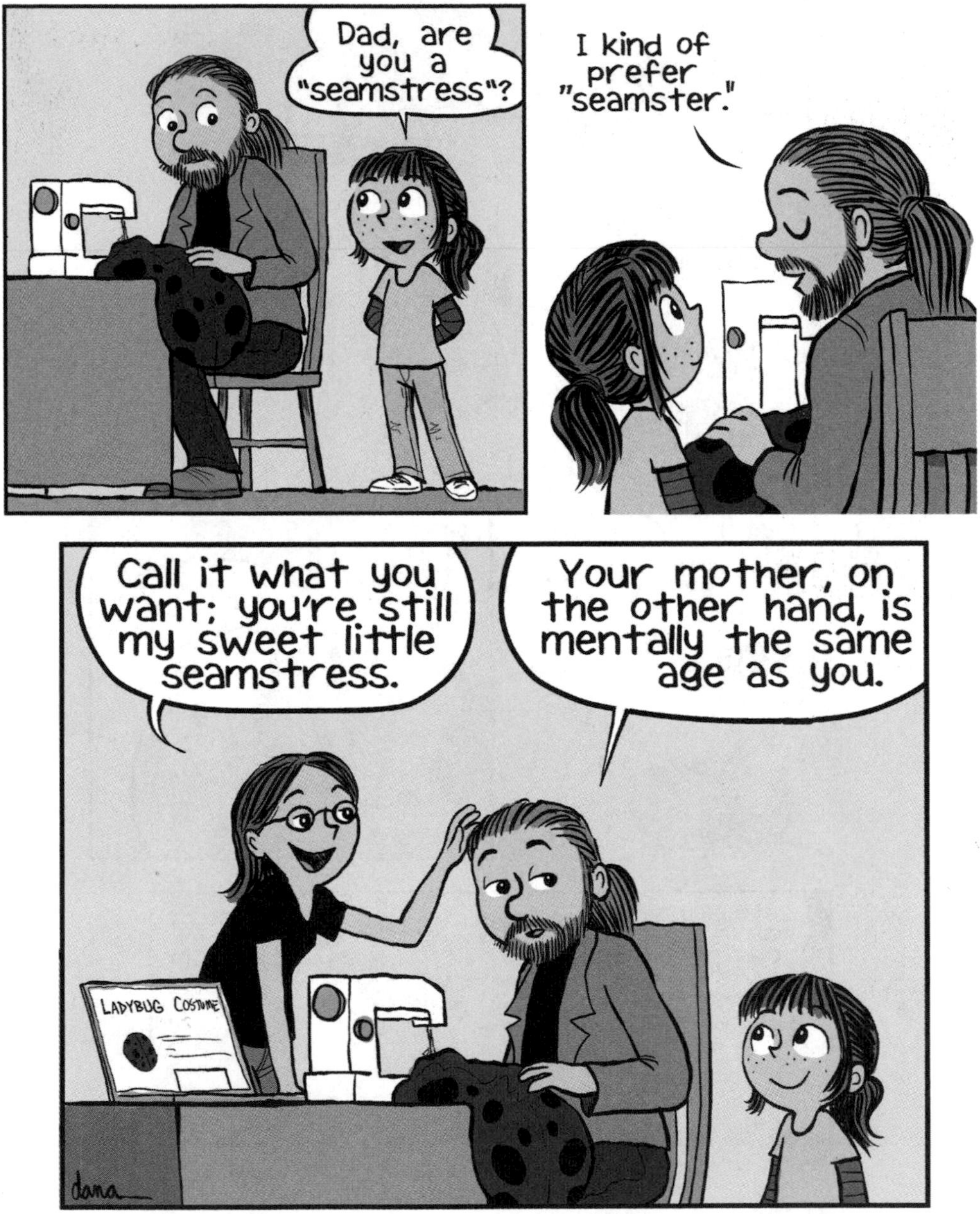
Dad, are you a "seamstress"?
I kind of prefer "seamster."
Call it what you want; you're still my sweet little seamstress.
Your mother, on the other hand, is mentally the same age as you.
LADYBUG COSTUME
dana

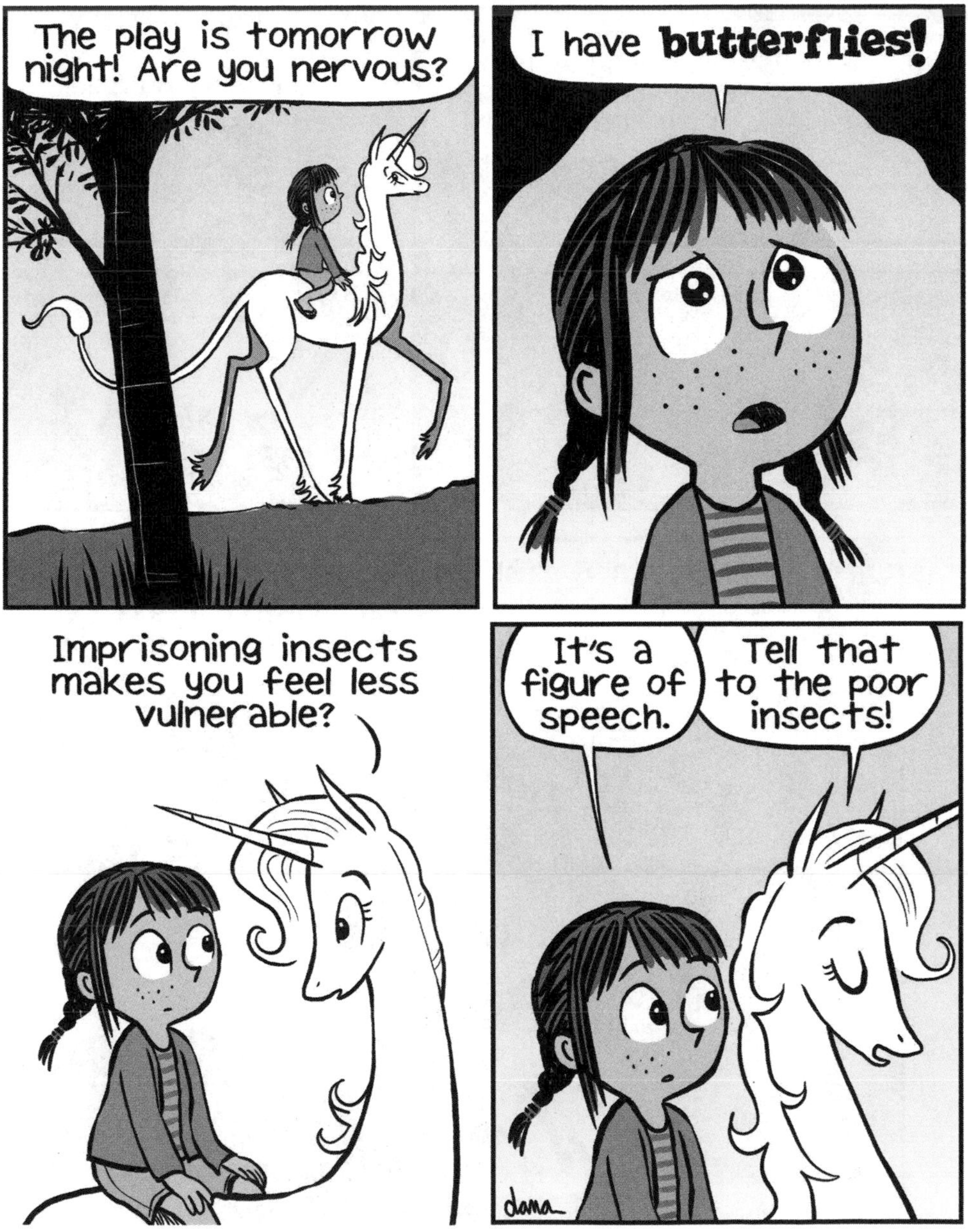
The play is tomorrow night! Are you nervous?
I have butterflies!
Imprisoning insects makes you feel less vulnerable?
It's a figure of speech.
Tell that to the poor insects!
dana

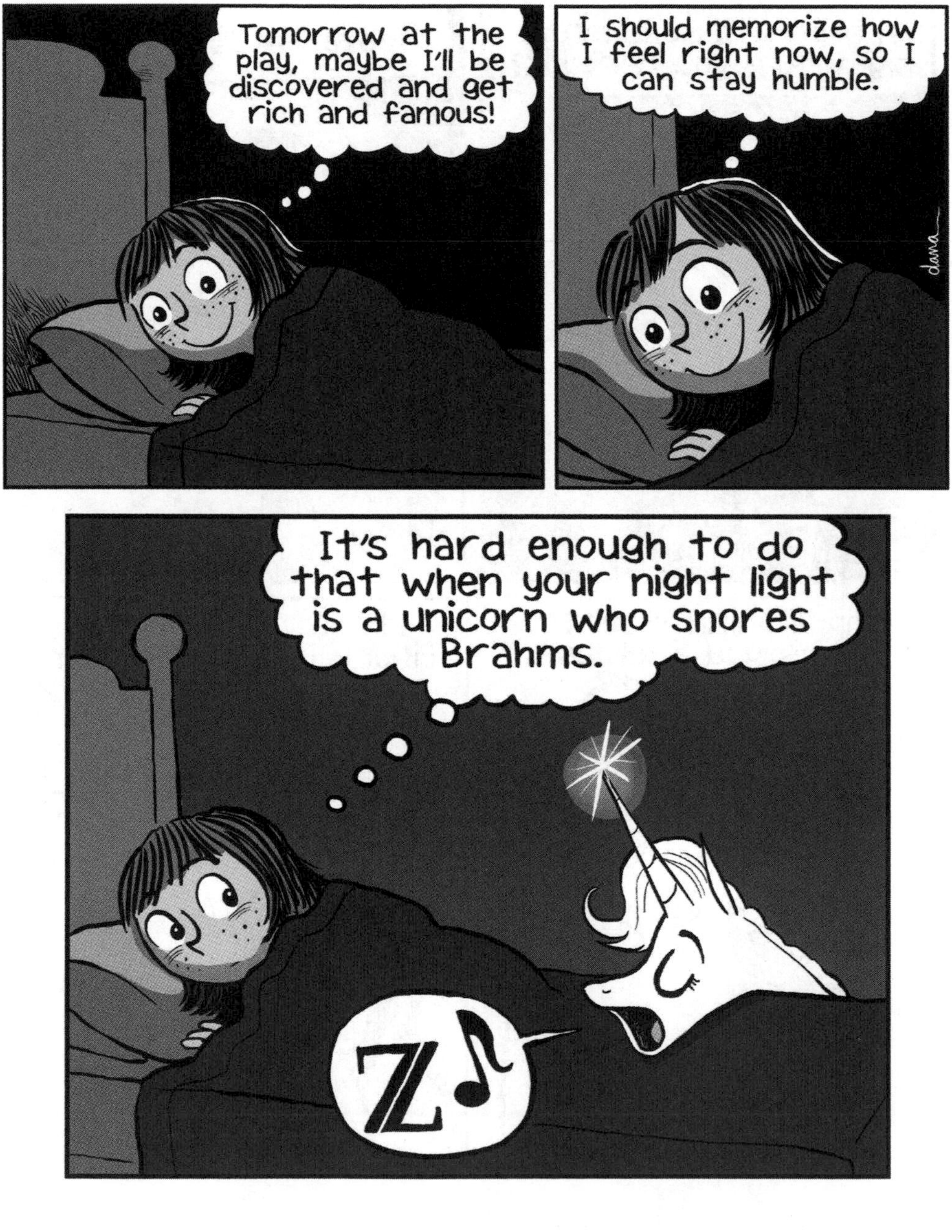
Tomorrow at the play, maybe I'll be discovered and get rich and famous!
I should memorize how I feel right now, so I can stay humble.
dana
It's hard enough to do that when your night light is a unicorn who snores Brahms.
Z

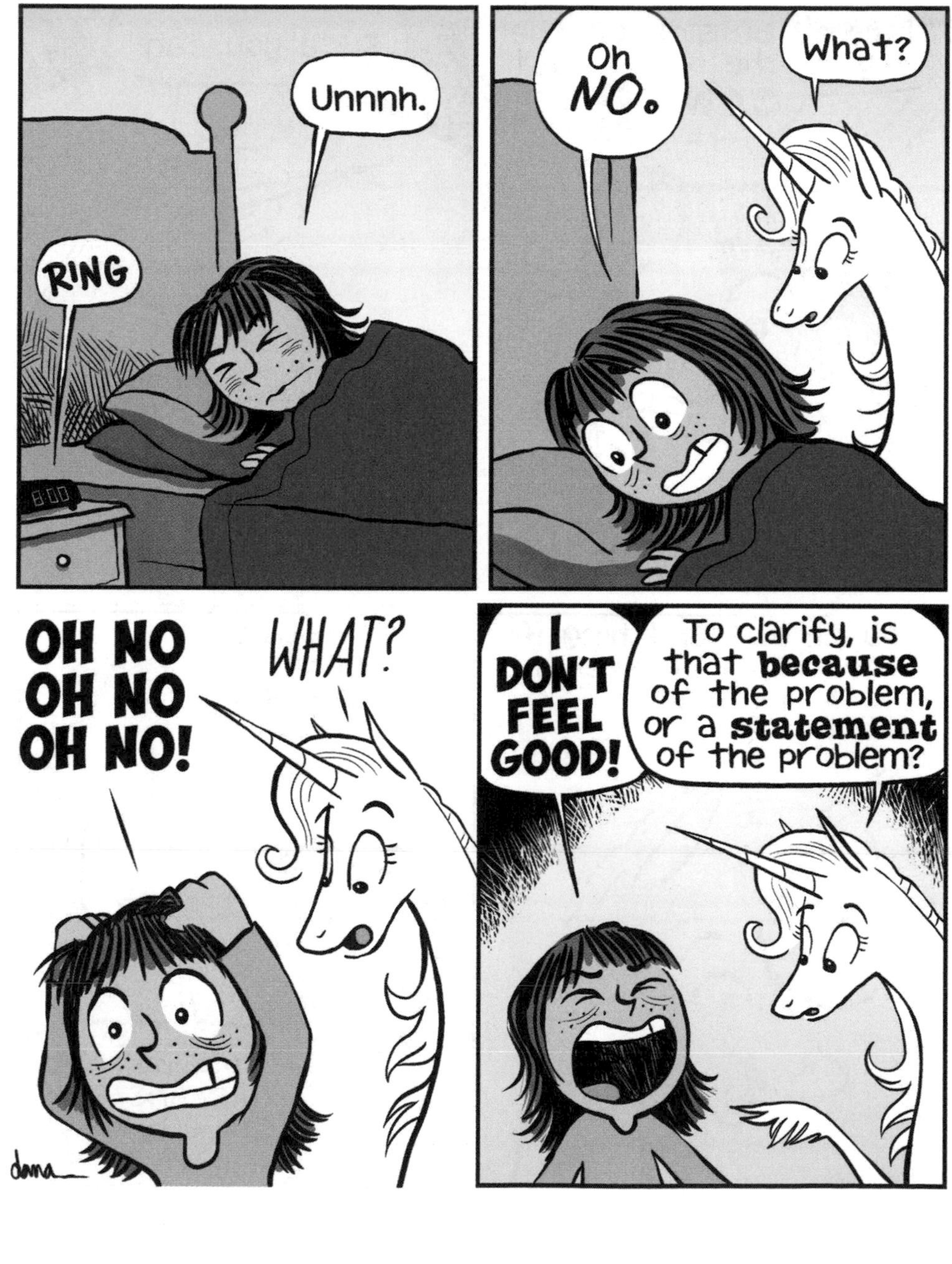
RING
Unnnh.
Oh NO.
What?
OH NO OH NO OH NO!
WHAT?
I DON'T FEEL GOOD!
To clarify, is that **because** of the problem, or a **statement** of the problem?
dana

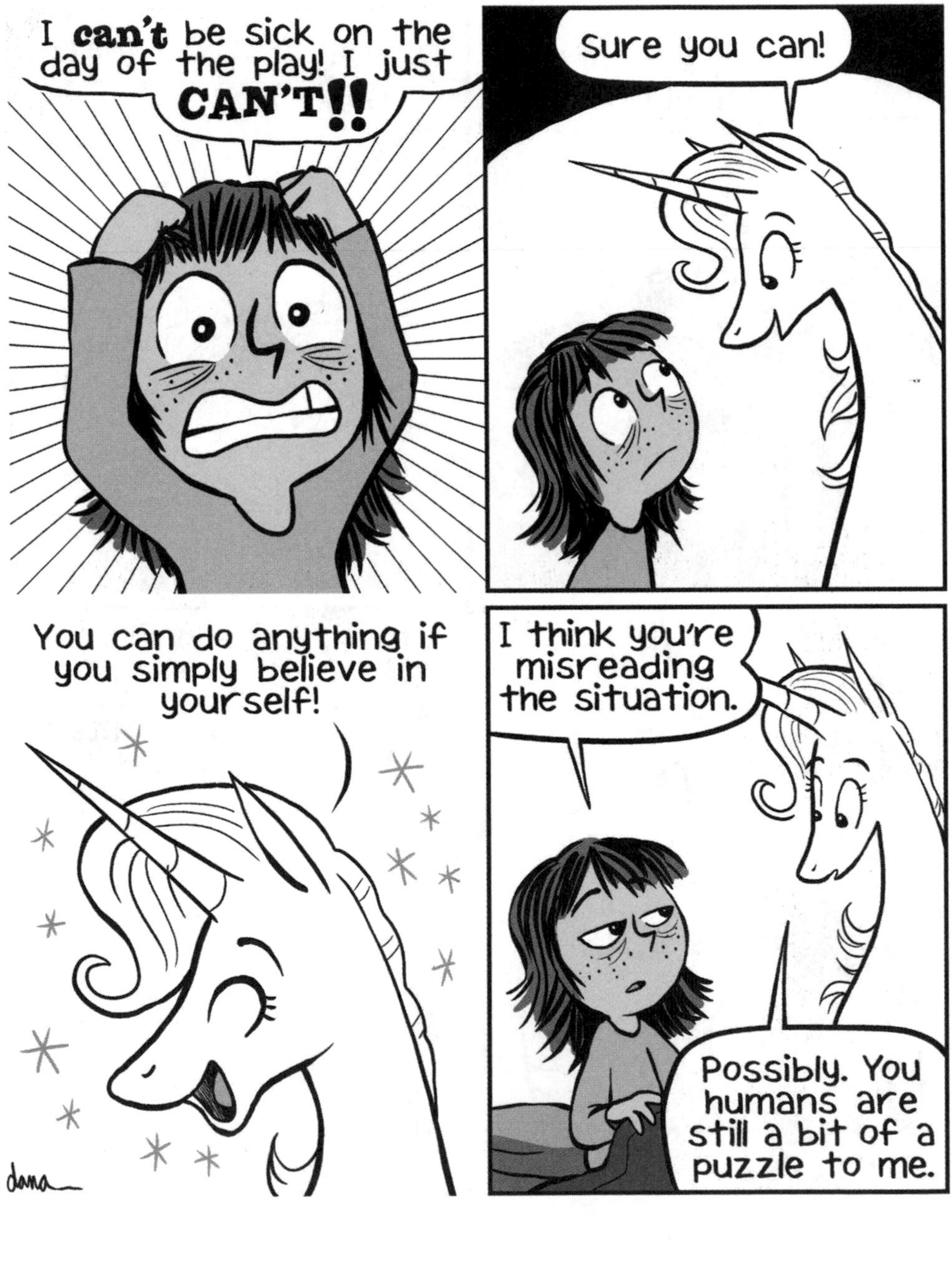
I can't be sick on the day of the play! I just CAN'T!!
Sure you can!
You can do anything if you simply believe in yourself!
I think you're misreading the situation.
Possibly. You humans are still a bit of a puzzle to me.
dana

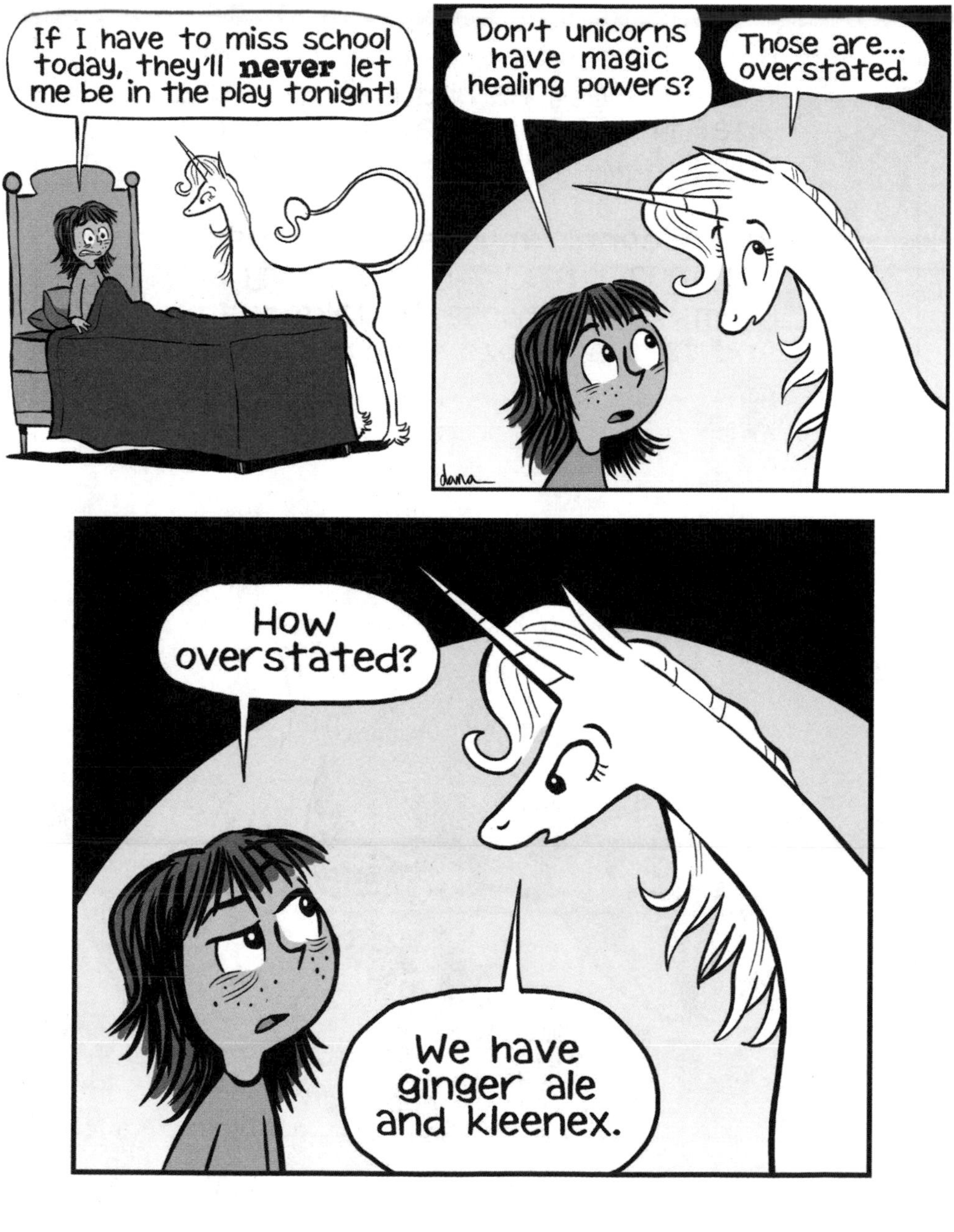

If I have to miss school today, they'll **never** let me be in the play tonight!
Don't unicorns have magic healing powers?
Those are... overstated.
dana
How overstated?
We have ginger ale and kleenex.

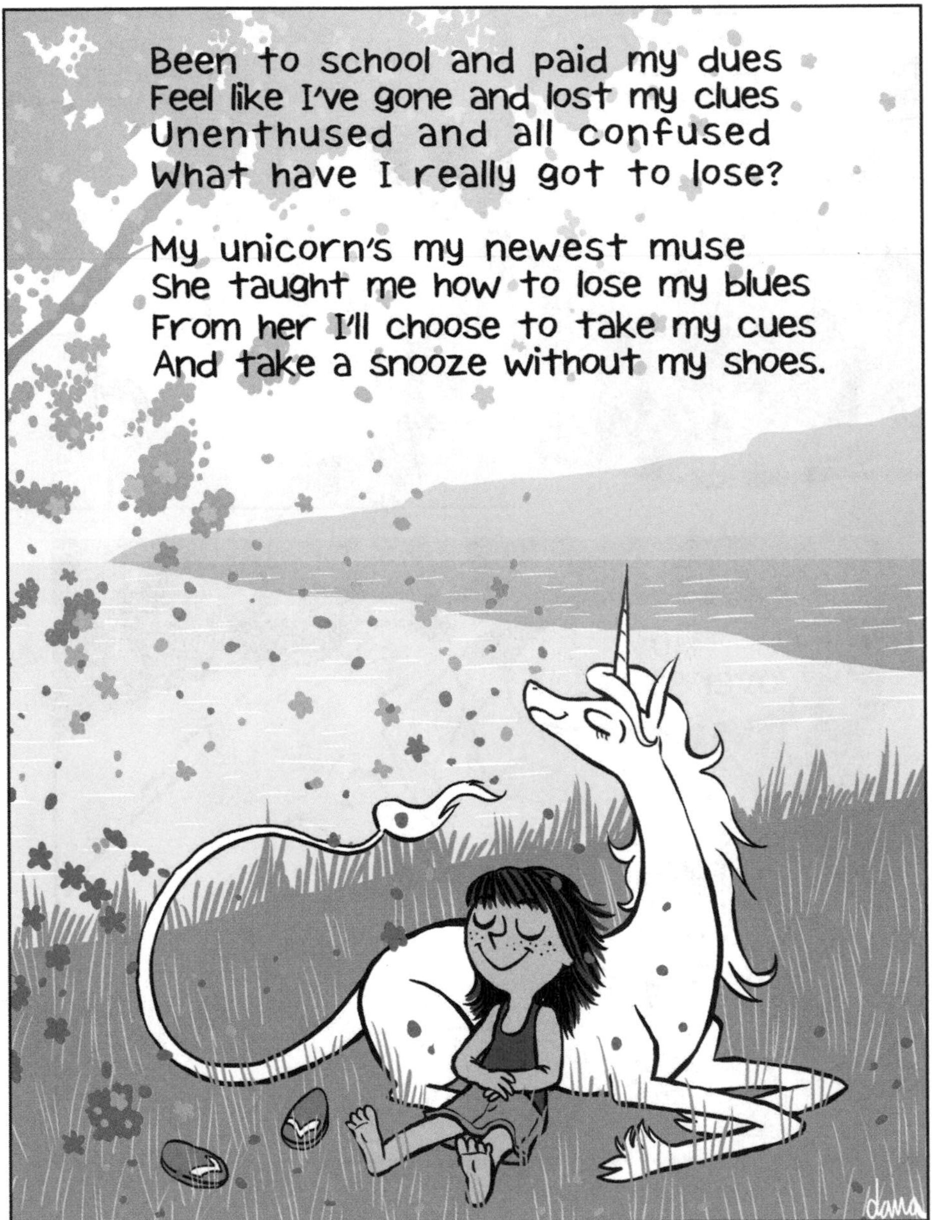
Been to school and paid my dues
Feel like I've gone and lost my clues
Unenthused and all confused
What have I really got to lose?

My unicorn's my newest muse
She taught me how to lose my blues
From her I'll choose to take my cues
And take a snooze without my shoes.
dana
with thanks to Ronnie Simonds

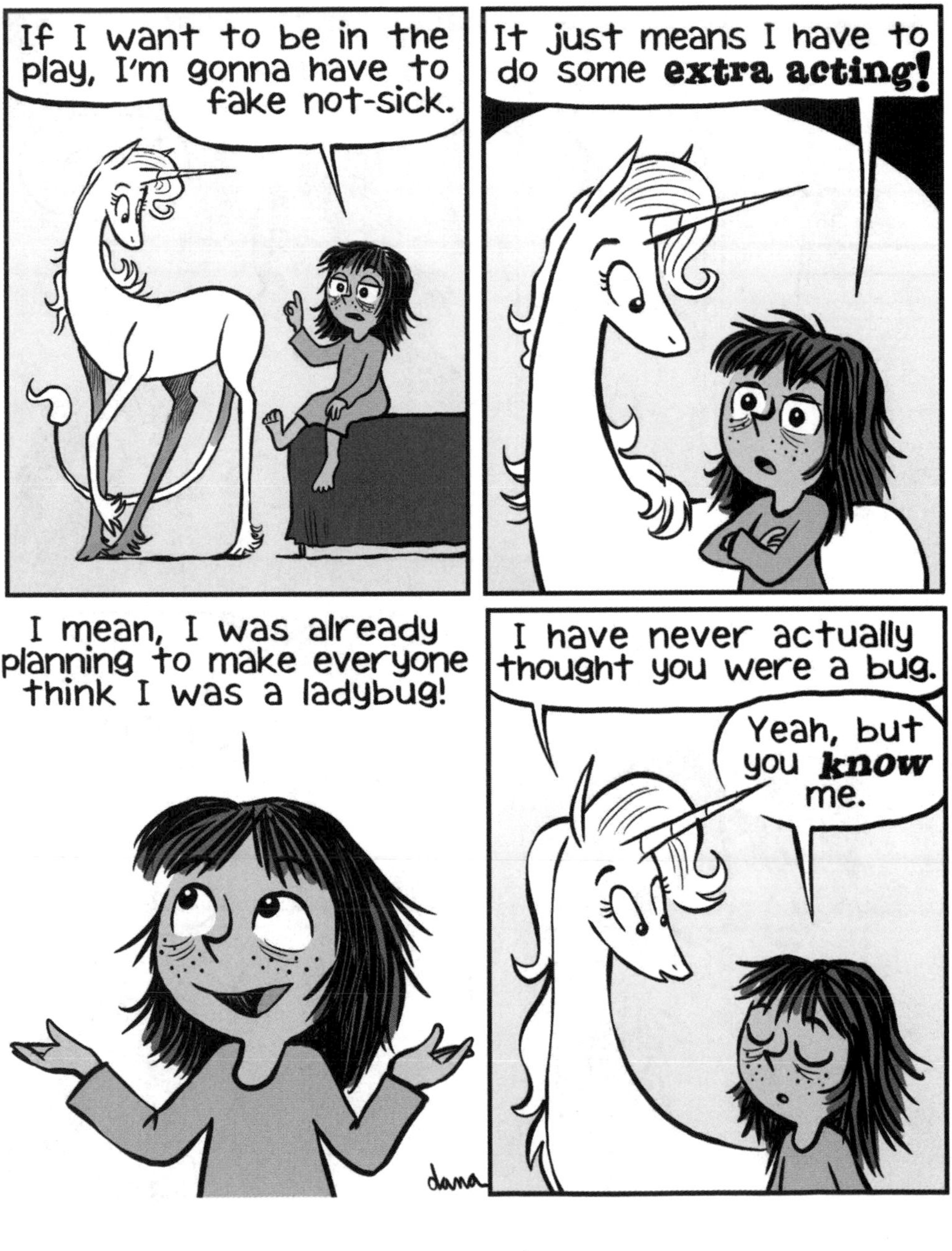
If I want to be in the play, I'm gonna have to fake not-sick.
It just means I have to do some **extra acting!**
I mean, I was already planning to make everyone think I was a ladybug!
I have never actually thought you were a bug.
Yeah, but you ***know*** me.
dana

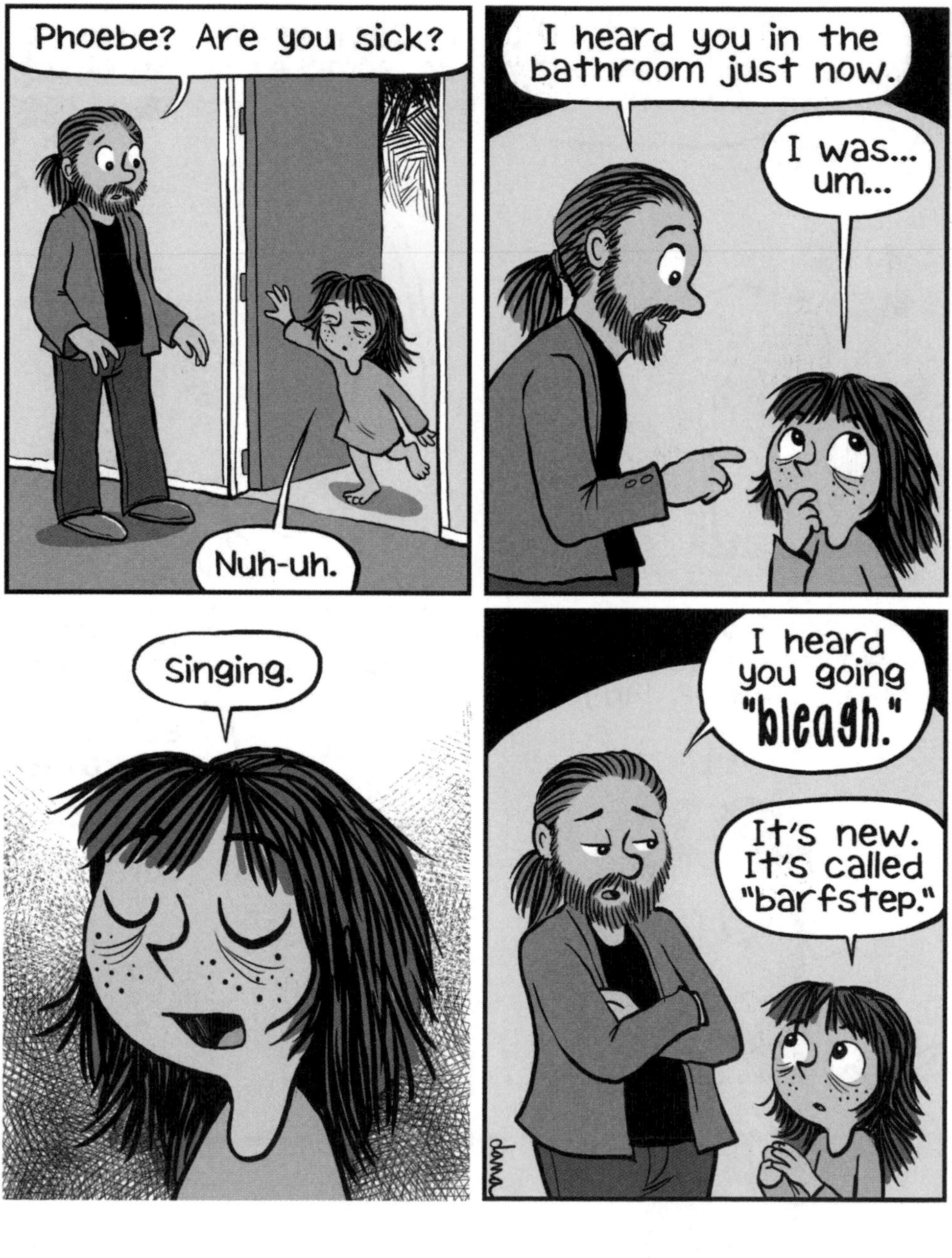
Phoebe? Are you sick?
Nuh-uh.
I heard you in the bathroom just now.
I was... um...
Singing.
I heard you going "bleagh."
It's new. It's called "barfstep."
dana

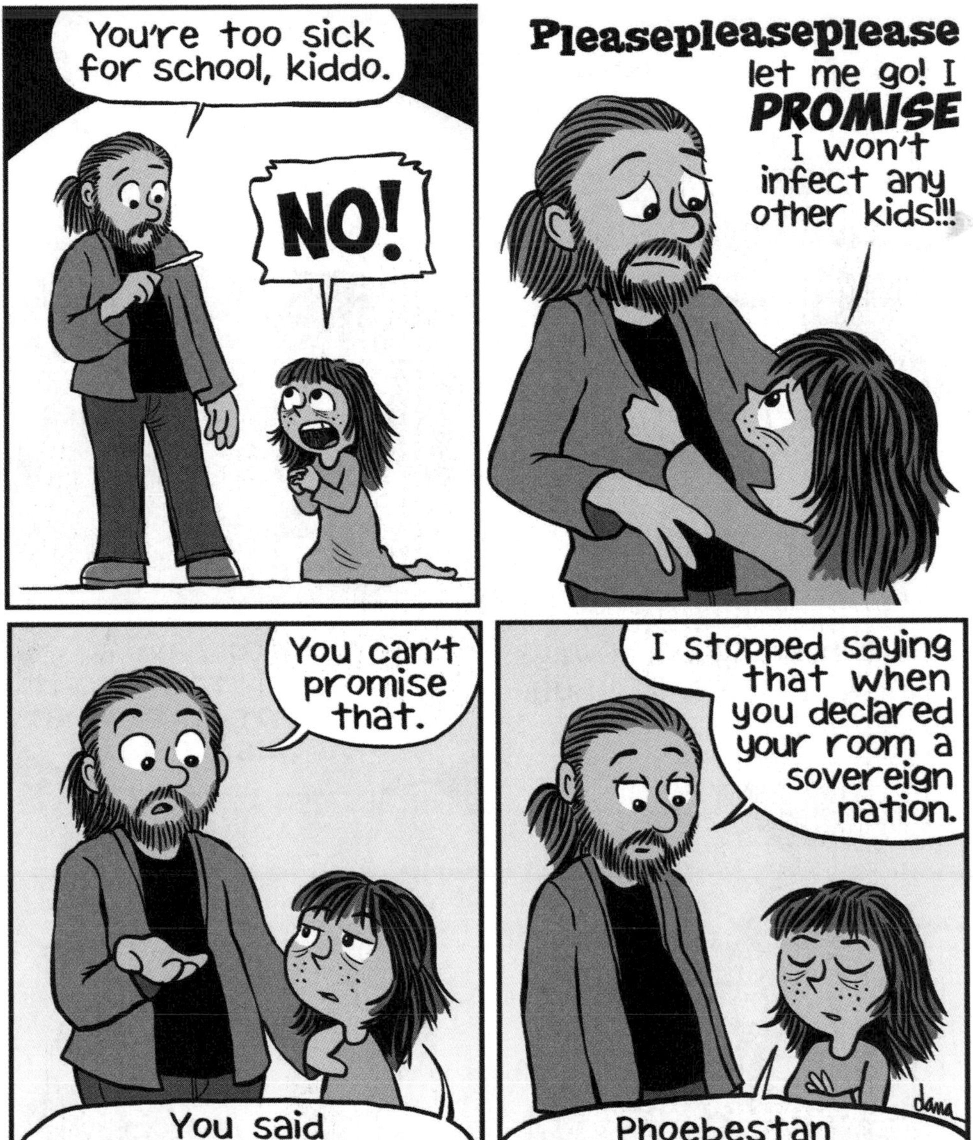
You're too sick for school, kiddo.
NO!
Pleasepleaseplease let me go! I **PROMISE** I won't infect any other kids!!!
You can't promise that.
You said I could do **anything** if I believe in myself.
I stopped saying that when you declared your room a sovereign nation.
Phoebestan still believes in freedom from room-cleaning.
dana

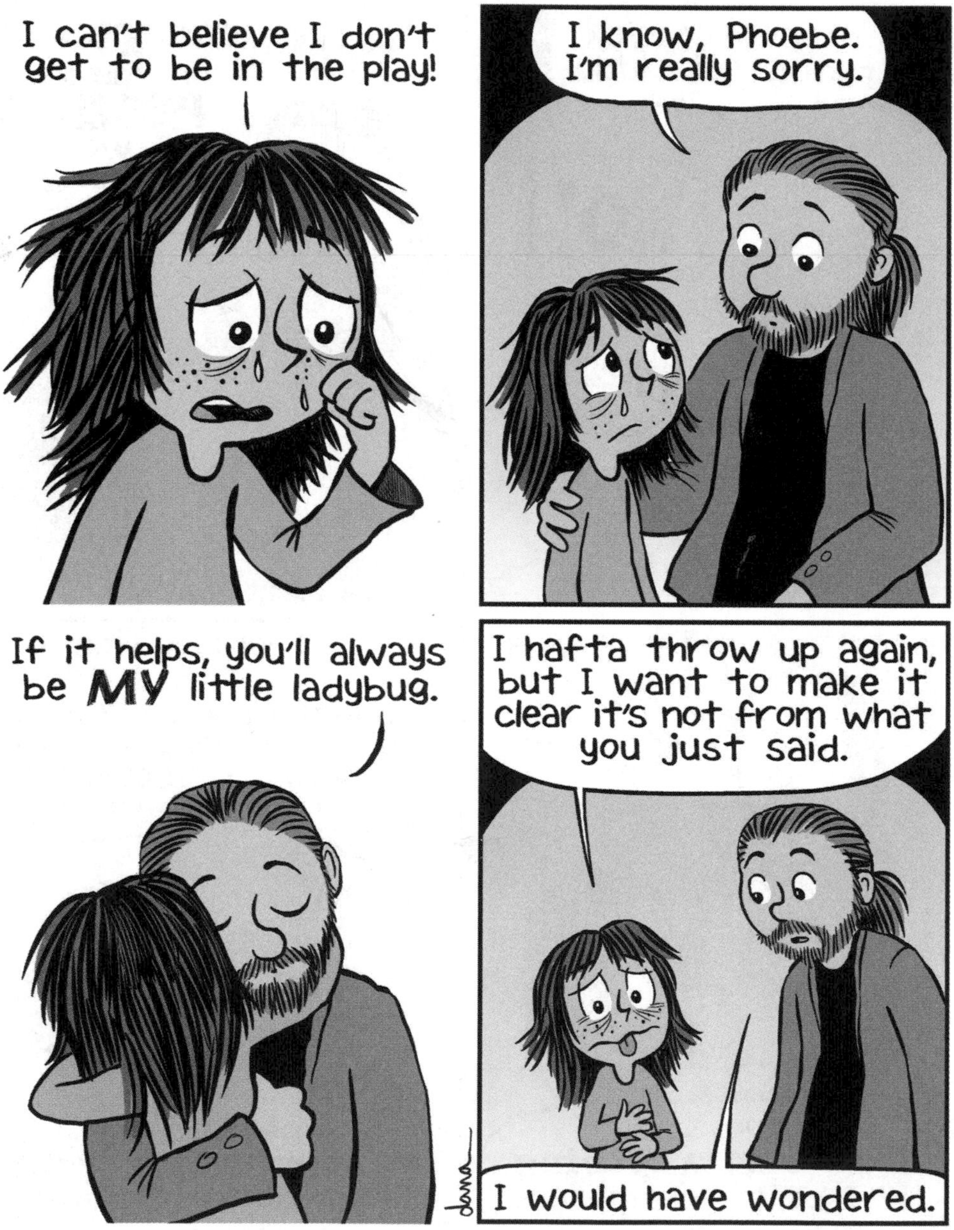
I can't believe I don't get to be in the play!
I know, Phoebe. I'm really sorry.
If it helps, you'll always be MY little ladybug.
I hafta throw up again, but I want to make it clear it's not from what you just said.
I would have wondered.
dana

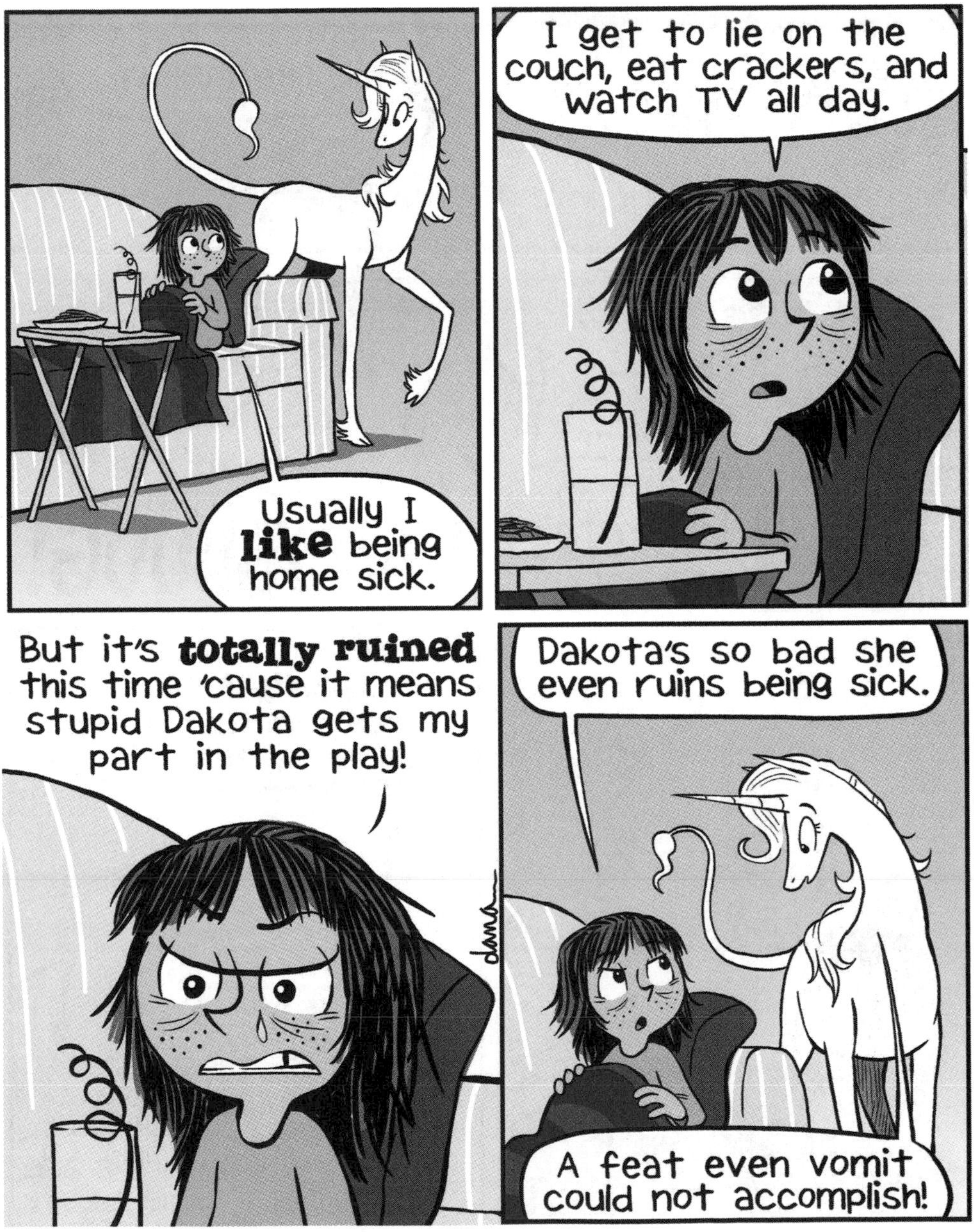
Usually I **like** being home sick.
I get to lie on the couch, eat crackers, and watch TV all day.
But it's **totally ruined** this time 'cause it means stupid Dakota gets my part in the play!
Dakota's so bad she even ruins being sick.
A feat even vomit could not accomplish!

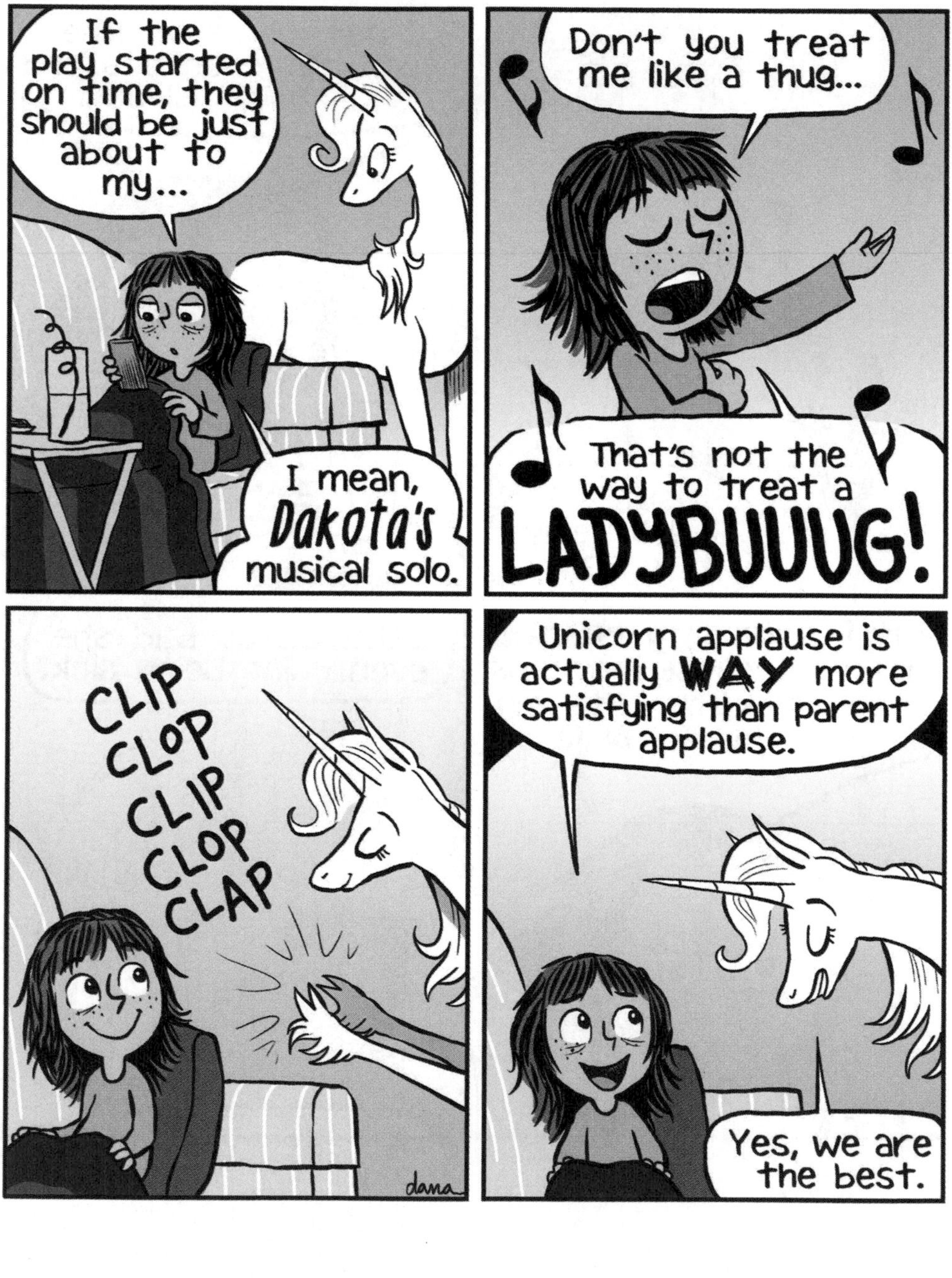
If the play started on time, they should be just about to my...
I mean, Dakota's musical solo.
Don't you treat me like a thug...
That's not the way to treat a LADYBUUUG!
CLIP CLOP CLIP CLOP CLAP
Unicorn applause is actually WAY more satisfying than parent applause.
Yes, we are the best.
dana

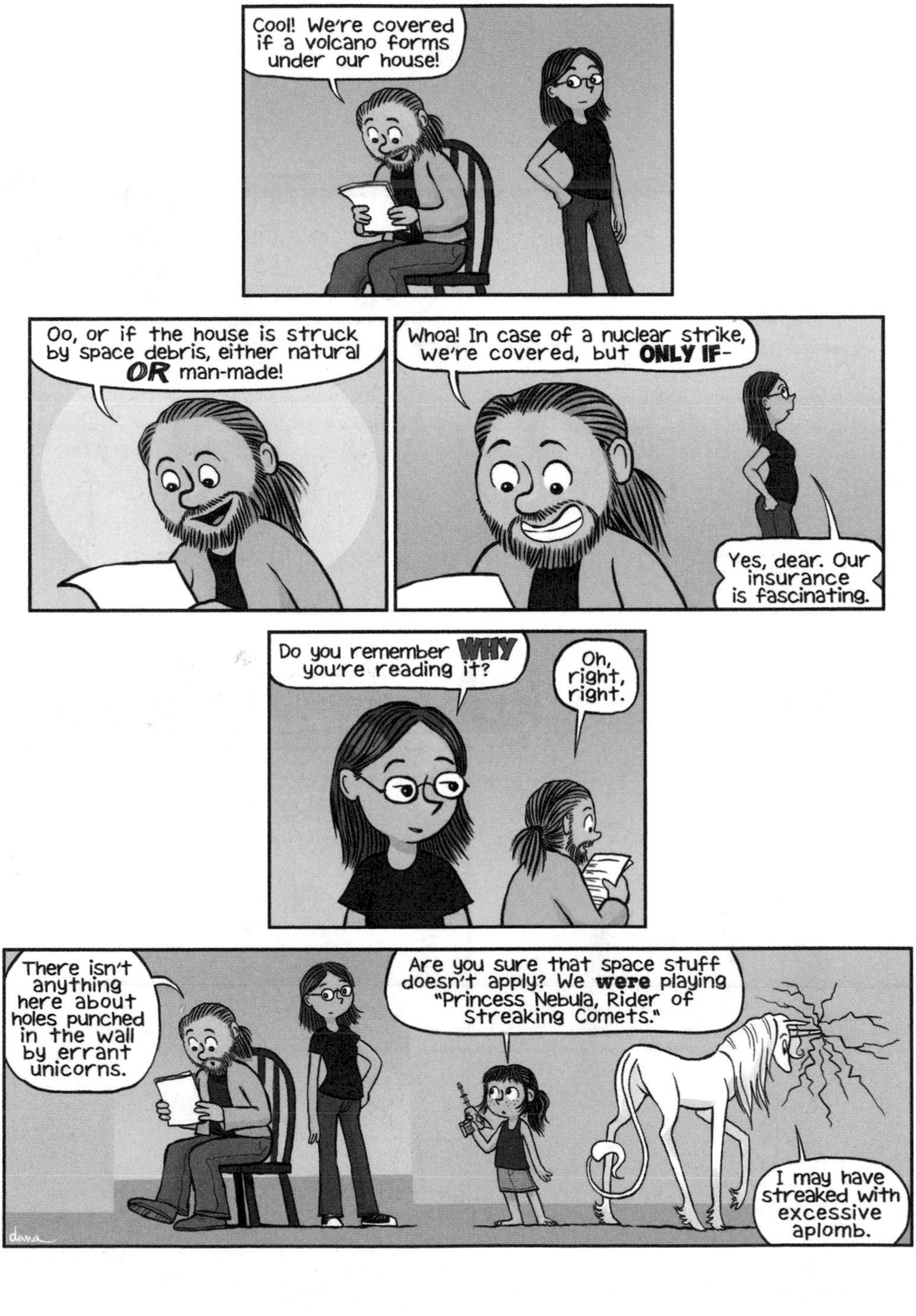
Cool! We're covered if a volcano forms under our house!
Oo, or if the house is struck by space debris, either natural OR man-made!
Whoa! In case of a nuclear strike, we're covered, but ONLY IF-
Yes, dear. Our insurance is fascinating.
Do you remember WHY you're reading it?
Oh, right, right.
There isn't anything here about holes punched in the wall by errant unicorns.
Are you sure that space stuff doesn't apply? We were playing "Princess Nebula, Rider of Streaking Comets."
I may have streaked with excessive aplomb.
dana

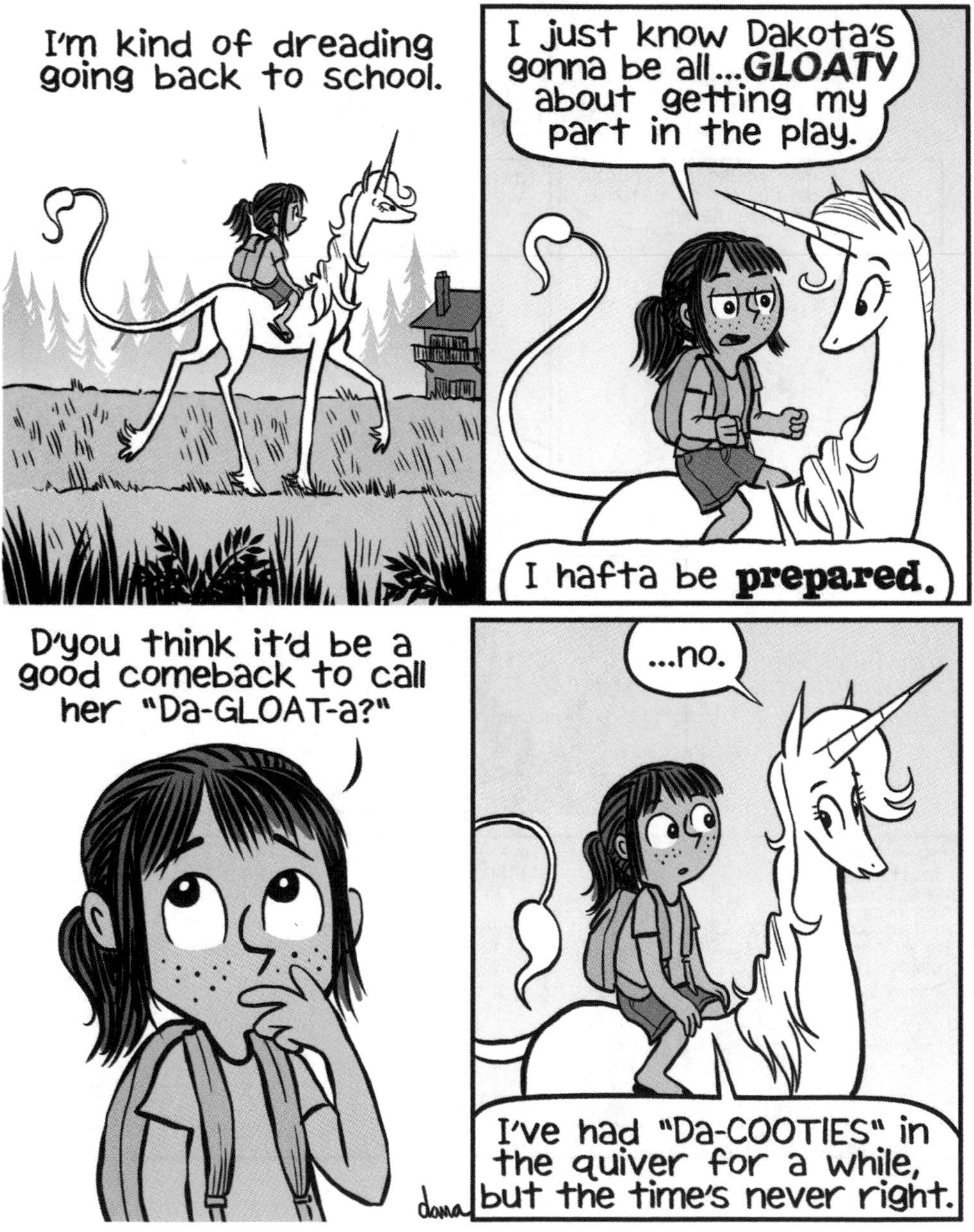
I'm kind of dreading going back to school.
I just know Dakota's gonna be all...GLOATY about getting my part in the play.
I hafta be prepared.
D'you think it'd be a good comeback to call her "Da-GLOAT-a?"
...no.
I've had "Da-COOTIES" in the quiver for a while, but the time's never right.
dana

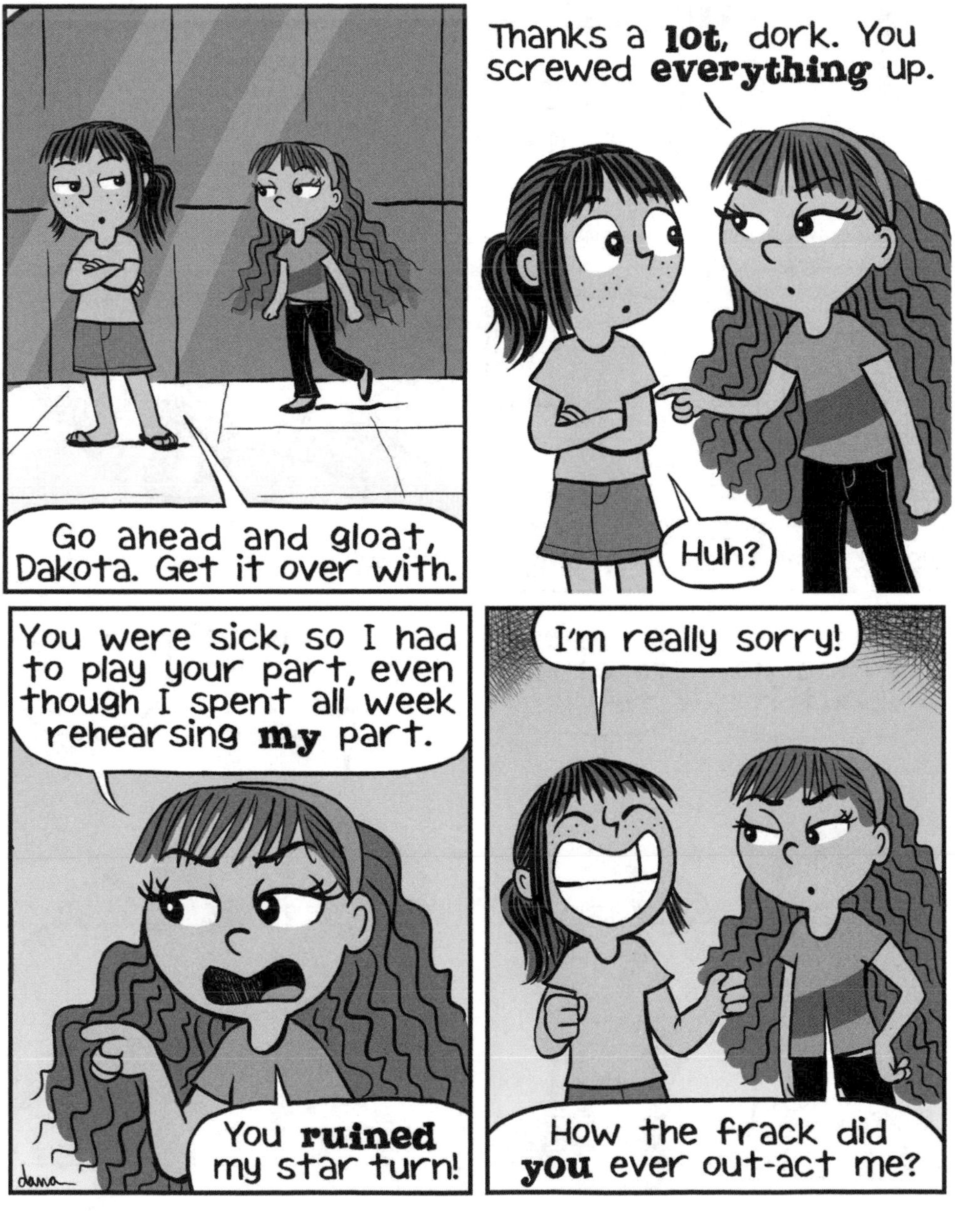
Go ahead and gloat, Dakota. Get it over with.
Thanks a **lot**, dork. You screwed **everything** up.
Huh?
You were sick, so I had to play your part, even though I spent all week rehearsing **my** part.
You **ruined** my star turn!
dana
I'm really sorry!
How the frack did **you** ever out-act me?

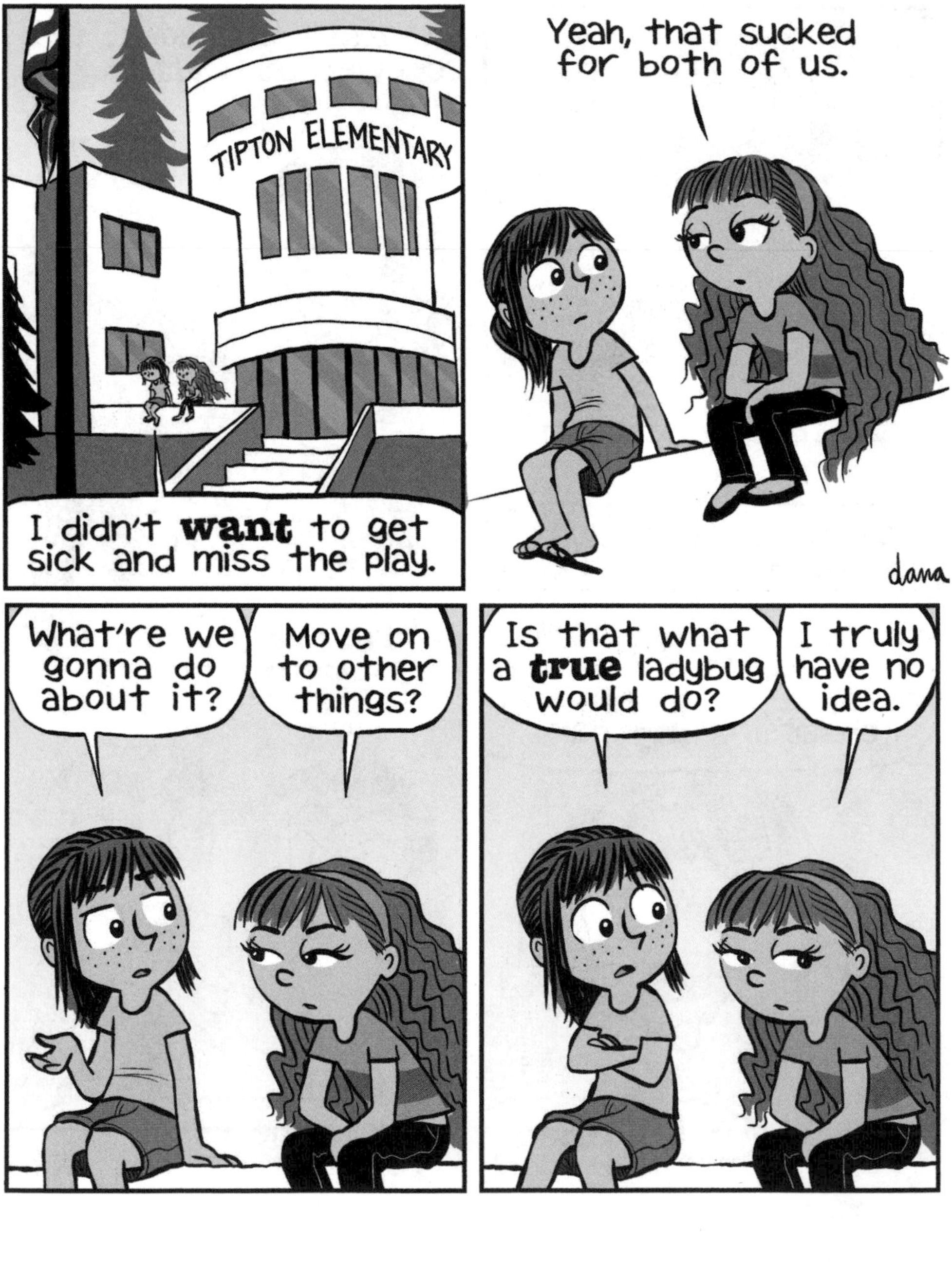
TIPTON ELEMENTARY
I didn't **want** to get sick and miss the play.
Yeah, that sucked for both of us.
dana
What're we gonna do about it?
Move on to other things?
Is that what a **true** ladybug would do?
I truly have no idea.

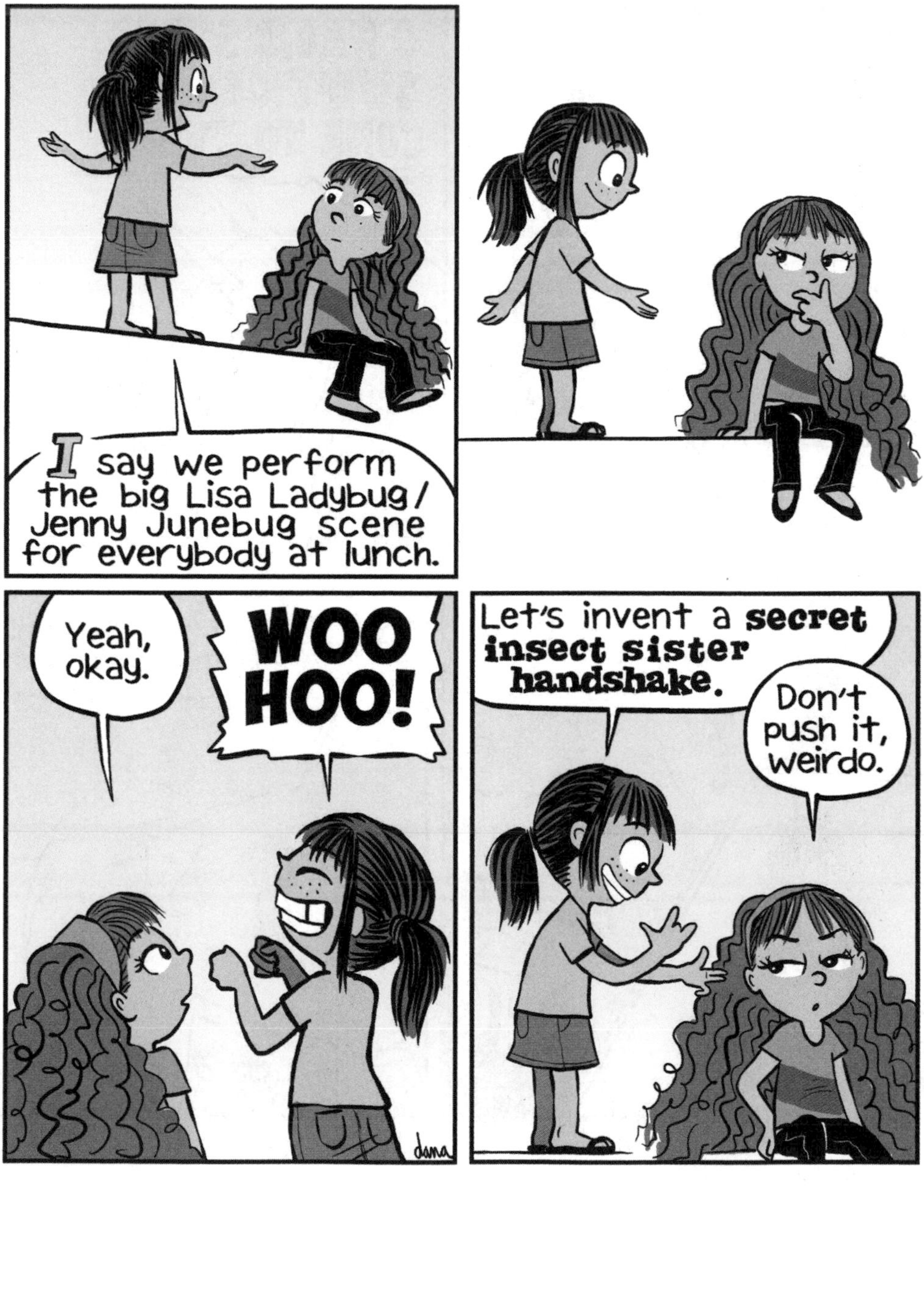
I say we perform the big Lisa Ladybug/ Jenny Junebug scene for everybody at lunch.
Yeah, okay.
WOO HOO!
Let's invent a **secret insect sister handshake**.
Don't push it, weirdo.
dana

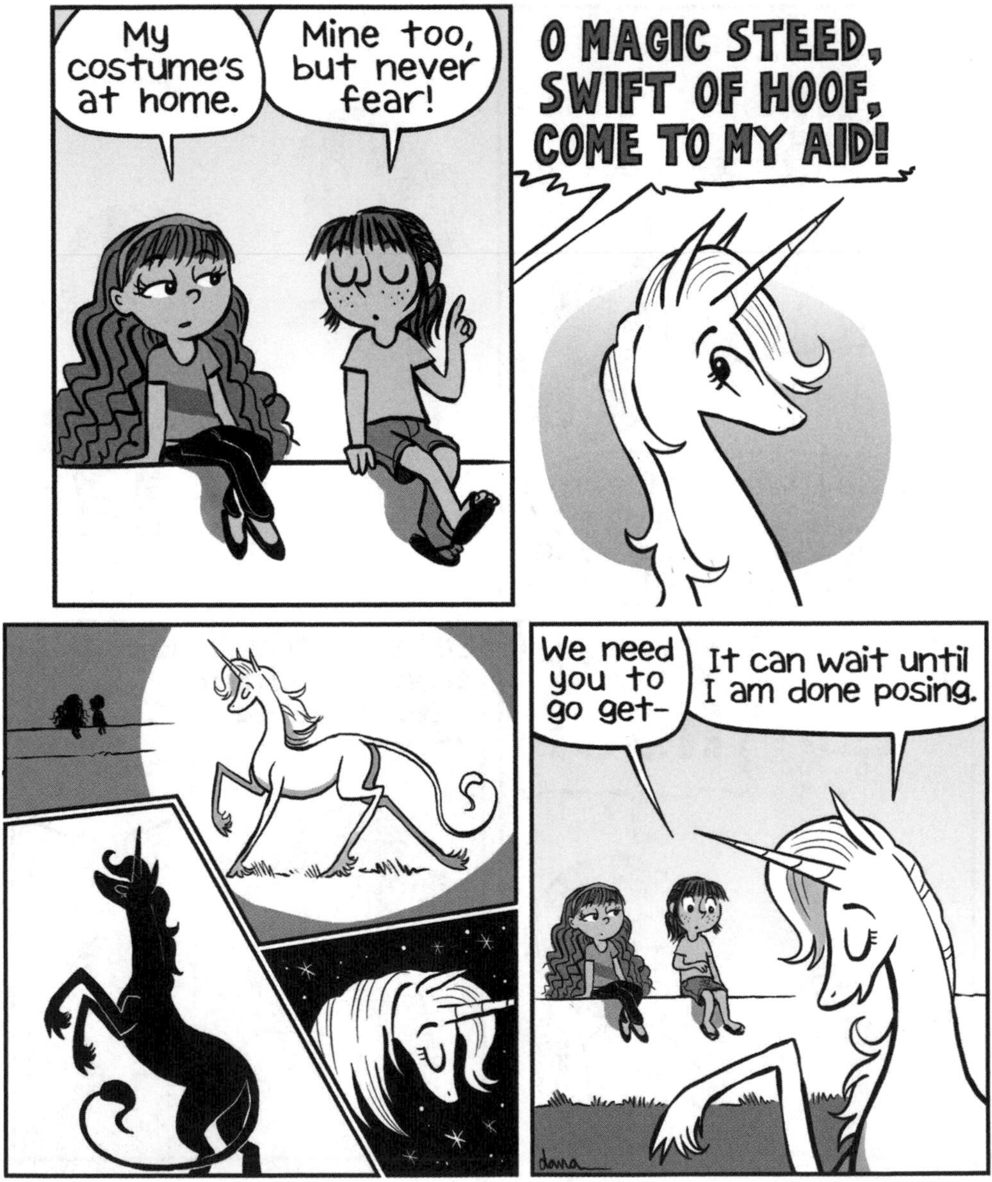

My costume's at home.
Mine too, but never fear!
O MAGIC STEED, SWIFT OF HOOF, COME TO MY AID!
We need you to go get-
It can wait until I am done posing.
dana

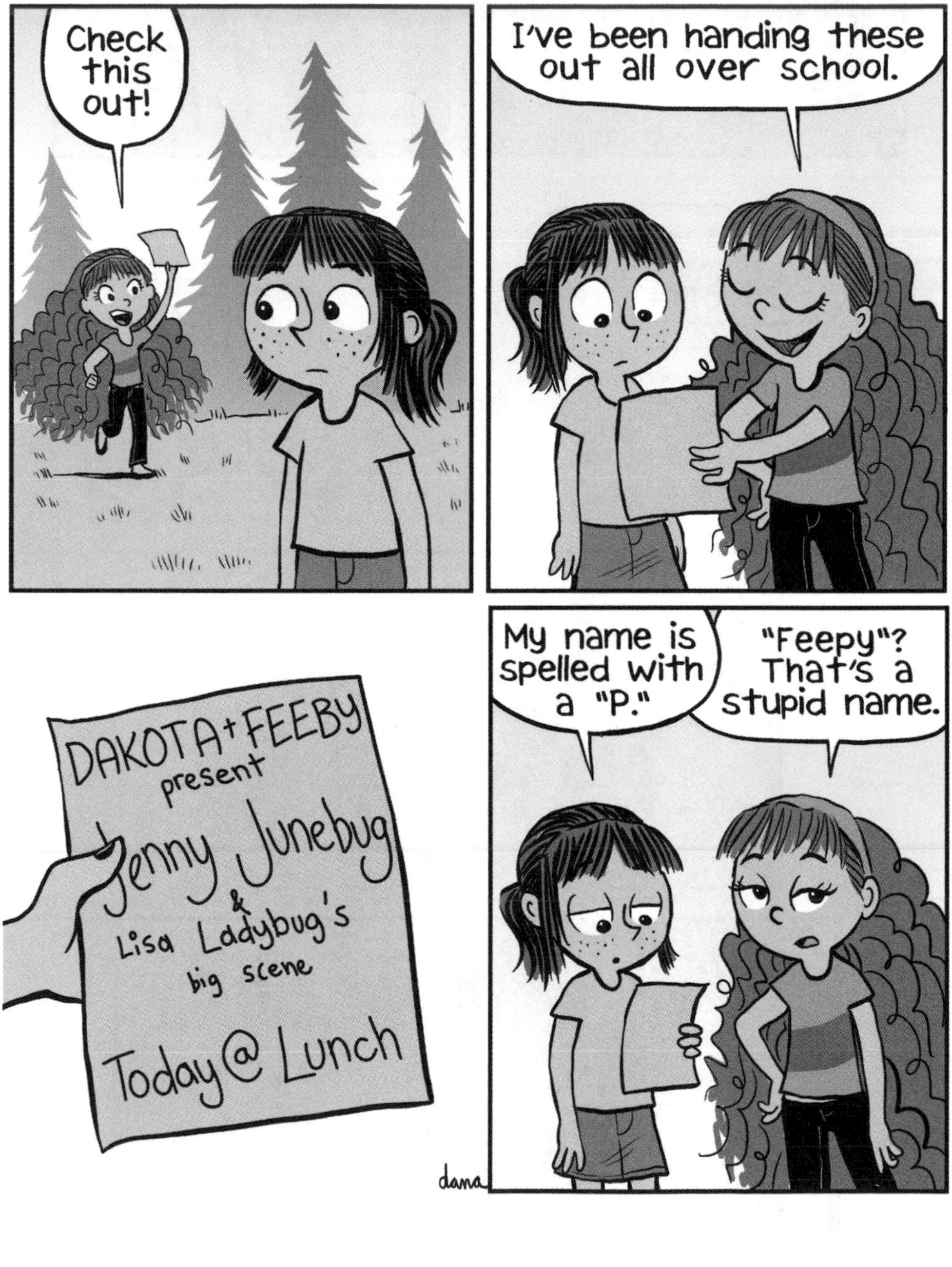
Check this out!
I've been handing these out all over school.
DAKOTA + FEEBY present Jenny Junebug & Lisa Ladybug's big scene
Today @ Lunch
My name is spelled with a "P."
"Feepy"? That's a stupid name.
dana

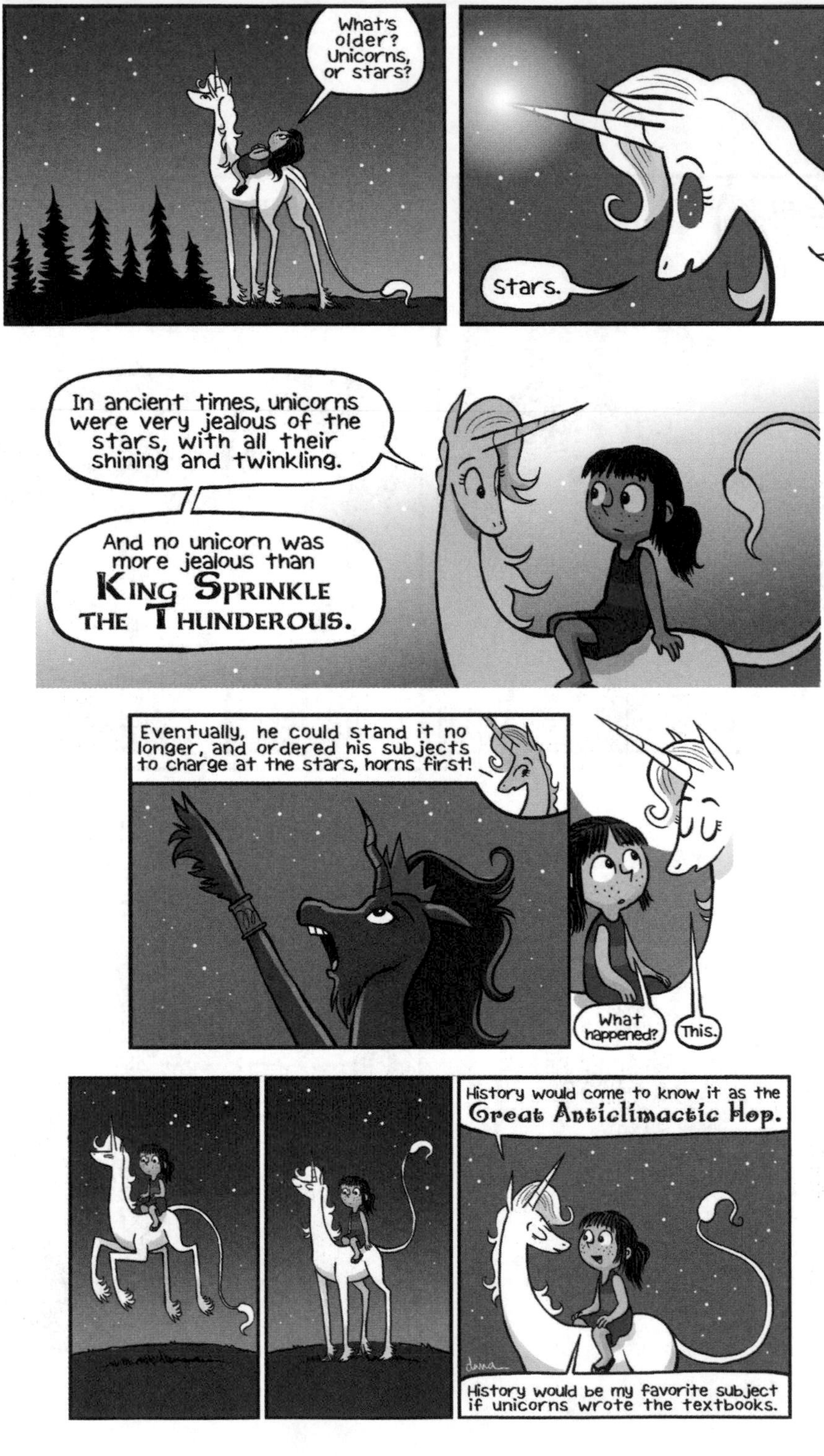
What's older? Unicorns, or stars?
Stars.
In ancient times, unicorns were very jealous of the stars, with all their shining and twinkling.
And no unicorn was more jealous than KING SPRINKLE THE THUNDEROUS.
Eventually, he could stand it no longer, and ordered his subjects to charge at the stars, horns first!
What happened?
This.
History would come to know it as the Great Anticlimactic Hop.
History would be my favorite subject if unicorns wrote the textbooks.

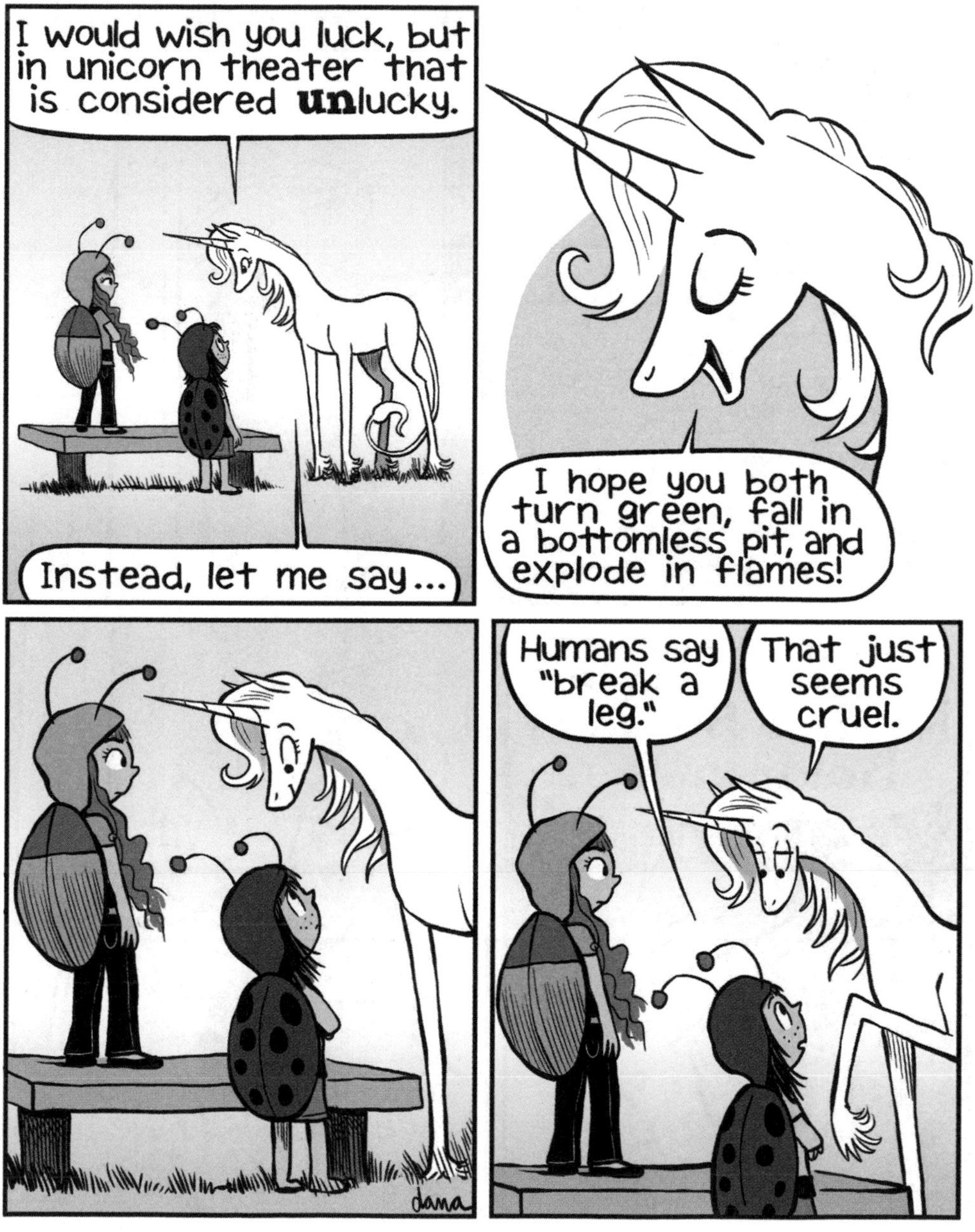
I would wish you luck, but in unicorn theater that is considered **un**lucky.
Instead, let me say...
I hope you both turn green, fall in a bottomless pit, and explode in flames!
Humans say "break a leg."
That just seems cruel.
dana

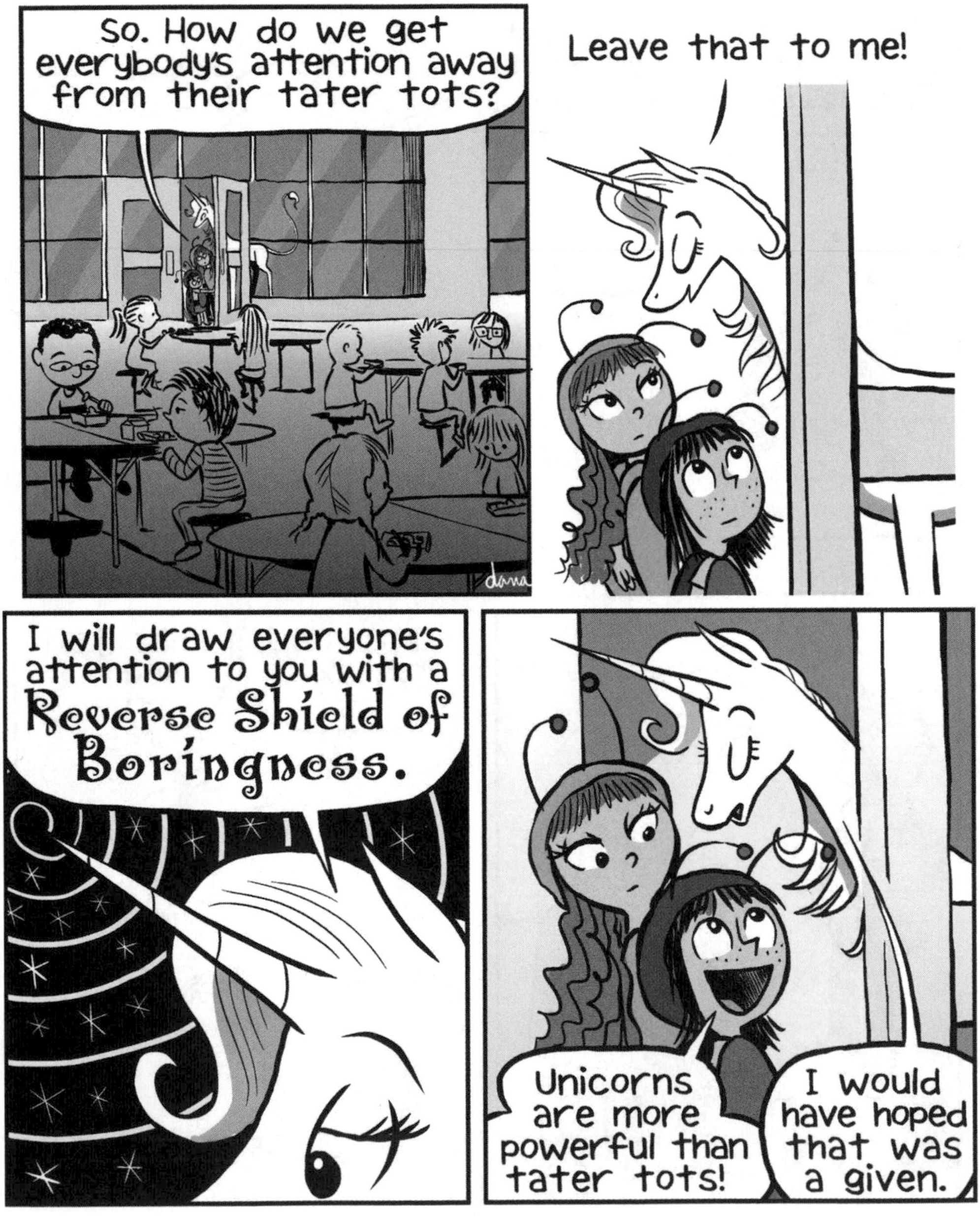
So. How do we get everybody's attention away from their tater tots?
Leave that to me!
I will draw everyone's attention to you with a Reverse Shield of Boringness.
Unicorns are more powerful than tater tots!
I would have hoped that was a given.

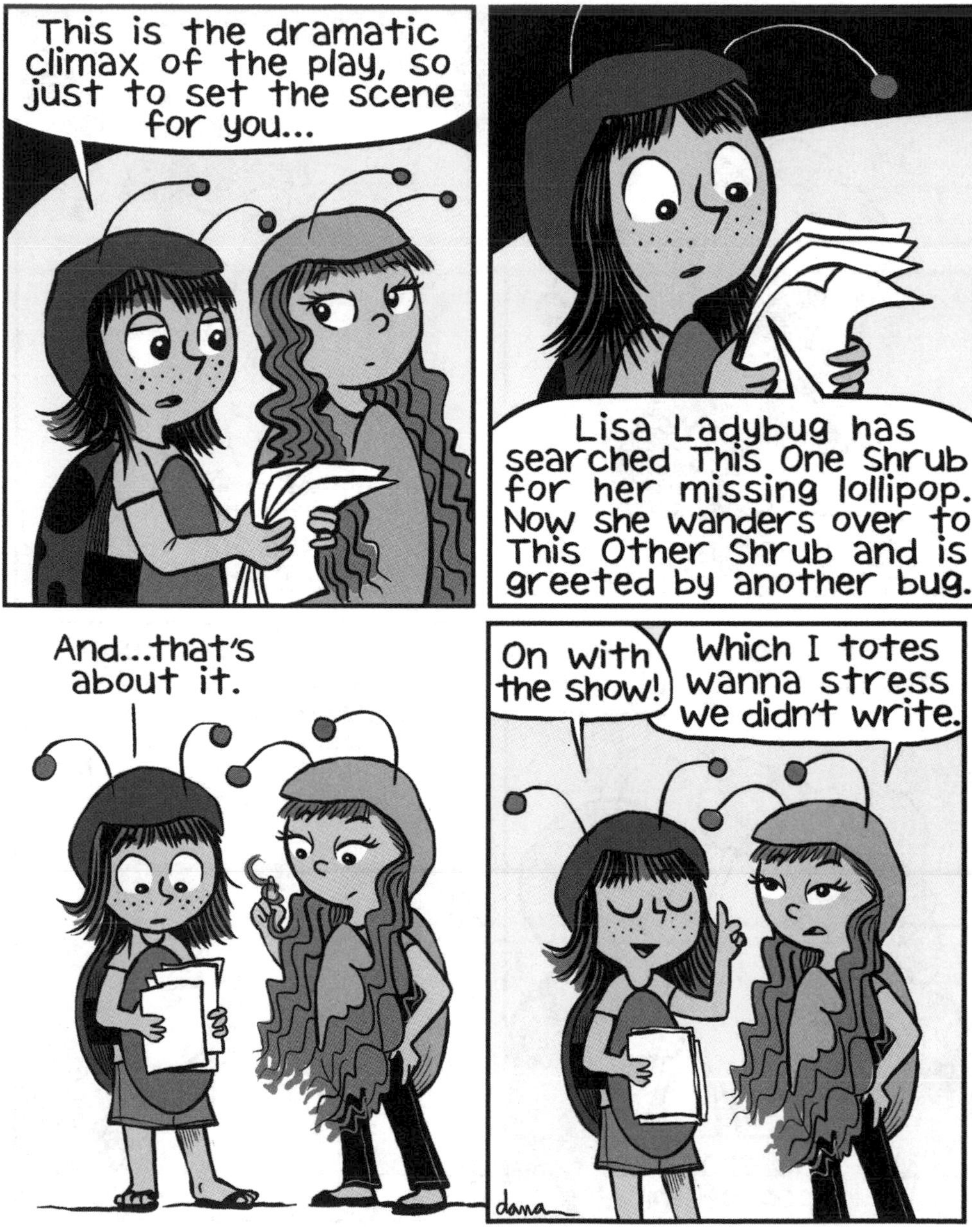

This is the dramatic climax of the play, so just to set the scene for you...
Lisa Ladybug has searched This One Shrub for her missing lollipop. Now she wanders over to This Other Shrub and is greeted by another bug.
And...that's about it.
On with the show!
Which I totes wanna stress we didn't write.
dana

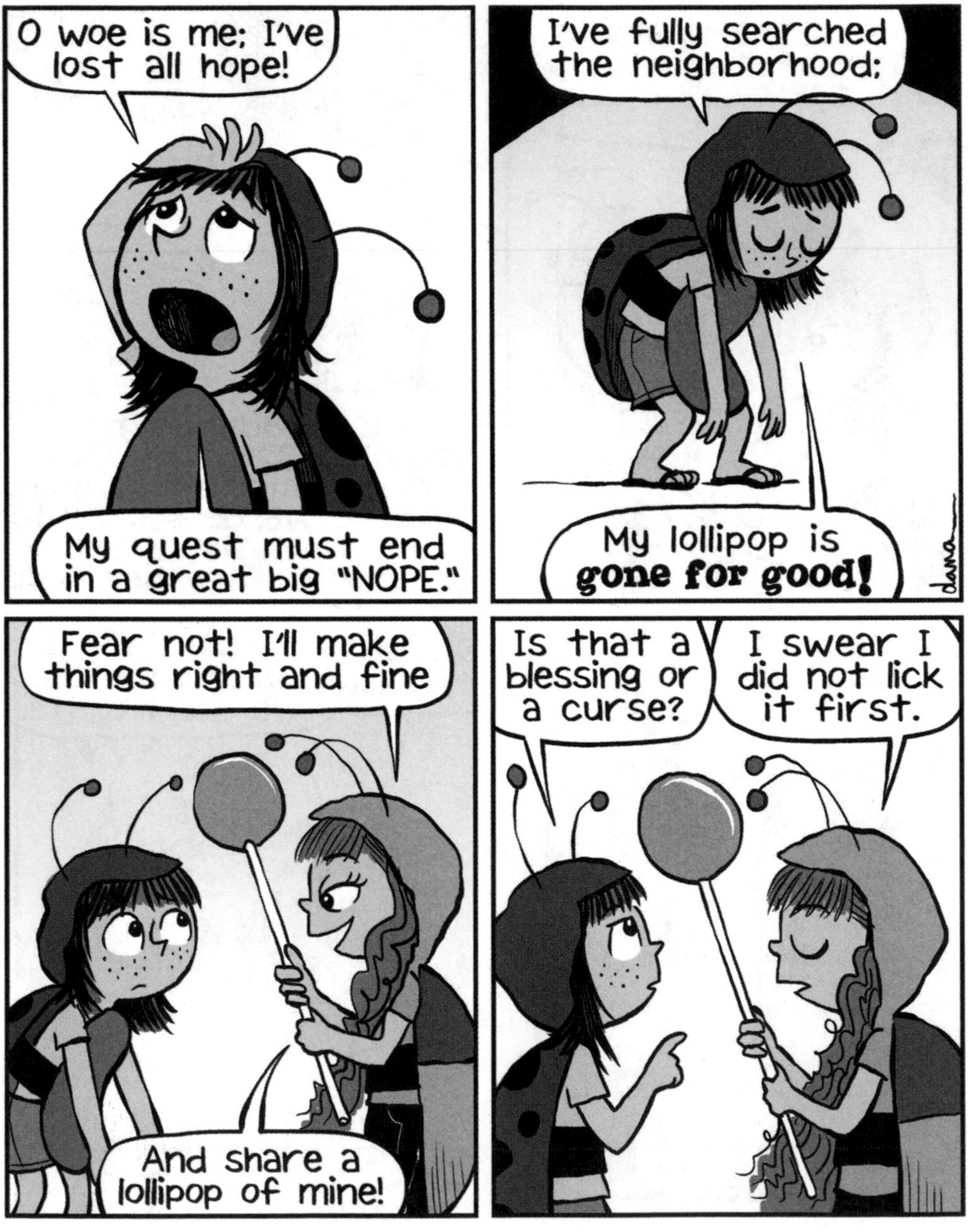
O woe is me; I've lost all hope!
My quest must end in a great big "NOPE."
I've fully searched the neighborhood;
My lollipop is **gone for good!**
dana
Fear not! I'll make things right and fine
And share a lollipop of mine!
Is that a blessing or a curse?
I swear I did not lick it first.

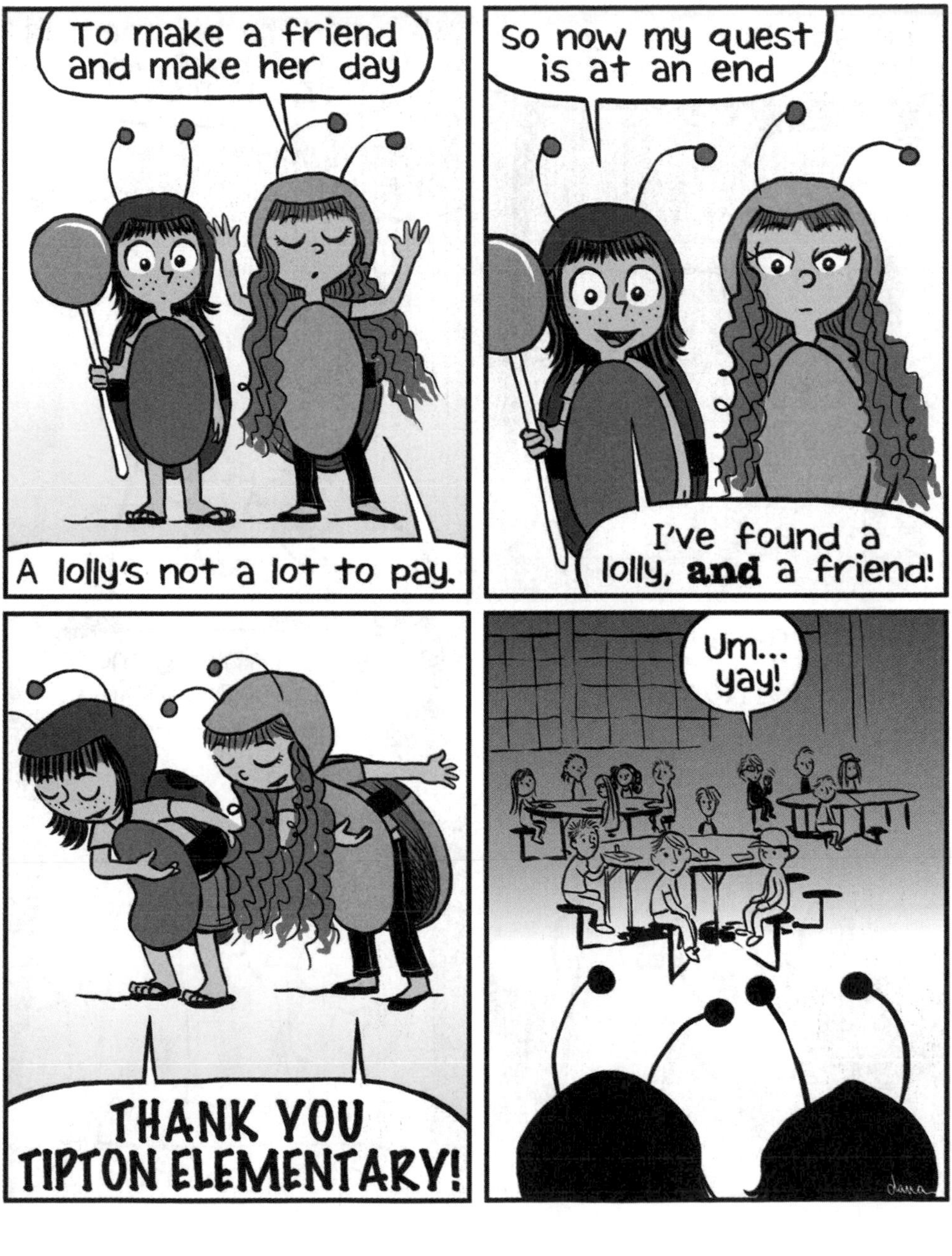
To make a friend and make her day
A lolly's not a lot to pay.
So now my quest is at an end
I've found a lolly, **and** a friend!
THANK YOU TIPTON ELEMENTARY!
Um... yay!

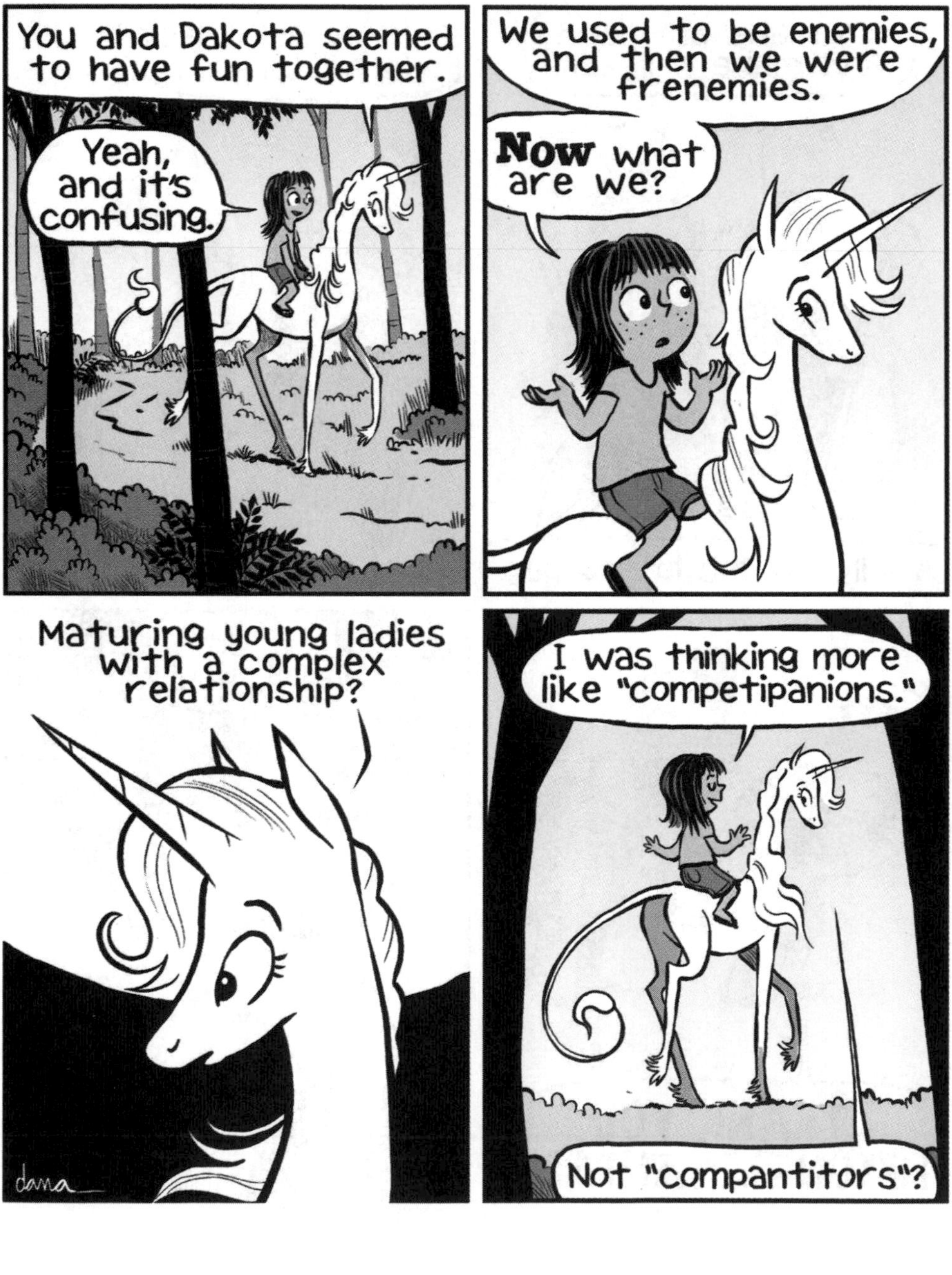
You and Dakota seemed to have fun together.
Yeah, and it's confusing.
We used to be enemies, and then we were frenemies.
Now what are we?
Maturing young ladies with a complex relationship?
I was thinking more like "competipanions."
Not "compantitors"?
dana

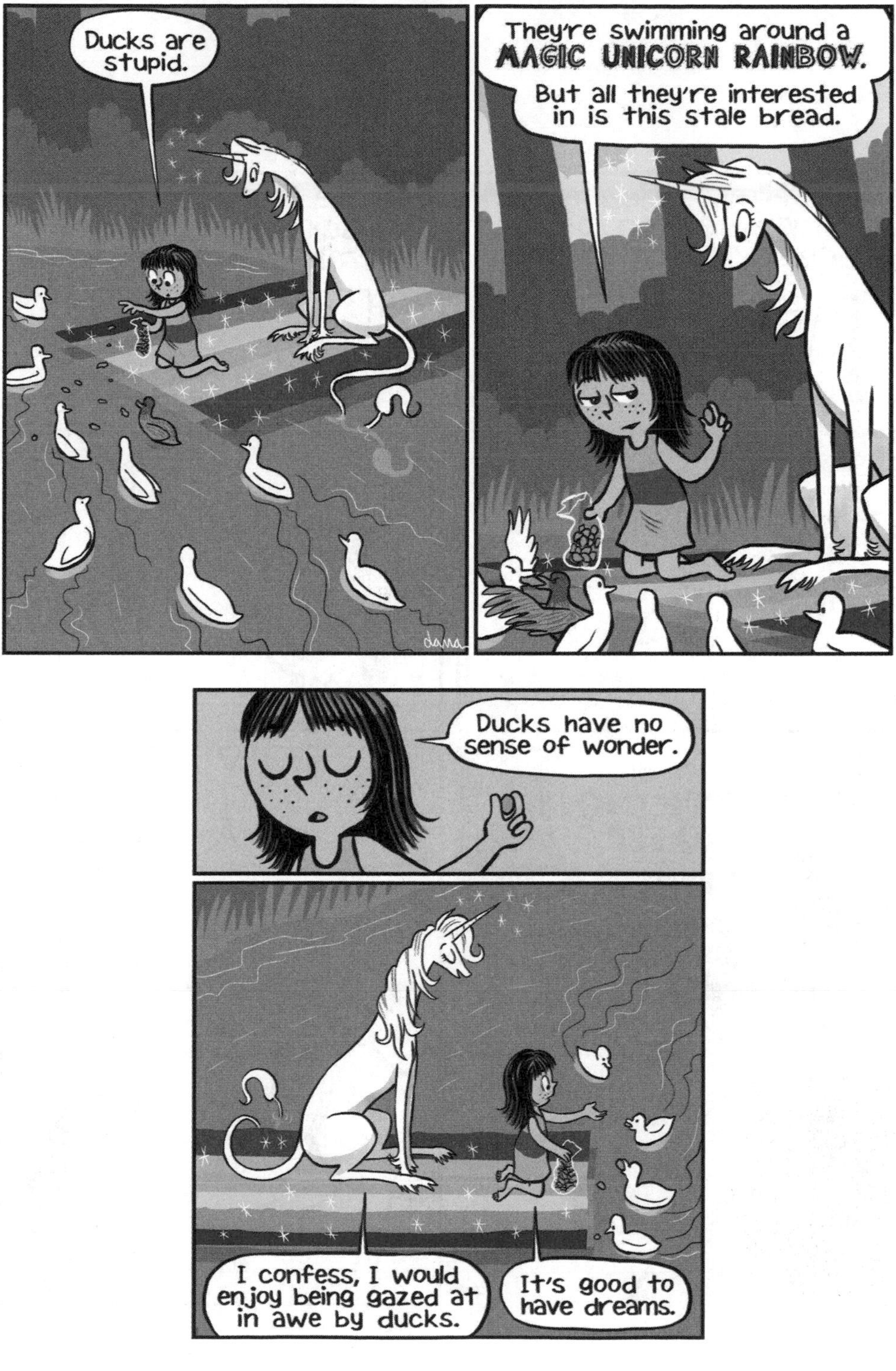
Ducks are stupid.
They're swimming around a MAGIC UNICORN RAINBOW.
But all they're interested in is this stale bread.
Ducks have no sense of wonder.
I confess, I would enjoy being gazed at in awe by ducks.
It's good to have dreams.

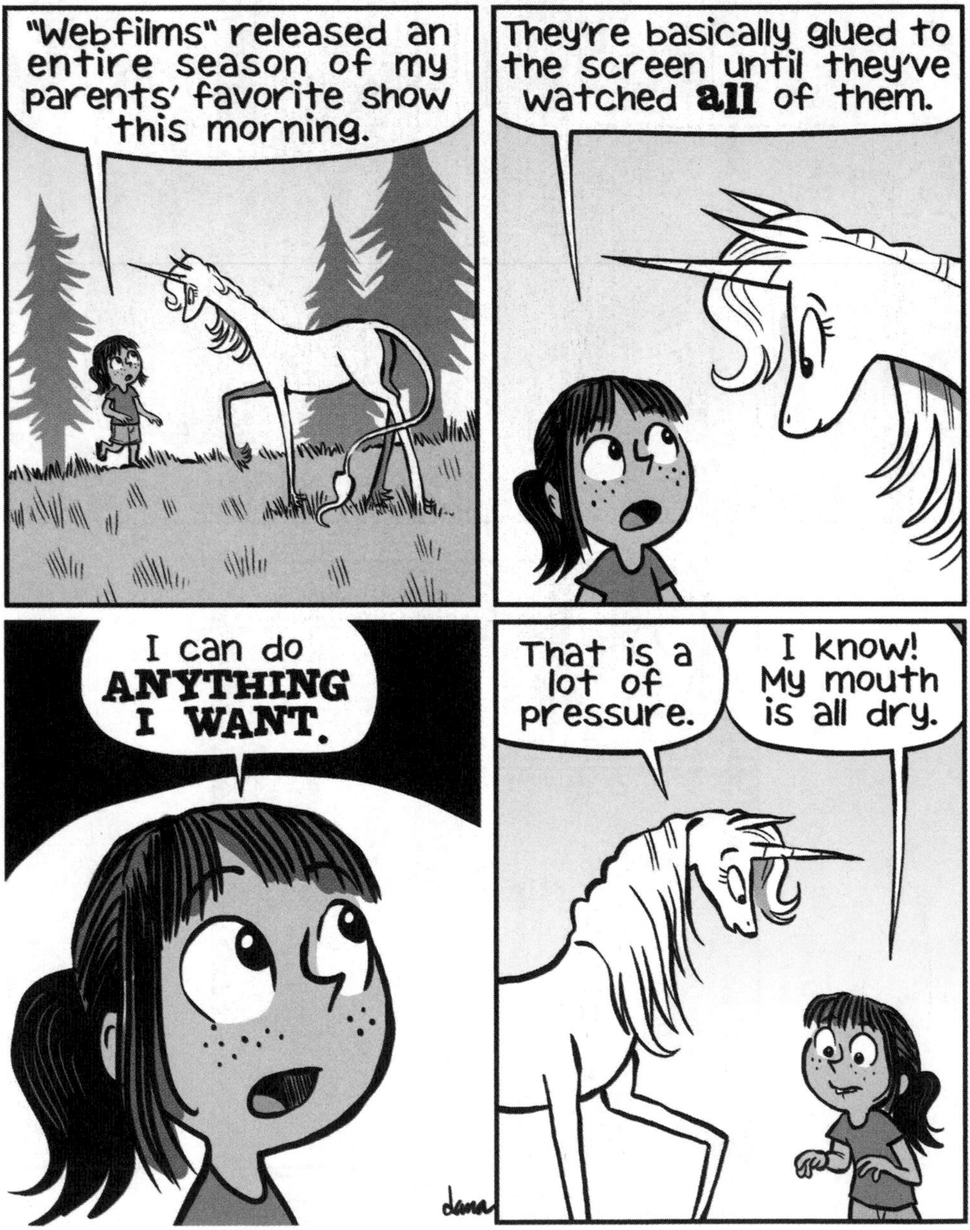
"Webfilms" released an entire season of my parents' favorite show this morning.
They're basically glued to the screen until they've watched **all** of them.
I can do **ANYTHING I WANT.**
That is a lot of pressure.
I know! My mouth is all dry.
dana

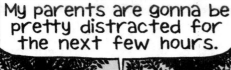

My parents are gonna be pretty distracted for the next few hours.

I wanna use the time to do something I'm not supposed to.

Like what?

That's the problem! I have no idea.

You clearly have not planned ahead.

Mom always says I should. Does **THAT** count?

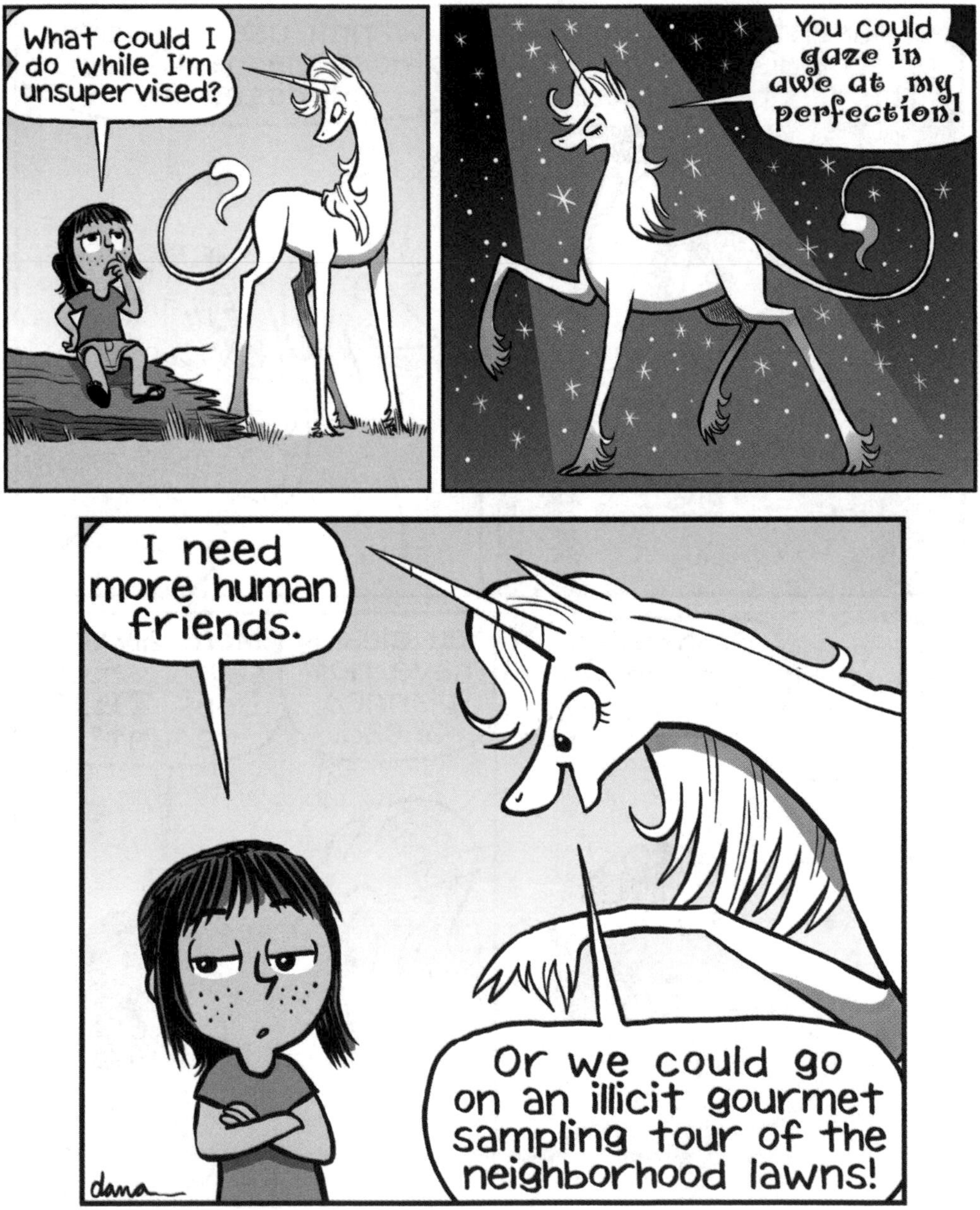
What could I do while I'm unsupervised?
You could gaze in awe at my perfection!
I need more human friends.
Or we could go on an illicit gourmet sampling tour of the neighborhood lawns!
dana

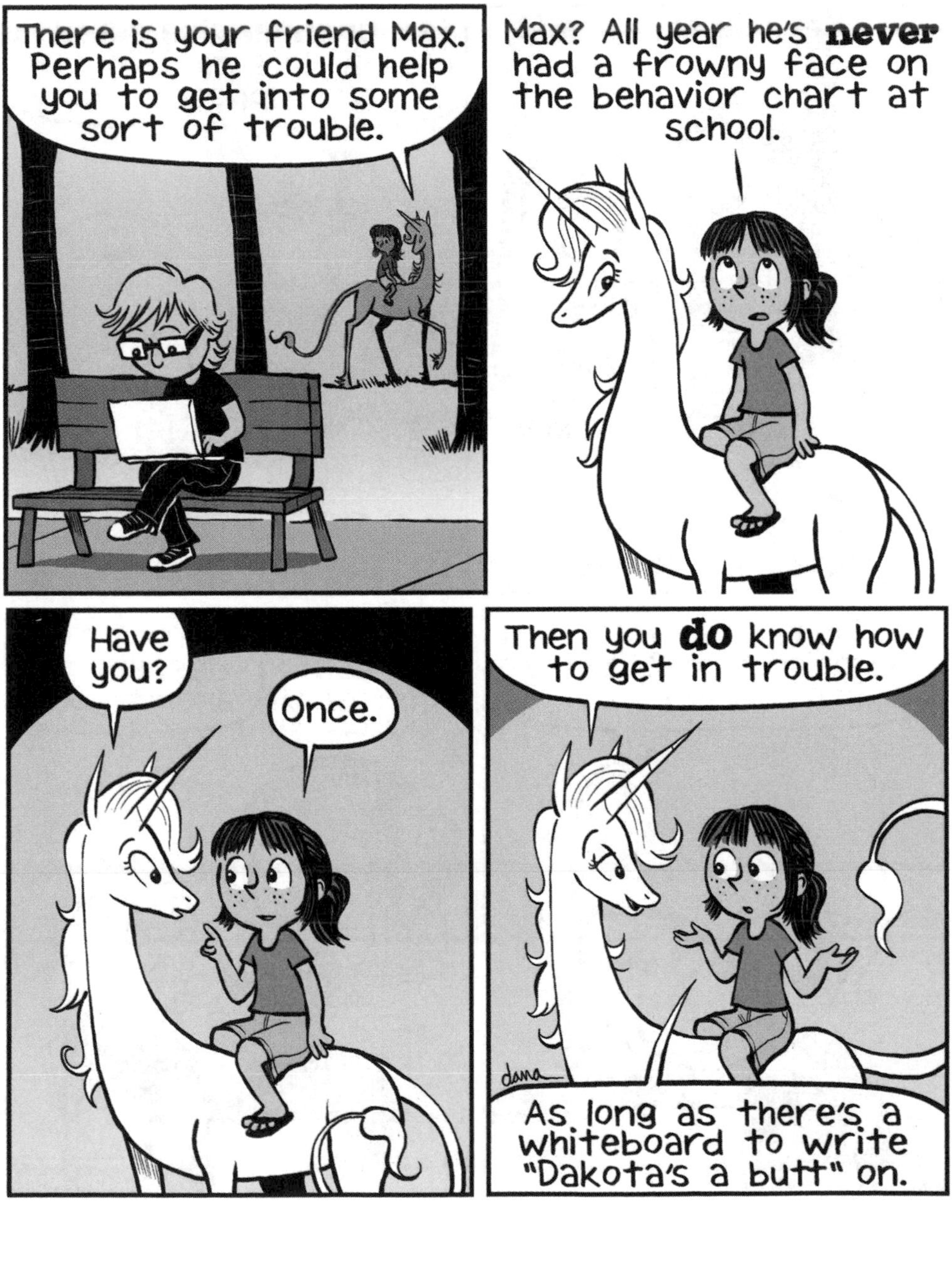
There is your friend Max. Perhaps he could help you to get into some sort of trouble.
Max? All year he's **never** had a frowny face on the behavior chart at school.
Have you?
Once.
Then you **do** know how to get in trouble.
As long as there's a whiteboard to write "Dakota's a butt" on.
dana

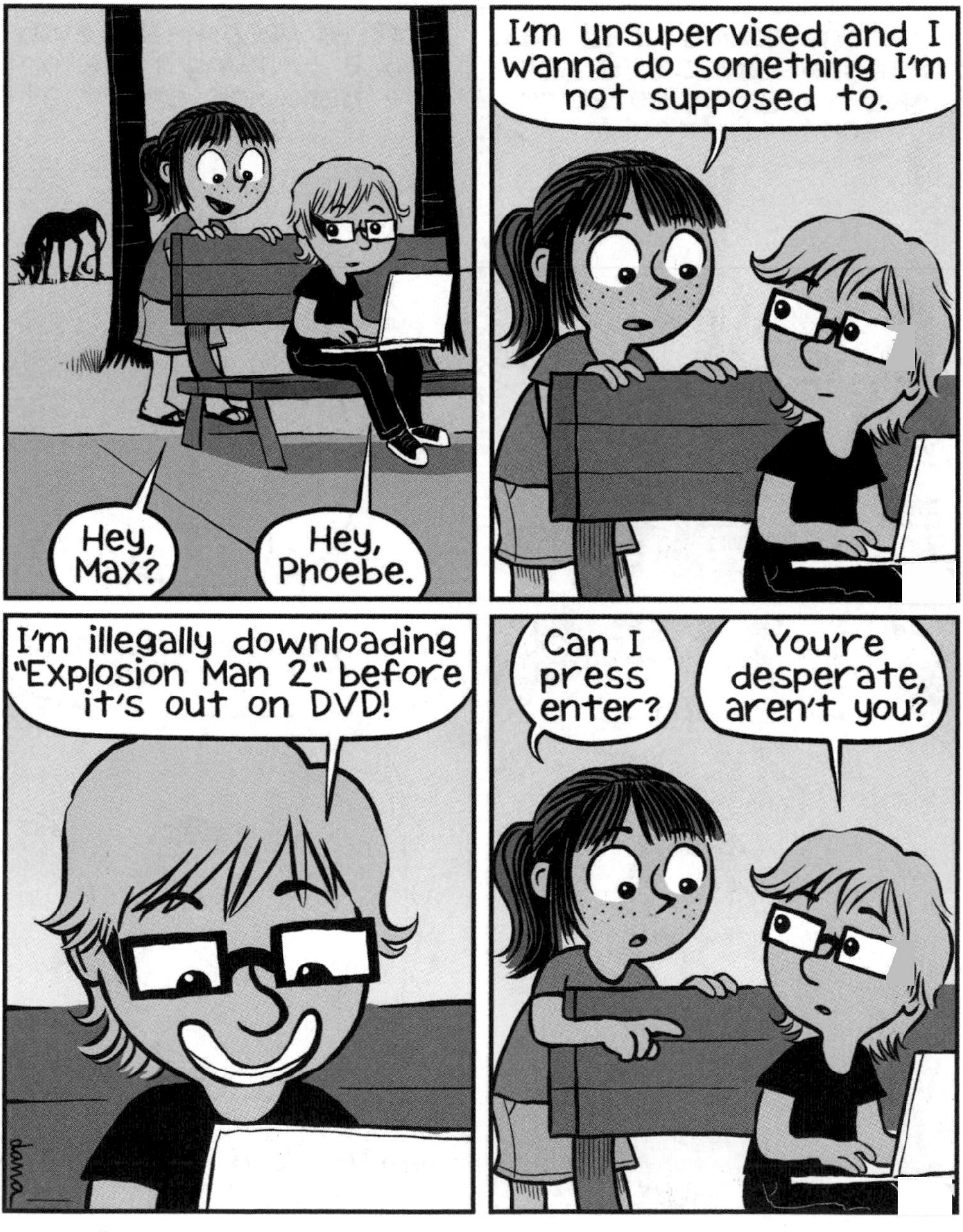
Hey, Max?
Hey, Phoebe.
I'm unsupervised and I wanna do something I'm not supposed to.
I'm illegally downloading "Explosion Man 2" before it's out on DVD!
Can I press enter?
You're desperate, aren't you?
dana

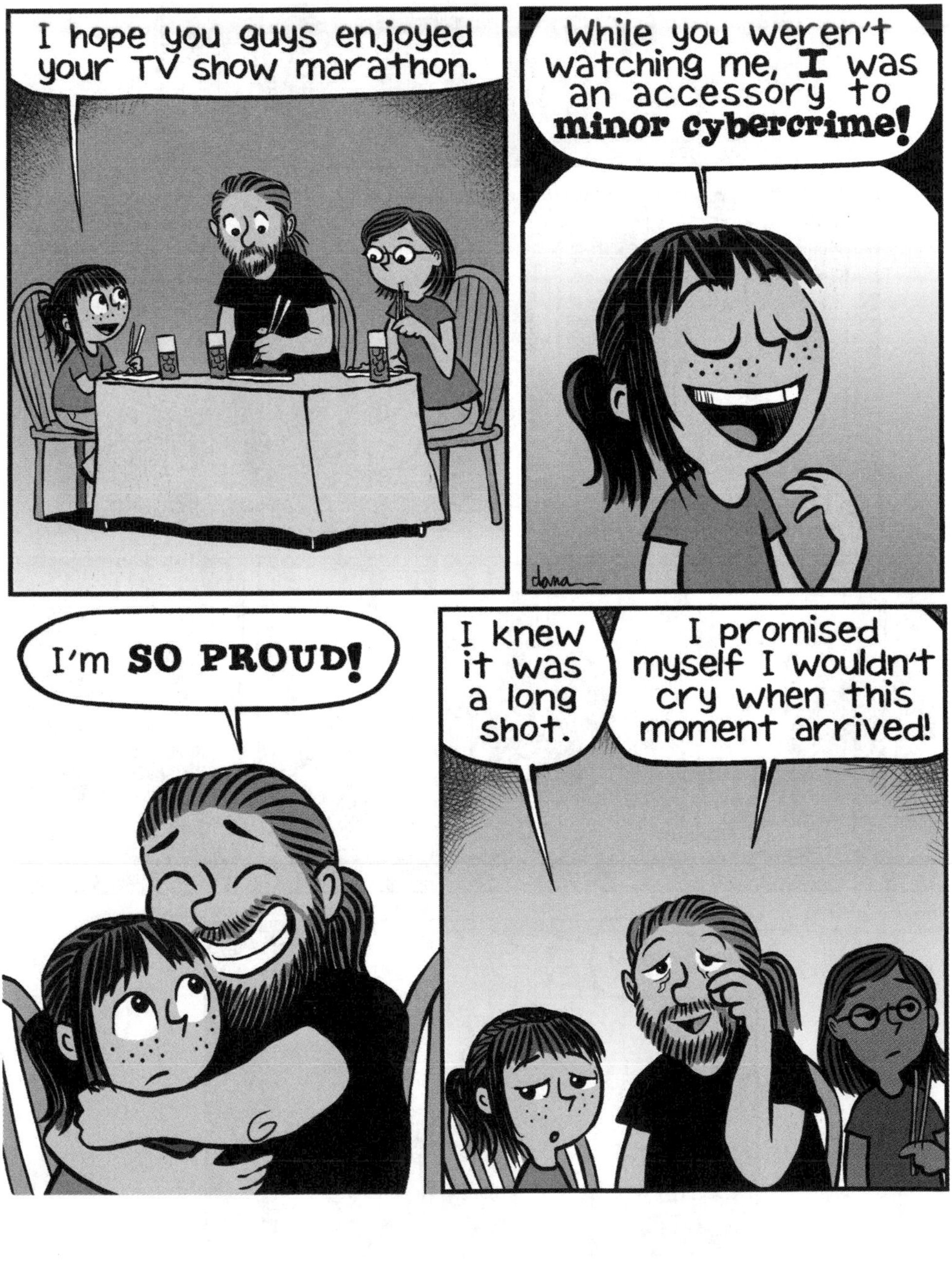
I hope you guys enjoyed your TV show marathon.
While you weren't watching me, I was an accessory to minor cybercrime!
dana
I'm SO PROUD!
I knew it was a long shot.
I promised myself I wouldn't cry when this moment arrived!

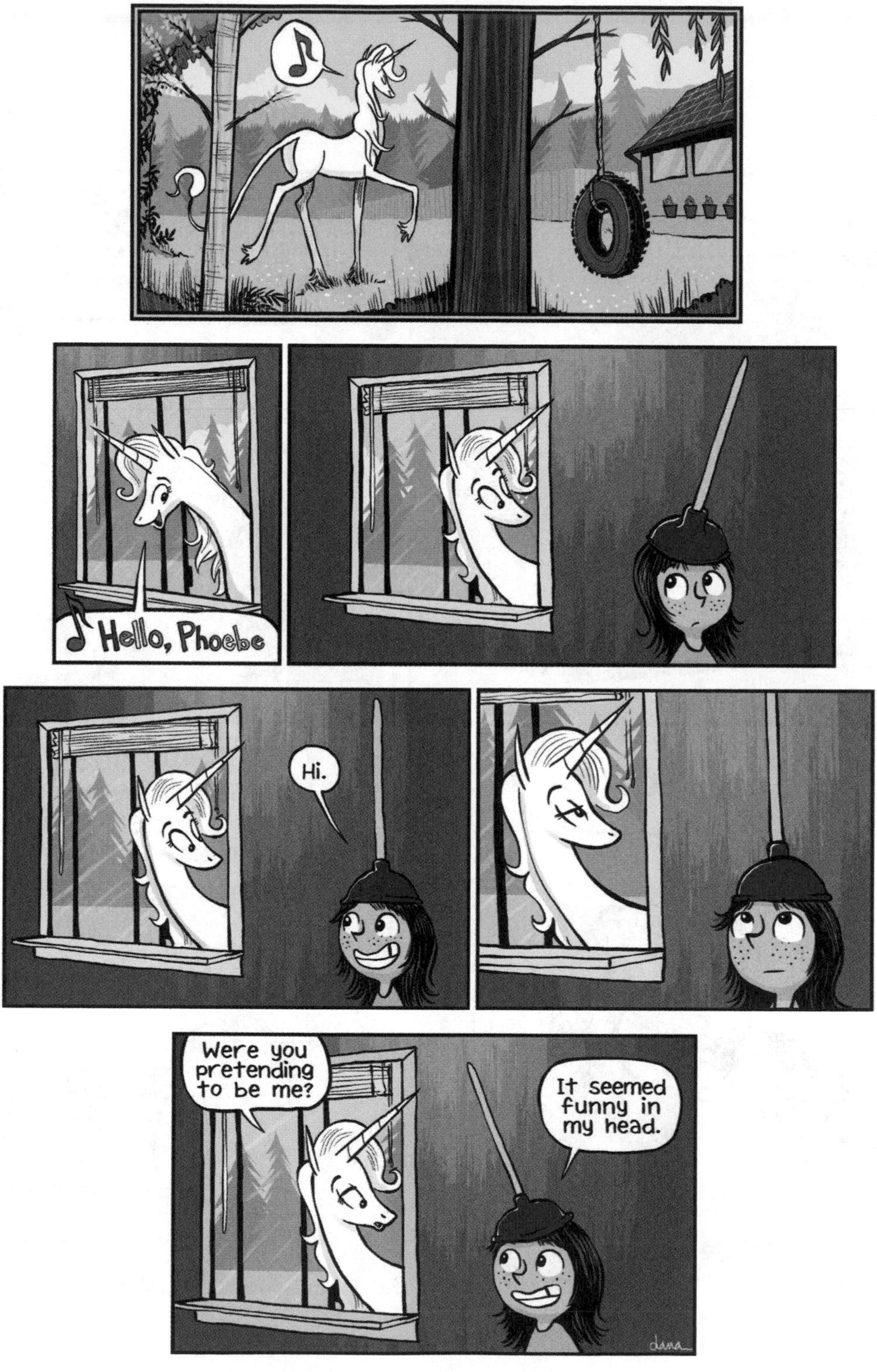
♪
♪ Hello, Phoebe
Hi.
Were you pretending to be me?
It seemed funny in my head.
dana

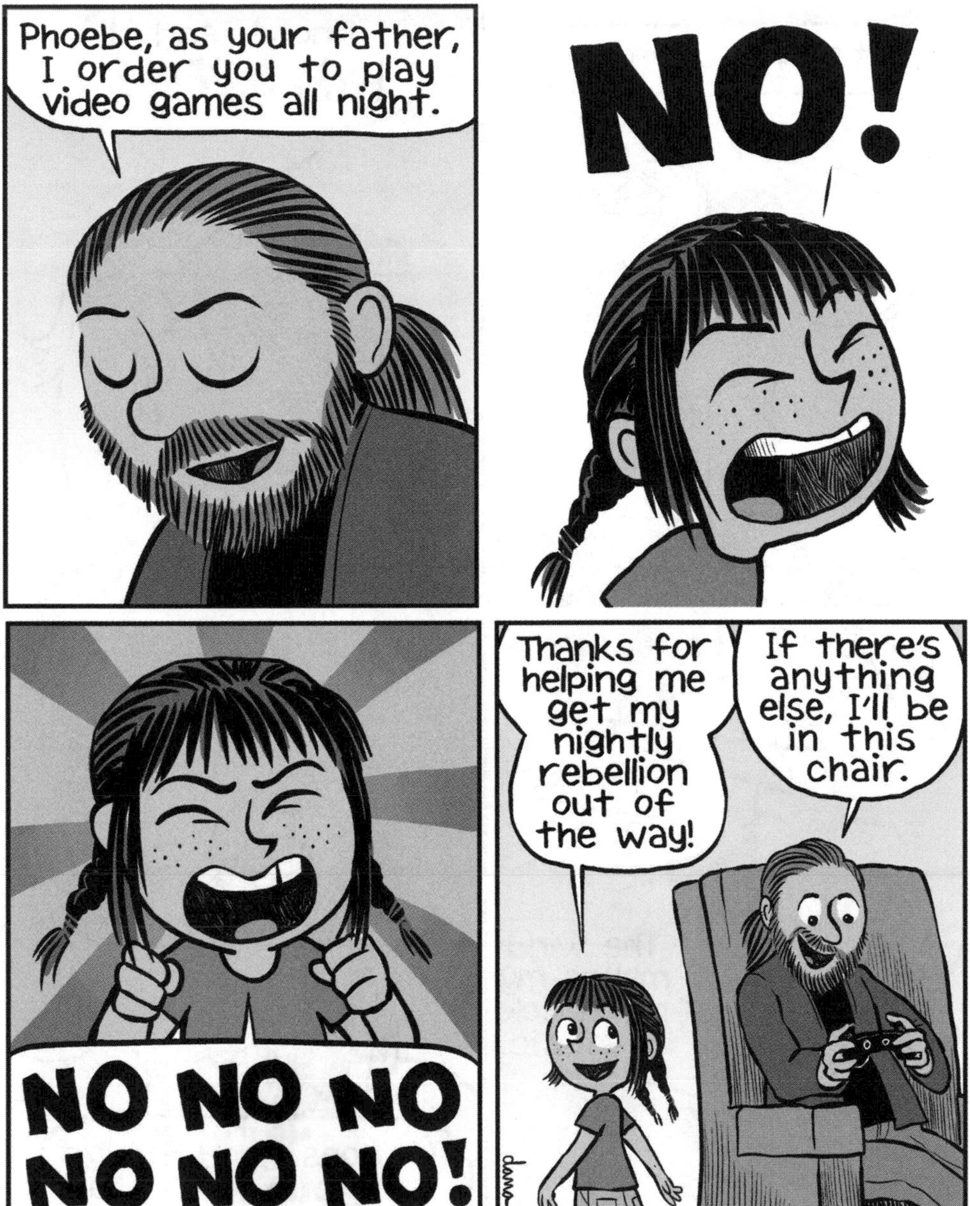

Phoebe, as your father, I order you to play video games all night.
NO!
NO NO NO NO NO NO!
Thanks for helping me get my nightly rebellion out of the way!
If there's anything else, I'll be in this chair.

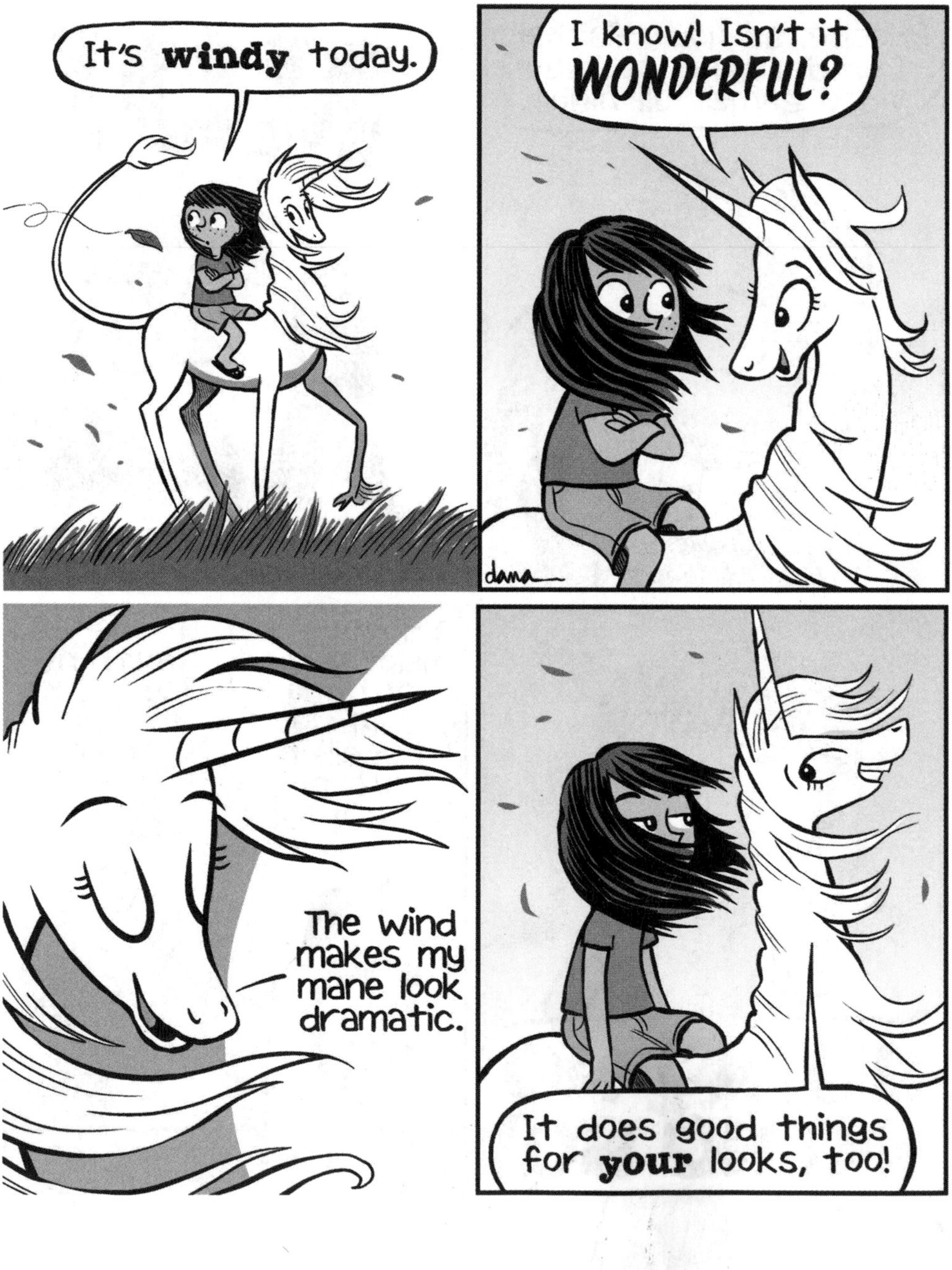
It's **windy** today.
I know! Isn't it WONDERFUL?
dana
The wind makes my mane look dramatic.
It does good things for **your** looks, too!

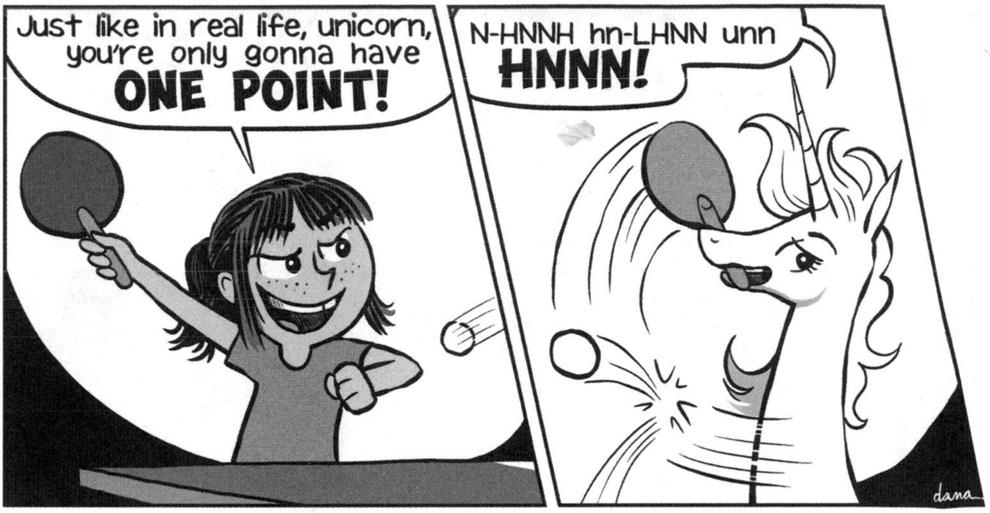
Just like in real life, unicorn, you're only gonna have ONE POINT!
N-HNNH hn-LHNN unn HNNN!
dana

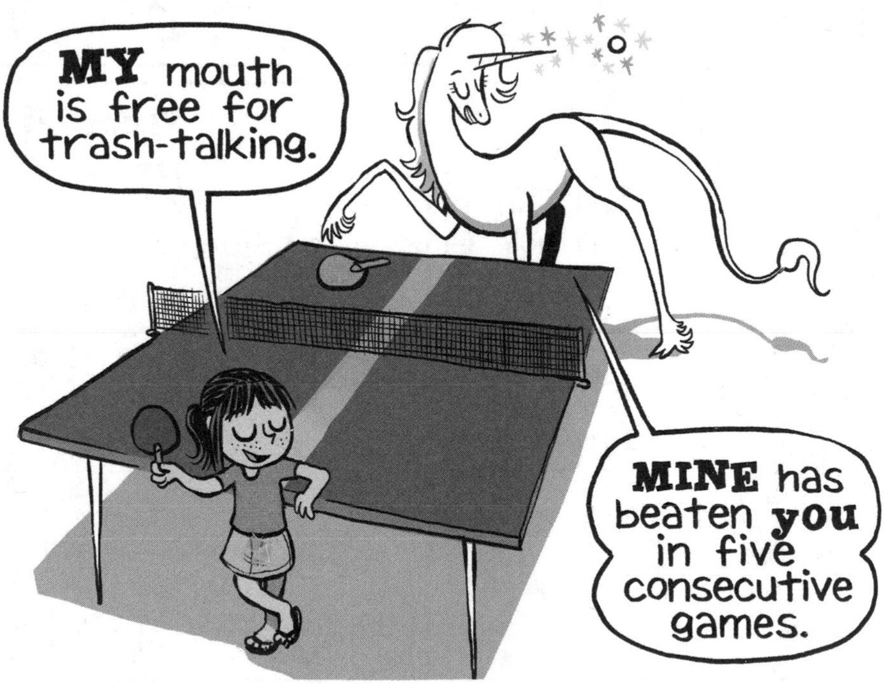
MY mouth is free for trash-talking.
MINE has beaten you in five consecutive games.

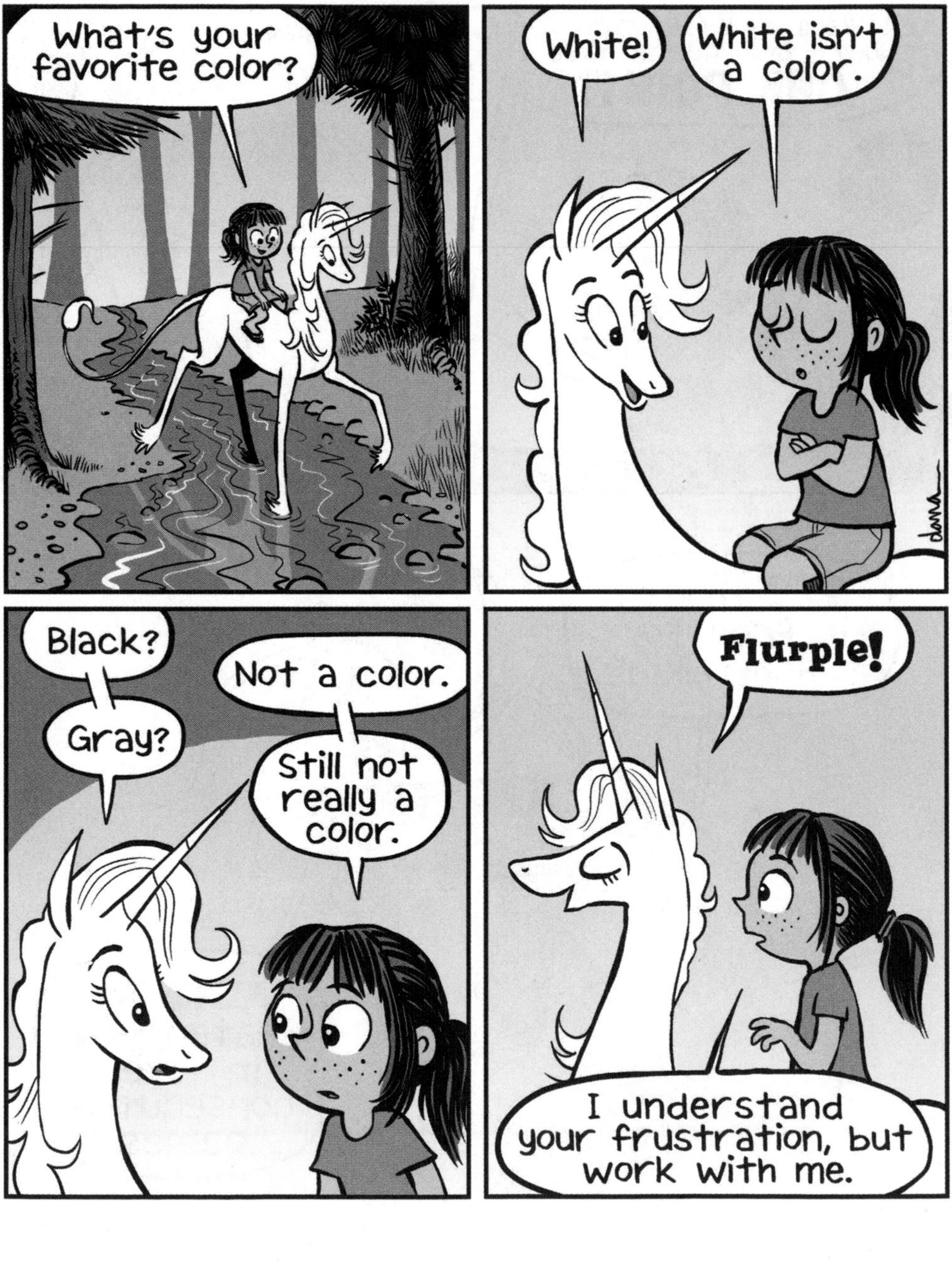
What's your favorite color?
White!
White isn't a color.
Black?
Gray?
Not a color.
Still not really a color.
Flurple!
I understand your frustration, but work with me.

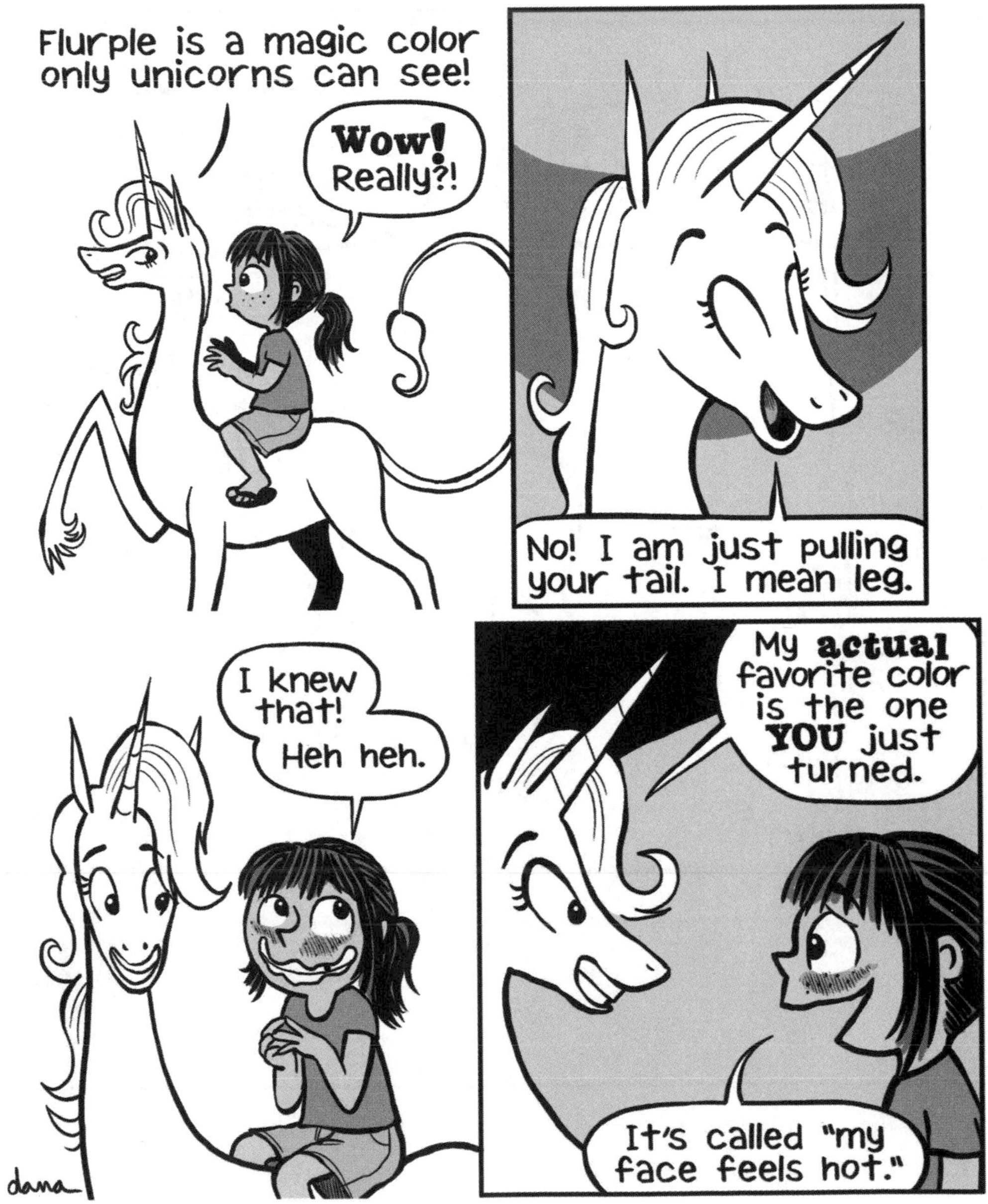
Flurple is a magic color only unicorns can see!
Wow! Really?!
No! I am just pulling your tail. I mean leg.
I knew that! Heh heh.
My actual favorite color is the one YOU just turned.
It's called "my face feels hot."
dana

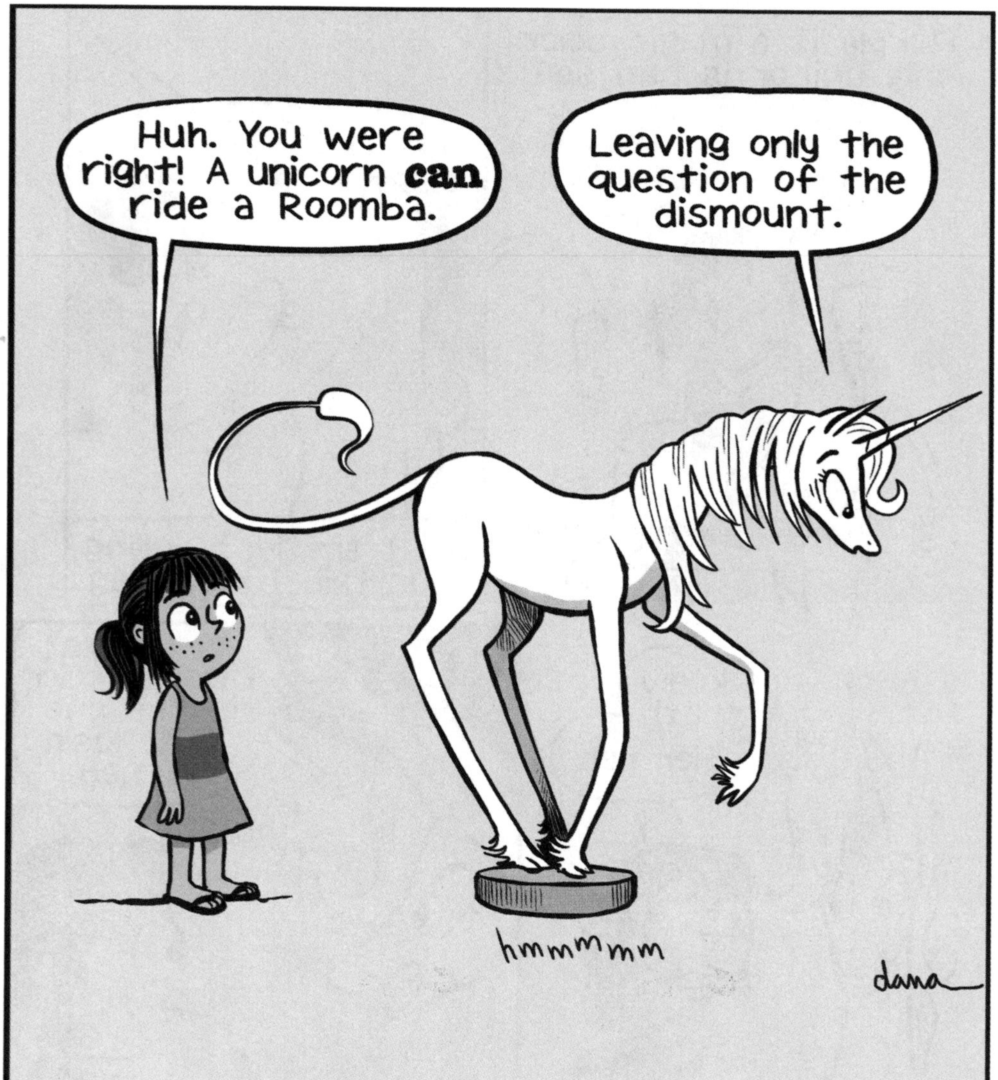
Huh. You were right! A unicorn **can** ride a Roomba.
Leaving only the question of the dismount.
hmmmmmm
dana

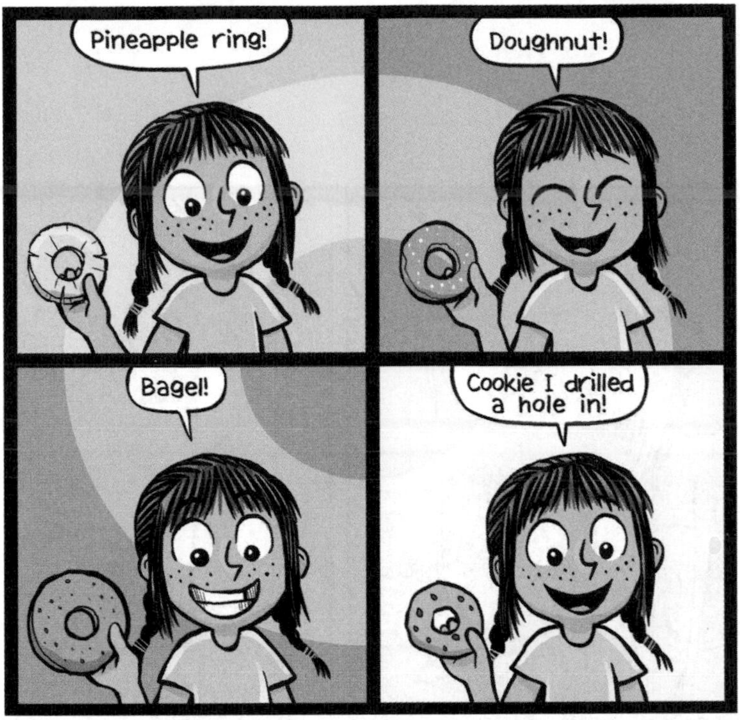
Pineapple ring!
Doughnut!
Bagel!
Cookie I drilled a hole in!

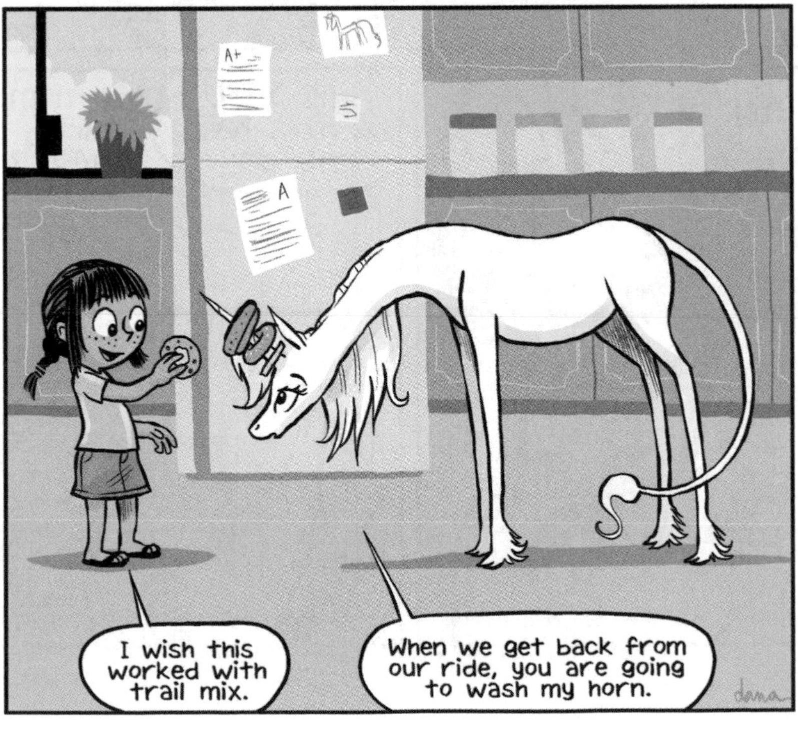
I wish this worked with trail mix.
When we get back from our ride, you are going to wash my horn.
dana

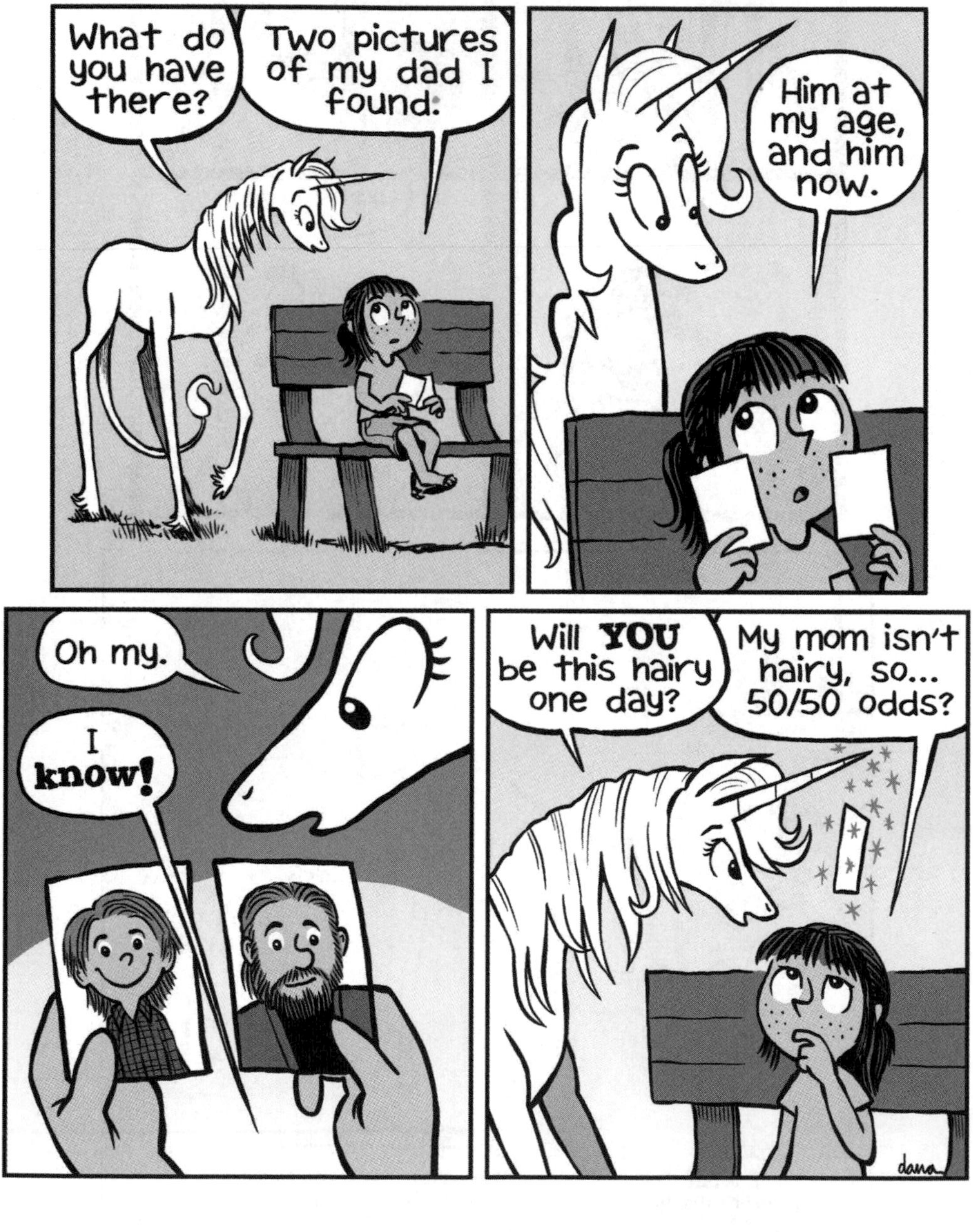
What do you have there?
Two pictures of my dad I found.
Him at my age, and him now.
Oh my.
I **know!**
Will **YOU** be this hairy one day?
My mom isn't hairy, so... 50/50 odds?
dana

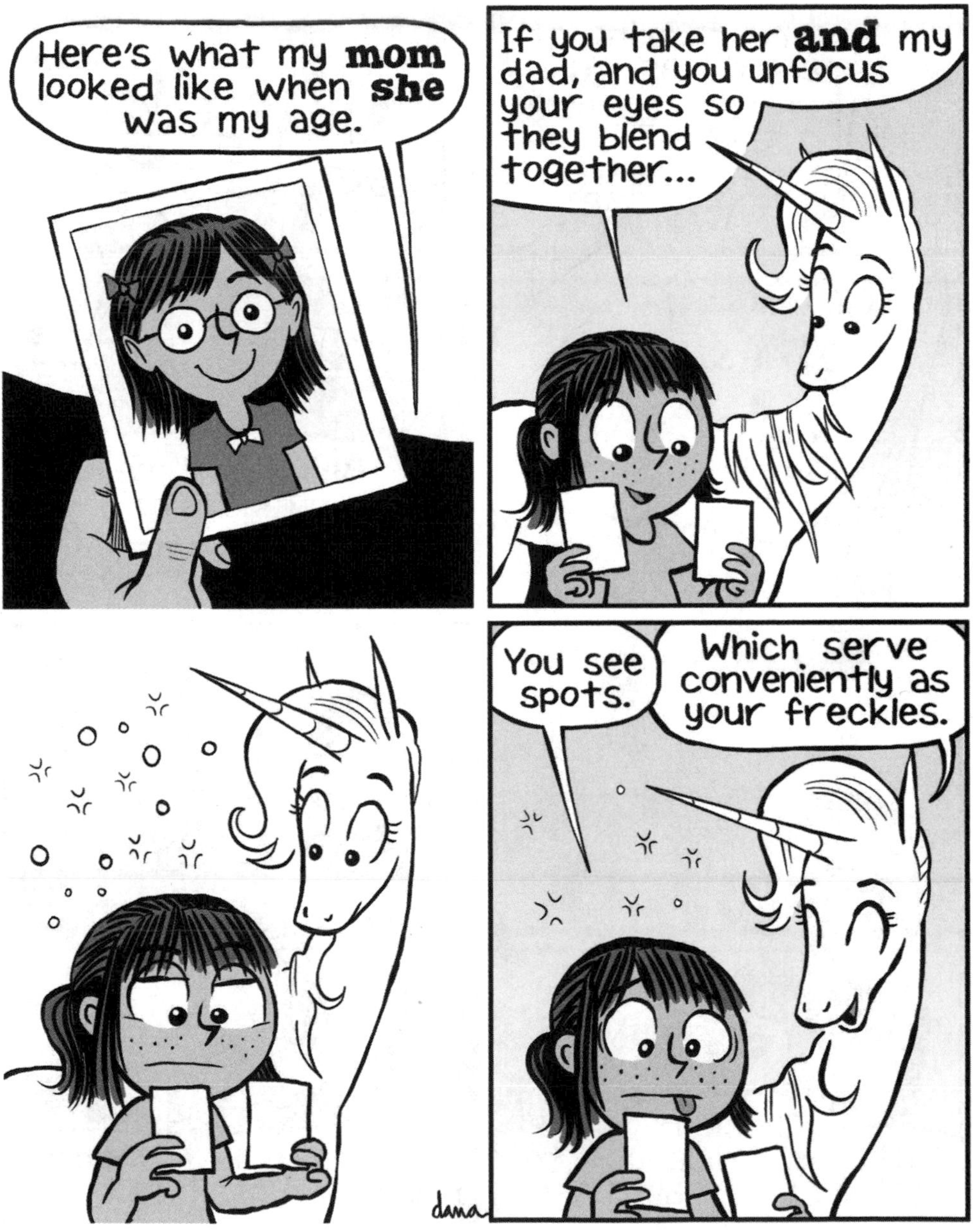

Here's what my **mom** looked like when **she** was my age.
If you take her **and** my dad, and you unfocus your eyes so they blend together...
You see spots.
Which serve conveniently as your freckles.
dana

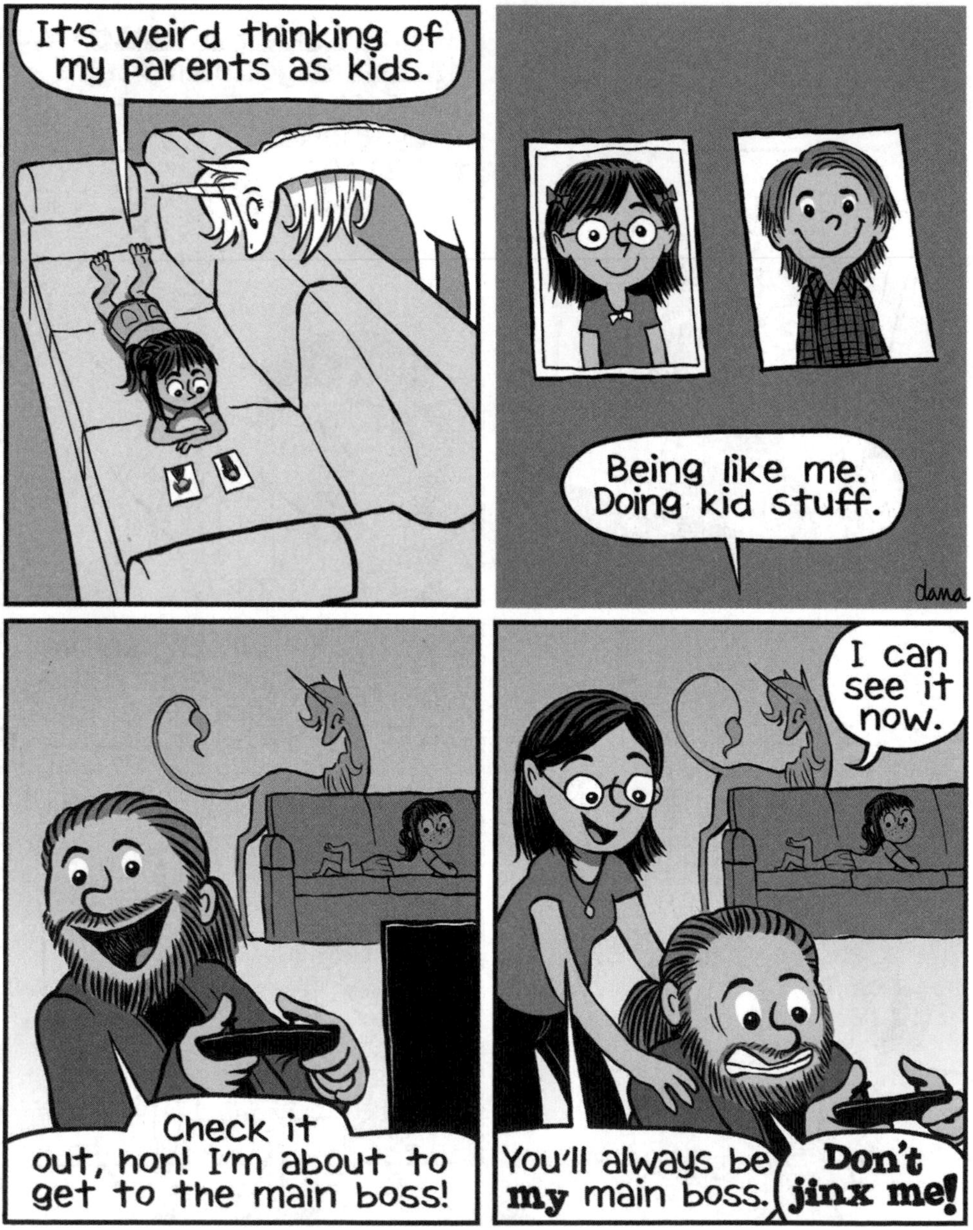
It's weird thinking of my parents as kids.
Being like me. Doing kid stuff.
dana
Check it out, hon! I'm about to get to the main boss!
I can see it now.
You'll always be **my** main boss.
Don't jinx me!

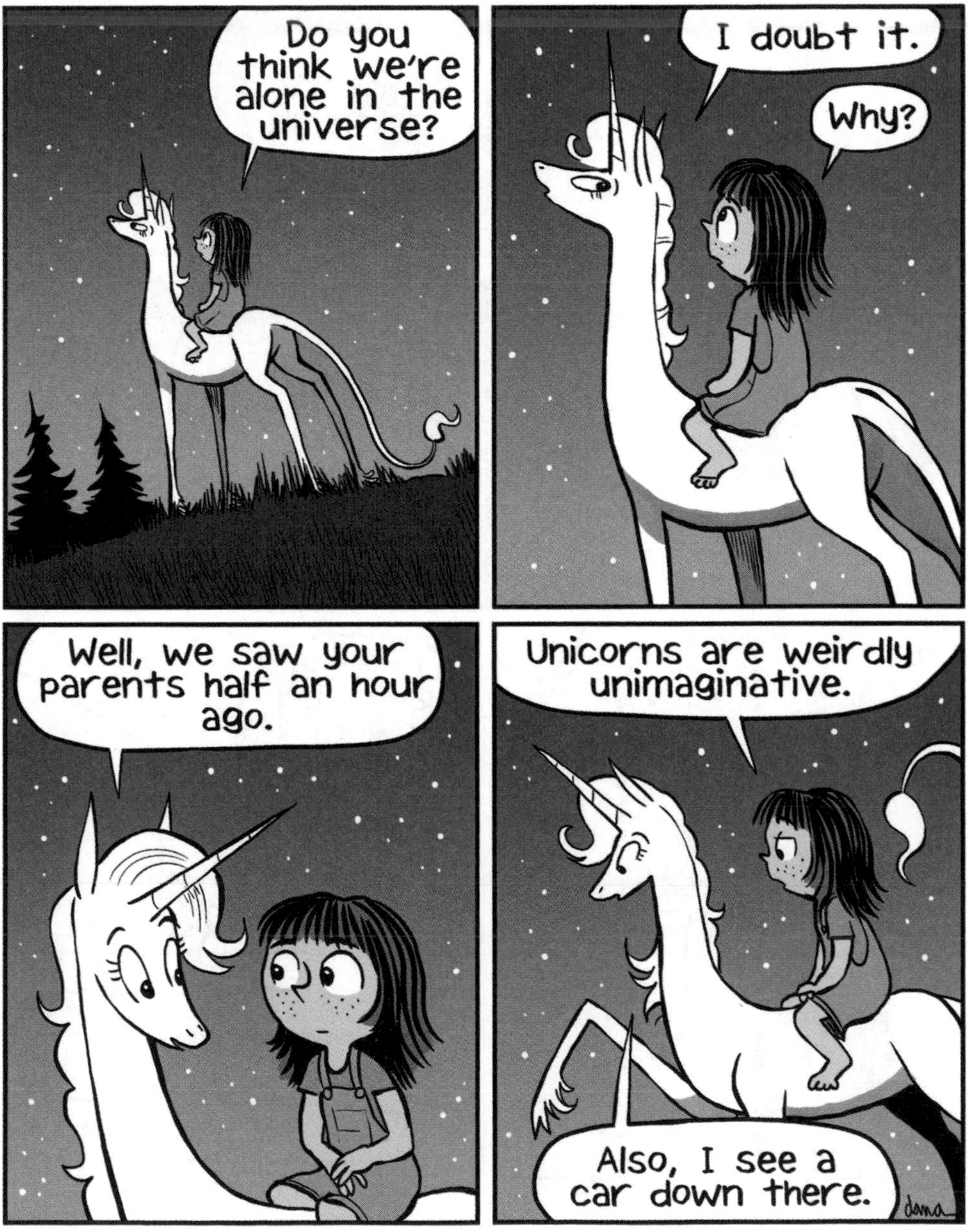

Do you think we're alone in the universe?
I doubt it.
Why?
Well, we saw your parents half an hour ago.
Unicorns are weirdly unimaginative.
Also, I see a car down there.
dana

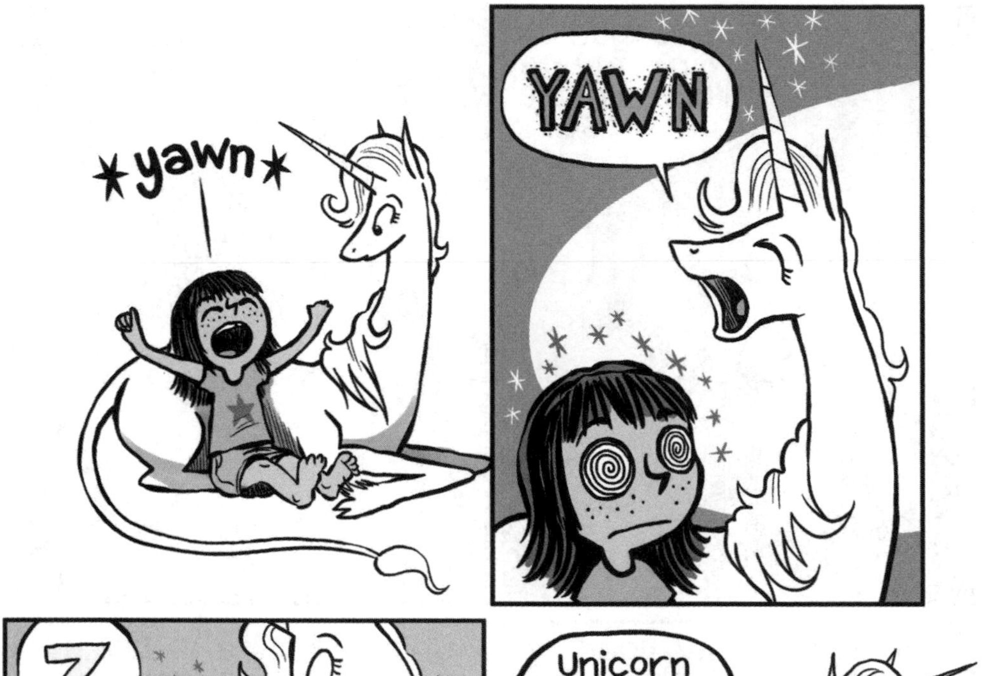
yawn
YAWN
Z
snrk
...wha?
Unicorn yawns are powerful magic.
And you did start it.
dana

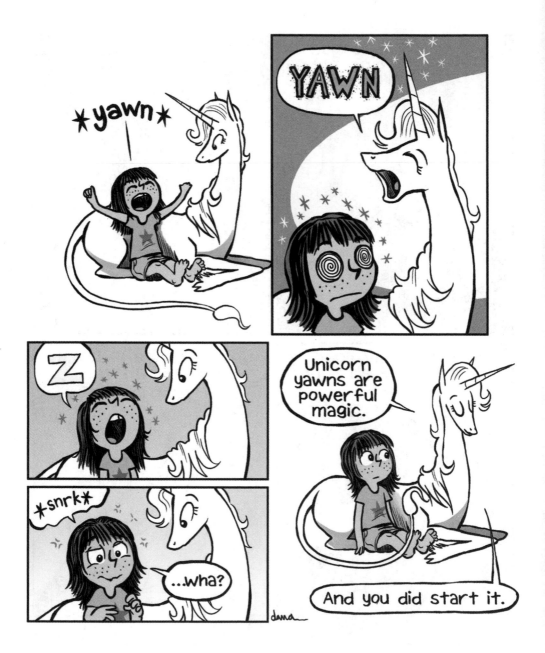

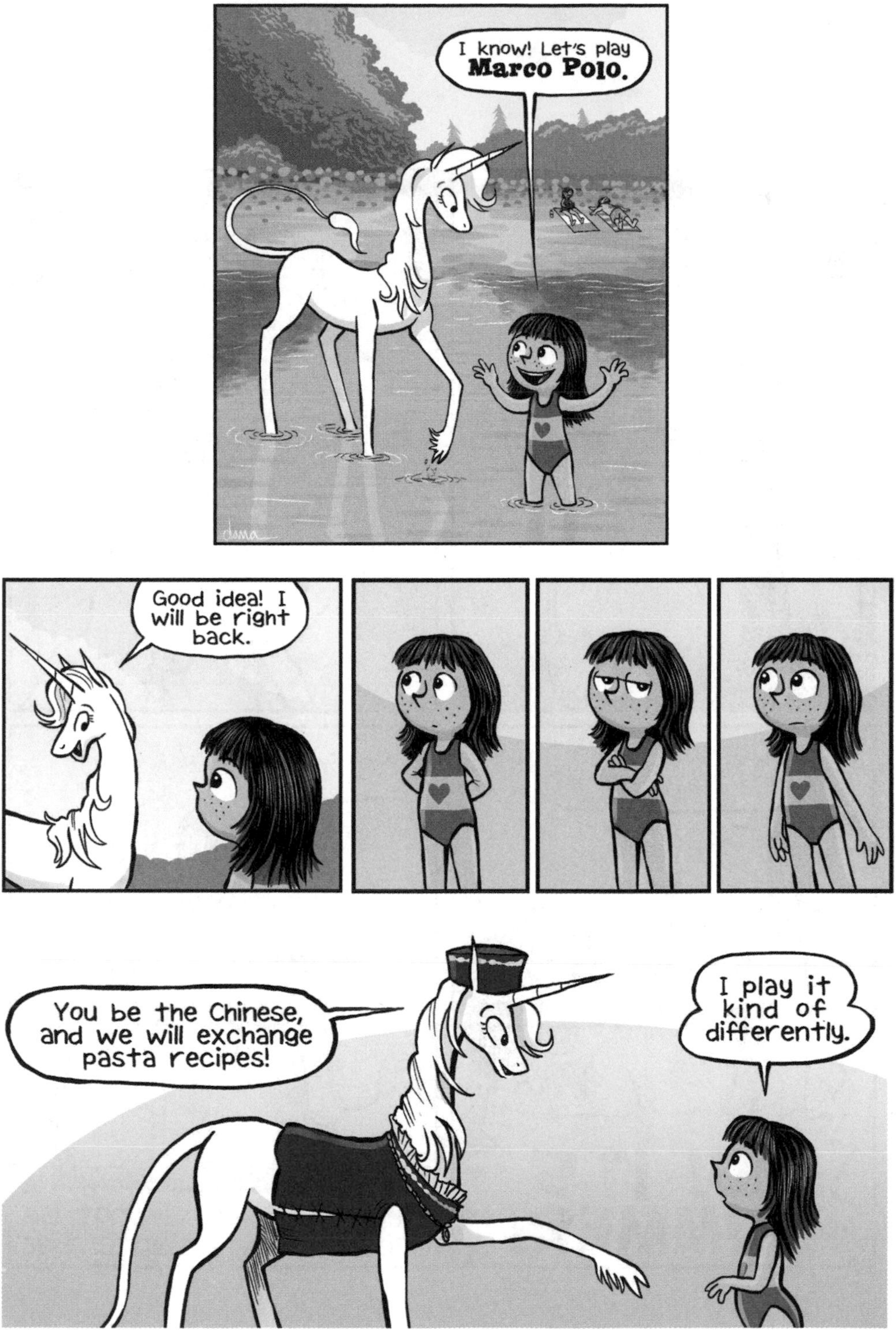
I know! Let's play **Marco Polo.**
Good idea! I will be right back.
You be the Chinese, and we will exchange pasta recipes!
I play it kind of differently.

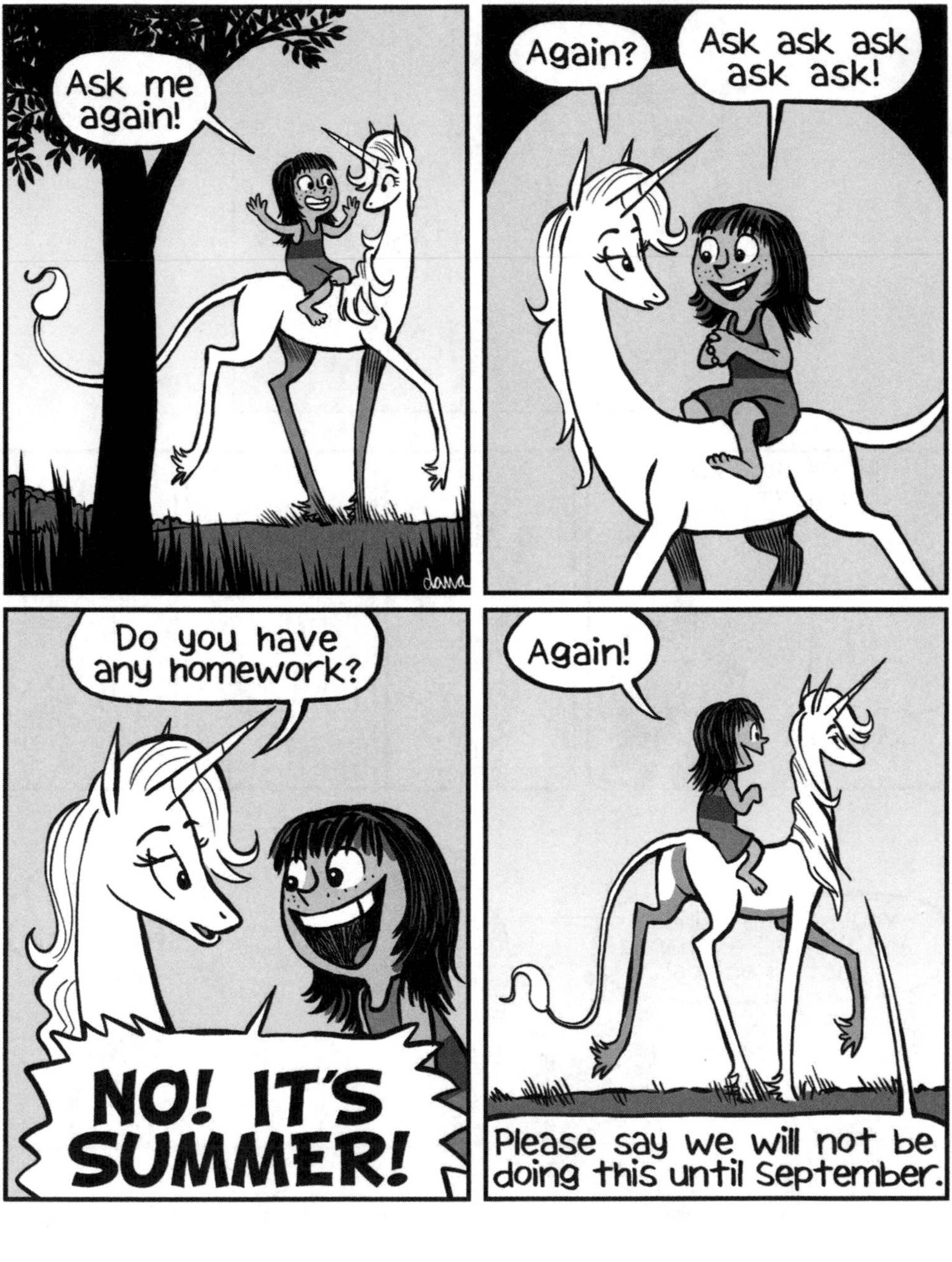
Ask me again!
dana
Again?
Ask ask ask ask ask!
Do you have any homework?
NO! IT'S SUMMER!
Again!
Please say we will not be doing this until September.

MORE TO EXPLORE! A special section featuring fun activities!

How to Draw Expressions

There are a lot of ways to draw expressions! There's really no single right way to draw any of them. But here's some of how I do it.

SERIOUS
(moments away from giggling)
Sometimes, Marigold's mouth is optional.
LAUGHING
HAPPY
yay!
Phoebe has a bigger mouth than Marigold, but Mari is far too polite to mention it.
SAD
this one hurts a little to draw!
ears droop (you could make her horn droop too, but that would be silly)
Draw a lot of tears if you want, but one or two gets the point across

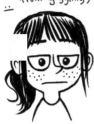

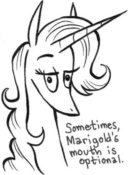

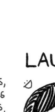

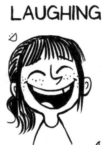

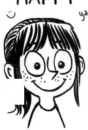

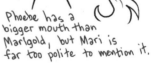

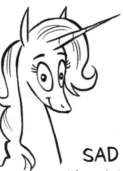

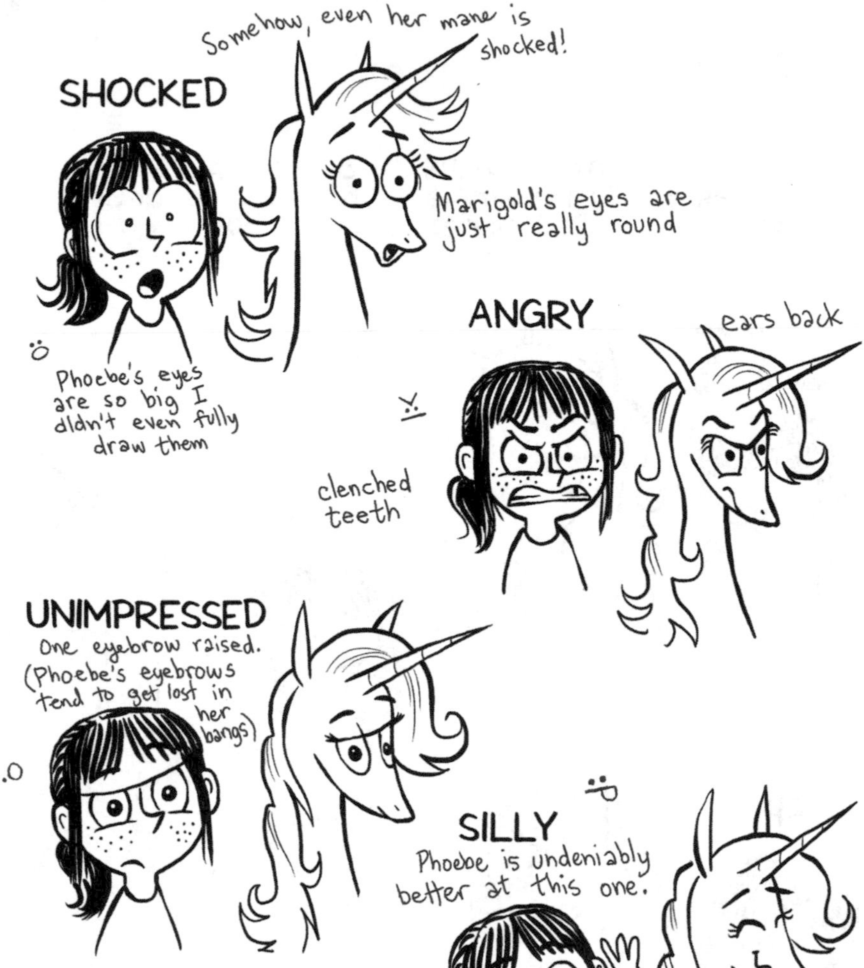
SHOCKED
Somehow, even her mane is shocked!
Marigold's eyes are just really round
ö
Phoebe's eyes are so big I didn't even fully draw them
ANGRY
ears back
clenched teeth
UNIMPRESSED
One eyebrow raised. (Phoebe's eyebrows tend to get lost in her bangs)
o.O

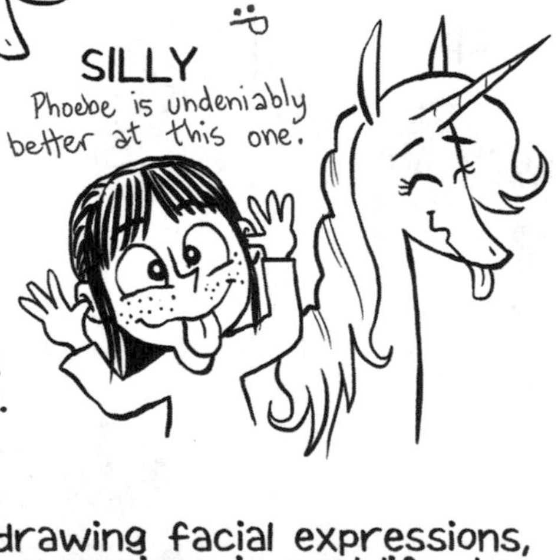
SILLY
Phoebe is undeniably better at this one.

Of course, you can (and should!) also just look at the expressions of people you know, too. Or just find a mirror!

(Fun fact: When I'm drawing facial expressions, I often make those expressions in real life, too, without really meaning to. Sometimes my husband looks at me and just starts giggling.)

Make Sparkly, Colorful Unicorn Poop Cookies!

Marigold is far too refined to ever use the word poop, but Phoebe knows delicious cookies when she tastes them! With an adult's help, make this sweet treat to enjoy with your friends.

INGREDIENTS: Store-bought refrigerated sugar cookie dough, four-pack of food colors, shiny sprinkles, edible glitter

INSTRUCTIONS:

1. Split the dough into four equal pieces and place each one in a separate bowl.
2. Add one food color to each bowl and stir to mix completely with the dough.
3. Refrigerate the bowls for 30 minutes.
4. Take a small piece of dough from each bowl. Roll each one on a counter or cutting board to make a rope-like shape. Then coil the four different colored pieces into a cookie shape until you've used all the dough.
5. Follow the directions on the cookie dough package to bake and cool.
6. Decorate with your favorite colors of sparkly sprinkles and edible glitter.

Makes about 24 cookies.

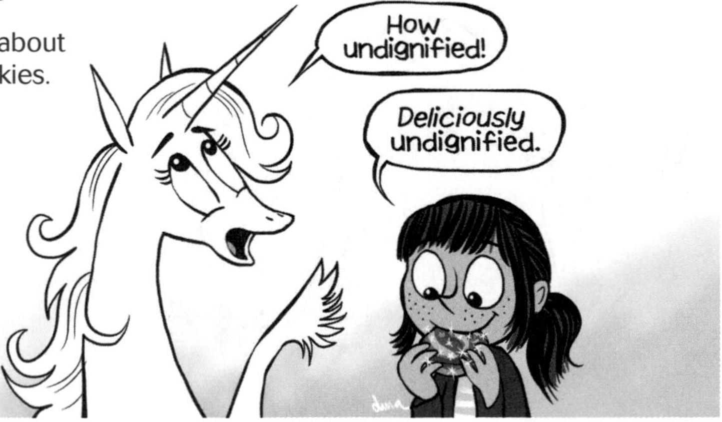
How undignified!
Deliciously undignified.

Make an Origami Figure of Marigold's Far-Removed Relative, the Happy Horse

First, make the Helmet Base.

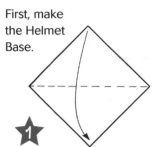

1 Take a square piece of paper and fold it in half as shown.

2 Then fold it in half again.

3 Fold left and right to center.

Helmet Base

Then make the Happy Horse.

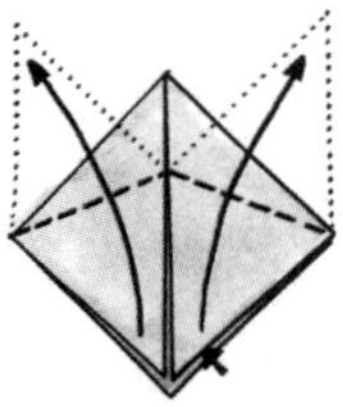

4 Start with the Helmet Base.

5 Fold sides and bottom to indicated point.

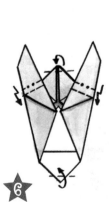

6

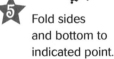

7

Happy Horse

Thanks to Jeff Cole, author of *Easy Origami Fold-a-Day Calendar 2015* (Accord Publishing, a division of Andrews McMeel Publishing) for the origami instructions.

Andrews McMeel Publishing
a division of Andrews McMeel Universal
1130 Walnut Street, Kansas City, Missouri 64106

www.andrewsmcmeel.com

16 17 18 19 20 RR2 10 9 8 7 6 5 4 3 2 1

ISBN: 978-1-4494-8349-4

Library of Congress Control Number: 2014921935

Made by:
RR Donnelley & Sons
Address and location of manufacturer:
1009 Sloan Street
Crawfordsville, IN 47933-2743
1st Printing—8/5/16

ATTENTION: SCHOOLS AND BUSINESSES
Andrews McMeel books are available at quantity discounts with bulk purchase for educational, business, or sales promotional use. For information, please e-mail the Andrews McMeel Publishing Special Sales Department: specialsales@amuniversal.com.

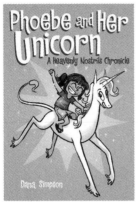

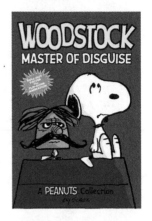
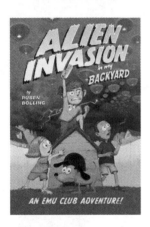

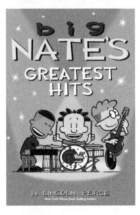

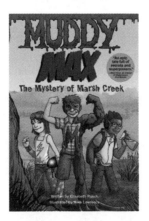